John Ironmonger was born and grew up in East Africa. He has a doctorate in zoology and was once an expert on freshwater leeches. He has also been part of a world record team for speed reading Shakespeare, has driven across the Sahara in a £100 banger and once met Jared Diamond in a forest in the middle of Sumatra, but that's another coincidence ... Follow him on Twitter @jwironmonger

www.thecoincidenceauthority.com

By John Ironmonger

The Notable Brain of Maximilian Ponder
The Coincidence Authority

JOHN IRONMONGER

PHOENIX

A PHOENIX PAPERBACK

First published in Great Britain in 2013
by Weidenfeld & Nicolson
This paperback edition published in 2014
by Phoenix,
an imprint of Orion Books Ltd,
Orion House, 5 Upper St Martin's Lane,
London WC2H 9EA

An Hachette UK company

1 3 5 7 9 10 8 6 4 2

A CIP catalogue record for this book
is available from the British Library.

ISBN 978-1-7802-2084-0

Printed and bound in Great Britain by Clays Ltd, St Ives plc

The Orion Publishing Group's policy is to use papers that
are natural, renewable and recyclable products and made
from wood grown in sustainable forests. The logging and
manufacturing processes are expected to conform to the
environmental regulations of the country of origin.

www.orionbooks.co.uk

for Zoe and Jon

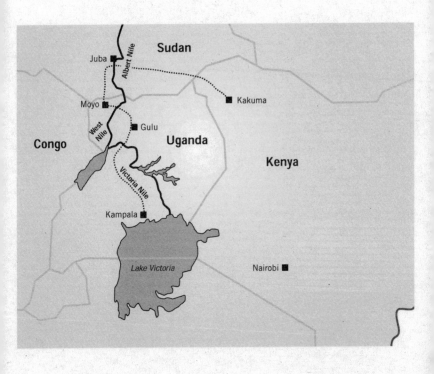

PART ONE

Finding Azalea

Mr Bond, they have a saying in Chicago:
'Once is happenstance. Twice is coincidence.
The third time it's enemy action'.

Ian Fleming, *Goldfinger*

1

June 1982

One Midsummer's Day, when she was only three years old, the girl they called Azalea Ives was discovered alone and lost at a fairground in Devon. It was late in the evening, when children of her age should surely have been at home, tucked up in bed. She was held in the fairground manager's caravan for an hour, or even more, while appeals were made over loudspeakers. This was a travelling fair, and we can imagine what a faint impression the public address system might have made against the caterwauling of shrieking teens, the clattering of the roller coaster, the thundering of the waltzer, the hollering of hawkers and hucksters, and the pounding basslines of fairground music. By ten o'clock when the noise had subsided, and when most of the revellers had dispersed into the night, no one had come forward to claim the little girl. A police car arrived from the town of Torquay and two large policemen, unfamiliar with the ways of very young children, did their best to communicate with the child. They asked her her name, and when she told them, one policeman carefully wrote down 'Azalea Ives', and this is what they called her from that moment on. They asked her where she lived, and she told them that she lived at Number Four.

'What's the name of the road where you live?' asked one of the policemen.

'Number Four,' said the girl.

'No, not the number of the house,' said the policeman. 'Do you know the name of the road?'

'Number Four.'

'Do you know the name of the town?' asked the policeman.

Azalea shook her head.

The second policeman tried a different tack. 'Do you know your daddy's name?' he asked.

'Daddy,' said Azalea.

'But does he have a name?'

'Just Daddy,' repeated Azalea with a shrug.

'What does your mummy call him?'

Azalea thought about this. 'She calls him Daddy too.'

The police in Torquay searched through phone books and the electoral roll and the police records for anyone called Ives. Phone calls were made. No one seemed to know anything about the missing girl.

'Is your house close by ... or is it a long way away?' asked the policemen.

'A long way away,' Azalea told them.

'How did you come to the fair? Did you come by bus? On a train?'

Azalea looked at them directly with clear green eyes. 'Mummy drove us here,' she said.

'Where were you going?'

'We were going to see Daddy.'

'Does your daddy live near here?' the second policeman asked, scenting a promising line of enquiry. 'Does your daddy live in Totnes? Does he live in Torquay?'

Azalea shook her head.

'Can you remember what time you set off from home?' asked the first policeman.

Another shake of the head.

'Did you have lunch on the way?'

'Yes,' the girl's eyes widened. 'We had *ham* sandwiches,' she said.

If Azalea and her mother had started their journey before lunchtime, enjoyed ham sandwiches and *still* only arrived at the fairground in the evening, then the search area could easily include most of England and all of Wales.

Back at the police station, a child protection officer called

4

Sergeant Jennifer Nails was given the job of looking after Azalea. A police photographer was summoned from his bed to photograph the girl. Social Services were awoken and instructed to check their 'at risk' registers for any child matching Azalea Ives's description. Photographs of Azalea, looking sleepy, were printed, and posted by first-class mail to the Department of Education, from where they would be forwarded to the head teachers of primary schools to see if anyone could identify her.

Azalea did possess one distinguishing mark. This was an inch-long scar running down her face just to the side of her left eye.

'How did you get that scar?' Sergeant Nails asked her. But the little girl just shook her head.

A police doctor examined the scar, but declared it to be an old wound – possibly even a forceps mark from birth. No signs of abuse or neglect could be found. Azalea was well nourished, suitably dressed and clearly well cared for; her hair had been combed and her fingernails trimmed. It all added to the general sense of mystery that clung to her apparent abandonment. Who would do this to a child like Azalea?

By nine o'clock the next morning, when Sergeant Nails and Azalea Ives appeared at the Torquay police station, the phones were busy. The police had widened their net. Calls were made to police forces in Cornwall and Somerset. Police computers (such as they were back then) were queried. People named Ives were visited and questioned across the South and West of England and the Midlands, and Wales.

By midday, with no sign of progress, a Chief Inspector from Exeter arrived in Torquay to take over the investigation. Sergeant Nails reported that there was a faint hint of an Irish accent when Azalea spoke. The girl also had red hair, and to Sergeant Nails's mind this indicated Irish origin. So a speech therapist from the Royal Devon and Exeter Hospital was called. She listened carefully to the tapes that the police had made and said that evidence of an Irish accent was thin, but that she wasn't strictly speaking an expert on accents, so she couldn't be sure. Recordings were then played over the telephone to a London expert in regional accents. He told the police that the girl's speech exhibited a number of distinctive characteristics, which might suggest that she was from an itinerant family, or perhaps that her mother had a different accent to her father. The expert proposed that they might want to look around Liverpool and North Wales, but he wouldn't commit to either. 'The girl has a rather neutral accent,' he told the police inspector. 'She has a high rising terminal which is a feature of Australian speech, where the inflection tends to rise rather than fall at the end of a sentence. Some Americans also talk in this way. But we can't really conclude that the girl is Australian or American.'

By the second day after Midsummer's Day, the puzzle surrounding Azalea Ives had reached the newspapers. Her photograph featured, with police consent, in the *Daily Mirror* and the *Daily Mail*. Extra staff were drafted in to the police station in Torquay to handle the resulting telephone calls. Child protection officers were included to help detect malicious callers. For operational reasons, the newspapers had not been given the name 'Azalea'. Instead, they were asked to identify the child simply as 'Girl A'. The reasoning was, with a name as unusual as Azalea, if anyone was to call the Torquay police station and volunteer the correct name, they would surely be bona fide.

But by the end of the second day, not one caller had suggested the name Azalea – or even the name Ives. A child psychologist was charged with trying to gain further information from the girl. She spent the third day playing with Azalea and coaxing her to talk. She discovered that Azalea knew her letters but had made very little progress in reading or numbers. She knew she had a mummy and a daddy, but no nana, and no brothers or sisters or aunties or uncles. She said she had never been to school. She had been to Sunday School, but she couldn't remember where. She didn't remember ever having visited London, or Blackpool, or Brighton. She may have been to a zoo. If she had, then it may have been a zoo with elephants. This led to more calls. Maybe if they could identify the zoo, then they could narrow down the search area. The Zoological Society of London confirmed that only a few zoos kept elephants, but these zoos were widely scattered around the country; they included Bristol, London, Chester, Whipsnade and Edinburgh, and you could, if you wanted, throw in Dublin as well, and safari parks such as Longleat. It was a rather unhelpful geography. The child psychologist showed Azalea some photographs of the different zoos, but her results were inconclusive.

The forensic people examined Azalea's clothes, but all were common department-store lines, with nothing to identify the particular shop where they had been purchased. Most of the items had been bought recently; they were, it appeared, all from the 1982 summer range of children's wear – but then children grow so fast, you would *expect* all her clothes to be new, unless perhaps they were hand-me-downs or items from charity shops. Which they weren't.

Several more ideas were explored to see if Azalea could help them to refine the search. They showed her station idents from different regional TV stations to see which ones she might recognise. She wasn't able to help. They showed her photographs of the sorts of places where children might be taken on outings. She recognised beaches and fairgrounds and parks, but only in a very general sense. Photographs of city centres or landmarks only resulted in a shake of her head.

'When did you last see your daddy?' the child psychologist asked.

Azalea looked at her, wide-eyed.

'Did you see your daddy this week?'

'No.'

'But you came here to see your daddy?'

'Yes.'

'Do you know where your daddy lives?'

Azalea thought about this. 'Daddy lives on a boat.'

'A boat? A boat or a house? Does your daddy live in a house?' She thought again. 'Yes, a house,' she said.

'Is it maybe … a houseboat?' asked the psychologist.

Azalea shook her head, but she looked uncertain.

'So it *is* a house. Yes? But maybe your daddy has a boat too? Does he have a boat?'

Azalea seemed puzzled. 'Yes,' she said at last.

'Do you know where the boat is? Do you know where your daddy keeps his boat?'

The child seemed to be thinking hard about this. 'Sheffield,' she said eventually.

The psychologist picked up the telephone.

Throughout the entire investigation, at the centre of a maelstrom of activity, Azalea remained remarkably untouched by the whole experience. The child psychologist, in her report, described Azalea as 'extraordinarily balanced', and 'apparently unconcerned by the absence of her parents, or any of the familiar features of her life'. She was a child, it seemed, of a cheerful disposition. She did not speak a great deal, except to respond to questions, but this she did with a politeness that would have done credit to a much older girl. Since her appearance at the fairground she had not once cried, nor had a tantrum, nor complained, nor asked for anything or anybody. She had absorbed herself in the toys she was given, the TV she was watching and the conversations that were intended to extract information. She seemed anxious to help, and disappointed, often, that the answers she gave were not more useful. In some cases, this desire to help made the adults more sceptical about her answers.

'Tell me about your house,' the psychologist asked her. 'Is it a big house?'

'Yes, a *big* house,' said Azalea, holding her hands wide apart.

'Or is it a small house? A teeny-weeny house?'

'Yes, it's a teeny-weeny-weeny house,' said Azalea, helpfully but unhelpfully.

'Do you go upstairs to bed?'

'Yes. Upstairs to bed.'

'And what can you see from your window?'

'Houses.'

'Do you live in a big town? Or a little town?'

'A big town.'

'Or a little town?'

'A little town.'

'How old are you, Azalea? Can you tell me how old you are?'

'Three.' Azalea held up three fingers.

'Or are you four? You're a bit of a big girl for three.'

'Four.'

'So you're four? Are you?'

'Yes. Four.'

The child psychologist and Sergeant Nails spent all day with Azalea. They played some games and they went out for a walk. At the end of the third day the girl was made a ward of court, and a temporary foster family was assigned. George and Eileen Robins from the Cornish village of Indian Queens came and collected Azalea, a lady from Social Services helped to complete all the forms and then a police car followed them home to check that everything was in order. Azalea joined George and Eileen's three older foster children and one biological child in a noisy but happy-sounding household. The Robins were briefed carefully and told to report any information that might help to identify the girl.

A sample of Azalea's hair and some fingernail clippings were sent off to a lab in London for isotopic analysis and geographic profiling. One of Azalea's first molar teeth was loose, and with a little encouragement this was removed and also sent for testing. But this was 1982, and these were early days for this type of analysis. Today, experts could probably use such tests to pinpoint a child's origin down to a county or even a village. In 1982 the results were inconclusive. The lab confirmed that Azalea may have spent the past few months of her life in northern Europe, most probably in northern Britain. But they couldn't rule out southern Britain. She may have shared her time between two locations – perhaps spending some of her time with her father in Sheffield, and some of her time with her mother in who-knows-where. There were no traces of cocaine (or any other drugs) in the girl's red hair, which suggested that Azalea's mother was probably not a dropout, nor an addict. The levels of fluoride in the tooth suggested that she came from an area where there was no natural fluoridation of the water supply, helpfully ruling out the West Midlands and the North-East of England and parts of Essex, but leaving open the possibility that the girl and her mother had lived almost anywhere else, that is, in practically ninety per cent of the United Kingdom.

By the end of the first full week after Azalea's midsummer appearance at the fairground, the Devon police were working on the theory that the girl had been abandoned deliberately. The assumption, based upon answers supplied by Azalea herself and on deductions made by experts and authorities, was that she came from a family that lived in the North-West of England – possibly in Lancashire or Merseyside. Her father may have walked out. Or else, perhaps, he worked away from home. Certainly he hadn't been seen by Azalea for a long time. He probably lived near Sheffield – but perhaps not in the city itself. His house was on a hill, close to a wood and next to a stream, if Azalea's account was to be believed. He sometimes lived on a boat. It was uncertain if Azalea and her mother lived with him. It seemed more probable that the couple had separated several months earlier, and that Azalea's mother had moved out and was renting a house somewhere – the 'Number Four' of Azalea's account. Azalea's mother, went the theory, had finally snapped. Unable to cope, she had bundled the girl into an old car that was light blue in colour and, telling Azalea that they were off to meet her father, she had driven as far away from home as she could before deciding that it was getting too dark to drive much further. She had spotted the bright lights of the fairground and had chosen this as the place to abandon her daughter. She had left Azalea sitting on a bench with some candyfloss, and then walked out of her life.

That, at least, was the proposition. There was no CCTV footage, and the only photograph recovered from the fairground that showed Azalea was a snapshot taken by a teenager from the top of the big wheel. There was an adult alongside the little girl, but she – or he – was in shadow, and the police could not be sure if this mystery person was Azalea's missing mother or just an innocent stranger. No unclaimed blue car was found in the fairground car park, or in the streets nearby.

By the end of the second week, the police operation in Torquay was already being scaled down. It was July, and the holiday season was in full swing. This was the busiest time of the year for the police in this part of England. One officer was still assigned to the case, but she was overdue for maternity leave and when she called in to the Chief Inspector to say that her waters had broken, the case was not reassigned.

Four months later, Azalea Ives was placed into the care of a second foster family, this time in Exeter. Two more months passed, and approval was given for her adoption. She was adopted by a childless couple from the Cornish village of St Piran. The couple were Luke and Rebecca Folley. They were teachers. So Azalea Ives became Azalea Folley, and the events of 21 June 1982, when a small girl was discovered to be lost at a travelling fair, were gradually forgotten.

But there are postscripts to the story of the foundling girl, and these are significant too. In none of these cases did anyone appreciate at the time quite how relevant each of the events might be to the life of Azalea Ives. The first such event occurred in May 1983, almost a year after Azalea's appearance at the fairground. The body of a young woman, very badly decomposed, was discovered on a beach in North Devon, near Bude. She had been dead for about a year. She lay unidentified in a refrigerated store for eighteen months until instructions were issued for her burial. In 1986, a police constable in Cornwall, carrying out a cold-case review, was able to point to a number of similarities between this case and the case of 'Girl A'. In particular, he noted, both the dead woman and Girl A had red hair. He speculated that the body at Bude could have been related to Girl A. In particular, he thought, the dead woman might have been Azalea's mother. His report was seen by an Inspector in Exeter who considered the theory briefly and then dismissed it. The conclusions were too circumstantial. The official explanation for Azalea's presence at the fairground was still deliberate abandonment, and the Inspector saw no reason to change this. There was no DNA testing, but crucially, the conclusions of the Cornish policeman were diligently recorded on the file.

The file on Azalea Ives was closed on 6 June 1986, and in 1992 all the documents associated with the case were sealed and sent to Exeter for long-term storage, where they still exist in a brown cardboard document box among several thousand others in a warehouse near the old docks. In all this time only one person consulted them – a private detective called Susan Calendar. We will come to her, in good time.

Neither Azalea nor the Folleys were ever officially told about the body discovered on the beach; not by the police, at least. There were insufficient grounds to warrant such an intrusion into their lives. And this could have been the end of the official story of Azalea Ives, and in many ways it was, except that the list of postscripts kept on growing. In 1990, eight years after the discovery of the girl, a fifty-year-old man called Carl Morse was arrested in Liskeard, accused of abducting a student nurse from a fairground and raping her. The girl survived the ordeal, escaped from a locked car by kicking her way through the rear windscreen and led the police to her attacker. At his trial, Morse confessed to an earlier abduction. According to Morse, he had been invited by a young woman into her car at a travelling fair in Totnes in 1982. He couldn't remember the exact date, but records confirmed a fairground had been there for the last two weeks in June. Morse denied having murdered the woman. Instead he made the unconvincing claim that the woman had thrown herself from the cliffs at Millook, not very far from Bude.

A second event occurred in the spring of 1993. A decorator in Cumbria came across two suitcases on the top of an old oak wardrobe. It was this discovery that set in train a sequence of events that led to the mystery of Azalea's origin being solved. But that story is still to come.

2

June 2012

The plain, painted sign on the office door reads 'T. Post, PhD', and beneath these words, in a smaller point size, 'Lecturer: Applied Philosophy'. It is something of a forbidding legend, its minimalist presentation not especially welcoming to casual callers.

But just above this uninviting plaque, someone has helpfully pinned a more informal notice. This one is on a sheet of drawing paper, fastened with a pin at each corner in such a deliberate way that you sense the occupant of the office must have placed it there himself. It is a caricature drawing, in charcoal, of the kind that artists do for tourists in Leicester Square or Montmartre, and it portrays a lofty, angular man with a wildly exaggerated nose and chin, a quiff of disobedient hair and a disproportionate set of rabbit teeth. No one could consider this a *flattering* portrait. Although, on closer inspection, there is a kindness to the eyes, a becoming smile and a look of gentle amusement about the subject. The man in the drawing is leaning forward over a table, across which he has scattered half a dozen dice. Every die shows the number six. Now the twinkle in the subject's eye has some meaning. He is, perhaps, a magician. Underneath the drawing, the artist has added a legend. 'Thomas Post', this caption reads, 'the Coincidence Man'.

We've leaped forward three decades from the fairground in Totnes, and the case of the foundling girl. This part of the story takes place in London, in the glorious Olympic year of 2012. We are in the upper corridor of a nondescript building in the university quarter of north London, and we are following Thomas Post, PhD down the dimly lit passage and into his office. We can see, at once, many of those features that the caricaturist chose to amplify. Thomas Post seems to roll along, a curious, angular fellow, a lummox, tall, awkward, in an ill-fitting jacket and large round spectacles. His arms swing clumsily, as if they are somehow too long to control. He pushes the door shut and folds himself down into his office chair and, in that moment, but just for that moment, he is the man in the sketch; all he lacks are the dice, and the inscrutable smile.

The small office obeys the principles and traditions of academe in its furnishings and its general sense of disarray. Sunlight streams in from an attic window. There is a solitary desk, its territory occupied with books, papers and computer devices trailing tangled, disobedient wires. There are bookshelves, themselves overladen, and an armchair and a whiteboard that carries faint fossil traces of charts and tables that have never been fully rubbed away. There is a small worktop, designed, or so it would appear, exclusively for the making of tea.

This is the workspace of Thomas Post, PhD. There are few personal touches, apart from his array of mugs and the books. A poster of a steam train, dog-eared and faded, looks as if it may have belonged to a generation of occupants of this room. A postcard of the seaside is pinned up beside his desk. Otherwise, the walls are populated by charts and more books. A photograph in a frame on the desk appears to be the only private image. It's a snapshot of a woman on a hillside with the coiling blue of a lake far below. It could be Scotland, perhaps, or Wales. The woman is laughing. She has been caught by the camera unawares, and her hands have flown up to rescue her hair – hair the colour of an autumn maple.

Thomas lets his upper body cantilever forward like a tree being felled in slow motion until he is face down on his desk, his hands locked behind his head. There is something desolate about his manner.

He stays like this for some time.

'Everything that happens,' says a very soft voice, 'happens for a reason.'

Thomas doesn't stir. Perhaps he didn't hear the voice. Maybe it was too quiet for him to hear.

'Everything that happens …' whispers the voice again.

Thomas levers himself up. He mouths the response through thick lips: '… happens for a reason.' He is distracted. He taps his fingertips on his desk.

Now that we look closely, there is no one else around. Did he imagine the voice?

There are footsteps coming down the corridor. He waits for them to pass.

'Everything that happens …'

It isn't a voice at all. It is nothing but the echo of a voice. The remembered echo of a voice. He isn't even hearing it. He is fabricating it, creating it from phantoms and figments of his mind.

His eyes flicker to a calendar propped up on his desk. 'Six days,' he whispers. 'Six days.'

Then, without so much as a knock, his door bursts open. He has a visitor.

'Clementine?' Thomas springs upright and starts to lift himself from his chair.

'Thomas, dear boy. Don't get up.' The visitor is a woman, comfortably twice his age. She wields a walking stick, and seems out of breath. She sinks heavily into the armchair without inviting a handshake. 'On second thoughts,' she says, 'you can make me a tea.'

'Of course,' Thomas says. He looks taken aback.

The woman casts her eye around the small office. 'So this is where you've been hiding away,' she says. 'On the fifth floor, where no one will ever find you.' She speaks with a faint accent. There is something Germanic or Eastern European about her voice, a huskiness, a hint of Lili Marlene.

'*You* found me,' Thomas says. He has made his way over to the worktop and is pouring water from a jug into a kettle.

'Only after an ascent worthy of a Sherpa,' says the visitor. She is looking this way and that, as if sizing up the room for sale. In response, Thomas Post starts to scoop up books and papers from the desk and floor. It is a transparent but hopeless attempt to tidy the avalanche of clutter.

'My dear boy, do leave all that alone,' Clementine says. 'If you shovel that stuff back onto the shelves you'll never find it again.'

Thomas stops, looking sheepish. 'You're probably right.'

'I'm always right.'

'It's just ... I don't get many visitors.'

'Five floors up, I'm not surprised.'

Thomas busies himself with mugs, waits awkwardly for the kettle to boil.

'This is your opportunity,' says Clementine, 'to ask me why I'm here.'

'Ah yes,' Thomas says, and he bobs his head like a nodding dog. 'So, Dr Bielszowska ... to what do I owe the pleasure?'

What an odd couple they are. Thomas Post, thirty-something, gauche and gangling; Clementine Bielszowska, surely past the honourable age for retirement, looking more like a grandmother than an academic: small and stout and sporting a shawl that can only have been hand-knitted.

The kettle boils and Thomas makes tea. He balances Clementine's mug on the arm of her chair.

'So?' Thomas says. He is back in his seat and waiting for a reply.

'I thought,' Clementine Bielszowska says, 'that we were friends.' She says this accusingly.

He gives a nervous shrug. 'We *are* friends.'

'So ... when did you last come to visit me?'

He starts to laugh, but stops in the face of her uncompromising gaze. 'I've been busy.' As he speaks, he knows these words won't suffice. Not for this visitor.

'Too busy to visit a friend ... for four months?'

It is a remark that can only be greeted by silence.

'Is it that girl?' she asks.

'Which girl?'

'The one you introduced me to. Or a bereavement? I only ask because every time I see you you look as if all the life has been punched out of you.' Clementine punctuates this observation with a loud tap of her stick on the wooden floor.

Thomas looks into his tea as if searching for inspiration. 'Am I that transparent?'

She looks at him unmoved.

He exhales very slowly and turns his face away. 'Clementine,' he says, 'sometimes I think you're the only person left who truly understands me.'

'Think of it as my job.'

He rises from his seat and makes his way over to the little attic window. It's a sunny day, and the rooftops of London roll away into a distant haze. But the weather clearly doesn't match his disposition. 'It *is* that girl,' he says. Then very slowly he adds, 'and a bereavement ... of sorts.'

'The girl is dead?'

He lets out a sigh. 'No. She isn't dead. I don't think so. Not yet.'

'Not *yet*? Is she terminally ill?'

Thomas is wringing his hands now. He turns back to face her. 'Do you have time,' he asks, 'for a long story?'

She takes hold of her tea mug and sinks down into her chair. 'Of course.' She purses her lips. 'I have as much time as you need.'

Thomas looks back at the window. There are so many thoughts. So much to say. A maelstrom of words awaiting an audience. 'It's complicated,' he begins.

'I like complicated.' She is patient, settling down to listen.

'You know I've been studying coincidences?'

'Every time we meet, you regale me with a dozen.'

He smiles at this. 'People think it's a whimsical thing. They love to come to me with a coincidence, and they challenge me to explain it. But it's never especially difficult. I can usually do some simple maths for them. Some events are unlikely, to be sure, but that doesn't make them miraculous. You understand?'

'I do.'

'One day, a woman came to see me, and she sat in that very

chair you're sitting in now. Azalea Lewis was her name.'

'Was she the redhead you introduced to me?'

Thomas nods forlornly. There is a silence between them for a while. 'Azalea's coincidences were off the scale,' he says quietly. 'They could not be explained. Not by mathematics, at least. In fact ...' he lifts his face and the sun catches his countenance with its glare, '... they might even be proof that our universe is not the place we thought it was.'

Clementine Bielszowska sips her tea slowly. 'This sounds profound.'

'I think it possibly is.'

'Azalea Lewis ... Azalea Lewis,' she tries the name. 'She had a little scar if I remember, right here.' She lifts a finger to her eye.

There is the soft trace of a tear in Thomas's eye. 'I can tell you how she came by it,' he says.

3

October 1978

While the case of the foundling girl – 'Girl A' – had been quietly shelved by the Devon police as long ago as 1986, the case of the identity of 'Ms C', the body found on the beach in North Devon, had never been closed. Murder has greater criminal longevity than child abandonment. Curiously, however, while the policeman from Cornwall had happily linked Ms C to Girl A, assuming that Ms C may have been Azalea's mother, no one in Devon had thought to make the reverse connection and to assign the name 'Ives' to the dead woman. This oversight undoubtedly closed off several avenues of investigation that might have helped to identify her earlier. In the end it was a blind man, a decade later, who helped to solve the mystery. But let's not get ahead of ourselves.

The woman whose decomposed body had washed up on that Devon beach was a twenty-four-year-old barmaid called Marion Yves. She probably pronounced her surname 'Ives'. You could forgive the police in the Azalea case for making such a simple mistake. Marion Yves was Azalea's mother. The Cornish policeman who wrote the report on the cold case had been right in that regard, and this without the corroborating evidence later provided by Carl Morse. Marion died when her head hit a rock on Millook Cliffs, and the reason her head hit the rock was because Morse had abducted her, had raped her and had thrown her from a clifftop. She had fallen, screaming perhaps, for one second, two seconds, until she reached the water and the rocks, and there she died. She may, of course, have been dead *before* she fell. Or she may have thrown herself from the cliff, just as her attacker had claimed. The sea has swept and cleansed the scene twice a day for thirty years; bladderwrack, barnacles and limpets have colonised the sharp and hostile stones. With virtually no forensic information available, we simply can't be sure. We don't even know which cliff she fell from, or which rock ended her life. All that Azalea would ever know of what happened to Marion in the days before her death she learned from a blind man, many years later.

Here is one thing that Azalea did eventually learn about her infancy. She learned the origin of the scar on her face.

At the christening service for Azalea, three years before Marion would meet her end on the rocks, the vicar accidentally dropped the baby into the font. The man responsible was the Reverend Doctor Jeremiah Lender. We shouldn't blame him too much for this mistake. It happened towards the end of a career which had seen him baptise almost a thousand babies, none of whom he had dropped. Also, in mitigation, the Reverend Doctor was sixty years old, with arthritis in his hands, which made him just a little too old, and a little too infirm, to be handling babies in a cold and draughty place like the old Church of Port St Menfre where the baptism took place. *Azaliah Yves*, the church records show, would be the last baby that the Reverend Lender would ever baptise.

The problem with baptisms, the Reverend Lender would later tell Azalea, is that they always made him nervous. There would be strangers among the congregation, and they would huddle around him in a way that simply wouldn't happen during any other service. If this wasn't bad enough, the baby to be baptised nearly always screamed objection on being passed from mother to minister. This happened in the case of the girl then called Azaliah. The vicar had, in the past, clutched babies rather too tightly, out of a fear that he might drop one. With experience, he had learned that this habit could contribute to the screaming, and so he had gradually developed a lighter grip until, in time, he barely held the baby at all. In addition, Azaliah, the vicar would later explain, wore a christening gown made of a glossy material. A very glossy material. The baby simply slipped through his arms and fell, while he, the good Reverend Doctor, clawed helplessly at thin air. With a clunk and a splash the infant hit the fourteenth-century font and the screaming stopped.

The prayer book in use for the baptism of Azaliah Yves was the 1662 version of the Book of Common Prayer, a book that can trace its lineage back to Archbishop Thomas Cranmer, who edited it – and probably wrote most of it himself – in 1552. Azaliah Yves was christened on 1 October 1978, two years before the Anglican Church finally dispensed with Cranmer's elegant words and introduced their new Alternative Service Book. So the words that the Reverend Doctor Jeremiah Lender was intoning when Azaliah slipped out of his grasp were the very same words that would have been spoken to generations of Anglican babies for the past three hundred years. 'We receive this child into the congregation of Christ's flock,' he would have read, 'and do sign her with the sign of the cross, in token that hereafter she shall not be ashamed to confess the faith of Christ crucified, and manfully to fight under his banner against sin, the world and the Devil, and to continue Christ's faithful soldier and servant unto her life's end. Amen.'

A thoughtful footnote to the 1815 edition of the Book of Common Prayer reads: 'It is certain by God's Word, that children which are baptised, dying before they commit actual sin, are un-doubtedly saved.' And for a moment or two after the dropping of Azaliah it seemed as if this amnesty might be needed to offer comfort to Ms Marion Yves. In the silence that followed the clunk and the splash there were, among the congregation, several who assumed the baby was dead. There was a gasp of almost theatrical proportions from the pews. The vicar snatched up the tiny body in its glossy wet christening gown, and all could see that Azaliah's little face was now awash with blood.

Then the baby gave a healthy enough wail, and the moment for the blessed absolution offered to the sinless passed.

What happened next was not especially edifying. Marion Yves tried to snatch her baby away from the vicar. She clearly felt that here was a man who could no longer be trusted to hold her precious offspring. By now the Reverend Lender had reverted to the tight grasp that characterised his early baptisms. He seemed determined not to allow the small matter of a dropped baby to interrupt the smooth flow of the service. He clung fiercely to Azaliah, and he attempted to avoid the lunging manoeuvre made by Marion Yves by taking a backward step. He was well into the next stanza of the service, which began: 'Seeing now, dearly beloved brethren, that this Child is by Baptism regenerate and grafted into the body of Christ's Church,' when Marion's voice rang out.

'Give me back my baby,' she demanded in tones that echoed around the fine acoustics of the Plantagenet church.

The vicar contrived to appear hurt by this, and attempted to shush the overwrought mother. 'We are quite near the end,' he said. 'Shouldn't we just carry on?'

'No bloody fear,' said Marion Yves, making another lunge for the baby. One version of the story has Marion using somewhat stronger language, but this may be due to the exaggeration that often accompanies tales repeated frequently over time.

Whatever words were used, the vicar was not to be easily diverted. In a thousand christenings he had never failed to reach the end of the service, despite the cries of some very vocal babies. 'Please,' he implored, 'we are nearly at the end. The baby isn't fully baptised yet.' He struggled to keep hold of Azaliah in what was becoming a rather unseemly tug of war.

The contretemps at the font was not the only unconventional feature of Azaliah's christening; another was the exceptional number of godparents. The usual pattern, prescribed since Cranmer's day, was for two godparents comprising one of each gender. But for this service, in a very uncharacteristic concession, the priest had agreed to Marion's request to admit three godfathers and a single godmother. All three godfathers looked acutely discomfited by the dropping of the baby and the subsequent attempts by Marion to seize her child back. This was when John Hall, one of the new godfathers, intervened.

Just moments before the fracas, we can presume that John Hall had been promising, in all solemnity, to renounce the Devil and all his works, to reject the vain pomp and glory of the world and equally (and highly improbably in John Hall's case) to renounce the carnal desires of the flesh. Now, however, he lumbered into the fray and relieved the vicar of the baby. For an instant it looked as if he might also deliver an uppercut.

'Please,' protested the vicar weakly, 'she isn't baptised yet.'

'She needs a bloody doctor, not a baptism,' said Hall, passing Azaliah to her mother.

'But we've so nearly finished.'

'Stuff it,' said Marion, taking the baby from Hall, 'we've had enough.'

'But my child,' insisted the vicar, 'in the eyes of the Church we have yet to …'

'Stuff your bloody baptism,' crowed Marion, 'and stuff all this.' She flung her Book of Common Prayer with all of Archbishop Thomas Cranmer's finely crafted words at the vicar. The book bounced off him and landed in the cold water of the font with a splash.

'Come on,' Marion cried to the congregation. 'We're going.' Whereupon she, and the three godfathers, and Azaliah Yves covered with her own blood and still only partially baptised, and a dozen or more of the assembled worshippers, stalked out of the church and into the secular world that lay beyond.

4

June 2012

There is jeopardy, Thomas Post thinks, in cultivating a psycho-analyst as a friend. How much of the friendship is sincere? Can he ever escape her instinct to analyse? If he whiles away time in her company, is she, perhaps, still at work, surreptitiously psychoanalysing him?

Dr Clementine Bielszowska may not be the most prepossessing of characters, sunk in her chair like a little weathered owl, peering through her half-moon spectacles, intemperately tapping her walking stick on the wooden floor; but as a psychoanalyst her reputation is exalted. No matter, as she would airily say to Thomas with a dismissive wave, that she hasn't practised for almost thirty years; no matter that she engagingly disavows the discipline. 'I don't even *believe* most of it,' she often says. Perhaps this is true; but she is nonetheless a disciple of Freud and Jung, and she does still tutor students in the dark arts. It isn't hard to imagine her with a notebook and pen in a wing armchair, lips tightly pursed, while a patient on a couch agonises over buried infatuations, complexes and phobias. It isn't difficult either, as she hunkers down in Thomas's fifth-floor office, to imagine her agile mind at work on Thomas's fragile psyche.

Thomas has turned away from the window and is looking forlorn. His visitor gazes at him with calculating eyes. 'Explain it to me,' she says.

'Explain what?' Thomas strikes a faintly defensive pose.

'A little while ago you said that you thought Azalea might be dead.' She is tapping on the floorboards with the rubber end of her stick.

'No I didn't. I said ... I said she isn't dead *yet*.'

'It's the "yet" that I don't understand. And you said that her coincidences were ... what? Proof of something?'

He is wide-eyed now. 'Evidence,' he says, 'not necessarily proof. But compelling, all the same.'

'Evidence of what? Destiny?'

'It's a good word, "destiny". Yes. I do like destiny.' He ponders this, tugging uncomfortably on his earlobe. 'Or "kismet", as the Turks say, which implies ... I don't know ...' he swings his arm around as if in search of a thesaurus, 'predetermination.'

'Predetermination?'

'Or something like it.' He gives a grin that radiates apprehension. He isn't comfortable with this line of questioning. His limbs are twitching as if assailed by invisible needles. He turns his face away. 'What if I don't have an explanation?'

'My dear boy,' she says, 'you *always* have an explanation.'

'Do I?'

'You do.'

He relaxes just a little. 'The Japanese have a good word: "hitsuzen".'

'"Hitsuzen"?' She puckers her lips on the unfamiliar term.

'Hitsuzen is an event that happens according to some pre-ordained plan or design. Something that was always *supposed* to happen.'

'A bit like Insha'Allāh?'

'A bit. "Deo volente" is what the early Christians would have said. If God wishes. Hitsuzen is more a property of a past event. Something happened because it *was* hitsuzen. Because it was supposed to happen. The Japanese also have the word "guzen", which is something that occurs by chance. A guzen doesn't belong to any greater scheme of things. It's just random, if you like. In Japanese philosophy, everything that happens is either guzen or hitsuzen.'

Clementine Bielszowska exhales. 'You're losing the thread,' she says. 'Can we stick to English?'

'If you insist.'

'I do.' She offers him a benign smile.

'You need to promise me something.'

'Usually when someone says that it's a good time not to promise anything at all,' she says.

'I don't want you to psychoanalyse me,' he says. 'This isn't that kind of problem.'

'In that case,' she says, 'it is a very easy promise to make.'

'I'm serious, Clementine.'

'So am I, dear boy.' She is observing him with professional relish.

'There is nothing in this story that you can help me with,' he says. 'There are no neuroses to resolve. There are no fixes. In six days it will all be over, one way or another. Azalea will be dead. Or she won't be.'

A shadow interrupts the stream of sunshine from the narrow window. A pigeon has landed on the windowsill. It bobs its head expectantly, peering through the glass.

'He comes for crumbs,' Thomas says. He takes a biscuit from a tin, crumbles it in his hand and opens the window. The pigeon retreats a little way. Thomas scatters the fragments on the sill, and in moments the bird is back.

Thomas settles himself again in his chair. 'Perhaps I should tell you the story of the seagull,' he says.

5

January 1978–January 1984

Azalea Lewis, the girl who was almost christened Azaliah Yves, owed her life to a seagull. The situation arose because Marion Yves was all set to become an unmarried mother. We should remember that in 1978, in villages like the one where Marion was born and raised, single motherhood wasn't the lifestyle choice it is today. Perhaps, in a city, Marion might have registered as just another statistic, and on city streets she might have pushed a pram unnoticed. But this wasn't Dublin or London. It wasn't even Douglas. This was the village of Port St Menfre, a clutch of whitewashed stone cottages that jostled down a precipitous hillside towards a small shallow harbour on the coast of the Isle of Man. Here, when Marion took to the street with baby and pram, heads would turn and tongues would wag, and this would be the only way that it ever could be, for her business was the business of the village, just as their business was hers. In Port St Menfre, every face was familiar. If a girl walked out with a man, people would know it from the top of Haven Hill to the far corner of the bay before the couple could even make it home. When Gideon Robertson, the fisherman, moved out of his dockside rooms in 1976 and moved into 4 Briny Hill Walk, where Marion had previously lived alone, this was the main subject of conversation for almost a week. When the community could bear it no longer, the Reverend Doctor Jeremiah Lender was dispatched to seek assurances from the couple that their living arrangements were purely commercial; a case perhaps of landlady and tenant rather than a matter of sinful cohabitation. The Reverend emerged from the cottage looking grim. Had excommunication been an option, then perhaps he would have exercised it.

But this, let us remember, was some years after the decade of free love, and now, even in Port St Menfre, a woman like Marion Yves could hold up a metaphorical finger to the world and do her own thing without fear of the ducking stool, even in the face of the disapprobation of the whole community. This, it seems, is exactly what she did.

Gideon Robertson moved *out* of the cottage on Briny Hill Walk in December 1977, around the time when Marion's periods stopped. He might well have been Azalea's father. But then again, that honour might have belonged to the young English barman Peter, who walked Marion home from work on dark evenings when Gideon was at sea. And equally possibly, Azalea's father might have been John Hall, a washed-up military man, retired from soldiering, now the landlord of the Bell Inn where Marion and Peter both worked; a man with a loud laugh, an overbearing manner and rather too much of a taste for his own ale.

When Marion Yves discovered she was pregnant, she was immediately aware of the dilemma she would have to resolve with respect to the paternity of the child. She checked back through the calendar and tried to work out possible dates, the who and when and where, but no clear answer emerged. She had never written these things down, so might it have been four weeks ago … or five … when she and Peter, or when she and John, or when she and Gideon …? Was that the Sunday when the tide was early, or the Sunday when the tide was late? There were no answers to these questions. She walked down to the bakery with her basket over her arm, and then she took the little cobbled street to the Parish Church of St Menfre and, alone at the back of the nave, she bowed her head and prayed to God for guidance.

Despite what we may have learned about Marion from the story of the christening service, she was a pious soul, the product of a fiercely pious community. Those who didn't visit the Anglican Parish Church of St Menfre could always attend the Hope and Faith Baptist Church in Port Erin, or the Elim Pentecostal

Church, or the Isle of Man Methodist Church, or the Christa-delphia Ecclesia in Dalby Patrick, or the Roman Catholic Church of St Columba in Port St Mary. The options for religious worship were wide and varied; it only really mattered that some level of observance should be seen to be made. The Anglican Communion was Marion's destination of choice. She had visited this church twice every Sunday for most of her life, and it was natural that she would turn to God here for advice on her predicament. She asked Him, as plainly as she could, to help her out. Her options seemed reasonably clear. Should she take the bus into Douglas and buy a ticket for the Isle of Man Steam Packet ferry service? This would secure a four-hour crossing to Liverpool over the unpredictable waters of the Irish Sea. Once in England, she could consult with the British Pregnancy Advisory Service; an agency whose principal, and enlightened, purpose was to secure for young women the services now permitted by the 1967 Abortion Act. She would need to establish an English residential address to qualify for an English abortion, but this should present little difficulty. It could all be done without anyone from Port St Menfre learning that a baby had even been conceived, let alone aborted.

Or should she, perhaps, confront Gideon when he next came ashore and tell him that the baby was his? It would probably lead to a resumption of their relationship, which was not something Marion particularly sought. But it was an outcome that might best suit the unborn child. It would at least provide him or her with a father and a household income somewhere above that of a barmaid.

She could try the same approach with Peter, the barman but he was too young and too impecunious to be a sound candidate for long-term fatherhood. He was from England, and planned to return soon to his native Cumbria. He wanted to join the navy. He longed to see the world. What life would that be for the wife left behind? Worse, even, than being married to a fisherman; at least a fisherman comes home with the tide. Nonetheless, she presented God with the option. John Hall was wealthy enough, and old enough to accept the responsibility, but his wife might have objections; and besides, he had a tendency to turn cantankerous when drunk. Marion considered excluding this option, but concluded that God was probably already aware of it, so she placed it squarely before Him along with the other choices. Should she raise the baby alone with no father in the picture at all? That was a real option too. Or should she demand that all three candidates submit to a blood test? Then the real biological father could be identified and perhaps persuaded to marry her and help her raise the baby.

There were altogether too many choices for Marion to make a decision herself, so she delivered the alternatives to God from her pew in St Menfre's church on a January day in 1978.

Little is known about Saint Menfre, who gave her name to the parish church and to the village in which it stood. She is believed to have been not Manx, but a Cornish saint – or perhaps even a Welsh saint, or possibly even Irish, depending on how far back you chose to go. She was one of the twenty-four children (by three wives) of the fifth-century Irish saint St Brychan, who married into the Welsh kingdom of Breckonshire. Unfulfilled by his life in Wales, and the county that now bears his name, Brychan travelled south into Cornwall to spread the Christian gospel. How, or why, or when his daughter came to the Isle of Man is not known. Menfre's claim to fame, if we can call it that, came when she threw her comb at the Devil. He had come upon her while she was combing her long red hair – Irish hair, no doubt. The Devil's intentions, it seems, were dishonourable. The throwing of the comb was a riposte that would have commended itself to Marion. From what we know of Marion Yves, we might well imagine her doing the same thing. She too was a redhead, as was her daughter Azalea.

So Marion prayed, but neither God nor St Menfre was forthcoming with advice. Leaving the church, she came upon the vicar arriving through the churchyard gate. He eyed Marion with a hint of suspicion as if, perhaps, she had been stealing the silver. The relationship between the two, pastor and parishioner, had not recovered from the visit that he had made to her cottage a year or so earlier, after Gideon moved in. Neither could the vicar bring himself to forget the frank, even *intimate*, revelations that Marion had felt obliged to share on that occasion. Nonetheless, because he was a holy man in a holy profession, he summoned a warm smile and wished her a good day.

'I wish it was a good day, Father,' Marion said.

'Is something troubling you, my child? Would you like us to pray together?'

'If you want.'

'It isn't what I want that matters,' said the vicar. 'What do *you* want?'

They sat together on a small bench that overlooked a knot of graves. Beyond the churchyard lay the slate rooftops of the fishermen's cottages on Menfre Hill, and beyond these the blue sweep of the bay flecked with the foam curlers of the incoming tide; and out on the bay, lost in the haze, were the lobster boats, and beyond them, smacks fishing for mackerel, and further still, beyond sight, the trawlermen and the pilchard ships. There you might find Gideon Robertson in his yellow rubbers and his striders, hauling on ropes until the salt burned his skin, slopping fish across the decks, packing down ice with his big hands, buried behind his beard, toiling against the waves and the wind like some creature who had been born upon the sea. For such men no other life existed; their brief spell on land, sleeping and waiting for the tide, were mere interludes in a life spent at sea. Could this big, silent man ever be a real father to her child?

Marion told the whole story to the Reverend Lender, sparing him none of the details. She pointed out to the sharp rocks beyond Haven Point, where the mist and the horizon were one, where Gideon might be with his fish and his buckets, his ropes and his nets. 'What if he's out there when my baby is born?' she asked. 'What if he doesn't come back?'

'I see,' said the vicar. They sat and looked out at the ocean. 'In my years here,' he said, 'and there have been many years, only four men have never come back.'

31

'One of them was my grandfather,' said Marion quietly, 'and another was my father.'

'That they were,' said the vicar. 'That they were.' They sat for a while in silence. 'So what are we to do, then?' he asked her. 'Are we never to fish?'

'Not if we want to be part of a family,' replied Marion. She said it quickly, as if it was something she had said many times before.

'I see.' The vicar took Marion's hand and held it gently. 'Gideon is a good man. He will take care of you – and your baby.'

'Is that God's answer, then? I tell Gideon he's the father and we settle down and play happy families for the rest of our lives? Until the sea takes him?'

'It seems the kindest answer. You said yourself that Gideon is probably the father.'

'But he might not be.'

'But even so … the baby needs a father. Every child needs a father.'

Marion turned to look the Reverend in the eye. 'I never had one. And my mother never had one.'

Above them the herring gulls wheeled and shrieked in the cold January sky. Marion released the vicar's hand and reached into her basket.

'Why don't we let God decide?' she said firmly.

'That's good, my child,' said the vicar. 'Put this matter into the hands of God.'

Marion drew out a loaf of bread from her basket and began, with some force, to break off small chunks. 'Yes,' she said, 'I'll give God the problem. Does God control the seagulls?'

'The seagulls?' The Reverend Lender looked puzzled.

'Of course he does. God controls everything.' She tossed a piece of bread onto the path. 'Let's see which bit of bread the gulls take first.'

'Look, I really don't think this is a good idea,' said the vicar, getting a sense of her intentions.

But Marion was not in a mood to be swayed. 'If they take that piece first,' she declared, 'then I'm having an abortion.'

Lender recoiled at the word. 'Look ... Please. Don't do this.'

She threw another chunk. 'If they take this one, then I'll raise the baby on my own, just like my mother had to do with me.' A third piece: 'And this one, God, is if Gideon is the father and you want him to move back in.' A fourth: 'And this is Peter. Peter the barman, Peter the Englishman, Peter the poet who wants to be a sailor.' A fifth: 'And this is John. John the landlord, John the husband already.' She clapped her hands in triumph. 'Come on, God,' she called to the sky. 'Give me your answer.'

'Marion, look, this makes no sense. This is no way to solve your problems.' The priest was clearly anxious now. 'You can't mean this.'

'Oh, I can,' said Marion, 'I absolutely can. If God can read my mind then he'll know I mean it. Otherwise what would be the point?'

Above them, the gulls were circling closer.

'This isn't the way to put your troubles before God,' said Lender. He was rising to his feet to scare the birds away from the bread.

Marion took hold of his arm. 'Wait,' she said.

A large gull all a-flap had landed on one of the gravestones. It hawked at Marion and Lender with its great yellow beak, tacking cautiously towards the trail of bread.

'This isn't a fair test,' protested the priest.

'Let God decide,' said Marion. A second gull dropped from the sky. A third.

'Stop this!' The vicar's voice drove the birds back, but only for a moment.

A fourth gull landed. A fifth. The priest was struggling to escape Marion's grasp. And then, of course, it was too late. With a flash of grey wings a bird swept in without landing and carried off a piece of bread. Emboldened, the flock surged forward, and soon all the bread was gone, carried aloft by the gulls.

Marion released the vicar and rose to her feet.

'Which one was it?' the priest asked weakly.

Marion gave him a twisted smile. 'It wasn't Gideon,' she said, collecting up her basket. She gave a rueful smile. 'And you'll be pleased to know it wasn't John. John the master of wandering hands. Maybe God does move in a mysterious way after all. Maybe He does.' And without looking back, she set off down the hill towards the village.

6

October 1978

The name 'Azaliah' was originally proposed by the Reverend Jeremiah Lender, the man who was later to drop the baby into the font. At the time Marion Yves was leaning towards the name 'Hazel'. She suggested this name to the vicar, but he gave her a disapproving look.

'With all the names we have in the Bible,' he rebuked her, 'and with all the names of all the saints in heaven, you want to call your baby after a nut?'

'But I like the name Hazel,' Marion had protested.

'In that case,' said the vicar, 'you should call her Azaliah. It's close enough to Hazel, isn't it? And it means "set aside by God".'

If you go back through the christening records for the parish of Port St Menfre you will find at least two more Azaliahs, along with a host of other biblical names. The villagers of Port St Menfre were Josephs and Ruths and Jacobs and Esthers and Rebeccas and Matthews; they were rarely Melvin or Roger or Veronica or Brenda. Clearly the Reverend had engaged in similar conversations with a generation of mothers. If you look up 'Azaliah' in a book of names, then it does indeed appear to mean 'set aside by God', or 'close to God', but curiously, if you search the Bible itself you will find this name only once, and in the event even the gender is ambiguous. Shaphan, we are told, was the son of Azaliah. So the original bearer of the name was probably male.

But, nevertheless, in her new life Azaliah became Azalea. The girl set aside by God became a flowering shrub.

*

The General Register Office in England has a process for the issuing of adoption certificates to foundlings. No birth certificate is issued, but a birth date is normally entered onto the adoption papers, marked, if necessary, as an estimated date. So as well as providing the foundling girl with a name, it was also necessary to establish an estimated date of birth. At the time Azalea came to live with the Folleys she was four years and three months old; but no one knew that, and with no known birthday the authorities were obliged to assign one for her. The doctor who had checked Azalea when she was found at the fairground had estimated the little girl's age as around four and a half, which would have made her almost five when she was adopted. We now know that she was only three years and ten months old when she was discovered. Her gangly frame may have made her look a little older, and her confident demeanour probably helped in this assessment. The doctor's judgement would have placed Azalea's birth date around December 1977. Her true birthday was in August 1978. But it was left to Rebecca and Luke Folley to agree with a registrar from Cornwall on an official date. The Folleys were anxious to resist a December date because this would be too close to Christmas, and had they been wiser they might have gone for January or later; but, in the event, the date they chose was an even earlier one – 1 November 1977, because this was All Saints' Day, adding a little over eight months to Azalea's age.

Eight months is a big gap for a four-year-old to make up. But the first intake in a school year will typically include children up to a year apart in age, so Azalea did not stand out as too young or too old when she joined the reception class at school within days of joining the Folleys.

Fate, of course, plays a part in all of our lives. As an adult, Azalea would often reflect upon the unlikely sequence of events that seemed to have directed her life. She would, many years later, visit the cliffs at Millook where Marion had perished, and there she would throw flowers onto the rocks in memory of a woman she no longer remembered. Had a hungry seagull snatched a different piece of bread, had a complicated train of events involving a faraway conflict in the South Atlantic not conspired to make her mother bundle her into a car for a six-hour drive, had the fairground lights not caught her eye, had Carl Morse not been prowling, had her mother been able to escape his clutches, had Azalea as a three-year-old known an address she could have given to the policemen, had the police in Sheffield possessed more imagination – then none of what was about to happen might ever have transpired. But all of us lead lives that twist and coil, and no one can truly say what might have been.

It wasn't until some years later that the young Azalea would learn of another cruel event that had happened on the very same day – 24 November 1982 – that she was adopted by the Folleys. It was an incident of such callous barbarity that Luke and Rebecca Folley would shield her from the news of it, even as she became slowly aware of the episode that was to determine her future in ways that no one could foresee. It was an event that may have been coldly unfolding, even as the Folleys hugged their new daughter and smothered her with new-found affection. Even as the car pulled up in the drive of the Folleys' home in St Piran, even as Azalea tore the coloured paper off the welcome gifts that her new parents had so lovingly wrapped, even then events were unravelling in a very distant land. Sometime on that day, as Rebecca Folley showed Azalea the little bedroom where she would sleep, as they looked out together at the boats that bobbed in the harbour, as they served up their first meal as a family – at some point a small conical slug of lead was starting a short and violent journey through the barrel of a gun, emerging into the bright sunlight of a town and a continent a great many miles from St Piran. And like the cascade of colliding balls on a snooker table, cold and inevitable consequences would accompany this fragment of metal as it crossed the void from its dark metallic tube. The repercussions of its flight would echo across years, and over continents, until the aftermath would engulf Luke and Rebecca and Azalea Folley – and eventually even Thomas Post as well.

One year after Azalea's adoption, the ripples had already reached the Folleys. By then the house in St Piran stood empty. Azalea and her new family were in Africa.

7

June 2012 / February 2011

'We met at Euston Station,' Thomas says. 'I don't think I ever told you that.'

He and Clementine are in the basement canteen of the university. They have lunched here many times before. Clementine picks at a healthy salad of unfamiliar beans and leaves. Thomas has goulash with chunky fried potatoes.

'Euston Station? How delightfully romantic,' Clementine observes. 'It reminds me of Trevor Howard and Celia Johnson.'

Thomas raises an eyebrow.

'*Brief Encounter*,' says Clementine. 'Please don't tell me you haven't seen that film.'

'I've heard of it,' Thomas says, lamely.

'They meet at a railway station. He helps to get something out of her eye. It's love at first sight.' Clementine hums a tune and lets her fingers dance over an imaginary piano. 'Rachmaninov plays in the background,' she says. 'Piano Concerto Number Two.'

'Ahh.' Thomas nods. 'It wasn't quite like that with us.'

'No Rachmaninov?' She is teasing him.

'None whatsoever.' He looks into his goulash and stabs at a potato.

It doesn't seem that long ago. How long was it? A year? A year and a half?

'It was February,' he tells her, 'February 2011.'

It had been cold; colder than winters in London have any right to be. There was ice still on pavements and swept-up snow in gutters. But the chill east wind was easing, and signs of a thaw were evident in the loosening of the coats and scarves of city commuters. There were fewer hats pulled down over ears than there had been just a week ago. Thomas, who rarely wore a hat, noticed these things.

They had never met. They were colleagues. But the University of London is Britain's largest; it is absurdly easy to pursue an entire career there without ever encountering the majority of one's colleagues. Azalea taught English literature and poetry to adult learners at Birkbeck, usually working unsocial hours at the college, where most teaching takes place in the evenings. Thomas was a philosopher, spinning out his days in an undistinguished annexe of the Institute for Philosophy in Russell Square. The two of them spent their working lives within the same few city streets; they undoubtedly swarmed down the same busy pavements to the same tube stations; they probably stood in the same queues for sandwiches in summer, and ate them on the same park lawn in Tavistock Square; they would have browsed together in the university bookshop, and must surely have squeezed into the same rowdy pubs after work. But huge universities and great cities deliver a cloak of invisibility, and so it was that when Azalea Lewis and Thomas Post mounted the top step of the escalator at Euston Station in the middle of the morning rush hour, neither would have afforded the other more than a courteous glance. They were strangers in a city of strangers.

That anonymity was about to change.

You may be familiar with the escalator at Euston Station; if not, you will at least recognise the general category of escalators that bear tides of people into the dark intestines of cities at all hours, but most especially at those times when, like one of the great animal migrations, the world's commuters take to their streets. Euston railway station, like a thousand city hubs from New York to Shanghai, is a portal, disgorging trainloads of workers from homes in the suburbs, propelling them down into the maze of tunnels that is the underground transport network. There is a moment every weekday morning when the sheer mass of humanity swarming onto the down escalator at Euston threatens to overwhelm the orderly unfolding of the steel steps, and a crowd begins to build and to push, as the urgency of the day's commute becomes more acute. Some workers filter off to the central stairway between the down escalator and the up escalator; they take the stairs in a hurry, often two steps at a time, anxious not to be overtaken by glassy-eyed travellers sweeping effortlessly down on the conveyor. Most commuters simply join the melee, waiting for the crush to carry them to the top step.

They are a diverse lot, the commuters of London; this one in an Italian suit off to get the Northern Line into the city; this one in fatigues off to clean a hospital; this one in the uniform of a nurse; this one in the uniform of a waiter. They clutch their bags and their newspapers and their laptop cases and their mobile phones, and they move with the precision of colonial insects driven by an unwavering programme to press forward. They make little eye contact. They rarely speak. They acknowledge fellow travellers with the faintest of nods. They are men and women on a mission, a familiar and practised journey from A to B. Thomas Post was one of this species, and so, on that February day, was Azalea Lewis.

There is a convention on the London Underground that the right-hand side of an escalator is reserved for standing passengers, while the left is a freeway for walkers. The walkers are impatient. The escalator is too slow to match the urgency of their commute. The convention fails when tourists, unfamiliar with the practice, find themselves on the left; then regular walkers get irritable and there can be pushing and bottlenecking. This is what happened that day. Two steps in front of Thomas Post (on the right) and Azalea Lewis (on the left), a pair of tourists were squeezed onto a step with large and unwieldy suitcases. A tetchy tail of commuters had sprung up behind. It should have been just another morning crush, but as the throng of people slid towards the depths, a man on the step behind Azalea tried to assert his right to push forward. Azalea was forced to steady herself by holding up a hand, which fell rather heavily on the tourist ahead; and the tourist, taken by surprise, tried to move and fell awkwardly over her suitcase. With creditable speed Thomas Post's hand flew out to catch the visitor, but she was falling too fast – and now Thomas was falling too, and Azalea was caught up in it.

And now the escalator reached the bottom. The twisted pile – two cumbersome suitcases, two frightened tourists and two employees of the University of London – was unceremoniously deposited onto the concourse. There was no time for anyone caught in the pile to extract themselves before commuters from two steps above also collapsed into the heap; and a second later another two, and then two more; and then a woman with a child in a pushchair and a man with a heavy parcel, and then two more people, and then two more.

It was astonishing how swiftly the mound of people grew. For those joining the stack, there was a grim inevitability about their destination. Unable to move backwards, unable to step sideways, they were carried forward and cast onto the pile. Screams grew from the press of people at the bottom and the cry carried back up the line, but the crowds joining at the top were blind to the commotion and they continued to press forward. Somewhere halfway up the escalator was an emergency button, but in the wave of panic that infected the crowd no one above the button thought to seek it, and those beneath it were unable to reach back.

The risk of injury was enhanced by those in the crush who struggled hardest to escape. The thrashing of legs and arms and the digging of heels made it worse for those who were being stamped upon, elbowed and punched by an increasingly panicked mob. Thomas had withdrawn his left arm from the woman on the stair below, and as they fell, he had gallantly extended the arm to protect the stranger who shared his stair. Now that arm was broken. Azalea for her part had broken a rib and was finding it difficult to breathe. Both of them stopped struggling to get out of the crush. By now any effort to move was painful.

At last someone found the emergency stop button and the relentless supply of new bodies was staunched. Even so, it took some time to disentangle all the limbs and to pull everyone to safety. Several commuters had been injured. One man was bleeding heavily from the face. A woman had possibly broken her neck. Another had a broken leg. A stiletto heel had been driven into the back of one of the Eastern Europeans and he was in a lot of pain. A student had seen her laptop computer trampled and crushed. Another had lost her glasses. Several people were in shock. The pushchair had buckled; but the baby, thank God, was unharmed.

First-aiders and paramedics started to arrive and Thomas and Azalea were pulled away and propped up on the cold stone floor, leaning against a wall. His broken arm was still draped around her shoulder as if they were a couple. In shock and in pain, neither of them sought to move it.

'Are you all right?' he asked her, unable – or unwilling – to move.

Azalea shook her head. 'I think I've broken some ribs. You?'

'My arm,' he said.

It was difficult to talk. They waited. Station staff tried to clear the crowd. Ambulance men arrived with stretchers.

'It's all right – I can walk,' said Thomas, getting to his feet and wincing with the pain.

'Are you two together?' asked an ambulance man. Thomas shook his head.

'In that case, if you can walk, can you go with my colleague?' he nodded towards a fellow rescue worker. 'Let's have a stretcher over here for this lady,' he called.

A first-aider tied a sling around Thomas's arm, and helped him to make his way back up the central stairwell to the station concourse. Thomas glanced back to see Azalea strapped onto a stretcher behind him. Her eyes were closed.

At the Accident and Emergency unit of University College Hospital, Thomas looked for the red-haired woman who had shared his step. But some of the ambulance cases were being directed to the Royal Free Hospital in Hampstead.

Thus quickly and unexpectedly our lives can change. None of us sets out to break a bone or to participate in an incident like the one that took place at the foot of the escalator at Euston Station that day. These things, when they happen, come as a surprise. Escalator pile-ups, as it turns out, are not especially rare. London Underground suffers dozens of incidents a year. This one was worse than many because of the intensity of the crush and because the couple at the front of the pile-up had heavy suitcases that blocked the way for anyone thrown into the fray. But the incident didn't even warrant a paragraph in the *Evening Standard*. A few bones were broken, but no one was killed.

In the days that followed the accident, Thomas found himself thinking about the woman with the broken rib. They had sat together in the corridor of the Underground station, waiting for the emergency services to arrive. His arm had been draped over her shoulder. He felt embarrassed to think about this. They had barely spoken a sentence to each other. Even in the chaos they had watchfully observed the Londoner's code of silence. But now he discovered himself trying to picture her face. There was a familiarity to her. Did he know her? He had struggled *not* to look at her. He had never asked her name, never enquired about her journey, never volunteered his phone number. He had, however, scented a delicate perfume, caught just a faint hint of organic fragrance from her hair, and now he longed to recapture the memory of this elusive aroma. For just a moment her head had rested upon his shoulder, seeking comfort like a lover's head, and he out of instinct had turned towards her, almost as if he might place a gentle kiss upon her hair. And then the moment had passed. But in his imagination and in his memory of the incident, this was the brief second that Thomas Post would revisit, this fragment of time and this indefinable scent. He thought of calling the accident unit at the Royal Free Hospital, just to enquire about the woman who had broken a rib, and on one occasion he did dial the number and he let it ring a couple of times, but he checked himself and hung up. The hospital would not share patient information unless he could prove that they were related, and how could he claim that if he didn't even know the woman's name?

The day of the escalator incident was a Friday. Thomas was

back at work by Wednesday morning, his arm in a plaster cast. He had an ordinary day. He taught a class on the social understanding of unusual events. It was one of his fields of expertise. Most of us, he argued, are bad at calculating the likelihood of quite normal events and we tend, therefore, to see them as remarkable, or divinely inspired. 'How likely is it,' he asked his class of twenty-five students, 'that you visit the theatre, and there in the audience is someone you just happen to know? Or let us say you stop at a motorway service station, or you go on holiday to Ibiza and there, in the same hotel, is someone you knew from school?' He let the students ponder this. 'I once flew to Madrid,' he said, 'and on the same flight were a couple whose wedding I had attended a year before. Was that a coincidence?'

He took a marker and did some calculations on a whiteboard. 'How many Facebook friends do you have?' he asked a girl in the front row.

She giggled. 'Around, maybe, four hundred,' she said.

'OK.' Thomas wrote *400*. 'Now if we add to these all your relatives, and your neighbours and people you've lost touch with, then four hundred probably becomes six hundred, doesn't it? Add all the people you'd recognise from school or university – not friends, just people you know – let's make it a thousand.' He crossed out the *400* and wrote *1,000*. 'When we look at it, that turns out to be a good estimate for the number of friends and relatives and acquaintances that each of us will typically have. So you'd probably recognise and go and greet a thousand people if you were to meet them in an unexpected place like an airport lounge or on a beach.' Again he sketched out the calculation on the whiteboard. 'How often are we in any kind of situation where there are two or three hundred strangers? At a theatre? In a supermarket? On a tube train? In the high street? Maybe four or five times a day.' He wrote the numbers up. 'Now your thousand acquaintances represent, say, one person in every fifty thousand in the UK. But you probably see the faces of fifteen hundred people every day. So you should have at least one chance encounter with somebody you know at least once a

45

month.' Thomas lowered himself carefully onto the desk at the front of the lecture theatre. His arm was in a sling and it was still uncomfortable.

'But that assumes,' he went on, 'that we're all randomly distributed around the country. In reality we can ignore big chunks of the population. We don't need to count children, or the very elderly, or stay-at-home farmers, or the housebound, or people in prison, or anyone you simply wouldn't bump into on a train from London. That should increase your likelihood of a chance encounter to one every fortnight. So the next time you meet a friend in Covent Garden, don't say, "What a coincidence meeting you here!" Because it isn't.

'So what are the chances,' he asked them, 'that two of us will share the same birthday?'

Many of the students had encountered this conundrum before. A quick poll of birthdays was held. In a gathering of twenty-three people, Thomas knew, there is more than a fifty per cent likelihood that two will share a birthday. The maths is counter-intuitive; most people would consider it a great coincidence if two guests at a party shared a birthday. In fact, with the twenty-five students in the room, it would be more unusual if *no* birthdays were shared. As each student called out his or her birthday, there was an air of expectation; but no two matched. Thomas held up his hand. 'There's one more person left,' he said, and he pointed to himself. 'My birthday is on the thirtieth of June.' There was a gasp and some applause. 'Who shares my birthday?' asked Thomas. 'Can you please stand up?'

A student towards the back of the lecture theatre rose.

'And can you remind the class of your name?'

The student grinned. 'My name is Jonathan Post,' he said.

'We have the same surname. How coincidental is that? And before you ask,' said Thomas, 'we're not related.' He took a longer look at the student who was on his feet. 'What did you do to your arm?' he asked.

Jonathan Post raised his arm. It was in a plaster cast.

'The same name, the same birthday and the same plaster cast,'

Thomas told his students. 'Now go away and calculate the chances of that happening.'

Back in his office, the telephone was ringing. A woman gave her name and asked to speak to Dr Post.

'Speaking,' said Thomas. He was still feeling a glow of satisfaction from his performance in the lecture hall.

'Are you the Coincidence Authority?' the voice asked.

Thomas laughed. 'I've been called a lot of things,' he said, 'but I don't think I've ever been called that.'

There was an awkward silence.

'All the same,' he added, 'I think I'm probably the person you want.'

'Oh good. I'm a colleague of yours,' said the voice on the phone, 'from Birkbeck. I've been reading your paper on coincidence.'

'Well you won't believe this,' said Thomas, 'but not only have I just come from delivering a lecture on coincidence, but I'm holding that very paper in my hand. Well actually I'm not, because I have only one good hand at present, and that one is holding the telephone. But I'm looking at that very paper on my desk. So we have a coincidence right away.'

The woman laughed, and her laugh was like the tinkling of a wind chime. 'What I should like,' she said, 'is to come and talk to you about it.'

'Of course,' said Thomas, feeling strangely light-headed, 'any time.'

'Is your office in the building in Russell Square?'

'It is.'

'Then I'll be there in twenty minutes,' she said. 'I shall see you then.'

So it was, that while Thomas was reflecting on the general gullibility of the population to the very ordinariness of encounters that they still consider remarkable, a soft knock came at his door, and around the door popped the unmistakable face of the woman he had met on the escalator at Euston Station – Azalea Lewis.

PART TWO

Losing Azalea

she dwells inside my picture frame
she has a face
she has a name
but i have neither sight nor sense
to trace her fading providence
engulfed in dreams i still await
the calculating hand of fate
but ash from fortune's spiteful cast
has sealed my celebration fast
and thus my providence amassed
its covenant and weight

p. j. loak

8

June 2012

'I need to digress a bit,' Thomas says.

They have finished their lunch, but Clementine Bielszowska has an aversion to lifts, so rather than brave the endless flights of stairs back up to Thomas's garret, they are still in the canteen. The lunchtime press of students and staff has eased. It is quieter now, and easier to talk.

'This whole story feels like one extended digression,' Clementine remarks, but she rests her hand on Thomas's knee to show that this isn't meant unkindly.

'It isn't easy to put it all in order,' Thomas says. 'There are different threads, and they all have a different starting point. Azalea's thread starts in Port St Menfre in the seventies. But Luke's thread starts much earlier.'

'Luke?'

'Luke Folley. The man who adopted Azalea.'

'I see. And we need his thread?'

Thomas shuts his eyes as if banishing the light will focus his mind on the narrative. 'Have you ever been to Uganda?'

'Uganda? No.' Clementine is emphatic. 'But I know where Uganda is. Have you been?'

'No.' He shakes his head and there is a suggestion of disappointment in the gesture. 'All I know is what Azalea told me.' He tries to imagine it, but how can you visualise a place you've never visited? He doesn't even have a photograph. He has scoured the internet for pictures looking for a mission that may, or may not, exist, and a township as remote from his world as any he might dream of; and he has tried to picture the hard red dust and the deep green hills, and the swirl of the great river. But imagination is no substitute for experience. Thomas knows this. He has heard these stories from Azalea. She can talk of the Albert Nile, and the markets of Gulu, and the voices of the Acholi people, and the cold eyes of the Lord's Resistance Army. But can he do the same?

'It starts,' he tells Clementine, 'in a little town called Langadi.'

9

1909–1984 / October 1969

The little township of Langadi lies north of the Nile River in that part of Uganda known as Moyo District in the province of West Nile. It is a remote place, the West Nile. It hugs the north and west borders of the country, cleanly severed from the rest of Uganda by the great river that snips off its top left corner. Only two fragile connections exist to link this secluded district to the rest of Uganda. One is an ancient ferry service that groans across the Nile at Laropi once every hour between sunrise and sunset, laden with lorryloads of produce from the south en route to the far-flung communities of West Nile and the markets of Sudan. The other is the great bridge at Pakwatch some two hundred miles or so, down perilous roads, to the west. Moyo town itself is little more than a straggle of buildings set around the confluence of half a dozen dusty murrum roads the colour of soft terracotta. There's a sprawling local marketplace and a handful of respectable buildings, and then a spidery network of poorly maintained dirt roadways and footpaths that link the town to its neighbours and to an endless succession of village communities each with its cluster of circular thatched Acholi huts, its farms, animals and ragged children. If you continue to travel north, past the patchwork of farms that roll out to the hills in the west and to the Nile Valley in the east, you will reach the border post with the country we must now call Southern Sudan – although in 1984, when Luke, Rebecca and Azalea Folley arrived in Langadi, the huge country to the north was all simply 'Sudan', and the region to the north of the border post was the Sudanese district of Central Equatoria. The great civil war that had raged since the mid-1950s in Sudan subsided in the early 1980s, but this was only a temporary armistice; in 1983 it erupted again and would escalate brutally for another two decades as the largely non-Arab, non-Muslim southern Sudanese rebelled against the authoritarian, Islamic rule of the north. For Ugandan border townships such as Langadi, Moyo and Arua, and even for the regional capital, the city of Gulu, two hours' drive to the south-east, the conflict that affected their northern neighbour would encroach upon their life too. Even during lulls in the civil war, the Sudan People's Liberation Army – the SPLA – would mount cross-border attacks. Armed militia groups would cross the border to raid farms and market stalls for food to take to their comrades-in-arms in Sudan; shots would be fired, and sometimes casualties would result.

Border skirmishes in Africa are nothing new, of course, and the five-hundred-mile border between Uganda and Sudan was never much more than an arbitrary pen line on an Imperial map, dividing villages and communities that shared a common culture and language long before the colonisers and their charts arrived. Like most boundaries in Africa, this one is not, and never has been, a border that can be policed in any realistic way, and this pragmatic feature of African geopolitics has always led to waves of immigration as refugees from unsavoury regimes go looking for a more benign place to scratch out a living. At the same time as the SPLA was waging its unpleasant guerrilla war in Sudan, and Sudanese militiamen were raiding Ugandan border towns for food, a less aggressive but more insidious invasion was taking place as southern Sudanese villagers, families and workers sought refuge from the travails of their country. Very few would cross the border legally, although for those who wished to take the formal road via the Jale border post, a small consideration to the border guards would normally be acceptable. Literacy was not high in this part of Africa at the time, and anyway, money has always been more reliable than paperwork in this part of the world.

The upshot of this little piece of history was an influx, every year, of tens of thousands of refugees into a part of the world with a limited ability to accommodate them. It wasn't a particularly proud time in Ugandan history, either. The brutal, syphilitic dictator, Idi Amin (or, if you prefer, 'His Excellency, President for Life, Field Marshal Al Hadji Dr Idi Amin Dada, VC, DSO, MC, Conqueror of the British Empire' to give him his assumed title) had been deposed in 1979; but the despot who succeeded him was the former Prime Minister, Dr Apolo Milton Obote, a man whose mismanagement of the country became almost as legendary as Amin's. The rule of Obote was characterised by widespread human rights abuses, corruption and torture. It was a period that became known locally as the 'Ugandan Bush War' when a whole gaggle of government and rebel groups with names such as the 'Popular Resistance Army (PRA)' and the 'Uganda Freedom Fighters (UFF)' pitted forces against one another. Tens of thousands would die in the skirmishes that followed. Child soldiers were regularly used by the NRA (National Resistance Army) against Obote's UNLA forces. The UNLA, in case you are keeping track of all this, was the Uganda National Liberation Army, not to be confused with its political wing, the Uganda National Liberation Front (UNLF). What the arbitrary mapmakers had done for the northern border of Uganda was hardly less ruinous than the mess they had made of Uganda itself, lumping together into a discrete geography a whole assortment of ethnic groups and tribes – many of whom had never particularly got on. Thus the majority Buganda people in the south were distrusted by the Acholi and the tribes of the north, much as the English are distrusted by the Scots and the French are distrusted by the English. And lest we are tempted to dismiss the bloodshed between tribes in Uganda as anything resembling the rivalry between the English and the Scots, or between the English and the French, it is helpful to remember how many years of bloody conflict arose from those disputes, and how many bodies ended up on battlefields. In Uganda the rule of Obote was threatened by the National Resistance Movement (NRM) of Yoweri Museveni – the man who would one day seize the presidency – as well as the NRA that we met earlier and a curious group called FUNA, the Former Ugandan National Army, most of whose members had once served Amin, and the Ugandan National Rescue Front (URF) who came from the same part of Uganda as Amin. In addition, the Uganda Freedom Movement (UFM) and the Federal Democratic Movement of Uganda (FEDEMU), both drawn from Buganda power bases in the south, emerged to oppose Obote. Even for students of this period the proliferation of armed groups, each with their proud acronym, is bewildering. To the Ugandan people it must have been a stressful and intensely wearying time. It certainly helped to bankrupt a country that was already very poor. The Uganda Ministry of Defence spent over a quarter of the government's revenue combating militias in 1983, and again in 1984, and yet the opposition kept on fighting, and the body count kept on growing.

This was the baffling, and rather intimidating, backdrop that confronted Luke and Rebecca Folley and their newly adopted daughter Azalea when they arrived in Langadi in January 1984. We first met the Folleys as primary-school teachers, but this was not their calling. Their true vocation was to be missionaries. Luke and Rebecca were to become teachers at the grandly named 'Holy Tabernacle Mission of St Paul to the Needy of West Nile'. It was a new and rather frightening venture for Rebecca Folley, but for Luke it was a return home; the end of a brief, ill-fated period of rebellion that had swept him up a decade earlier. It began as a turbulent attempt by the young Luke to thwart his destiny, to defy providence and to carve out a life a long way from the northern hills of Uganda. Moving to Langadi wasn't a calling from God for Luke; it was an acceptance of his fate. Luke Folley was a *third generation* missionary. This was, if you like, the family *business*. Luke's grandfather, the Reverend Lester Baines Folley, a Cornishman and a preacher of the 'fire-and-brimstone' variety, had founded the first Holy Tabernacle Mission of St Paul to the Needy at Langadi as long ago as 1907, when he was only thirty years old. These were early days for the white man in Africa, and Lester Folley was a pioneer, carving his way with considerable courage, and not a little recklessness, into the dark heart of Africa to bring the Good News of God to the villages of the West Nile. He was joined a year or so later by Elizabeth Jane Folley, the bride he had left behind in St Piran, and we can only imagine that she, too, was as redoubtable as he. Lester Bryant Folley, their son, was born in the newly built Langadi Mission Hospital in 1909. The younger Lester grew up to inherit the running of the mission from his father. It was the first indication that each successive generation of Folley children would inherit an obligation to succeed to the family calling.

The earliest photographs of the Folleys that still exist are from the 1960s. It is possible that before this time, no one at the mission had thought to squander God's money on a camera. There are some snapshots of the second Lester (perhaps we should call him Lester Folley II). They appear to show an elderly man, for although Lester was only in his fifties at the time, Africa had taken a fierce toll on his constitution. He is slightly bowed at the back, with a wild silver beard, and is making an uncomfortable attempt at a smile. In every photograph he carries a carved ebony walking stick – a reminder of the parasitic diseases that afflicted him badly in his childhood, and which left him with limited movement in his right arm and leg.

Lester Folley II married a French mission doctor in 1942. The couple's first son, also christened Lester, made his appearance in 1944. Why don't we, for clarity and consistency, call him Lester Folley III? Luke Folley, his brother, the man who would later adopt Azalea, was born in 1948. Both sons were born at the same mission hospital in Langadi.

The little mission stumbled by from year to year on meagre donations, most of them from the United States. Each year the mission office would post out twenty thousand leaflets to churches and missionary associations in Europe and America detailing the good work that the St Paul Mission was doing and appealing for funds; and every year the donations would trickle in. In the warm evenings on the veranda of the mission house under the sweep of a great jacaranda tree, Lester and Monique would write, by hand, letters of thanks for every donation, however small.

In each envelope they would enclose one small black and white photograph of a child from the mission orphanage with messages such as 'A very big thank you from Moses', or 'Many thanks from Mariah' crudely written on the back. Six weeks before Christmas, a small hand-coloured card would go out to each donor from Moses or Mariah, or whichever child had sent the first picture, and soon after, more donations would arrive.

This, then, had been the home of the Folley family for three generations: the whitewashed mission house, the church with its leaky corrugated-iron roof, the little four-room clinic and dormitory that called itself a hospital, the open-air mess and the two-room schoolhouse where generations of Langadi children had learned their reading and their numbers and their gospel stories.

There is a languid sense of abandonment that settles upon mission families, a comfortable torpor, an easy-going routine advanced by the agreeable climate and the slow pace of life, and the dust, and the singing of hymns, and the ringing of the mission bell. As history swept up the peoples of Uganda and Sudan, tossing them hither and thither like chaff in a wheat bowl, as European empires rose and then departed, and as the fireworks from independence parties gave way to the gunfire of new despots and transient militias, the mission, with its cluster of buildings, its school, its farmstead, its Sunday services and its quiet sense of duty became just another part of Langadi life. The white-painted board proclaiming *The Church of the Holy Tabernacle Mission of St Paul to the Needy of West Nile* became so faded that first-time visitors might have struggled to read it. But first-time visitors were rare, and why would local people need a sign? The farmstead grew bananas, sweet potatoes, maize, groundnuts, cassava, sorghum and sesame. The schoolrooms catered to gaggles of local children. The dormitories offered shelter to orphans. The clinic ministered to the sick.

The funds for the mission itself might have been in short supply, but church missionary societies in London had generous provisions to support the education of the *sons* of British missionaries. By the time the 1960s arrived, both Lester III and young

58

Luke were back in England kitted out in grey worsted suits and bright straw boaters as pupils of a public school in Kent. Lester III, the elder brother, ever the star pupil, shone at Latin and Greek and history, and rugby and fencing and tennis; and despite the suspicion that none of these skills might be especially useful for a career in an orphanage in the centre of Africa, Lester nonetheless set his sights upon a return to Uganda to continue the family tradition. While his contemporaries were packing to go to Oxford or Cambridge, Lester departed for a theological college in Canterbury, and there he began to learn the lore and teachings of the Church of England. No doubt he would have studied the fine words of Archbishop Cranmer, the very ones intoned by the Reverend Doctor Jeremiah Lender just a decade or so later over the infant Azaliah Yves. Perhaps he would have learned the best way to hold a baby in a glossy christening gown over an old stone font. Unquestionably he would have employed his Greek and Latin to better understand the great scriptures that informed his faith. In that pivotal year of 1969, when the decade of free love was coming to a close, Lester Folley III was ordained as a priest; and with the ink still wet on his certificate of ordination, he returned to Langadi.

There is a saying in Uganda: 'The older son inherits the farm, the younger son goes astray'. This is how it was for Lester and Luke Folley. Lester the diligent elder son had devoted himself to preparing for his return to the family mission; but could it ever be that simple for Luke? The times were a-changing, and Luke chose not to return. Although he might have said that he didn't exercise any choice at all. In a sense it was never a decision for Luke; it was, at best, the *deferring* of a decision. It was the brief rebellion of the prodigal son. As a non-decision, as a deferred decision, it was something that grew easier to bear with each day that passed. Luke Folley, a continent away from parental advice or family disapproval, did not excel in Latin or Greek or even, particularly, in history. He felt no calling to the priesthood. He developed a disdain for the prose of Thomas Cranmer. He dropped out of school and grew his hair. In the amiable language of the time, he found that he had somehow become a *hippy*. Comfortable with this new identity, Luke set about relishing the dying years of the 1960s. It was a career arc familiar to many of his generation. Together with a group of friends and like-minded dropouts, he moved into a squat in Ladbroke Grove. Burning with enthusiasm, the squatters changed the locks, repainted the walls with paisley swirls and psychedelic motifs, spread posters on the walls of Hendrix and Dylan and Che Guevara and drew Ban the Bomb symbols on the doors in pink and yellow paint. With the decoration complete, they opened those doors to fellow squatters. At one time ten, or twelve, or even fifteen people might have shared the four-bedroomed home. Sleeping arrangements were free and easy. Property was theft. Luke flirted, as many did, with Marxism and dialectical materialism and free love and LSD. He made a little money doing casual jobs: stacking shelves in a chemist shop, offloading vegetables at Old Covent Garden Market, selling small quantities of marijuana. He learned to play the guitar, and wrote songs that were vaguely Dylanesque; he wore sandals and tie-dyed shirts and an inside-out sheepskin coat and a headband from Peru. It was the uniform of his day. His hair was uncut and unwashed. Soap was an invention of the bourgeoisie. He washed in cold water and smelt of patchouli oil. He read discarded copies of *Oz* magazine, and comic strips by Robert Crumb, and books by Ken Kesey and Allen Ginsberg and leaflets by Timothy Leary. He burned incense sticks and listened to the music of The Grateful Dead and Iron Butterfly and Jimi Hendrix. He protested against the war in Vietnam. He joined CND, and practised the ironic two-fingered V with its accompanying drop of the head and unhappy smile and dutiful chant of 'Peace, man'.

With the great courage afforded by hindsight, Luke would later describe these as his 'lost years'. He grew thin on his new vegan diet. He developed a morose look. He stopped replying to letters from his parents in Langadi, or from his brother Lester at the seminary in Kent. He gave up his job at Covent Garden Market because he couldn't manage the early-morning starts. He was sacked from the chemist shop because his appearance was unsuitable for a family business. He resisted the bourgeois temptation to sign on the dole, and took to playing his guitar in a subway at Marble Arch, effectively begging for small change. It was a desperate move for a desperate young man.

Luke Folley turned twenty-one in the autumn of 1969. One evening he came home to find that a security firm with black and gold vans had forcibly repossessed the squat in Ladbroke Grove. It wasn't a great surprise. A dispute over the ownership of the house and the rights of the squatters had been running for several months, and it was said that the house had been sold at a comfortable discount to a foreign buyer who was confident that the freeloading residents might be persuaded to depart. That moment seemed to have arrived. A manifestly persuasive group of large men of African origin had arrived at the house while Luke had been strumming his guitar in the subway, and by the time he had drawn up at the house, the men had persuaded the other occupants to vacate. The locks had been changed again, and Luke's belongings, what few there were, had been roughly packed into cardboard boxes and abandoned on the pavement where they now lay like the strewn wreckage from a hurricane. From a cold, grey sky it was raining softly. The boxes were already damp.

A gaggle of Luke's fellow squatters stood about looking shell-shocked. One of the girls was wailing. Others were remonstrating with two of the African security men, who seemed unmoved by their appeals. Drained of energy, Luke slid down onto the pavement and sank his head into his hands to contemplate his bleak existence. His great dreams and ideals had evaporated. Now here he was – weak, homeless and virtually penniless, sitting on a London pavement looking at the contents of his life in two brown boxes and a guitar case.

A limousine slid up to the kerb. From it emerged a tall African man in a grey suit, and a pale European girl wearing Bardot plastic boots and a paisley miniskirt. They were plainly the new owners of the house from which Luke and his feckless companions had been so brusquely evicted. The African man ignored the hippies and let loose a stream of remarks aimed at the two security guards in a language that was so familiar to Luke it might just as well have been English. What he said to the guards was in Acholi, the language of the West Nile. The translation that Luke often quoted to Azalea when he told her the story included the African invective, 'Get these effing wasters off my effing land before I effing bury them here.'

The shock of hearing the Acholi language made Luke sit up and look at the man. 'Okot?' he found himself saying. The name 'Okot' means 'Born in the rains'.

The African man swung around to look at the thin hippy whose body was littering his pavement. 'Luke?'

Luke rose weakly to his feet. Talking in Acholi he said, 'You're a long way from the mission, Mr Okot Lakwo.'

'As are you, Mr Luke Folley,' said the African, and he broke into the heartiest laugh the Englishman had heard in months.

We don't often think of laughter as a means of communication. We laugh as a reaction to a comic situation; we laugh to relieve stress; we laugh to join in socially with the laughter of others. For Luke, however, bedraggled, cold, homeless and hungry, Okot Lakwo's laugh was none of these. This laugh was a cruel polemic; it was a sermon in sound. It was a laugh that spoke of triumph and exultation. It drew its comedy from the deepest wells of Schadenfreude. While Okot Lakwo laughed the world stopped for Luke Folley; laughter that echoed and amplified around the Georgian terraces of Ladbroke Grove.

When it was done, Okot Lakwo slapped his arm around Luke Folley's back. 'My dear, dear, friend,' he said, now speaking in English. 'Your father is worried about you.'

Luke shook his head. Long wet strands of hair clung to his face.

'Why do I find you in this state?' the African asked, the slightest gesture of his head indicating everything.

Luke found himself unable to speak. The great elation of his rebellion had vanished. He could not summon up a peace sign, or a Marxist metaphor, or a single slogan in support of free love. He could not begin to compute the sheer unlikeliness of an orphan from the mission in Langadi buying the very house in which he had been squatting. He was struck only by the penetrating echo of the laugh and by the sheer hopelessness of his situation.

'It's OK,' he managed to say. He turned as if to walk away.

'Wait, wait, wait.' Okot's hand was on his shoulder. 'Are these your things?'

Luke surveyed the wet boxes. He hesitated. 'No.' And truly they no longer felt like his things. They felt like the loveless impedimenta that occupy the shelves of charity shops. They felt like the clothes and the books and the records of a different, distant person.

'Let me offer you some hospitality,' Okot smiled. 'Come inside. Let's get you dry. We'll find you somewhere to stay until you can get back on your feet.'

'No. But thank you all the same. I'm all right.' Luke hoisted his guitar case onto his shoulder.

The African looked at him suspiciously. 'So,' he said, 'we are to meet a continent away from home, and you are to turn and walk away?' He drew closer. 'You remember what we say in Acholi? *Okom oyoko langwec* – the stump of a tree can fell a running man. I think, my friend, you have run into a tree.'

Luke tried to wipe the tendrils of hair from his eyes. 'I think perhaps I have.'

'Then the running man must pick himself up and run on.'

'It isn't always as easy as that.'

'Oh yes it is. Believe me, it is.'

What could Luke say? With his private education and all the benefits of his birth, what words could he utter that would make any sense to this man who had fought his way from a civil war orphanage in Africa to stand above him on this pavement beside his limousine and his trophy girlfriend and his London house? Luke just shook his head miserably.

'Do you remember another saying in Langadi, *Yoo aryo oloyo lalur*, the hyena is defeated by two roads? He's in full chase of his prey but he comes to a fork in the path. Which way should he choose? He stops. Maybe this way? Maybe that way? Now instead of running he's standing alone in the road, unable to decide. I think this has happened to you, my friend.'

'Maybe.'

'So tell me ... what are the forks that have left you here?'

Luke thought. 'In one fork,' he said, 'I will be a famous musician, playing my guitar in the Albert Hall, selling a million records.' He managed a weak smile.

'And in the other fork?'

'I go to teacher-training college. Then maybe I teach for a while in England. Maybe one day I go back and help Lester and my dad at the mission.'

Okot nodded his understanding. 'These are both good forks,' he said. 'But now, you're like the hyena. The fork in the road is your prison instead of your way out.' He offered a genial grin. 'What kind of music do you play?'

Luke shrugged. 'Dylan, Simon and Garfunkel.'

'Then you're ten years too late, my friend.'

Luke grimaced. The comment stung.

'How many demonstration tapes have you made for record companies? How many auditions have you been to? How many doors of record producers do you knock on every day to demand that they listen to your music? How many have you spoken to *today*?'

Luke shook his wet head. 'None,' he admitted.

'Then you truly are stuck,' said Okot. 'You haven't chosen to be a famous musician, and you haven't chosen to be a teacher.'

'But if I choose to be a teacher ... if I do ... then I know what would happen. I would have to go back to Langadi.'

Okot laughed. 'No you wouldn't. You don't have to do anything you don't want to do.'

'Oh, but you don't know the pressure I would get from my father, and my mother, and from Lester.'

'Oh but I think I do.' The African gave Luke a kindly smile. 'Would it be so bad? To go back?'

'*You* never went back.'

The big Ugandan man laughed again. But it was not the same

laugh as before. It was kinder, more understanding. 'It was different for me, my friend. What would I do in Langadi? Milk the cattle? But for you – you could run your own mission.'

'That isn't the biggest problem ...'

'So tell me the biggest problem.'

'I don't believe any more.'

'You don't believe in the work of the mission?'

Luke looked miserable. 'I don't believe in God.'

For a third time the African exploded into a great gale of laughter. He pounded his big hand like a paddle on Luke's back. 'My friend, my friend, my friend,' he said in between snorts of hilarity, '*nobody* believes in God any more.'

'My brother still does.'

The big Acholi man grinned widely. 'Then get him to do the God stories,' he said. 'You teach everything else.'

Luke bobbed his head weakly.

'But all the same, I'm not telling you which fork to choose. I'm saying don't make the mistake of the hyena.' Okot reached into a jacket pocket and peeled a dozen large banknotes from a roll. 'Here is what you do, my friend. You take this money and you turn and you walk away. You leave all of this behind.' He gestured at the boxes, now limp in the rain. 'Either you go now and start calling on record producers – shall we say, four a day – or you get a haircut at the first barber you pass. You buy a good meal. You buy some good strong clothes and you go down to your father's house in Cornwall. You write to your father and you tell him you're well. Tell him that we met, but never tell him *how* we met. You find a job and you find a girl. And then you enrol in your teacher-training course, and one year from today you visit me here in my house.' He grinned. 'You know the house – right?'

Luke nodded.

'One year from today. You visit me in my house and you pay me back my money.'

'I will.'

'One year from today?'

'I will.'

'Go then.'

Luke raised his head, and for the first time he looked Okot right in the eye. He reached out a hand and took the money. '*Apwoyo*,' he said. Thank you. And then, because this was the Acholi way, he turned and walked away. One of the hippies called after him, but he didn't break his stride. He had run into a tree stump but the stump hadn't killed him. It was raining hard when he turned the corner and left it all behind. Across the road was the red and white pole of a barber shop.

10

January 1978

It wasn't long after the incident with Marion Yves and the seagull that the story took hold in the Manx village of Port St Menfre. The Reverend Jeremiah Lender, who must have been bound by *some* obligation regarding clerical confidentiality, nonetheless recounted the story of the seagull to his wife Ruth, making her promise faithfully not to share these secrets with a soul – *not with a single soul* – a pledge that Ruth Lender solemnly extracted later that same day from her sister Mary. Mary, in turn, swore secrecy with her cousin Eve; and after that the trail has faded. But it does appear that within twenty-four hours the tale was common currency among all but six members of the village population: Marion herself, the vicar, Gideon Robertson the fisherman, Peter the barman and Mr and Mrs John Hall at the Bell Inn.

Versions of the seagull story varied in their particulars, especially when it came to the final outcome. Marion had left the Reverend Lender without revealing the course that God had chosen through the medium of the seagull. But the vicar told his wife that *he* was sure that the piece of bread snatched up by the first gull had in *fact* corresponded to one of the potential fathers, and not to either of the less palatable options of single parenthood or termination of the pregnancy.

Eventually, of course, the story *did* find its way to the three putative fathers.

The first to appear at the gate of 4 Briny Hill Walk was the landlord of the Bell Inn. John Hall was a bulldog of a man, a former SAS soldier, built like a rugby full back and with a face as red as a strong rosé wine, a neck as wide as a cider barrel and a look of permanent outrage. He stormed up the pathway and rapped belligerently on the door. Marion admitted him, and the door was closed for almost an hour before he left the cottage, as scarlet-faced and furious as he had been on arrival. It hadn't been an easy encounter. He demanded to know what Marion thought she was doing, spreading rumours through the village; rumours that he, Sergeant Hall, the innocent and irreproachable landlord of the inn, had somehow fathered a child by her. He, the blameless husband, the ex-soldier with the spotless reputation, was now tarred with the brush of suspicion.

'Don't you remember fucking me, down in the beer cellar,' she asked, 'with your trousers around your ankles and me pressed up against boxes of cider, while your wife pulled pints in the bar above our heads? Don't you remember lying me down on an old wooden pallet, and tearing my knickers in your haste to get your thing inside me? Don't you? Don't you?'

He might have wished to protest his innocence, but how could John Hall deny it? He was a military man; he was possessed of a code of honour. He squared up to the truth. 'In that case,' he said, 'you must tell me if the child is mine.'

'Can't you tell yourself?' Marion replied. 'Did you fire blanks from that thing? Didn't I have to douse myself with bottled water before going back to the bar, in case the smell of your spunk should give me away to your wife?'

It wasn't the only exchange that took place between Marion and John Hall that evening, but it was the one that mattered. One hour after he arrived, John Hall left 4 Briny Hill Walk in little doubt that the child in Marion's womb was his, but resolved to admit it to no one.

Gideon Robertson lumbered up to Number Four as the sun set, just a few hours after John Hall's visit. He did not march up and strike the door like the ex-soldier had done; instead he stood hesitantly at the gate of the cottage he had once shared with Marion, and for a while he sat on the low wall looking out at the tide, watching the last of the mackerel boats returning. The sun had disappeared beneath the Irish Sea before he headed gingerly up to the front door and tapped as gently as a child. He too was admitted.

How did this conversation go? There was much more history between Gideon and Marion. Theirs had not been a hasty knee-trembler in a beer cellar; they had shared a bed like husband and wife, had rolled nightly into each other's arms, had slept and caressed and loved and argued and done all those things that lovers do. Gideon was more hurt than angry; more concerned for Marion than for himself. He had no reputation to protect. 'How are you taking all this gossip?' he asked her. 'How will you manage this pregnancy on your own?'

He begged her to let him stay, flattered and cajoled in his big, cumbersome way. He made promises. He would look for work on the island. He would raise the child as his own with no care if it were his or some other man's. And there is no doubt that Marion found his suit difficult to resist. She cared for Gideon. So why didn't she relent, and let him take his place beside her and raise the child as his own? Was it the seagull and the bread that swayed her? Perhaps. Was it the fear that one dark night when the swell was high he would sail out and never return? Certainly this preyed on Marion's mind – she, who was the daughter of a man who had died at sea and the granddaughter of another. Did she look at him and see no future for herself or her baby? We do not know. All we know is that the interview took about an hour.

No one saw Peter the barman visit. He came after midnight, after the inn had closed its doors.

'They are saying,' he said dramatically to Marion, 'that you have fallen pregnant.'

Marion laughed at this ponderous accusation. 'Fallen pregnant? *Fallen*? Is that how it happens? Why didn't they teach us this at school? Well, well. And I always imagined there would be some screwing involved.'

Peter sheepishly corrected himself. 'They're saying you are with child.'

Marion was weary of these encounters by now. She was in her dressing gown and the two were standing in her kitchen. 'Are they really,' she said with some sarcasm in her voice. 'Well it must be true then, if that's what they're saying.'

'They are saying,' insisted Peter, 'that I'm the father.'

'Well, well,' said Marion again. 'And could it be true?'

'You must tell me,' said Peter. 'Tell me if it's true.'

'Don't you remember being in my bed?' asked Marion.

Peter looked bowed. 'Of course I remember.'

'And do you remember wearing any protection?'

The boy shook his head.

'And didn't they teach you at school in England what might happen if you come into a girl with no protection?'

'I thought ...'

'What did you think, young Peter?'

'I thought you were on the p-pill.' He stammered this out.

'And did you ask me? Did you ask if I was on the p-p-p-pill?'

He shook his head again.

'No,' she said. 'You didn't. You just assumed.'

'So I *am* the father then?'

She looked at him. He was eighteen. He was slight and pale and he was frightened of what she might say, of what this might mean.

'Do you remember that day ... up by the stream?'

He bobbed his head.

'We lay in the long grass.'

'I remember. We were underneath a hornbeam tree.'

'Is *that* what it was? You quoted poems to me as the sun went down.'

'"Shall I compare thee to a summer's day?"'

'That was one of them.'

'"Thou art more lovely and more temperate".'

She slid an arm around him.

'Was it that day?' he whispered.

'Of course not.' She allowed their eyes to meet. 'That was September.'

'... And this baby?'

'Was conceived in November.'

'Ah,' he said. '"Winter when icicles hang by the wall ..."'

'Is this another poem?'

'"And Dick the shepherd blows his nail, and Tom bears logs into the hall, and milk comes frozen home in pail".'

She laughed and pretended to slap him but he caught her hand and held it.

'So, is it mine?'

'Where were you in November?'

'You know where I was in November.'

'Then you know as much as I do.'

He released her hand. They were both breathing heavily now. Softly he recited, '"Not yesterday I learned to know, the love of bare November days, before the coming of the snow".'

'Is this another poem?'

'Robert Frost.' He held her then, and whispered the lines into her ear. And a little while later they went up the small staircase to bed.

11

June 1992

In Langadi the day began early. Anyeko, thirteen years of age, was the oldest child in the orphanage. She would rise when the cockerels started to call, when the sun was still an orange gleam on the eastern hills. She would pull on her blue school dress and would scamper out of the dormitory. She would lead the nanny goats from the night shed and tether them in the grass yard, and she would throw open the shutters of the chicken roost and laugh out loud when the birds all flew down at once.

When it was time to milk the goats, Anyeko would go to the window of the mission house and tap on the glass. Azalea, now also thirteen, lanky and tanned with a boy's cut of hair and not a single girlish curve on her figure, would slip out from beneath her mosquito net, and, barefoot, still in her nightdress, she would tiptoe outside. The two girls would run back to the goat yard, and snatching up the buckets, laughing together, high, happy voices floating over the compound, they would milk the nanny goats in time for breakfast.

Breakfast at Langadi was at seven o'clock with the sun still low in the sky. Odokonyero, the big Acholi cook, would be waiting for the goats' milk. He would splash it straight from the bucket into the pan ready to make cassava porridge. Tebere, one of the older boys, would fetch rolls of charcoal for the stove, and two more girls, Okema and Kila, would stir it. When seven o'clock arrived, Odokonyero would nod towards Anyeko and Azalea and the two girls would tug on the bell rope, and the bell high in the bamboo rafters would summon the mission to the table.

The mess hall was a high wooden gazebo, open on all sides

around a cement floor, shaded by a roof of deep black thatch. The kitchen was no more than an alcove, featuring a barbecue fashioned from the two halves of an oil drum and a lock-up cupboard for storing pans and provisions. Mrs Rebecca Folley, her long hair tied back in a bun, would sit at the top of one long table smoking her first cigarette of the day and slowly savouring a tin mug of tea. She favoured her tea freshly brewed, using tea leaves from western Uganda, still green, bought in bundles from the market in Moyo. Luke Folley, on the other table, preferred coffee. His favourite beans were from Mbale in the far east of Uganda, freshly roasted each morning by the cook.

The smell of Luke's breakfast coffee roasting slowly over the charcoal would become one of Azalea's abiding memories of Langadi. Long after this day was over, this day that would change her life for ever, the smell of coffee would be one of those delicate index smells that could trip delicious cascades of memory, so that even as an adult, even in the winter streets of London, she could walk past a coffee shop and catch just the faintest hint of Mbale beans rich with all the smells and sounds of Africa: the chuckle and whoop of the gonolek bird and the flash of its scarlet and black wings, and there in the distance would be the sounds of the motor scooters on the road to Moyo and the high, excited voices of the orphanage children; and if she closed her eyes just for the briefest of moments, there would be Pastor David droning out grace and Odokonyero doling out the meals.

It was a morning such as this, a hot African morning. The fifteen orphanage children and the Folleys, the cook, the six farm workers, and Stanton who drove and maintained the mission bus, and the old Buganda preacher Pastor David, and Maria the orphanage matron, and Elizabeth the nurse, and two maids who cleaned and washed and helped in the kitchen, and two boys who swept and minded the compound, and Ritchie and Lauren the VSO students still pale from the English winter, and old Mzee Njonjo, a Kikuyu man from Kenya, who served as the nightwatchman; all thirty-six sat down for breakfast, and another sixteen breakfasts would be cooked and served to patients in the hospital. You might argue that only thirty-five sat down for breakfast, since Odokonyero never quite took a seat at the table – he was too busy with the porridge and with Mr Luke's coffee – but a place was set for him nonetheless.

The five farm boys were first at the table. They had already milked the Ankole cows and walked them out to pasture, and now they were hungry. They bantered and jostled until Mr Oweko the farm manager came to take his seat beside them.

No one could eat until Pastor David had recited grace, and he would always appear ten minutes or more after the breakfast bell, by which time the farm boys and the orphans were shrieking his name and the porridge was cooling fast on the table. 'Please hurry, Pastor David,' Matron Maria would reprove him, 'or our orphans will starve.'

'One more minute and I'd have said grace myself,' Azalea would say.

The language spoken at the St Paul Mission was English. This was a tradition begun by Lester Folley I. Acholi was spoken too, informally, and other Luo and Sudanese dialects like Dinka and Madi. Fragments of Swahili were used as a lingua franca in marketplaces and on the streets, for this was a melting pot of a place and snippets of English and Swahili were necessary to carry out business here. Sometimes there would be Arabs in the marketplace, swathed in Bedouin headscarves, walking tall and erect, speaking Sudanese Arabic, shunned by the Acholi. There could be Kenyans, who had drifted across from the difficult farmlands of Lake Turkana looking for greener fields to work. There were young Tanzanians who had fled from conflicts down on the southern border. There were, sometimes, Karamojong from the north-east, tall and elegant. Their religion forbade the wearing of clothes, but successive regimes had taken to punishing public nakedness, and these days the younger Karamojong were apt to relax the rules and to dress. There were short, dark people from the lands to the west – Congolese – in their colourful cottons, here to trade with animal skins and bush meat and forest fruits and beads made from the teeth of crocodiles. A handful of Indian traders who had survived Amin's purges by moving over the borders into Kenya and Sudan were now back in Moyo District. There were Chinese here from time to time, emissaries from Peking looking for opportunities to engage with the ever-changing regimes. There were Europeans, too – Britons mainly – farmers and missionaries for the most part, like the Folleys, but some who came to work on projects for the UN or for businesses back in Europe. Any journey from Karama to Gulu and north on the dirt road to Moyo would pass a whole collection of missions and clinics, their signboards proudly proclaiming their presence to passers-by. Never, the Acholi must have felt, had there been so much interest in their immortal souls.

Then there was commerce of a less spiritual kind. There were representatives of charities and foundations whose aims were related to aid, healthcare, education or wildlife. And often in Gulu, around the pool at the Acholi Inn, or limbering with cold beer at a roadside bar, would be the occasional mercenary soldier from Belgium or from England, kitted out in neutral khaki, displaying biceps with tattoos to advertise their unsavoury trade.

But this international assortment was, in reality, little more than a dust of seasoning among the growing numbers of native Ugandans and Sudanese for whom this forgotten line on a colonial map had become a refuge from a conflict zone – and this only when the borderland managed to escape from being a conflict zone itself.

Azalea would later talk about these days in Langadi as the happiest of her life. The Folleys had a network of friends in the communities of the West Nile, and these families would come to visit in their Land Rovers or in their old Toyota vans. Out on the verandas in the evenings the adults would talk and play bridge and click Scrabble tiles, while Azalea and the children would make endless explorations of the farmstead, climbing the trees and collecting insects in jars. When Lester Folley I bought the farmstead in 1907 it was a remote place, off every beaten path. By the time Luke and Rebecca arrived at the mission in January 1984, the track had become a thoroughfare and the cluster of huts that had once comprised the village had grown into a township, now with its own school and church and a welter of uninviting shops and bars. For two hours every evening, between four and six, the mission would open up its gates to provide access to the standpipe that drew water from an aquifer, and this singular act of charity saved local families the long walk to the river for water and the longer walk back. A queue would begin to form by the gate early in the afternoon, women mostly, bearing jerrycans and plastic bottles; and by the time Odokonyero (whose job as cook also made him head of security) swung open the gate at four o'clock, there could be two hundred people waiting for water. In the early days of the mission, Lester Folley II had unwisely provided round-the-clock access to the standpipe, but this provision had been withdrawn as the mission compound threatened to turn into an encampment. Now the two-hour limit applied, with no more than one minute at the pump for any one person. There were Acholi ladies who sat at the gate of the mission and wove baskets to sell to passers-by, especially to those who might appreciate a basket in which to carry their water bottles. There were women who sold mangoes to the people in the queue, and children who sold scavenged bottles and cans. Traders would appear with such an assortment of goods for sale that it was difficult to see the connection. An old man sold a little pyramid of tomatoes and plastic shaving razors and batteries. Another sold toothpaste and a heap of yams and tinned sardines. Gaunt young men with frayed trousers, riding bicycle taxis, would wait expectantly for fares back to the village.

Odokonyero would count the villagers in – he knew them all by name – and he would police the whole operation with his watch. Every day this involved an awful lot of hand-waving, raised voices and squabbles.

'Can't you all be a little quieter?' Rebecca Folley would appeal to Odokonyero. Her schoolroom was right next to the standpipe, and the daily commotion disturbed the children.

'But it isn't me who is making the noise,' Odokonyero would exclaim, quite untruthfully for his was the voice that soared above them all. But no matter: the inefficient routine of the water pump was too much a part of village life ever to interrupt it.

'Do you know what we ought to do?' Luke would say to Rebecca and Azalea. 'We should raise some money to run a new pipe all the way into the village. Then all the villagers would have as much water as they liked, and we would be left alone.'

But no new water pipe was ever installed, except in some of the grander homes in Langadi, so the daily ritual continued. 'We would miss the queues if they went,' Azalea said. And she was probably right. The daily trip for water brought the mission closer to the people, and this in turn helped to ensure that no one was suspicious of the place, and few had any motive to wish them harm. Local people would come to Pastor David's services on a Sunday to sing African organum harmonies to English hymns, and from time to time they would arrive with a family that was in hardship – usually a Sudanese mother abandoned or widowed by the civil war with as many children as had survived – and Luke Folley would let the family sleep in the mission hall as long as the parents (or parent) worked on the farm and the children attended the school. Then he would set about finding something more permanent for them, which would mean calling in favours from all the farms and businesses that had ever dealt with the mission.

Every now and then the villagers would appear with a child. The child would become the immediate responsibility of Matron Maria, who would look after his or her welfare until the parents or other relatives could be found. Luke Folley would complete the necessary government paperwork and would photograph the child, then send the papers off to the police control in Gulu where a show would be made of looking for the missing family. Often, of course, the parents were never found. There were fifteen children in the orphanage this morning, although there had sometimes been as many as twenty-six and once as few as five. Orphans didn't always stay long. As soon as they were stronger, well fed and partly educated, a distant family member would often come to claim them, especially if they were old enough to carry water, or to help in the fields. There was little that the

Folleys could do when this happened. Ugandan security forces would not take the mission's side in a family dispute. So the reclaimed child would be vaccinated and hugged and dispatched with the new family; and every now and again one of the Folleys would happen to drive past the village where the child now lived and, if all was well, a happy reunion would take place.

Some orphans, of course, stayed longer. Odokonyero had been an orphan at St Paul's. So too had one of the maids, both of the yard boys, all of the farmhands, Stanton the driver and Elizabeth the nurse. Most of the long-stay orphans, however, would drift off into the towns or cities in search of work once they reached the age of fourteen or thereabouts. Many would write long letters home, and these would go up on the walls of the schoolhouse for all to read.

By nine in the morning the day would already be hot. Schoolchildren from Langadi township would start to arrive in their dark blue shorts and pale blue shirts (for boys), or their dark blue cotton frocks (for girls), clutching their exercise books and pencils, in twos or threes, often holding hands and chanting songs. There were two rooms in the schoolhouse. Luke Folley taught the younger children, Rebecca Folley taught the older ones. There was no grading or streaming by age; rather it was done by height and general ability, and by the need to keep around thirty children in each class at two to a desk. Luke taught reading and writing and numbers, and since most of his starters spoke little or no English, he also taught the English language. He taught with a great deal of chanting and repetition because this, he knew from his own childhood, was a technique that commended itself to Acholi children. Every day they would chant the alphabet and multiplication tables, and then they would break to sing songs, and often Luke would strum along on his guitar. They would sing English and American songs: 'Puff the Magic Dragon', and 'Blowing In the Wind', and 'In the jungle, the mighty jungle, the lion sleeps tonight'. And if there was a noticeable absence of gospel tunes or hymns, well, nobody remarked upon it – and anyway, the children would sing these with Pastor David at Morning Prayers and

78

again at Afternoon Prayers, so perhaps it didn't matter. Luke read poetry to the children, and every morning he would tell them a tale from Aesop's fables. 'Today we will hear the story,' he would say, 'of the lion and the jackal and the donkey. All three agreed to go hunting together, and all three agreed to share the kill.' All voices would hush and all eyes would turn to the teacher. Later they would learn more English words, and Luke would draw the pictures and write the words on the blackboard so that the children could chant them – lion – elephant – snake – bicycle – gun – fish – pencil – banana, and then the children would write down the words and there would be a lot more chanting, for Luke Folley never taught in silence except when he was telling a story.

'Can't you teach more quietly?' Rebecca Folley would complain. 'How can you expect my class to learn *anything* with all that singing and wailing going on in the next room?'

But Luke only knew one way to teach, and this was it, a successful enough formula for him. Six-year-old Acholi children – or children of about that age – would arrive at the start of term, often with no uniform, no shoes, no pencils, no understanding of English, no appreciation, even, of why they were there at all. Luke would apprehend the parents to explain the rules. Attendance at St Paul's was free of charge, but certain conditions applied: the parents would need to make a solemn oath that once their children started at the school, they would continue until at least their thirteenth birthday; they would not miss classes except for a family funeral; they would wear a uniform, and they would uphold the reputation of the mission at all times. The family would be expected to make a contribution to the mission: whatever they could afford, that would be enough. The contribution could be in the form of money, or it could be produce from the family farm, or it could be hours spent working in the mission fields. Either way, Luke told them, they had to understand the value of education for the children, and what better way to appreciate value than to contribute something. Luke would base his decision on what that contribution should be on his own assessment of each family's ability to pay. But given that most of these children were from the poorest families in a region that was already poor, and some lived not with parents but with the brothers or sisters of parents who had died, there was little expectation that the contribution would make any real difference to the mission coffers.

There was, of course, a final condition, which would normally be that the family attend the mission's Sunday service, but Luke was never particularly vigilant about this requirement. Pastor David would complain that mothers in Langadi were sending their urchins to the school yet were not attending the church, and Luke would hold his palms upwards, feigning despair – *What can we do?*

The six-year-olds who started in Mr Luke's class normally demonstrated an aptitude for learning that might have surprised an outsider. Language skills came quickly to them. Numbers seemed to come even quicker. Perhaps in the environment these children occupied, the ability to count and calculate was an essential survival skill.

Rebecca Folley's class of older children was an altogether quieter regime. Rebecca herself was no singer, and the requirement for chanting no longer applied to children who by now knew their numbers and their letters. Rebecca taught an eclectic mix of skills. She had a textbook on Ugandan history, and she taught this to the children because this was a National Requirement, and if ever a government inspector should happen to call, which was rare, it was nonetheless helpful to have the book open on the top desk and a map of Uganda already drawn on the board. Then Rebecca could select a child with the requisite knowledge and demand, 'Onyo – please tell our esteemed visitor about Yoweri Museveni, the President of Uganda,' and the child would happily oblige. But apart from coaching her most accommodating pupils, Ugandan history was not an especially large part of Rebecca Folley's curriculum. She taught First Aid, and human biology; how children were conceived, and how AIDS was transmitted. She taught practical nursing and simple paramedical skills: how to treat broken limbs, how to recognise the symptoms of malaria, how to avoid parasites, how to protect against mosquito bites. She taught fundamental life skills – basic economics and business. She taught agriculture and horticulture, how to improve the yield and efficiency of small family farms, how to treat and care for the soil, how to water, till, crop, rotate and plan for the next season, and while these were skills that most of the children would learn in other ways, they were proficiencies that Rebecca was sure would benefit the children when it came to making their own farms succeed. Rebecca also taught some geography, and she tried to get the children reading. The mission would receive occasional parcels of books sent out from kindly charities in the West, and these would be registered into the school library and then lent out, and frequently they were also returned (because only by returning a book would a child be allowed to borrow another). On trips to Gulu and to Kampala, Rebecca would buy comics and comic books because these were always a way to encourage reading, and every afternoon the older children would have their reading hour in silence while Rebecca settled into a deep chair with a book of her own, the glorious peace only interrupted by the chanting from the primary class and the raised voices of the water queue.

In the evenings the farm boys would lead the cattle into the barn and tether them there out of reach of opportunist thieves, and then they would do the same with the goats. The hens and the cockerels would find their own way into the shed, and the farm boys would shut and bolt the doors and clip the padlocks into place. By the time they had finished, the bell in the mess hall would be ringing for tea; Azalea and Anyeko would be pulling on the bell – ding … ding … ding – a slow and steady ring because *that* was the rhythm for the mess bell, one ring every second like a steady pulse; a reassuring rhythm, a comforting call to dine.

There was another ring this bell could make, but then it wouldn't be the dinner bell. The other ring was fast and urgent – a dingdingdingdingding – rapid and fierce, loud and deafening, a rhythm that panicked and called out 'danger danger danger'. These were the rings that they only did in practice, and Luke would prepare them in advance; this was the *alarm* bell ring. 'When you hear the alarm bell ring,' Luke would tell everyone at the mission, 'then this will be your order to flee. When you hear the alarm bell, you must *run*!'

The orders for the alarm bell were clear, but all the same they rehearsed them. The village children would flee the compound. In any direction – or all directions – they would escape the mission with every ounce of energy they could muster. Some would run back up the driveway, others would cross the fields, others would head into the farmstead and loop around; but whichever route they took, the instructions were very plain – the schoolchildren should get home to their villages, to their circular Acholi huts, as fast as they could and seek out their parents or elder siblings. There they should hide in the hidey-holes and small dark places that had been prepared for them, and they should not return until their families were confident that it was safe. For the mission orphans the instructions were much the same. For each of them there was a hiding place in Langadi town. If the compound was surrounded, then they should scatter as widely as possible. If the danger did not seem imminent, then they could run for the mission bus – but *only* if one of the mission staff was driving.

For the adults of the mission, the alarm bell spelled out a different message. The adults were to assemble by the mission buildings, with no sense of panic; they should not suggest by voice or by gesture that the children had taken flight. Whatever the crisis that had summoned the alarm, the adults were there to project calm.

This was the day in Langadi when everything changed for Azalea, and yet everything about the morning was normal. The goats were milked, the breakfast was served, grace was said. The farm boys squabbled. Maria the matron barked sharp commands at the orphans. Rebecca lingered over her tea and her cigarette. Luke savoured his coffee. The VSO couple sat uncommonly close to each other and whispered things that no one else could hear. Odokonyero oversaw the whole meal with the righteous bonhomie of the cook, and Mzee Njonjo, the nightwatchman, hobbled to his hut to sleep away the day. This was June 1992. The mission dogs were drinking old milk from the cooking pan. A yellow-backed weaver bird hopped among the tables looking for crumbs; a gonolek bird flickered across the dusty yard. Crickets were calling; cockerels were scratching. The orphans began to trail off towards the schoolhouse in twos and threes, holding hands. Matron Maria lifted herself heavily out of her seat and started putting Little Michael, the only baby at the mission, into a wrap to tie on her back. The VSO couple disappeared off to their rooms in the mission hall. The nurse wandered over to her clinic. One dog barked and the gonolek flew up into a tree.

And then it was uncommonly quiet, for just a brief and precious moment. Azalea slid down from her bench, and still in her nightdress she walked out of the mess hall and into the yard. A little dust devil, whipped up by the wind, tumbled past the mess hall and was gone. The dog barked again. And then there was a man in the drive.

Azalea saw him first. He looked like an army man, in camouflage fatigues with a gun slung over his back like a quiver. He stopped when he saw Azalea, but now the dogs had seen him too and they rushed towards him, barking.

Odokonyero came out, in his position as head of security, to investigate the commotion. He stopped as if struck by a stone, and shouted to the man in Acholi. The man shouted something back in a language unfamiliar to Azalea. Probably he was saying 'call off your dogs'.

Odokonyero whistled and the dogs drew back.

There followed an exchange between the two men. It did not sound friendly.

Luke Folley emerged. 'What's going on?' he demanded.

Odokonyero spat on the ground. He grumbled something in Acholi.

A second, younger man came sauntering down the driveway wearing the same combat uniform. The first man spoke to him. They approached Luke.

'What do you want of us?' Luke asked.

The first man began a long, angry-sounding tirade.

'Wait, wait, wait,' Luke flattened out his hands as if trying to calm the situation down.

The second man started now. There was a demanding urgency to his voice. Luke replied, and suddenly all three were speaking at once, and the volume was rising as each man competed to be heard.

Then Rebecca Folley floated out, blowing smoke rings, and all three fell silent. 'Darling,' she said, 'what is all this noise? I can barely hear myself think.'

'This man says … he is LRA,' said Luke.

Rebecca took a long pull on her cigarette. 'My dear, if he's a visitor you shall have to invite him in for tea. Or coffee. I suppose Odokonyero will have some of that disgusting brew left.'

'My wife says you must join us for tea,' said Luke, talking in Acholi.

'And get him to explain to us what an "LRA" is,' said Rebecca in English. She had never made much progress with the local languages. 'I think we get every acronym known to man in this godforsaken shithole. NRA, UPDA, SPLA, God-knows-what bloody A. It's so nice to be able to add another one to the list.'

'Rebecca, it may be wise not to upset this man,' said Luke.

'They all end in A, don't they? Have you noticed?' Rebecca gave a sweet and wholly insincere smile to the LRA soldier. 'You're just a bit too late for breakfast,' she told him. 'But I can offer you a cigarette.' She held out a packet of menthols.

The LRA man seemed taken aback by the gambit, but he took a cigarette with the demeanour of a man who had learned never to refuse a gift, however small, and the second man did likewise.

'Do you speak English?' Rebecca asked, adopting an imperious tone as she lit the man's cigarette.

'I do,' he said. 'My English is very excellent.'

'Splendid,' said Rebecca. 'In that case, we shall get on.' She turned and drifted back into the mess hall. 'Odokonyero,' she called, 'tea, please.'

Rebecca Folley had not been the most willing of recruits to the mission in Langadi. It might be more truthful to say that she had *resisted* the move from Cornwall to Uganda with the fiercest determination. Nevertheless, now that she was here, she was not the kind of person to let a fracas with a make-believe soldier spoil her morning.

Rebecca and Luke had met at university while both were studying for a degree in education, and somehow, more by chance than judgement, they had ended up together. As a student, Rebecca had been a serial dater, never in a relationship for much longer than a term or so, the kind of person who always has the next boyfriend lined up and ready before the tenure has expired on the present one – and it just seemed to happen, like a roll of the dice, that Luke Folley had been the incumbent suitor when Graduation Day came round. Another term might have seen the romance fade, as so many had done before. But there wasn't to be another term. Somehow Rebecca and Luke ended up at the big empty family house in St Piran, and it just seemed right and sensible to make a home there with no rent to pay. It was even exciting for a while. Luke started teaching at the local village school and Rebecca started work at another, in a village just around the headland. And so it was, just weeks after graduation, that they were settled and happy and earning. The school terms came and went. Rebecca became Mrs Folley, and they threw open the big windows of the old rambling home, they swept out the dust and waited for a family to arrive.

But none came.

The old Folley house on the cliff paths overlooking the bay cried out for children. There were empty bedrooms galore. Rebecca took brisk walks along the cliffs to improve her circulation. She swam off the shingly beach. She ate healthy meals. She gave up smoking for a while. But each month came and went, and with each passing season the hope Rebecca had seemed fainter.

The doctors diagnosed polycystic ovary syndrome. 'It's a hormone dysfunction.' The doctor in St Piran shook his head when he delivered the bad news.

Rebecca, it must be said, was made of stern stuff. When Luke arrived home from work, she sat him down in the kitchen. 'Darling,' she said, 'I've got bad news and I've got good news. Which would you like first?'

'I think I'll start with the good news,' said Luke.

Rebecca lit a cigarette. 'Well, the first good news is that I'm smoking again.' She took a long drag on her cigarette and let the smoke leak out between her teeth, half closing her eyes to savour the moment. 'And as for the second bit of good news ...' she said, pausing to allow for effect, then looking Luke directly in the eye, '... I've made a decision. We're going to adopt a baby.'

12

March 2011 / November 2009

Azalea slid a slim paperback volume across the desk to Thomas Post. 'Take a look.'

It was the day that they met in Thomas's office, the day that Thomas had returned to work with his left arm in plaster. Both had registered surprise when Azalea popped her head around the door.

'Good Lord – it's you! From the escalator. Did you track me down?' Thomas had asked, aware, as he did, just how awkward this question sounded.

'Of course I tracked you down. But that was because of your paper.' She held the document up to show him, and they both found themselves looking at it with expressions of surprise. 'It had nothing to do with what happened at Euston.'

Thomas suffered a moment of bewilderment. 'Are you ... are you all right?'

Azalea screwed up her face. 'All right how?'

'You know – after the accident.'

'Ah.' She put her hand on her side. 'I did break a rib.'

'Of course. You thought you'd broken a rib, didn't you? I mean ... you said at the time you thought ... you know, you'd broken one. A rib.' Thomas found his grasp on the English language crumbling. 'Is it ... you know ... in plaster, or anything?' Another stupid question. Of course it wasn't in plaster. Was he blind?

'No, it's not,' said Azalea. She gave Thomas a sideways smile. 'It hurts like hell, though. How's the arm?'

'Bloody awful.' He held up the cast.

'At least people can *see* you've been injured. With me I just get the pain and no sympathy.'

Thomas gestured for her to take a seat. 'So let me get this right,' he began, 'you sought me out because of a paper I wrote on coincidences?'

Azalea lowered herself carefully into the proffered chair. 'Shouldn't we introduce ourselves first?'

'Oh, how rude of me.' Thomas extended his good arm. 'Thomas Post.'

'You'll forgive me if I don't shake hands. I'm Azalea Lewis. I teach at Birkbeck.'

Thomas withdrew his arm. 'Sorry,' he said. 'Pleased to meet you, Ms Lewis.'

Another smile.

'Isn't that funny?' she remarked. 'After all, we *have* already met. After a fashion.'

'Yes. But we were never properly introduced,' Thomas said. 'Can I rustle you up a tea – or maybe a coffee?'

'Do you do real coffee, or instant?'

'Ahh.' Thomas looked apologetic. 'Only the plastic stuff, I'm afraid. I'm a bit of a tea drinker myself.'

'Well then, I shall have tea.'

While Thomas busied himself with the kettle, they talked about the incident on the escalator. Azalea confirmed that she had been taken to the Royal Free Hospital. She told him that no one she had seen there had been seriously hurt. Thomas told her that one woman at UCLH had broken her neck. She was all right, but it could have been touch and go.

They talked about the whole risky business of commuting in London. Azalea declared that she would never go on an escalator again. 'Not unless there are hardly any people on it,' she added.

Thomas returned with the tea. 'I almost tried tracking you down,' he confessed. 'I thought about phoning the Royal Free. Only I bottled out.'

'What would you have done if you had phoned, and if they *had* given you my name?'

'I don't know.' He looked sheepish. 'Sent you some flowers, maybe.'

Azalea offered a disarming grin. 'You old romantic.'

'Less of the "old", if you don't mind.'

Azalea looked into her tea. Thomas reflected that she was prettier than he'd remembered; perhaps she was prettier than he wanted to remember.

Now aged either thirty-two or thirty-three, depending on which birthday she might select, Azalea Lewis still possessed the willowy frame of the thirteen-year-old Azalea Folley and the russet hair of the foundling Azaliah Yves. Her features may have been unremarkable – nose and mouth and chin – but she had a subtle asymmetry to her face, like an imperfect painting, mismatched freckles on her cheekbones, smile lines that turned this way and that and of course that trace of a scar. Perched carefully on the edge of the armchair, with one arm cradling her ribs, there was, Thomas noticed, an intensity about this woman. He could feel it. She turned her face upwards to look at him and the glance of her deep green eyes felt almost physical; he felt captured in their beam, unable to break her stare until she released him and he could cast his eyes away. He found himself recalling that faint scent, the dark olfactory memory of the day they had squeezed together on the cold stone floor of the subway. With deliberation he inhaled through his nostrils. There it was again – a musky, feminine odour, unfamiliar in the dank masculinity of his room.

On that day they talked about the coincidence of meeting after the escalator pile-up. 'And as you know, I've been reading your paper on coincidence,' Azalea said.

'Ah, that.' Thomas Post was in a light mood. 'And what is your interest in the subject, Ms Lewis?'

Azalea seemed to reflect upon this. She nodded slowly, resting her teacup on his desk. 'I seem to be afflicted by coincidences, Dr Post.'

'Afflicted?'

'Afflicted. Affected. Benighted. Bedevilled. Whatever word you wish to choose. They seem to follow me, or infect me. I don't really know how to explain this. I was hoping perhaps you might help.'

Thomas raised his eyebrows. 'Help? How could I possibly help?'

'Well, not in any practical way, I don't suppose. I mean, I'm not looking for an exorcist. I don't expect you to mount a white charger and take on the forces of nature, or anything.'

'Pity,' said Thomas, 'I quite fancy the white charger.'

'It wouldn't suit you,' said Azalea, sweeping away the fantasy. 'I was hoping you might be able to help me to understand it. To make sense of it.'

'I see.' Thomas narrowed his eyes. 'And now, I suspect, you'll add this very meeting to your list of strange coincidences.'

Azalea nodded. 'I think I was less astonished than you,' she said. 'I'm getting used to the universe springing surprises.'

'Would it help if I were to explain why coincidences happen? Why it is that we frail humans have to find patterns in nature?'

'It might help.'

'I'm not a psychiatrist.'

'I don't need a psychiatrist. I'm not going mad, Dr Post.'

'Good.' Thomas pulled a sheet of paper from his desk and slid it across to her. 'Do you have a pen?'

Azalea produced one from her bag.

'I want you to draw a squiggle on this sheet of paper. Just a scribble – as random as you like.'

'Like this?' Azalea let her pen zigzag and curl over the page.

'Splendid.' Thomas drew the paper back to his side of the desk. 'Have you played this game before?' he asked. 'You draw a scribble, and the other person has to turn it into a picture. So if I turn this loop here into a hat,' he added a few lines, 'and if I give him an eye, and maybe this bit here could be a moustache …' He sketched for a moment, then stopped. 'There.' He flipped the page back to Azalea. 'Charlie Chaplin.'

She took the picture and laughed. 'You're an artist, Dr Post.'

'Thomas.'

'So what's that supposed to prove?'

He grinned at her. 'It doesn't prove anything. But it does illustrate the extraordinary human capacity to see patterns in random shapes. We look at the moon and we see the face of a man. We look at clouds and we see animals. Pareidolia. That's the name for it.'

She smiled at him. '"Do you see yonder cloud that's almost in shape of a camel?"'

'Is that a quotation?'

'It's Hamlet. He's teasing his girlfriend's father. Polonius says, '"'tis like a camel, indeed". Then Hamlet says, "Methinks it is like a weasel", and Polonius has to agree. He says, "It is backed like a weasel." Hamlet says, "Or like a whale?" "Very like a whale," says Polonius.'

'There you go, then.' Thomas gave a laugh. 'That was very good.'

'I teach English literature.'

'I see. The point is that we human beings have a great ability to take random events from our lives and construct patterns around them. Synchronicity is a curious thing when it happens to us, but only because we neglect to include in our calculations the seven billion people in the world that it didn't happen to. One person wins the lottery and that person has just experienced a fantastic coincidence, an almost unbelievable piece of serendipity, a fourteen-million-to-one chance that the very six numbers they chose on their ticket were the exact same numbers that came out of the machine during the draw. But we don't call that an amazing coincidence, do we? That's because we know that twenty million people have tickets that didn't match.'

'But you've studied this, haven't you ... Thomas?'

'I have,' said Thomas Post. He was enjoying this. He offered a broad and self-satisfied smile – his boyish smile that was part of his armoury for dealing with the opposite sex.

'So you know that what you've just said is a load of bollocks?'

It wasn't the reaction he'd expected. He felt surprised and faintly hurt. 'Why bollocks?'

'Because no one would suggest that one person winning the

lottery is a coincidence. What *would* be a coincidence is one person winning the lottery twice.'

He leaned back and gave one of his shrugs. 'You're quite right, of course, but then nobody ever actually wins the lottery twice.'

'Maybe after the first win they stop buying tickets.'

'Maybe that's it.'

Azalea took a sip of her tea and let the moment hang. After a while she said, 'So if I see patterns in my life that seem to be … I don't know … fate, destiny … then I'm just a simple girl seeing patterns in the clouds that aren't really there?'

Thomas opened his mouth to reply, but then he caught himself. He was suddenly unsure if he wanted to dismiss this woman quite so quickly. He tugged abstractedly on his earlobe. 'I tell you what,' he said, 'why don't you start right at the beginning and talk me through it?'

'All of it? That could take some time.'

'We may have to break for lunch,' he said, 'and it could take more than one session.' He felt a strange sensation like bubbles floating up his spine. He tried to catch himself from beaming too widely, and looked suddenly down to conceal his expression.

'Thank you,' said Azalea, 'that is what I was hoping you might say.' Her voice was like a melody in his head. This was when she slid the slim paperback across the desk towards him.

A book of poems. He picked it up almost cautiously. The cover bore a rough finger painting of hills in black and a stream in grey.

'What is this?'

'*Dark Lakeland*. It's by p. j. loak. Have you heard of him?'

Thomas shook his head. 'I don't really do poetry.'

Silly thing to say. Damn damn damn.

She surveyed him. Self-conscious now, he opened the book. Poems in unremitting lower case with minimum punctuation. He coughed. 'Is there any particular poem I should read?'

'No, it's OK. I'm not going to make you *do* poetry.'

He grimaced.

'I teach poetry,' Azalea explained. 'For my master's degree I needed to find a modern poet to study. I chose p. j. loak. His writing is quite plain. Unadorned. I like that.'

Thomas nodded. He leafed through the book.

'Now here is the thing. Why did I choose Loak? I wrote a thesis on his poetry. I invested two years of my life dissecting every line he's ever written. I tried to interpret him. I deconstructed his poems like Jacques Derrida taught. I argued about his use of rhythm and metre, and I looked for hidden meanings in between the lines. These are the sort of things you do when you study literature, Dr Post.'

'Thomas.'

'But why did I choose Loak? I wanted a modern poet, but there are hundreds I could have picked. Shall I tell you why?' Azalea looked at Thomas and held him again with the earnestness of her gaze. 'Loak always wanted to be a Lakeland poet. I'd never been to the lakes before I discovered his writing, so maybe I was curious. I don't know. But it turns out that Loak isn't really a Lakeland writer, he's a *damaged* writer. That should be a genre of its own. He fought in the Falklands War. I say "fought", but he didn't actually do any fighting. In 1982 he was on a Royal Navy ship called HMS *Sheffield*. He was a communications officer. They'd been on tour in the Middle East and they were on their way home when the war began and so they were rerouted down to the South Atlantic. Loak was on Deck Two, somewhere near the galley, when the *Sheffield* was hit by an Exocet missile eight feet above the waterline. It was 4 May 1982. Twenty men were killed.'

Thomas exhaled. 'But not Loak?' he said.

'No. Not Loak,' Azalea said. She paused, nodding gently. 'The missile didn't explode. It was faulty, thank God. But it severed a power main and set light to a fuel store. Loak was lucky,' she said, 'if you can call it luck ... He was blinded.'

'Permanently blinded?'

'Yes. They invalided him out of the navy and he went back to Buttermere.'

Thomas opened the book.

'Why not read one?'

He flicked through the pages, not wanting anything too long. He found a poem and cleared his throat. 'Shall I read it aloud?'

'I'd like that,' Azalea said.

This is the poem that Thomas Post read:

> an owlet slight alighted by a stream
> where foxgloves grew
> where all of nature scented and aglow
> did rise anew
> where spanned aloft a small stone bridge
> where sprang a salmon up the ridge
> among the stones and the pale cascade
> where dragonflies and stoneflies played
> where naked as a boy i laid
> with all the canvas of a world displayed
>
> and when the gunshot sounded plain
> as a whistle from a distant train
> and i half turned and turned again
> i saw the bridge
> i saw the salmon leap upstream
> i felt the splash of spray
> as one might dream
> of sunlight and shadow
> of presence and place
> where naked as a man i laid
> with blood upon my face
>
> there are no guns on red pike crag
> no missiles on scafell
> there is no sound of cannon fire
> no tolling of the bell
> there are no cries from wounded men
> no one to weep for solace when
> the blood upon your face runs thin

and darkness takes away your pen
where naked as an ancient now
i beckon back and turn my brow
and think of her who lay with me
beside the stream
beneath the tree

Thomas closed the book. 'Is it good?' he asked.

'You tell me.'

'I don't know. What do I know about poetry?'

'No, it isn't especially good,' she said. 'The metaphors are superficial, the language is very plain, the passion is pretty muted. He isn't always faithful to the metre, and the rhymes are simple – thin/pen, brow/now, stream/dream; but he has a following of a sort, and I wanted to explore that. I wanted to understand what draws people to his poetry.'

'So what drew you to him?'

'His blindness.'

'You wanted to know what it might be like … to be blind?'

Azalea nodded. She held back her head as if decanting a tear.

'Do you have blindness in your family?'

'I once met a man who said he was my father. He was blind.'

'You met a man who said … he was your *father*?'

'Long story.'

'And he was blind?'

'Yes.'

'And that drew you to this poet. This Loak?'

'Yes.'

'So where's the coincidence?' Thomas asked.

She gave a gentle groan as if recalling this story would be painful. 'A little while ago I resolved to meet p. j. loak,' she began. 'It was while I was writing my thesis on his poetry. So I wrote to him, via his publisher of course, and I asked if we could meet. He wrote back – eventually. He doesn't do email, you see. But it wasn't a very helpful reply. All he said was, "Do drop in if ever you're passing." No phone number. No way of contacting him.

But I did, at least, have an address, and of course it was way up in Cumbria. Anyway, a day came when I really didn't have a lot to do, and I found myself deciding to do exactly as he had suggested. Only it wasn't quite so simple. I packed a little overnight case, and I took a train up to Oxenholme and a bus to Cockermouth and then a taxi to his cottage in the hills. I don't really know what I expected. It was November. I should have thought about miserable hail and wind, but somehow I'd read so many Lakeland odes that in my mind I'd imagined this land of perpetual springtime and daffodils and babbling brooks.'

'Wordsworth,' said Thomas.

'Indeed. Anyway, by the time I reached Loak's driveway it was almost dark and it was raining hard. The taxi dropped me at the gate, but the cottage itself was up a long steep driveway and there I was, in a ridiculous city coat, no umbrella, heels, with a silly little suitcase on wheels. I paid the taxi and then I sheltered under a tree for a long while, asking myself what the hell I was doing there. I tried to look down into the valley but everywhere was steamy and misty and all I could really see were a few drystone walls and some sad-looking sheep.'

'Should I be writing any of this down?' Thomas asked.

Azalea shook her head. 'So here's the first strange thing. I was standing there in the rain, trying to shelter under a tree with no leaves, when suddenly I had this overwhelming feeling of déjà vu. I thought perhaps I'd read so much Lakeland poetry that now I felt as if I'd already visited this place. It was unsettling. I thought, "If I follow that little path, I know where it'll lead – it will climb slowly up to the left, and it will curl around the hill to the right, and then it will cross a beck over some stepping stones, and there will be an ancient tree with roots like a giant's fingers bursting out of a buried glove." That's what I thought.'

'That's poetic.'

Azalea smiled. 'I didn't mean to come over all purple. But you see, it was such a strange feeling. How could I possibly know a strange pathway in a county I had never visited? Even if I'd read the most lucid poems, even if I'd studied the maps, even if I'd seen photographs – well, even then I wouldn't have felt the way I did right then. It was something eerie – something other-worldly.'

Thomas gave a gentle cough. 'I think perhaps it's a feeling we all get from time to time.'

Azalea shook her head. 'But you need to let me finish,' she said. 'You see, there are some things you don't know about me, Dr Post.'

'Thomas.'

'Well, one thing you don't know about me is that I never knew my mother. My real mother. She abandoned me when I was three.'

'Abandoned you?'

'Well, no. Not exactly. But we used to *think* she had abandoned me. That was the story I grew up believing. It was the story my parents – my adopted parents – believed right up to their deaths, and I believed it too until that day, the day that I went to visit p. j. loak. That was the day I learned the truth. My mother didn't abandon me. She just took me to a fair, and then she was abducted. And murdered.'

'Oh my God!'

'But what matters is that I have no memories of her. No real memories. I have some memories that I may have made up, but there is no picture of her in my mind.'

'That's a shame.'

'Yes, it is. But here's the funny thing. As I stood there, I could somehow feel my mother with me. My real mother.'

'Are you claiming to be psychic?'

'No, not at all. I don't even believe in that sort of thing. This was more like a deep memory. I could see myself clambering over the stile and running up the pathway and in my mind the sun was shining, the daffodils really were blooming and with me there was a woman and I could feel her next to me and there was this enormous sense of warmth between us.'

'I'm starting to see where this is leading,' Thomas said, tugging again on his earlobe.

'So anyway. I waited for a lull in the rain, but none ever came.

Finally I just thought, to hell with it, and I made a dash for it up the driveway, and all the time I was cursing myself for not bringing an umbrella, or even a coat with a hood. And then, when I got to the front door there was no porch. I stood there for about five minutes, in the downpour, ringing the doorbell. I almost gave up. I thought I was going to have to walk all the way back down to the valley. Then finally he came to the door. p. j. loak. Not an old man, particularly. He was twenty-two when he lost his sight, so he was only forty-something when I met him. You'd think from that poem that he was decrepit, but I suspect that's just how he thinks of himself. He looked fairly trim. He wasn't wearing dark glasses or anything, but his eyes looked glazed. We sat in his front room. He had a little electric fire. He didn't make me tea, or offer to let me dry myself. He's blind, so he couldn't see how wet I was. So we just sat, and I realised that I hadn't really prepared much for this meeting – hadn't really thought what I should say. I didn't want to come over like some crazed groupie. I told him I was the woman who had written to him, and he said that he used to get quite a lot of letters, but not so many now.

'The funny thing was, all this time, coming in through his little hallway, sitting in the front room – I had this eerie sense that I knew this house. I knew the hallway, I knew this room; I knew there was another room that I hadn't yet seen, and in that room there would be a piano and somehow, in a parallel universe, I could hear it playing, something soft, dreamy, a lullaby perhaps. I could see a door that led to another room, and I wanted to get up and snatch the handle to prove that I was wrong. Maybe it was just a broom cupboard. Or maybe behind that door there would be a room in which the sunlight flooded through the windows, where a man would sit at the piano and his fingers would become musical notes; and maybe there would be a woman in the shadows and maybe she would sing, with a voice as pure as an organ pipe, and the words she would sing would speak of love.

'But of course I didn't. I didn't get up and open the door. I was scared. Something was making my heart race. Then I told Loak my name was Azalea Lewis. It was an uncomfortable moment.

My head was still swimming from the turmoil of images I'd experienced. Loak paused for a very long time. "Tell me how old you are, Azalea," he said. So I told him my age – I was twenty-nine. He seemed to think very hard about this. Then he asked me my birthday. I told him it was the first of November. "That's good," he said, and he seemed to be off in a dream somewhere. Then he said, "I knew an Azalea once – a long time ago; a very long time ago. She would be twenty-nine now, too. But I have no idea where she is, or how to find her. Her birthday would be in August.'"

Azalea paused, as if the effort of telling the story was too great to bear.

'Go on,' Thomas coaxed.

'The thing you need to know, Thomas, is that I'd heard these words before; almost these exact same words. Do you know what it's like when somebody quotes something back to you that should be familiar, but just for a moment you can't place it? Well, that was what his words were like to me. It was as if he was playing me a recording of a conversation that had taken place at another time in my life. I was … unbalanced by it. Like when you cross a beck on stepping stones and one of them suddenly wobbles.'

'I'm beginning to understand why you teach poetry,' Thomas said.

'The thing is, Thomas. Well, the thing is … my real birthday *is* in August. I've never bothered to change my birth certificate. After all, you get used to your birthday, don't you?'

'I suppose you do.'

'Anyway – now I was spooked. I said, "If … just *if* … I was born in August … and *if* I was the same Azalea you knew a long time ago – well, then you would be able to tell me what part of England I was born in."

'He just sat there and shook his head very slowly, in some kind of reverie. Finally he said, "If … just *if* … you were the same Azalea I knew a very long time ago – well then, I would be able to tell you that you weren't born in England at all."

'Now I was almost shaking. He said, "If I tell you the name of the place, can you tell me the name of the village?" I said I could. Then he said, "*If* ... you were the same Azalea I knew, you would have been born not far away ... not far away at all as the seagull flies ... but far enough for it to be a different place and a different country way across the Irish Sea. You would have been born in the Isle of Man."

'And I could barely say it, Thomas. I could hardly speak. My mouth and tongue just locked and I couldn't get the words out. I was crying. It was so sudden. Down by the gate I'd seen a shadow of my mother, the first I'd seen since I was a toddler, and now he'd pulled away the floor, and I was just floating ... not even floating, I was sinking. So at last I just choked out, "Port St Menfre," because that was the name. The name of the place.'

'And then what?'

'There was a long moment when he didn't speak at all. I just looked at him with my mouth wide open. I was trying to find my voice again. Finally I said, "How do you know all this?" and he just started to laugh. And then as he laughed it wasn't a laugh any more. He was sobbing. He was crying into his hands. When he looked up, I could see that even if his eyes no longer worked, his tears still ran.

'"The Azaliah I knew would have had ..." and I took his hand, because I knew what he was about to say. His hand felt big and cold. I put his fingers here.' Azalea brushed her hair away from her face to reveal the faint trace of a scar.

'I knew then what he was going to say, and I was almost willing him not to say it. "The reason I know all that, Azaliah ... the reason I know that ... is because I'm your father." That was what he said.'

Thomas held Azalea's gaze. 'I see. So this ... Loak ... he *was* the blind man – the blind man who said he was your father?'

'Not exactly, Thomas,' she said. 'No.'

'But I thought you said ...'

'I did.'

'So this chap Loak ...' Thomas was floundering.

'This is my coincidence, you see,' said Azalea. 'This is why I'm the person who won the lottery twice. You see, Peter Loak wasn't the first blind man that I've met quite out of the blue who told me he was my father.' She shook her head slowly. 'Oh, no.' She looked directly into Thomas's eyes. 'He was the second one.'

They walked from Thomas's office through the green park in Russell Square, past the British Museum, and found a small café – one where Azalea could savour the rich smell of roasting coffee and find herself on a different continent half a lifetime away. Azalea drank her coffee rich and black, the way Luke Folley had once done. Thomas drank tea.

They sat in a corner on two inadequate stools. Thomas ordered a ciabatta, Azalea a salad. She was muffled in a stylish overcoat and matching scarf. He was unsuitably dressed in a plain blue shirt and a loose brown cardigan – all the better, he had thought in the morning, to protect his plastered arm, but now he looked like an invalid at large.

'What do we look like?' Azalea said. 'Like a couple of survivors from Waterloo – you with your arm and me with my rib.'

Thomas offered up a grudging smile.

'Creeping into the dark shadows of a little coffee house,' said Azalea, demonstrating something of her flair for the dramatic, 'to nurse our wounds and share battle stories.'

Thomas stirred sugar into his tea.

'It's just as well,' said Azalea, 'that we're not sneaking off here to have an affair! Imagine trying to do that with your arm and my rib.'

'Imagine,' echoed Thomas Post.

They found their way back to the story of p. j. loak, and Azalea told Thomas about her childhood. She explained the events at the fairground in Totnes, and filled him in on the scant details she had learned about her mother.

'Peter Loak was convinced that he was my father,' she said.

'And you're not so sure?' asked Thomas.

'I don't know what to think. They didn't marry – Peter and

Marion. She was quite a few years older than him. He offered to marry her, but she refused. She said that God had told her to raise me on her own, just as she'd been raised by her mother. So, by and by, he went back to England, just a few weeks after my christening; back to his father's old house in Cumbria, while Marion stayed on in Port St Menfre.

'Then Peter joined the navy. It was what he'd always wanted to do. He was nineteen, and I think it was something he needed to get out of his system. One day when he was back on shore leave, my mother turned up at the Buttermere house with me. I must have been around two, or two and a half. I don't remember it, of course. And then they made up their differences – at least some of them – and for a while, Marion would return to Port St Menfre when Peter was at sea, and then cross back to England when he was home on leave. Then, in the autumn of 1981, Peter set off on HMS *Sheffield* to the Middle East, and they toured there for a few months until the spring of 1982. She was thirty, and he was twenty-two. It can't have been easy. He promised her this would be his final trip. She was terrified that he'd be lost at sea. And they had words. From the way Loak tells the story, they just about stopped speaking. He didn't know if she'd be waiting for him back at the house in Buttermere, or if he would ever see her or his daughter again. He cabled to tell her that the *Sheffield* was on its way home. But of course it wasn't. The *Sheffield* got sent off to the Falklands. And then – *kerbang*! One duff Exocet missile later, Marion paid off the rent on her cottage in Port St Menfre, packed all she had into two suitcases, bundled them into her old car and took the ferry over to Liverpool. Then she drove up to Buttermere and let herself into the empty house. She hadn't spoken to Peter on the phone, but she'd been in touch with someone on the hospital ship where he was taken. That hospital ship, by the way, was called the *Uganda*. Anyway. Somehow a message got through to her to say that Peter had been hospitalised in Uruguay, and that he was coming back to a naval hospital in Plymouth. So Marion left her belongings at the house, packed a small overnight bag and strapped me into the car. We drove all day from Cumbria to Devon so that we could go and see him in hospital. Only that never happened. We never got as far as the hospital. We didn't even get as far as Plymouth. I was found wandering alone in a fairground. And Marion wasn't seen from that day to this. No one knew, for a long time, if she was still alive.

'When Peter Loak was eventually discharged from the naval hospital, he went home to Cumbria. Marion hadn't been to visit him in hospital, of course, and he figured that she was probably gone from his life. She never answered his letters. He wrote to the vicar of Port St Menfre, and he received a reply saying that Marion had never returned to the village. Someone else was renting the cottage on Briny Hill Walk. So he stopped writing. What else could he do?

'Loak drew a services disability pension from the navy, and that's what he lived on – and still does – apart from a very modest income from his poetry. And then, about ten years after moving back into the house, he employed a decorator to do some repairs and other general improvements on the house. The decorator said, "What do you want me to do with these two suitcases?" Marion's cases were still on top of the big oak wardrobe in the bedroom, exactly where she had left them. Loak, being blind, had never seen them – and his various cleaners had simply dusted over them and never mentioned them. The decorator opened up the cases and told Loak what they contained. That was when he realised that something must have happened to Marion. He called the police out from Cockermouth, but no one seemed interested in ten-year-old suitcases or a missing woman and child. Eventually he lost patience with the police. He had given up all hope of ever seeing Marion again, but he was desperate to see his daughter. I use the word "see" the way a blind person uses it – the same way Loak uses the word. Of course he would never see either of us. But he still wanted to *see* his daughter, as a blind man does. He had a photograph of me as a three-year-old on his mantelpiece – a strange thing, you might think, for a sightless man to have. But every now and then, if he had visitors, he would direct them to the picture and he would ask them to describe me. Then he would write down their descriptions, and sometimes he would turn them into poems.

'Finally Loak went to a private investigator in Keswick – a lady called Susan Calendar. It took her less than two weeks to uncover everything he needed to know. She was thorough. She drove all the way to Exeter to examine the police files, and then she wrote up a report and delivered it to Loak in person. She had a Braille copy made especially for him. Loak still keeps the report in the desk in his front room.'

Azalea looked across the café table to Thomas. His tea had gone cold.

'Am I boring you?' she asked.

'No,' he shook his head. 'Tell me what the report said.'

Azalea drew a breath. 'The report said that Marion Yves had been abducted and raped by a man called Carl Morse. This was the very first time I'd heard this story. Morse had murdered her and had thrown her body into the sea from a place called Millook Cliff in North Devon. When she was finally washed ashore there was no way to identify her body. The daughter was adopted in November 1982 by Luke and Rebecca Folley, teachers from a village called St Piran in Cornwall.' She nodded thoughtfully and turned her face away. 'Luke and Rebecca were my parents,' she said.

'I see.'

'In January 1984 the Folleys went to run a mission school in Africa, taking me with them, of course. That's what the report said, and that's what happened. Then, in June 1992, according to the report, just one year before Susan Calendar's investigation, the mission in Uganda was raided by a militia group called the Lord's Resistance Army. Four orphan children were taken to become child soldiers. The Folleys and their daughter were slaughtered.'

There was a long silence at the table; elsewhere, the clinking of crockery and the hiss of the espresso machine and the murmur of voices.

'Of course, that isn't what happened,' said Thomas. 'Or you wouldn't be here.'

'It isn't exactly what happened,' said Azalea.

They listened for a while to the coffee-shop noises.

'Have you ever visited the spot where your mother was killed?' asked Thomas Post. 'Your birth mother, I mean, Marion.'

Azalea looked down. 'No,' she said. 'Why would I want to do that?'

'I don't know. Maybe to lay some flowers.'

There was another long silence. 'I would like that,' Azalea said.

The espresso machine emitted a geyser of steam and someone in the café started a loud conversation on a mobile phone.

'What were you planning to do this weekend?' Thomas Post asked.

13

June 1992

The day had begun so well. The two LRA men and the Folleys settled themselves inside the mess hall. It could have been a cosy business meeting.

Odokonyero, who rarely sat for meals, came and placed himself firmly between them. When Rebecca cast him a reproving look he said, 'Mrs Rebecca – I know these people. You don't.' And that was that.

Luke Folley took his familiar place at the head of the table. Now comfortably into his forties, Luke had arrived at a time in his life when the intersecting paths of providence were well behind him, and where the work he did and the role he played rested easily upon his shoulders. The faint echoes of youthful rebellion had long been silenced. His past and his future had melded into a single broad river; he knew where he came from and he knew where he was headed, and while there may still have been invisible rapids around the bend, the riverbanks themselves presented no diversions. His destiny was clear. He was the fourth Folley to run the Holy Tabernacle Mission, stepping confidently into the shoes of Lesters I, II and III. Lester III, of course, had been his brother. One day, he felt, he would hand it all on to his daughter. Azalea would make a fine teacher. Luke was sure of that.

He had never rediscovered his lost faith; but many a clergyman in a fine house, drawing a comfortable salary, had found ways to balance the contradictions between personal faith and professional duty, and Luke, in a much more modest way, would make the same concessions. He had learned to enjoy the fragile sliver of status that came with heading a small mission in a small township in a forgotten corner of an overlooked country. He didn't have to wear a suit and tie for work. No one appraised his performance. He didn't battle his way through commuter traffic, or worry too much about a pension plan. There were anxieties, of course; the strained political map of northern Uganda was a constant focus of harassment by political or militia groups. And then there were the events that had befallen his parents and his brother, Lester III. Their deaths were always there in the background, a reminder that he should never grow too complacent. But the years came and went, and the mission routine survived all attempts to derail it, and Luke acquired the skills of a manager, a teacher, a fundraiser and a politician, and all of the related talents required to steer the little enterprise through the years of the Uganda Bush War and into the uncertain new millennium that lay just a few years ahead.

Luke stretched out his arms and entwined his fingers. He may have been shaking – but only slightly. 'If you're here to meet with us, gentlemen, perhaps we should introduce ourselves.' He glanced around the table as if seeking approval for this very Western formality. 'OK, then. Let me begin. My name is Luke Folley, and I'm the director of this mission. The mission was founded by my grandfather, Lester Folley.' He indicated the whole compound with a broad sweep of his arm. 'We have a school here where we teach sixty children from Langadi village. We have an orphanage where we look after fifteen children. We also operate a small medical clinic, a hospital of sorts with around sixteen patients, and a church. We employ a full-time nurse and three part-time nurses, and three – or is it four? – nursing assistants, who don't have any professional training but who help out in the hospital. Our clinic takes place twice a week, led by a Swahili doctor who drives up from Gulu. Is this helpful to you?'

The two LRA men seemed discomfited by the sudden formality of the meeting. The more senior man nodded.

'Very good,' said Luke. 'In 1982 I was in England with my wife Rebecca,' he identified Rebecca with a generous gesture, 'and our daughter Azalea. While we were there,' he said, and he tapped the table in thought, 'while we were there ...'

'Luke,' said Rebecca, 'you don't need to do this.'

'No, it's all right. It's all right.' He gave a thin smile at the men. 'While we were in England in 1982,' he said, 'two SPLA men walked into the camp. Just the way you did now. Straight after breakfast. One of them had a Kalashnikov.' Luke pointed at the gun slung over the first man's shoulder. 'Just like the one you've got there.'

The two men shuffled in their seats.

'*You* know what happened next, don't you?' Luke asked. 'Of course you do. You gentlemen are Acholi, aren't you? You probably know the story very well. My parents, my brother ...'

The man with the rifle reached over his shoulder and unclipped the weapon. He lifted it onto the table. 'Of course, Mr Luke,' he said. 'We know what happened here.'

'In that case,' said Luke, 'you can understand why we don't welcome people who come marching in here with guns.'

'We are not SPLA,' said the man, as if this would excuse everything.

'Perhaps not,' said Rebecca, adding some urgency to the conversation, 'but this is an orphanage, not a bloody shooting range. Anybody is welcome to come in here and talk – but not with guns.'

'Missus – my gun is on the table,' the LRA man protested, pushing it a bit further away. 'We have not come here to make trouble.'

'Then why have you come?' Rebecca demanded.

The two men conferred softly in Acholi. Then the first man said, 'If you please, Mr Luke, Mrs Luke, it is my turn to make my introduction.'

Luke leaned back and raised a hand to silence Rebecca. 'Very well,' he said, 'your turn.'

'I am a man of God,' the soldier said, 'I am a preacher like you.'

Luke nodded without correcting him.

'I am known throughout all of Acholiland as a holy man. That is right. Your man will tell you.' He nodded towards Odokonyero.

Odokonyero looked down. 'It is true what he says.'

'You say everybody knows this man?' Luke asked.

'Everybody knows him,' Odokonyero replied.

'And he is a holy man?'

The cook nodded. 'He is a holy man to the Acholi.'

'I've never seen a holy man wearing an army uniform,' said Rebecca.

The holy man – or the man who claimed to be holy – said, 'Is it only the white man, then, who can fight for the Kingdom of God?' He looked around the table and his eyes settled on Rebecca. 'You are a child of God, are you not? Are you not commanded to take up arms to defeat the forces of evil in the world?'

The softly sinister implications of this question floated above the little meeting and settled like moths on the rafters to watch the way the conversation went.

Rebecca said, 'Our God commands us to love our enemies; to turn the other cheek.' She flinched as a fly landed on her face, and swatted it away. Outside in the compound an unnatural silence prevailed.

'So,' said the holy man in the army uniform, 'you do not know of the LRA?'

'I was hoping,' said Rebecca, 'that you might enlighten us.'

Luke made a show of looking at his watch. 'You gentlemen must excuse me for just one moment. I am as anxious as my wife to hear about the LRA, and what your aims are. But we need to ring the school bell. Classes should be starting.'

'So soon?' asked the soldier.

'Oh yes,' said Luke. 'Forgive me just one moment.'

He stood up and walked over to the bell rope.

'Are you familiar with the hymn "Onward Christian Soldiers – marching off to war"?' asked the solider of Rebecca.

Rebecca shrank slightly. 'It's marching *as* to war.'

The mission bell began to ring.

'*As* to war,' she said, 'not *off* to war. It has a completely different meaning.'

Dingdingdingdingdingdingding

'It is a command for Christian Soldiers to fight,' said the man, 'to go off to war and fight.'

'No, it isn't,' Rebecca said. 'It's a metaphor. The hymn is telling us that we must face up to evil – but not with violence.'

'"With the Cross of Jesus going on before",' said the solider triumphantly. '"Onward into battle, see his banners go".'

Dingdingdingdingdingdingding

The LRA man's attention began to turn towards Luke and his urgent ringing of the bell.

'I think that's enough, dear,' said Rebecca to Luke.

The ringing stopped and Luke returned to the table. A little river of sweat was coiling down his face. He wiped it away. 'You were going to explain to us about the LRA,' he said, settling back down into his seat.

Luke and Rebecca Folley, as it happened, needed no explanation of the three humble initials. In reality, they needed no introduction to the man who sat opposite them in the uniform of a soldier with his roughly trimmed beard, his make-believe medal bars and with his beret angled firmly across his scalp; this man who claimed to be a holy man who had levered his gun onto their table. They knew him from photographs and newspaper reports and a dozen first-hand and second-hand accounts. They had seen him from time to time in Gulu and in Moyo, always with his ragtag army of hollow-eyed, gun-toting acolytes. They had seen the way pedestrians would dissolve from the streets as he passed, had seen how mothers would scoop up children and whisk them into the shadows, had seen how the news would be telegraphed down the street so that hiding places could be found. They had talked about this man, on the veranda here in the mission, on other verandas, over coffee in the day and over cold gin cocktails and beers as they watched the sun set over a land that no one could understand any more. They had given coins to callers in exchange for information about this man, had paid to find out where he was. Where had he been seen? Who was he with? Where was he heading? He had haunted their dreams and their waking hours. And now here he was, alone except for a batman with no teeth, sitting among them, drinking their coffee, smoking their cigarettes, misquoting hymns.

The man's name was Joseph Kony. He still *is* called Joseph Kony, although if God and providence can ever join forces and do the right thing, then by now he and his tangle of associates will have been scoured from the face of the earth, and Kony will be rotting in a very deep and undiscovered grave. His people are the Lord's Resistance Army, although that wasn't always their name. When Luke and Rebecca and their daughter Azalea came to Langadi, there was no LRA. There were dozens of ragtag groups, of course, and a few of these represented the general grievances of the Acholi people. But when a president from the south, Yoweri Museveni, seized power in Kampala, then the murmuring among the northern peoples grew louder. First they were the Lord's Army, and then they were the Uganda People's Democratic Christian Army, and finally they became the LRA – but in truth it mattered not to the Folleys, or to the mothers of Acholi children, or to the Sudanese or Buganda or Karamojong. To them they were only ever Kony's men, the vacant-faced, brutalised, undead army that did the bidding of Joseph Kony and did it without question, mercy or remorse.

Early in 1992, the same year that Kony came walking into the Langadi mission, LRA men had attacked two schools at Aboke, near Gulu. One was the Sacred Heart Secondary Boarding School for Girls; the other was St Mary's Girls School. In an act that has become infamous in Ugandan history, forty-four girls were abducted. They were taken to become child soldiers and sex slaves for the nascent militia group. They were not the first, nor the last children to disappear from schools and missions in northern Uganda, but this public abduction was a startling message to Luke and Rebecca Folley, and to every school and every parent, that the ambition and brutality of the LRA was on the rise. Long after the events told in this story – and not long before Azalea had given this account to Thomas Post – the International Criminal Court would estimate the number of children snatched by the LRA at thirty thousand. Some estimates would put the number at sixty thousand. Ten-year-old boys and girls were expected to fight. The youngest armed soldiers in Kony's resistance army were often said to be five years old. They carried light arms, and could be relied upon to fire and kill with natural indiscrimination. Those children who were seized but who did not cooperate were not killed by Kony or his men. Instead they would be mutilated. Lips would be cut off. Ears and hands would be amputated. Genitals too. The mutilated – and often dying – child would be dumped back close to their home town as a warning to any future abductees. This, as the West went about its business; as we busily circled our world with satellites and criss-crossed the planet with roadways and watched our TV shows and piped our music into foreign lands – this was the fate handed down to hundreds upon hundreds of children. As we wept for a dead princess in London, as we hunted for weapons in Iraq, as we queued for our touch-screen mobile phones, children were lining up to have their hands hacked off. We are good at hiding ugly events, and after all, this was Africa, a continent effectively invisible to the outside world – not because light will fail to penetrate the darkness, but because very few will choose to look at what is revealed.

But for Luke and Rebecca, and the Mission of St Paul to the Needy of West Nile, there was to be no hiding. Joseph Kony, the butcher of Acholiland, soon to be labelled one of the most wanted criminals on earth, had brazenly walked into their compound, had accepted one of Rebecca's cigarettes and had un-shouldered his Indian-made copy of a Russian machine gun onto the table where children, just minutes earlier, had been devouring cassava porridge.

On this June day in 1992, Luke and Rebecca were not the only Britons present in the compound. Working alongside them were two VSOs, young people doing voluntary service overseas. Their story, too, became entwined with Azalea's. On the day when

Joseph Kony strolled into the mission, the VSOs had been in Uganda for exactly five days. They were doctors, each newly qualified. Or not quite; which is to say that both had concluded the arduous years of study and examination required of a physician, and only a few weeks stood between this and the awarding of a degree. Lauren Marks had just completed a five-year degree course at the University of Edinburgh, and now, before taking up a post as a junior doctor in a city-centre hospital, she had chosen to spend four months at the mission hospital in Uganda. The boy's name was Richard Lewis, known to everyone as Ritchie. He too had just completed his degree in medicine; in his case, at Liverpool. Lauren and Ritchie had been on the same flight from London but had not met, and did not meet until they assembled with a dozen other VSOs at the airport in Entebbe, there to be peeled off to their respective assignments. There was a great deal of excitement and not a little trepidation.

At the airport, the pair were introduced by their VSO minder to a tall, aloof-looking English woman wearing an African cotton frock, smoking a mentholated cigarette and clutching the hand of a teenage girl. It was their first introduction to Rebecca and Azalea Folley. Rebecca threw their bags unceremoniously into the back of a battered twelve-seater minibus with a faded mission logo on the side, and their African adventure started as they wound their way out of the Kampala traffic for the four-hundred-mile, ten-hour journey to Moyo District.

It happens that Rebecca Folley *knew* that Ritchie Lewis and Lauren Marks would end up as a couple. She said this later to Luke. She knew it even as the minibus battled along the Lido Beach Drive past the steamy shallows of Lake Victoria, even before they left the built-up area around the airport, even as the two doctors were coming to terms with really being in *Africa*. Already, Rebecca could smell the sexual chemicals starting their ancient reactions, despite the fact that introductions at the airport had been hesitant and ridiculously polite: 'Hello, I'm Ritchie'; 'Delighted to meet you, I'm Lauren'. Even as the two would-be doctors sat deferentially on separate minibus seats, one gazing out of the left window and the other out of the right, and as they avoided looking directly at one another, even despite all this Rebecca could almost hear their raised heartbeats, could scent the pheromones, could practically count the days until they would be sharing a mosquito net.

They drove up the fertile Nile Valley through countless villages spread out among the hillsides, past the endless African array of farms and businesses – up past Masindi Port, where the Nile pours out of Lake Kyoga, where fishermen sold black piles of finger-sized fish along the roadside, where the soil was as red as Azalea's hair. They stopped for a warm Coca-Cola at a make-shift grass-roofed café, and Lauren treated Azalea for a bee-sting with a potion from her bag. Azalea looked at her with instant affection.

They drove north, skirting the Karuma game reserve. Now Ritchie and Lauren were on the same long seat with a perfect excuse, for the wildlife would be out in the park to their left. Azalea came to join them in the back of the bus while Rebecca sat stoically in the front with Stanton the driver.

That had been the introduction to Africa for Lauren Marks and Ritchie Lewis – that ten-hour drive. Lauren would eagerly write in her journal the names of all the animals she had spotted – distant giraffe hiding among the tall trees, baboons lingering along the roadside in search of discarded scraps, and huge bald marabou storks lurking like dirty old men in the ditches. She would record how she saw children gathering maize, women carrying firewood, men pedalling wobbly bicycles, boys herding cattle with horns longer than a human arm, children in bright pink uniforms coming home from school, toddlers selling mangoes and charcoal. Soon after Kampala, the tarmac roadway gave way to a dirt track and the minibus slowed to negotiate the potholes. Ritchie took photographs, cautiously conserving his film. They stopped by the bridge at Karuma where the broiling froth of the Victoria Nile hurtled beneath the road, and Ritchie photographed the whole group standing by the barrier – including Stanton the driver. Then Stanton took a photograph of Rebecca and Azalea and Ritchie and Lauren, and already they were so close they were touching.

The roadblocks started soon after Karuma, wire barricades strung across the track manned by soldiers in torn, unwashed uniforms. They were searching for LRA. Rebecca obdurately refused to bribe, so the delays were long. In the dark hours before they got to Langadi, Rebecca told Ritchie and Lauren what they needed to know about Uganda.

For all her dispassionate demeanour, Rebecca Folley had a good heart. She would never have endured nine years at a godforsaken mission in a civil war zone without one. She didn't deliver the voluble European invective so often heaped upon the poor of Africa. Rebecca, almost to her own surprise, had grown to love the country, could almost call it home. She told the young VSOs about the mission, and what she could about the medical needs of the hospital. 'We are hopelessly understaffed,' she told them. 'But we simply can't afford to pay more wages. We have sixteen inpatients because we have sixteen beds and sixteen mattresses – not because we have the staff or the medicines or the doctors or the money to treat sixteen patients – not because that is the right number to serve the population of a town like Langadi. So what do we do when a child comes in with malaria? We send someone else home. Someone else with malaria, or TB, or sleeping sickness or AIDS.'

It was almost dark when they got to the ferry at Laropi. A colonial-era barge, the last of the day, bore them heavily over the dark waters of the Nile. Now they were truly separated from the world they had left behind. The ferry slammed into the sandy bank and Rebecca said, 'Welcome to West Nile. There's no way back now,' and she laughed. 'Unless you fancy your chances in Sudan.'

They arrived a little before midnight. Azalea was asleep on Lauren's knee.

Rebecca knew that the *proximity* of the little bedrooms that they had cleared at the end of the mission hall for the two young doctors, with nothing but a brushwood wall between them, would only fuel the sexual tension. But what could she do? No better accommodation was available. She shrugged silently to herself. Lauren and Ritchie were adults, she figured. By the time she was their age, she had been through a dozen partners or more. They could work things out for themselves. They would only be in Langadi for sixteen weeks.

She was wrong. It would be only five days.

When the alarm bell sounded out over the thatched roof of the mission mess – the dingdingdingding urgent call – it was a rhythm unfamiliar to Lauren and Ritchie, who had yet to rehearse the ritual of the alarm. Each, still with their own mosquito net, was enclosed in their own small room behind the mission hall when the bell sounded. Lauren was cleaning her teeth with bottled water. Ritchie was shuffling items among his luggage.

Lauren, alerted by the noise, glanced through her window to see the disappearing heels of children fleeing into the bush. One child sped past her window, arms flailing, her face set in such a look of consternation that Lauren was immediately infected by a sense of apprehension. She slid from her room and knocked lightly on Ritchie's door.

'I think something's wrong,' she said when he came to the door.

'Wrong? How?'

Ritchie Lewis was a quiescent young man, and it would take a very significant crisis to ruffle his nonchalant demeanour. He was broad-shouldered, casual and blokeish, with a raffish smile and a quiff of hair that constantly threatened to obscure his vision unless it was affably flicked back into obedience. He wasn't about to let Lauren's anxiety upset his agreeable mood.

'Wrong, like the bell is ringing like crazy and all the kids are running for the hills,' said Lauren.

'Maybe it's sports day … or something?' said Ritchie.

Lauren looked at him slightly agog. 'Ritchie,' she said, this time in an urgent whisper, 'it isn't sports day. Something's going on.'

It would be an exaggeration to say that Lauren Marks was the 'ying' to Ritchie Lewis's 'yang'. They were not chalk and cheese, these two. Lauren too had a feisty reputation – a shrinking violet does *not*, after all, volunteer to spend sixteen weeks in a civil war zone. But on this occasion at least, Lauren demonstrated a more pragmatic, cautious attitude than her colleague.

Ritchie, unruffled Mr Practical, said, 'OK. Let's go and have a look.'

Outside it was already uncomfortably hot. The bell had stopped and tranquillity appeared to reign.

'There,' said Ritchie. 'Nothing's up.'

'But what about the bell?' protested Lauren.

'Probably just the school bell.'

'Ritchie, it's a quarter to eight. The school bell goes at nine.'

'Does it? Well, then. Probably just one of the orphans playing a prank.' Ritchie made to go back indoors, but Lauren blocked his way.

'Richard Lewis,' she said in a firm tone, 'we're not going back in there until we find out what this is about.'

Ritchie drew himself up to his full height. Nothing so motivates a man of Ritchie's temperament as the urgent command of an attractive woman. But there was to be no skulking around. Ritchie would approach the situation head on. He marched out into the driveway to look for someone to ask. The wizened figure of Mzee Njonjo appeared behind the bulb of a makote tree. 'Excuse me!' Ritchie called over to him, 'What was the bell for?'

Mzee Njonjo's response was an unexpected one. He crouched down suddenly and gestured to Ritchie, with quick patting motions of his hand, to do the same. Lauren, who had seen the old man's reaction, gave a short gasp and grabbed Ritchie's arm.

'It's the LRA,' she said. They had learned about the LRA on the journey from Entebbe.

Ritchie's bravado, however, was not to be so lightly punctured. 'Hang on,' he said, 'there's someone coming. We'll ask them.'

Down the drive in a billow of red dust, far too fast for the ruts and potholes, came a truck. Ritchie, smiling widely, set off to greet it. The truck braked hard and the dust began to subside.

'It's just a load of kids,' said Ritchie.

But Lauren, still clutching his arm, had not relaxed. Down from the back of the truck leaped half a dozen boys – teenagers – most in faded t-shirts and patched-up cotton shorts. One of them wore a beret and was shouting out commands.

Ritchie raised his arm to issue a convivial wave, but the gesture was not reciprocated. There was a sinister metallic click, and Lauren Marks and Ritchie Lewis found themselves looking up the oiled and shiny barrels of two locally made G_3 assault rifles, and into the vacant and incurious eyes of the child soldiers of the Lord's Resistance Army.

14

June 1992

In the mess hall at the St Paul's Mission, the tension was now palpable. Rebecca tapped out a second cigarette, this time avoiding any offer to Kony or his henchman.

It was important, Rebecca knew, to keep these men talking. She imagined the children fanning out across the fields, heading for their safe houses. They needed time to get away. The farm lads too, and the nurses; they would need to be well away from the compound by the time the LRA men started looking around – which they surely would. She wondered where Azalea would be. Azalea had nowhere to fly to. Azalea's alarm plan was to run for the mission minibus and to conceal herself inside until one of the staff could find the keys and drive them all to safety. Rebecca's heart fluttered at the thought. Anyeko, too – Azalea's best friend – she would certainly be with her; those girls were inseparable.

How strange it was, Rebecca Folley had often thought, that no sooner had her own childlessness led them to adopt Azalea than fate conspired to deliver to her a family of fifteen needy children and plenty of needy adults besides. There was not a child in the orphan hall that she, Rebecca, had not sat with and cradled, had not sung to, had not read to. In the early evenings when the children were ready for bed, the boys from the boys' dormitory would gather on the beds of the girls' dormitory and Rebecca would read aloud to them. A soft silence would settle over the room. Azalea would be there too, cosied up alongside Anyeko. Outside the crickets would call, and inside mosquitoes would hum. Maria the matron would appear with her spray of pyrethrum insecticide and around the beds she would go, pumping out the mist above every bed as Rebecca began to read.

Whatever the age of the children, there was a spell cast upon them when Rebecca was reading. Some of the little ones spoke no English. Some of the older ones would struggle to relate to the stories. It mattered not. At bedtime, Rebecca, who was so formal in class, who demanded such discipline among her pupils, could unravel her temperament to become mother to a dozen or more children, from a world so far away, who had no mothers of their own.

And the books and stories that she would read! The favourites among the younger orphans were the stories of Dr Seuss. 'The sun did not shine. It was too wet to play. So we sat in the house, all that cold, cold, wet day,' read Rebecca, to children for whom the sun would never *not* shine, who would never know a cold, cold, wet day. She would hold up the pictures for all to see, and boys and girls who had never known what it was to sit bored in a house waiting for a mother to come home would share the excitement and the anxiety generated by *The Cat in the Hat*.

Then sometimes she would read stories for older children. Anyeko, at thirteen, would still suck her thumb while the stories were read. August and Okot and Abola – the older boys – would squat close to Rebecca and peer around to look at the pictures on the pages. Lanyomi and Ruth and Little Rebecca, the youngest of the girls, would all be together in a single bed with only their eyes peeping over the top of the covers. Rebecca would read them the stories of Peter Pan and Wendy and the menacing crocodile, and she would read them the stories that she, Rebecca, had loved as a child. She read *Black Beauty* to children for whom horses were a rare sight, and if ever seen were always whipped hard, and thin. She discovered that orphans were common enough in children's literature; *Pollyanna*, the story of an orphan girl with an unquenchable tendency for optimism; *Oliver Twist*, an orphan boy who finds his place in society; and *Heidi*, raised by her grandfather, who overcomes her disabilities through strength of character and determination. It seemed to matter not a jot that none of the children at Langadi had ever been to Vermont or London or the Swiss Alps – the stories delivered their own powerful message. Whenever Rebecca would finish a chapter, she would firmly shut the book and the children would chant, 'More, Mrs Rebecca, more, more.' And sometimes, with a twinkle in her eye, she would open up the book again. 'Just one more chapter,' she would declare.

Now, in the mess hall, with the AK47 rifle resting like an alien corpse on the breakfast table, Rebecca wondered if she would ever read to the children again. Would this be the day it all ended for the Holy Tabernacle mission of St Paul? She thought about each of the children. Abola with his passion for football, able to sprint barefoot across the stony playground, able to send a ball high into the flame trees with a flick of his long toes; Lubangak-ene with her predilection for wearing trinkets in her hair – beads and posies wound in with rubber bands; August, who came to St Paul's as a youngster (maybe six or seven years old) and was so traumatised by something in his past that he barely spoke for a year, but who now helped Odokonyero in the kitchen carrying sacks of pulses on his shoulder like a man; Little Rebecca with eyes like mysteries, who would dissolve away into the darkest shadows, who would steal the heart of every visitor to the mis-sion. All of these, and so many more. Rebecca found herself shaking deep within her being. She imagined Little Rebecca with her lips and nose cut off; Lanyomi and Ruth and Cota and James with no hands. It was too horrible. Too, too horrible.

Joseph Kony was saying something to Luke. Something about God's plan for the world. He was quoting the Ten Command-ments. Rebecca found herself rising to her feet, struggling to control the deep emotion that was choking her. She felt a hand upon her arm: Odokonyero. It was a touch – just a subtle touch – a feather-light, fingertip touch of his large hands. She flicked her eyes towards the big cook, but he was focused on Kony. His touch upon her arm was telling her, 'Wait, wait, wait. Wait while this man wastes his time with us. Wait while he fills the air with his miserable polemics.'

But Rebecca could no longer wait. She shook off Odokonye-ro's hand and stubbed her cigarette firmly out on the wooden table.

'Why don't you just tell us what you want with us, Mr Kony?' she said sharply.

Outside there were noises. A truck was barrelling down the drive in a universe of dust.

'I am a man of peace,' said Kony, although his eyes said otherwise. 'I am here to help you. I am here to help your mission.'

'And how do you intend to help our mission?' demanded Rebecca.

Kony's hand crept back towards his gun. The tone of the meeting had changed. 'I can offer employment to your children,' he said in Acholi, 'to your orphan children.'

'What is he saying?' said Rebecca.

Luke stretched out his hand to calm her. 'He is telling us he can find jobs for the children.'

'Well, tell him that our orphans don't need jobs,' Rebecca snapped. She started to fumble with her packet in search of another cigarette.

'Mrs Luke,' said Kony in English, 'these children are not *muna muna*. They are not white men. They are Acholi. The Acholi people are at war with the murderers and child-killers of the Museveni regime. Every Acholi man, woman and child is bound by blood to rise up and support the struggle. Every one.' He swept his gun back off the table and slung it on his shoulder, rising from the table as he did so. There were shouts emerging from the truck that had swung into the compound. 'You will not stop us, Mrs Luke,' said Kony, 'because we have God and Jesus on our side; because we are the Acholi. If you try to resist, then we will say you are a part of the Museveni regime.' He swung his gun around so that the barrel was an inch from Rebecca's face.

'Now look here,' said Luke, 'we're not looking for trouble.'

'*Are* you a part of the Museveni regime?' asked Kony of Rebecca. There was a heartbeat of silence. Two boy soldiers came bounding into the mess hall with G3 rifles and also levelled the guns onto the Folleys.

'Well, are you?' asked Kony.

'Of course I'm bloody not,' said Rebecca.

Kony lowered his gun and the boy soldiers did the same.

'Good answer,' said Kony.

'This mission has looked after Acholi children for ninety years,' said Luke. 'We only care about the welfare and health of the children.'

'Very good,' said Kony. 'Then we are on the same side.' He barked something to the child soldiers in Acholi. Rebecca couldn't understand, but Luke knew exactly what he was saying. What he said was, 'Find all the children you can and put them in the truck.'

A second truck now rolled up the driveway and more young soldiers spilled off the back. Kony barked some orders, then he turned to Luke.

'Do you have any vehicles?'

Luke shook his head.

'Don't lie to me, Mr Luke!'

There were two vehicles in the compound. One was the Folleys' Land Rover, the other was the mission minibus. Luke reached into a pocket. 'You may borrow the Land Rover,' he said, and he tossed the keys onto the table. 'The bus isn't working. The engine is broken. It needs parts from Europe.'

'Is that so?' said Kony. He turned to one of the older boy soldiers and gestured with his gun. There was a series of shouts outside, and a militiaman in uniform emerged from one of the trucks leading a man by his collar. The man was Stanton – the minibus driver.

'Is this bus working?' demanded Kony.

Stanton looked down at his feet. 'It is not working well,' he said, in Acholi.

'Do you have the keys?'

'I … have lost the keys,' said Stanton. But he paused too long before he spoke and one of the boy soldiers was onto him, striking him across the face with the barrel of his rifle. Stanton fell to the ground weeping loudly. The boy with the rifle flicked his hands like a professional pickpocket into the driver's jacket and extracted the keys.

'That man is not a true Acholi,' said Kony in mock sorrow. 'Please send him for some education in how to defend his own people.'

The soldiers hauled Stanton out of the mess hall.

'You are not to touch a hair of his head!' shouted Luke.

Kony tut-tutted. 'He is no longer your concern, Mr Luke.' He tossed the Land Rover keys back at Luke. 'You may keep your Land Rover. We will take your bus.'

Rebecca said, 'I have one or two personal items in the minibus that I would like to remove.' She shot an imperious look at Kony and started off towards the compound. No one tried to stop her.

Some boys came running up. They had Tebere and Kila and Lubangakene and James; four of the orphans who had not run fast enough. There were no other children in the orphanage, the boy soldiers told Kony; only a matron and a baby. Kony shouted at them to search the rest of the mission buildings. He was joined now by a couple of his more senior-looking commanders.

As they emerged from the mess hall, Luke and Rebecca spotted Lauren Marks and Ritchie Lewis standing against a truck while a child of little more than ten waved a machine gun at them.

'Would you please tell your men not to wave guns at my guests,' Luke said to Joseph Kony.

Kony issued the command and the child with the gun withdrew.

'You two are to do exactly what I say,' Luke said to Ritchie and Lauren in a brief moment when Kony and his men were out of earshot. 'Don't waste any time. Don't attempt any heroics. These men are LRA. They are very, very dangerous. In one minute I shall create a diversion. When I do, just turn and walk out of this compound and never come back. Don't stop for your personal belongings or your passports. Just turn and walk calmly out into the town. Get a lift back to Gulu and go to the British High Commissioner in Kampala. They'll get you back on a plane. Now nod if you understand what I just told you.'

What could Lauren and Ritchie do? They nodded.

As Luke was instructing the VSOs, Rebecca was making her way over to the minibus. This was a routine, it appeared, that they had practised.

Eyes followed Rebecca to the bus. She slid open the door. 'Don't make a sound,' she whispered.

Cowering in the back were Azalea and Anyeko.

'As soon as I say so,' said Rebecca, 'open the back door and run to Pastor David's house. Run as fast as your legs will carry you and don't look back.'

She made as if she was collecting some items from the seat, then stepped out of the bus with the faintest of nods to Luke.

'Aaaaah!' Luke cried suddenly, falling to his knees. 'A devil! A devil!' He was looking up at the makote tree, his eyes wide. 'A devil!'

All eyes swung back his way.

'Now!' commanded Rebecca. Across the compound Luke let loose the wail of a banshee. He threw himself on the grass and began to thrash about like a fish plucked from a stream. The unlikely performance had the desired effect. Men with guns came running from every direction to investigate the commotion, and as they did, the two teenage girls slid unseen from the belly of the minibus and fled behind the mission house.

Rebecca, too, ran over to Luke. 'Please, please,' she cried, 'let me through.' She knelt beside him. 'He gets like this when there are devils around. Please – no one must move until the devil has departed.' Rebecca froze. One by one the child soldiers also obliged. 'Has the devil gone yet?' Rebecca asked Luke.

'Not yet.'

Kony and his commanders appeared. 'What is going on?'

One of the boy soldiers replied, 'This man has seen a devil.'

Kony looked worried. He stalked up to the place where Luke was lying. 'Tie him up,' he ordered. He waved his gun to call all his men and boys back. 'We will return for more children,' he told Rebecca. 'They are needed for God's work.'

As Luke was being restrained, he managed a glance back over

125

his shoulder towards the road. Lauren and Ritchie had made good their escape. His last sight of the couple was the flash of Ritchie's blond hair over the top of the compound hedge, and then they vanished into the network of little paths that led towards the village.

Two LRA men commandeered the mission bus. 'We need this vehicle,' Kony said.

'Don't tell me,' said Rebecca, 'for God's work.'

Kony shot her a look that indicated this sudden sarcasm was not lost on him. 'Where does your pastor live?' he asked her.

'We don't have a pastor,' said Rebecca.

Kony turned to speak to one of his men. Stanton, the driver, was offloaded from one of the trucks. 'Take him,' said Kony, 'he will show you where the pastor's house is. Bring him to me.' He gave a sideways sneer. 'And search the house well,' he said.

Then, without looking back, Kony climbed into the front seat of a truck and in a flurry of dust they were gone.

15

March 2011

The trip to North Devon, to see the place where Marion Yves had met her end, did not go without a hitch. For a start, Thomas wasn't sure if he could drive with only one good arm. Azalea drove instead, but after just a few miles she complained that her rib was hurting, so they stopped in a side street and swapped seats. Thomas could steer with his right arm while Azalea could change gear. This arrangement wasn't much better, however. It relied on good communication between them, so Thomas would say, 'Ready to change into third,' and Azalea would chant, 'Ready'. Thomas would depress the clutch, Azalea would slip the gearstick, Thomas would release the clutch and on they would go. But they had failed to account for the traffic driving out of London and the constant demands upon the gears, so that for the first half-hour or so of their trip, their conversation consisted of little more than prompts to change gear and apologies when one or the other got the whole thing wrong.

This wasn't quite the start that Thomas had envisaged. To make matters worse, the persistent gear changes soon gave rise to frayed tempers, and by the time they hit the M4 heading west, they had been beaten into silence, and they saw about a dozen miles sweep past without either one uttering a word.

Eventually it was Azalea who broke the impasse. 'Are we going to continue like this all the way to Devon?' she asked. 'Only it's five hours' driving, and I don't know if I can go all that way in silence.'

'There's always the radio,' Thomas suggested.

'Turn it on then,' said Azalea.

'I can't,' said Thomas, wobbling his plastered arm.

'Well then neither can I,' said Azalea, 'because if I take my hand off this blessed gear knob then I'll get my head bitten off.'

'It's a gear*stick*,' said Thomas, 'not a gear knob.' To be fair to Thomas here, he was trying to lighten things up, but this may not have been the best way to do it.

'Oh pardon me,' said Azalea caustically, 'I should have known. The gear knob is the one driving the car.'

It really wasn't a good start. Thomas began to wonder about the wisdom of even suggesting this excursion. What had he been thinking? How could he have imagined that a shared trauma on the Underground, and a very odd consultation about coincidences, could ever have been a suitable basis for a whole day in each other's company? Yet now there seemed no turning back. He glanced towards Azalea. Her right hand was firmly clutching the gearstick but her face was pointedly turned away, watching big airliners lumbering into Heathrow.

'I'm sorry,' he heard himself saying. 'I *am* the gear knob.'

'You are,' she said. There was no reciprocal apology.

'Shall we start again?' said Thomas. 'I could tell you about my life.' He turned his face to look at her, and this time she returned the look. 'Just to pass the time,' he added, 'until we both get our nice personalities back.'

'Nice personalities?' Azalea echoed.

'Not very poetic, I know.'

'Well,' said Azalea, 'you don't *do* poetry.'

She hadn't forgiven him yet, then.

'I was born in Belfast,' said Thomas.

'You don't sound especially Irish,' said Azalea.

'I'm not,' said Thomas. 'At least, not all Irish. Northern Irish. My mother was a Belfast girl. My father was English.'

'That must have made you popular,' said Azalea, with irony.

'Indeed. And to make things worse, my father was a security consultant. His job was to work with shops, hotels, companies in town to help make them safe from terrorism. He would do a survey of the premises and then advise them to lock any doors or cupboards, to brick up holes, to make sure there were no hiding places where anyone might conceal explosives. He used to seal up the manhole covers and block over the drains, and show them where to put up concrete bollards to stop cars getting too close. He was pretty good at his job, but in the end there isn't a lot you can do to stop a committed bomber. Anyway, his job meant that he wasn't just *English*, but he was a part of the regime too.'

Azalea was silent. They had passed the M25 and now the green fields of the Thames Valley beckoned.

They drove for a while without saying anything, then Thomas picked up the story again. 'So we lived in a state of constant alert,' he said. 'We lived in the middle of a loyalist estate, surrounded by Protestant families and UVF lookouts and British Army checkpoints.'

Azalea seemed to be getting restless. 'I don't know if I want to hear this,' she said suddenly.

'Oh.' Thomas fell silent. 'OK,' he said, after a while.

The countryside of Berkshire rolled past.

'How old were you?' asked Azalea, softly.

'How old was I when … what?'

'When your father was killed?' Azalea was looking at him now. 'That's what you were going to tell me, wasn't it? You were going to tell me that one dark night the IRA broke into your house and blew up your father.'

Thomas looked at her and then looked away. He didn't speak.

Azalea released the gearstick and reached out to turn on the radio.

'Wait.' Thomas caught her hand with his heavy, plastered elbow. 'Is this a special skill of yours? Do you magically know what everyone is about to say? Maybe you want to tell the story for me?'

Azalea looked down. 'I guess it's my turn to say sorry,' she said. She gave a slow grimace. 'I'm the gear knob now. Tell me the story.'

'You've already told it,' he said. 'Some of it. I was five years old when the hunger strikes were on. That was the year it all began to change.'

'When was that?'

'Nineteen eighty-one. Ten Republican prisoners starved themselves to death in the Maze Prison at Long Kesh. You couldn't cross the city without passing half a dozen army barricades. There were soldiers everywhere, big sectarian slogans on the sides of buildings, and every night there was some atrocity or other. We all knew kids that were caught up in it. It was like this deep tribal divide. There was no logic to any of it. It wasn't even about religion, or Republicanism, or what your accent was; it was all about the mantras that had been drummed into you as a child.'

'Your parents were Protestants?' said Azalea.

Thomas nodded rhythmically. 'My mother was a Protestant,' he said.

'And your father?'

'... Was an atheist. But as my mother would always say of him, he was an atheist in the Protestant tradition, not in the Catholic tradition.' Thomas smiled as he made this remark. It was a kind of joke.

Azalea smiled too. 'How old were you?' she asked again.

A loud motorbike roared past them and was gone. Azalea flinched as if it might have been a gunshot.

'Would you rather I slowed down?'

'No. No, I'm OK.'

Thomas slowed a little anyway. He watched the car ahead pull away. A Motorway Services sign appeared. 'Do you want to stop for a tea?'

'Already?'

'I think I need one.'

Azalea seemed to relax. She let her head fall back. 'Will they do real coffee?' she asked.

'I'm sure they will.'

'OK then.'

Thomas flicked the indicator. 'I'm going to need you on gear-knob duty,' he said.

'Right-ho, Cap'n.' She saluted.

He pulled into the slow lane. 'I was eleven,' he said as Azalea nodded. 'It wasn't a bomb. Gear!'

They managed a slick change from fifth to fourth.

'They stalked my father home from work one day.'

Azalea was holding her breath.

'Gear!'

Down they changed into third.

'We were all sitting in the front room, watching television.' He turned to look at her. 'Gear.'

Down to second.

They pulled into the services. Thomas found a space and parked the car. Azalea slid the stick into neutral. They stayed sitting, looking forward, as the engine died.

'A bullet came through the window,' said Thomas.

'I'm sorry,' said Azalea.

'My father had just sat down. The bullet whipped past his ear and then it bounced off the radiator with one hell of a bang, but of course all of that happened at once – all in one single instant – then there was glass everywhere. And I was screaming. And my father was screaming. And I remember thinking, Why isn't Mum screaming too? Why is she just sitting there?'

Now Thomas was looking at his feet.

'I think,' said Azalea after a few heartbeats had passed, 'that we may have more in common than just a couple of broken bones.'

After the refreshment break, they drove again in silence, but this time it was a different *sort* of silence. Azalea pushed back her seat, kicked off her unsuitable shoes and put her bare feet up on the dashboard. For Thomas this was an unnerving distraction, although politeness intervened to prevent him looking too directly at Azalea's feet, or from watching the way that she would twiddle her toes, or from observing the way that her second toe seemed so much longer than her first. Neither did he notice the faint, but slightly intoxicating, odour, or the soft curve of her ankle.

'Do you think losing your mother the way you did explains

why you're such a rationalist now?' Azalea asked him after a while.

'Why would it do that?'

'Because it was such a random event, perhaps? The bullet might have ricocheted anywhere, but it didn't; it struck the one person who might have believed in a divine protector.'

'You should meet my mentor at the university,' Thomas said, 'Dr Bielszowska. That's the kind of theory she always likes.'

'Were you ever married? I mean – I take it you're not married now. You're not married, are you?'

Thomas grinned. 'No,' he said, 'I'm not married.' He turned to look at her 'I'm not ... in a relationship,' he said.

'Oh my God. You're not gay? I mean ... it's perfectly cool if you are. Are you gay?'

Thomas gloried at the question. It wasn't so much that she had recovered from her first 'oh my God', it was more the fact that she had reacted like that in the first place. Why would she have done that if she hadn't, in some way, been sizing him up as a possible ... a possible ... what? A possible partner? The suggestion sent a sweet electric thrill along the very bones of Dr Thomas Post, philosopher. 'I'm not gay,' he said, and he could feel his heartbeat quickening.

'I'm sorry,' said Azalea, 'I didn't mean to pry.'

'I was engaged for a while,' he said. There was a flutter of space-time. 'It didn't work out.'

'What constitutes "a while"? I mean, how long is a while? Are we looking at weeks? Months?' enquired Azalea.

'... Or even years,' said Thomas.

'Years?'

'Three.'

'That,' said Azalea, 'is one long engagement. No wonder the poor girl didn't go through with it. I mean – who gets engaged for *three years*?'

'Well. Like I said ... it didn't work out,' Thomas said. They were somewhere in the Wiltshire countryside.

'Did she leave you, or did you leave her?'

Wasn't she going to let go of this? Thomas said, 'It was six of one and a dozen of the other.' He caught a reflection in the window of Azalea smiling at this. 'I was the awkward one,' he said. 'I wouldn't leave London. She wanted to up sticks and go off to County Durham, or some other godforsaken place and I … well, I had my job, my flat …'

'So you had to choose between her and London – and London won,' said Azalea.

'It wasn't quite as simple as that,' said Thomas. 'But in the end, I suppose that was the last straw. Anyway. Have you ever been to County Durham? It's a miserable place.'

'I'm sure the people who live there don't think so,' said Azalea.

For you, thought Thomas, I would move to Murmansk. But he didn't say this. Instead he asked, 'How about you?'

'What?' she laughed. 'Are you asking if *I'm* gay?'

He laughed with her now. 'Well,' he said, 'are you?'

'Would it matter if I was?'

'Of course not,' came back Thomas. Any other answer might have seemed wholly presumptuous. Although, he might like to have added, cautiously, I would be a little disappointed.

'Well I'm not.'

He avoided saying, 'Good'.

'And before you ask, I'm not in a relationship either. But that's by choice. I don't do relationships.' She shot him a satisfied smile. 'We can all choose what we do. And what we don't.'

They arrived at Bude at lunchtime, and stopped at a pub on Marine Drive on the way out to Widemouth Sands. Their mood had lightened a great deal on the drive, but now that they were close to the spot where Marion died, Azalea became contemplative. They sat at a table in the window like the two invalids they were. The weather wasn't especially kind; a stiff wind was blowing in across the sound, but at least, as Thomas remarked, it wasn't raining.

'Does it seem like a silly thing to do?' Azalea asked. 'Driving all this way just to chuck some flowers off a miserable cliff for someone I have no real memory of?' She turned away from him, but there was moistness in her eye.

Very soon after Widemouth Bay the road wound steeply uphill towards Millook, and there, to their right, were the Penhalt Cliffs and beneath them, the sharp rocks and churning waters of the Irish Sea. They parked and walked together over a short grassy field. Not a long way to carry a body, Thomas thought. He tried to imagine Carl Morse here with the lifeless body of Marion Yves.

At the top of the cliff it was easy to see why Morse might have chosen this spot. The tide was neither high nor low, but the waves, picked up by the cold Irish wind, were slapping the cliffs way down and the rocks looked grey and wet and sharp.

'Don't go too close,' Thomas said, unnecessarily. He held out his good hand to steady Azalea as she edged towards the rim, and the rocks below seemed to beckon with malign intention.

Azalea was clutching a small spray of flowers, daffodils – the first of the season. They made Thomas think of Wordsworth and of Peter Loak in his permanent dark Lakeland.

'Do you think this is where he did it?' Azalea asked softly.

'Yes,' said Thomas.

'The funny thing is, I do remember some things. I think I do. I remember a tortoise.'

'A tortoise?'

'Yes. It must have been either at Marion's cottage on the Isle of Man, or else maybe at Peter Loak's house in Cumbria. But I remember it. I remember unwrapping him from a box at the end of the winter and watching him creak away into the bushes. People don't keep tortoises any more, do they? But we did. He was an old tortoise. I remember we used to call him Prairie Tortoise; that was my name for him. And then I remember years later telling my mum, Rebecca, about him. She laughed, and she said, "That's the name for the Lord's Prayer." I didn't understand what she meant. Not at first.'

'The prayer He taught us,' said Thomas.

'It's always made me laugh,' said Azalea. 'When the priest says, "Let's all stand and say together the prayer He taught us". Because it always makes me think of Prairie Tortoise, and I wonder if he's still alive, and who wraps him up in the autumn and puts him into a box, and who unwraps him in the spring?' Azalea started slowly to unpeel the cellophane wrapping from the flowers.

'I don't even know what she was *like*,' she said. 'My own mother ... I'd like to know what she was like.'

'She was probably just like you,' said Thomas. 'They do say, like mother, like daughter.'

'But I don't think she *was*. How could she sleep with three men and not know which one had fathered her child? I couldn't do that.' They watched the ocean billow and surge against the cliffs, and Azalea pulled her coat a little tighter. 'Do you want to know a strange thing?' she asked. 'I've been avoiding telling you ... but I shall have to tell you sometime, I suppose.'

'You can tell me anything.'

'I was worried that this one might freak you out. It's another coincidence. Tell me if you don't want to hear it.'

'Coincidences never freak me out. Of course I want to hear it.'

'Marion Yves died on Midsummer's Day, 21 June 1982. She was my birth mother. Rebecca and Luke Folley died on Midsummer's Day, 21 June 1992. They were the parents I knew and loved. Rebecca and Marion died ten years apart. To the day.' Azalea plucked a daffodil from her bunch and cast it into the wind. 'So this is for you, Marion Yves.' She threw another. 'I'm older now than you were when your life was so brutally taken from you.' She threw a third. The wind picked up the flowers and swirled them against the cliff beneath in a welter of petals and spray. 'We're all victims of savage, bastard inhumanity,' she cried into the wind. 'Marion, you were taken by a wicked, violent monster.' She cast another flower into the wind. 'Peter Loak, the man you loved, was mutilated by war.' Another flower. 'Rebecca and Luke Folley, who loved me and raised me, were slaughtered trying to protect me.' A final burst of yellow daffodils all flung into a gust of wind. 'And my friend, Thomas, lost his mother too, to another murderous thug with another stupid gun in another fucking stupid war.'

They watched the daffodils slip down the rock face and vanish into the waiting foam; just the way Marion, cold and lifeless, must once have done. The wind had increased, as if a guilty spirit out in the bay was shouting back. Thomas placed his hand on Azalea's arm – just the gentlest of pressures to suggest that perhaps she should step back now, just a little way, from the edge. But Azalea's face was set towards the storm. 'I don't care who you are,' she shouted suddenly into the face of the squall. 'I don't care who you think you are ... trying to rule my life!'

'Azalea, please.'

She shook free of Thomas's hold. 'I don't care what games you're playing with me,' she yelled into the wind. 'I don't care who you kill. Do your worst. Do your fucking worst!'

They stood as the gale buffeted them like stoic statues set against the tempests. There was salt spray in the air and it flashed against their faces as the hulking waves below rolled across the rocks and shattered into droplets and mist.

'Shall I take you home?' said Thomas.

For a while neither of them moved. Then Azalea turned and buried her face into his shoulder. 'Yes please,' she said. 'Take me home.'

16

June 1992

The low building that was Pastor David's house was built in the style of a circular Acholi hut and roofed with grass, but the building material was cinder block and not traditional adobe mud brick, and there was glass in the windows and a concrete yard with a bench and a rocking chair and a cooking stove. Inside the front door was a small anteroom, and leading off from this, two awkwardly shaped rooms like the slices of a pie. One was the room where the pastor slept, and the other was where he lived and conducted his business. Behind the roundhouse was the toilet hole, a rain barrel and a separate lean-to arrangement of corrugated metal sheets, behind which the pastor could carry out his ablutions in reasonable privacy.

When the alarm bell sounded from the roof of the mess hall, Pastor David had just returned from breakfast and was in his washroom soaping down, and maybe this is why he failed to hear the bell which should have summoned him back to the hall; or maybe – and perhaps more likely – Pastor David was growing a little old and his hearing was not so good. Whatever the reason, by the time he had finished washing, the bell had stopped. Pastor David had no need of a towel. He would dry off in the sun on his porch. He had laboured around to the little concrete yard and was lowering himself into the rocking chair to contemplate God's glorious creation, when down the path like a pair of cane rats came Anyeko and Azalea.

'LRA! LRA!' Anyeko was shouting.

Among the Buganda people, of whom Pastor David could be counted, there was no love for the Lord's Resistance Army and very little fear of the magic they claimed to perform. The pastor lifted himself back out of his chair, still wet from his morning wash. 'In there,' he commanded, and the girls disappeared into his sleeping room.

The wise thing, now, to have done would have been for Pastor David to have settled once more into his rocker, giving the appearance of a man undisturbed enjoying his morning nap. Instead the good pastor took up a position outside his front door, like a soldier guarding a palace, and this is how the two LRA boys found him when they came running down his path just a few moments later.

'Who are you?' Pastor David demanded of them in English. This took them aback. It was not a language they could reply in.

'Are you the pastor?' asked one of the boys in Acholi.

'I am,' said the old Buganda man, replying in their language. 'What do you want?'

'You are wanted,' said the boy. He carried a very old rifle.

'Who wants me?'

'Joseph Kony wants you,' said the boy.

'Why does he want me?'

'To chase away a devil.'

The pastor looked shaken by this information. 'Tell him to come and get me,' he said.

The boy looked frightened. 'You must come,' he insisted. 'You *must* come.'

The second LRA boy, whose gun was equally antique, made for the door of the house, but the pastor blocked his way. 'Very well,' said the priest. 'I will come. Lead the way.'

'You're hiding someone!' shouted the first boy in excitement.

'No,' said the pastor, 'I am hiding nobody. Now take me to Kony.'

The first boy hesitated. He was used to taking orders and perhaps, before his own abduction, he may have learned to respect the elders of the church. But the second boy, it seemed, did not share his qualms. He pushed past the elderly pastor, who could do little to stop him, and burst into the house. A moment later

138

he emerged, and at the dangerous end of his gun were Azalea and Anyeko.

This is what Azalea remembered of that day. She remembered being marched at gunpoint back to the compound. There was a sense of general pandemonium. Kony had left, and the men and boys who remained seemed wild-eyed and unsure quite what they should be doing. There was a lot of shouting.

It was as well, perhaps, for the delicate psyche of the thirteen-year-old, that Azalea was spared the opportunity to witness much of what followed. She and Anyeko were thrown roughly into the back of a truck, joining Tebere and Kila and Lubangakene and James. She felt a knee sharply in her back, and someone wrenched her arms behind her and pulled a plastic cable-tie tight around both her thumbs. Then she was shoved aside like a bag of cassava and with a jolt the truck was off, bouncing down the potholed mission drive.

In the annals of human recklessness or stupidity, what happened next might well deserve an entry. Despite his undertaking not to engage in heroics, Ritchie Lewis, now outside the mission compound and on the road to Langadi township, had struggled against this irregular instruction. When Luke had thrown his devil act, Lauren had grabbed Ritchie's wrist and had marched him firmly away from the compound. But it felt wrong to Ritchie. No sooner had they escaped from the confines of the mission than Ritchie dug his heels in. 'You go,' he told Lauren. 'I might be needed.'

'Needed! How?' Lauren demanded. But there was no restraining Ritchie once his gallantry had been awoken. They crept to the roadside a short way from the mission gate and concealed themselves behind a makote tree.

'Get down!' Lauren commanded in a stage whisper. 'They're coming.'

The truck carrying Joseph Kony and his henchman came barrelling out of the compound, flying past them in a dust cloud.

'You know who that was?' Lauren said. 'That was Joseph Kony. The most dangerous man in Africa.'

'We don't know that for certain,' Ritchie said.

'I've seen his photograph,' Lauren hissed.

'In that case,' said Ritchie, his mettle wholly undented by this possibility, 'they need us even more.'

'What are you intending to do?'

'I'm not exactly sure,' said Ritchie. He pulled Lauren towards him and, on impulse, kissed her firmly on the mouth.

'Is that in case we die in the next ten minutes?' Lauren asked. But the kiss had robbed her of some of her resistance.

'We won't,' Ritchie said reassuringly. And if the possibility of mortal danger had failed to occur to Ritchie before the kiss, it seemed even more remote after it. They crouched down and watched the road.

'What can you see?' Lauren whispered.

Ritchie was peering through the undergrowth. 'I think they've got the kids in the truck.'

'What? All the kids?'

'No. I think they just have four … or five. I don't know.' He paused. 'Azalea's with them.'

'Oh, shit!' said Lauren. 'Don't do anything rash, Ritchie. There's nothing we can do. They've got guns.'

'They're coming,' Ritchie said suddenly. He scrambled to his feet.

'Where are you going?'

'I'm going with them.'

'What? Are you mad?'

'I might be able to help,' Ritchie said. 'You stay there.' He stepped out from their hiding place behind the makote tree.

'Ritchie – you idiot.'

He was standing now in the middle of the track. The second LRA truck was on its way out of the mission compound heading towards them.

'Oh, for God's sake.' Lauren was on her feet too. 'You'd better kiss me again, you cloth-head,' she said.

They kissed, and less than two minutes later, with cable-ties around their thumbs, Ritchie and Lauren were in the back of the pick-up with Azalea and Anyeko and the rest of the children.

They drove for perhaps four hours, possibly five. The captives lay, tied and uncomfortable, on the floor of the truck, while an assortment of LRA soldiers sat on the wing plates with their guns, enjoying – it would seem – their appearance of gangster-like intimidation. When they pulled up at their destination and all the soldiers had whooped and jumped clear, a man who had the appearance of a senior commander came to inspect the catch. He was visibly disturbed by the presence of Azalea and the VSOs. 'Muna muna!' he yelled with some alarm. A crowd of armed and thin LRA conscripts and soldiers swarmed up to the truck. There were loud exchanges of view. Azalea's command of Acholi was fairly good. To her ear, the commander – or whatever his designated rank might be – was terrified that white captives would attract the attention of the Ugandan army. A welter of opinions and suggestions was forthcoming from the other LRA men. One suggestion was to shoot them right away and dump them on the road, but the senior man, to his credit, could not see how that would help. It would only enrage the army more. A suggestion that drew more support was to demand a ransom. The LRA were not proficient kidnappers – not for money, at least – but the idea clearly had some merit. Ritchie was identified as the spokesman. 'Are you British?' the LRA man demanded of him in Acholi.

'Tell him "Ee",' said Azalea in a whisper.

'Ee,' said Ritchie, uncertain what he was saying, or why.

The soldiers conferred.

'He asked if we were British,' said Azalea. 'You said "yes". They respect the British more than some of the others. Also they think the British would pay a good ransom for us. And they are scared that if they hurt us, then the British might come and track them down.'

After quite a bit of shouting, orders were given to unload the captives from the truck. As this happened it looked, for a moment, as if the St Paul's orphans might be going somewhere else. 'They stay with us!' shouted Azalea, in Acholi. A stunned lull in the bedlam greeted this declaration. 'If they don't stay with us, then the British will send planes to cut you all down!'

Eyes turned to the senior soldier, who was clearly the only man capable of making such a serious decision. He rolled his eyes and responded with a curt flick of his gun, and that appeared to be an instruction to keep the group together. Still bound at the thumbs, all eight of the prisoners were jostled off the tailgate, roughly herded underneath a jacaranda tree and ordered to sit in the dust.

'You can cut these things off our thumbs,' shouted Azalea, belligerently.

'I really don't think you should upset them,' said Lauren.

'Don't worry,' said Azalea. 'They won't dare hurt us.' She turned to a round-faced boy who seemed to have been ordered to watch them. 'And you can bring us some water!' she yelled.

The boy trembled. Then he shouted something over his shoulder and two girls came running with plastic water bottles. One girl held the bottle out to Azalea.

'We can't drink these with our hands tied,' Azalea said. She turned again to the trembling boy. 'Cut these ties from our thumbs,' she repeated, 'or I will speak to Joseph Kony. I'll tell Joseph Kony that you refused to let your British guests go free.'

At the mention of Kony's name, the boy shook even more. He relayed the threat back to a larger boy and the message was passed to the senior commander, who came over to investigate. He barked something at Ritchie.

'Talk to me,' said Azalea. 'Those two are just tourists.'

The commander looked anxious again. Taking tourists could be a dangerous gambit – even by the standards of the Lord's Resistance Army. He stared at the willowy girl wearing nothing but a nightdress, who seemed to be shouting instructions at his men. 'You know Joseph Kony?' he asked.

'Of course I know Joseph Kony!' Azalea snapped. 'Do you?'

The two held each other's gaze for a long moment. Azalea, who might not normally have counted herself a good liar, felt quite justified in her claim. Hadn't she been the first to see Kony at the mission, standing alone in the driveway as breakfast ended?

The commander looked away, apparently convinced. 'What do you want?' he said.

'First, get your men to release our hands,' said Azalea. 'Do you have any idea how uncomfortable this is? Then we want clean water and a hut. We won't run away.' She stared obstinately at the man. 'And bring us some bananas, we're hungry,' she said, 'and a melon.'

The commander was breathing heavily. Once again he gave a flick of his gun, and a boy ran up with a long cane-knife to cut the cable-ties from their thumbs. To assert his authority the commander took the knife from the boy, and, holding it up against Azalea's belly, he brought his face very close to her face and shouted a stream of Acholi words. Then, for good measure, he turned and did the same to Lauren Marks. Lauren, to her credit, had now learned from the sangfroid shown by Azalea. She kept her composure as the LRA man finished his tirade and stalked away.

'What did he say?' Lauren said to Azalea.

But Azalea, despite her bravado, had been shaken by the outburst. She shook her head, and for the first time there were tears emerging in her eyes. 'He said we must stay here,' she managed to say. 'We shouldn't try to escape.'

But what the soldier had really said was later told to Lauren by Anyeko. And what he said was, 'Set one foot out of this camp, muna muna girl, and I'll slice you from your little white pussy to your little white neck.'

And so, back to Langadi for the scene that Azalea was spared. We need not dwell too long on it. It was, after all, an episode, like the slaughter of Lester and Monique Folley and their son Lester Folley III, that does not call for embellishment. This was 21 June 1992, ten years to the day since Marion Yves was abducted from a fairground in Devon. And what transpired at the mission was indeed the violent shooting of Rebecca Folley, the second of three mothers that Azalea would learn to love. But in one important respect it was not quite the slaughter that Azalea had always imagined.

When the trucks left the compound taking with them Rebecca's only daughter and five of the orphans she loved, Rebecca's world fell apart. The lioness in a snare, say the people of West Nile, will devour her own leg to reach her cubs. The pandemonium that had greeted Azalea and Anyeko as they were tossed into the LRA truck was, for the most part, caused by Rebecca. As the truck carrying Azalea and the VSOs and the orphans bounced out of the mission, Rebecca broke free from two of the young soldiers who were restraining her and she ran after the truck with her arms waving. We will never know what she hoped to achieve by this. Probably she knew that the gesture would be futile and dangerous. But what is a lioness in a snare to do?

The boy who shot her was no older than August or Tebere. He wore a bandana on his head, like a South American freedom fighter, and a faded t-shirt with Dennis the Menace and Gnasher on the front, with red and black stripes like Dennis might wear. On his feet he wore sandals cut from an old car tyre. He was a thin boy with a lopsided face and one eye that looked the wrong way. We will never know his name or his story. Somehow, somewhere he had found himself enslaved to the cruel despotism of a mad preacher who swore to protect the Ten Commandments, and who did this – who still does this today – by abducting, mutilating and raping young children. Had he, the lopsided boy, like so many children, been kidnapped from his village by raiding militiamen? Had he been snatched from the fields, perhaps, or dragged out of a school? Or had he, like many abandoned children in Uganda and Sudan and Congo, simply drifted towards the LRA camps looking for food? We will never know. This was not a killing that would unravel in front of a jury. No laboratory would examine the bullets. No doctor would dictate a report. Only one journalist would ever come this far, and, crucially, he would get the story wrong.

When Rebecca ran out after the truck, the lopsided boy simply squeezed the trigger on his gun. He looked as much in shock as Rebecca when the shot sounded. Perhaps it was simply a nervous reaction, his finger already on the trigger, his nerves already frayed; we can speculate on this because the boy dropped the gun the second after the bang, put both hands on his head and wailed. Probably the boy knew he would face punishment for this transgression.

Rebecca toppled forward like a tree.

In panic now, in absolute alarm, the remnants of the Lord's Resistance Army fled towards the minibus and tore out of the compound.

When the reporter from the Olsen Press Agency arrived a day and a half later, the crime scene had been cleared by the Moyo District police. The new man in charge of the mission was old Pastor David, who could be found sitting on the red cement floor of the mess hall with his head deep in his hands. The reporter had driven all the way up from Kampala and was anxious to get back to a decent hotel in Gulu before nightfall, before the last ferry made its languid way back across the Nile. He spoke to one of the nurses and a big Acholi man who was the cook. There was very little to photograph; just a poor mission compound in a poor corner of a poor country. The reporter took a self-guided tour of the mission, and on the desk in Luke Folley's office he came upon a family photograph – Luke, Rebecca and Azalea standing outside the mission hall. He slipped the photograph into his satchel. On the way back to Gulu he wrote his report. He would stay a few days at the Acholi Inn in case there were any further developments in the incident. His report would be wired back to his news desk in Nairobi. The reporter was an old hand at this. He would stay by the poolside in his hotel for two or three days until the story subsided. If there were other reporters there, they could share a few beers, play a few hands of poker, swap details of the story.

The story that the reporter sent, while colourful, was not wholly untrue – at least in its conclusions, although it did mislead in its particulars. The reporter built his story around the photograph. Rebecca Folley, he wrote, had died in a hail of gunfire. Luke Folley and the couple's teenage daughter were missing, presumed dead. Five orphans were missing. The story failed to mention the VSOs, and this was because no one in the compound had thought to mention them. No one had seen them being bundled into the truck; the last that anyone had seen of Ritchie and Lauren was their hurried escape from the mission, en route – everyone would have suspected – back to Britain.

When the story and the photograph, now grainy from a fax machine, made it through to Nairobi, the subeditor gave it a headline that read, 'English Missionary Family in LRA Slaughter'. And this headline, over the touching photograph of the Folleys, led the news editor to make one or two adjustments to the reporter's prose. In particular the 'presumed dead' of his text was considered too soft for a story of this importance. Better, thought the news editor, to ask for forgiveness later than for permission now. He knew in his gut that the LRA had murdered the whole family, and the photograph seemed to confirm this assessment. So that is what he said. The story appeared in the Kenya *Daily Nation* as 'Mission Family Murdered', and it told in graphic detail how all three Folleys had perished in the raid. The bodies of two, the story said, had been taken by the LRA and were now missing.

The news item reached the London papers on 24 June, and the *New York Times* covered the story the following day in the context of a wider piece exploring terrorism in the developing world. The photograph, re-faxed, was by now too poor to publish, and this robbed the story of much of its impact. Some of the quality papers in Europe carried the item, and this was where, one year later, an investigator called Susan Calendar working for a blind man called Peter Loak sourced the conclusions for her report.

But while news of the shooting made very few ripples in London, things were different in Moyo District. Here the story of the incident at the Langadi Mission took hold like a bush fire. Police and army units were dispatched all the way from Kampala. Pastor David held a special service in the mission hall and a thousand people came. And sometime later, a helicopter flew in with Vice-President Samson Kisekka and a representative from the British Foreign and Commonwealth Office, and they walked solemnly around the mission and shook hands with Pastor

David and with Odokonyero. Photographs were taken, and some footage was shown on the Uganda television news. The Vice-President promised that those responsible for this outrage would be hunted down like rats, and he cautioned his people not to show the LRA any quarter.

In the city of Gulu, two hours' drive south of Langadi, an un-washed and battered Land Rover might have been seen in the car park of the Acholi Inn just hours after the shooting in Langadi. And if you had been in the pool garden, where waiters in white uniforms served iced drinks to the mainly Western clientele, you might have seen an urgent conversation taking place in the shade of a huge bougainvillea. A man of peace, who once might have given you the two-handed peace sign, who once sang protest songs in a subway in London with 'Peace' painted on his guitar, was sliding an envelope filled with American dollars across a table to a man of war, a man who had fought in jungles for the SAS, a man who was promising violent and bloody retribution, a man with the slogan 'Who Dares Wins' tattooed down the biceps of one arm.

17

March 2011

The journey home from the cliffs at Millook felt like an anti-climax. They had driven for five hours to stand for ten minutes in a gale, so that Azalea could rant against the cruelties of fate. Now they were headed back on the same road, aimed squarely towards the M5 motorway, and Thomas could feel the moment of opportunity that this day might have represented somehow slipping through his fingers. Azalea's feet were strapped back into her unsuitable shoes. She was gazing wistfully out of her window, and Thomas felt unable to interrupt her reverie.

Eventually, however, she turned towards him. 'Thank you,' she said. 'Thank you for taking me all that way.'

'You're welcome,' he said, and now it was all worthwhile.

'Do you believe in my coincidences? My midsummer coincidence?'

'Of course I do,' said Thomas.

'But what do you think it means?' said Azalea.

'What do I think it *means*? I could tell you. But I don't know if you'd want to hear it.' Thomas looked at her, wondering perhaps if she might want to remove her shoes again. And then he felt cross with himself for such a selfish thought. Then he told himself that this was why Azalea had made this journey – not because she relished the opportunity to spend a day in his company, but because she wanted to understand the strange existential events of her life. So he started again.

'Do you believe in luck?' he asked her.

'What kind of luck? Good luck? Bad luck?'

'Any sort of luck.'

Azalea shrugged. 'Of course.'

He smiled at this. It amused him that Azalea's view of the world could fall so far from his own. 'Are some people naturally lucky? Do some people get all the luck?'

She smiled her half-smile. 'It seems like that.'

'OK.' He appeared happy with this answer. 'This isn't a test.'

'Good.'

'There's really only one question that matters when you talk about luck and coincidence. Do you believe that it's all down to the mathematics of chance? Or do you prefer to believe that there are other forces at work, influencing our lives?'

'Well *you're* the coincidence man,' she said. 'What's the answer? You tell me.'

'I'd like to know what *you* believe. Does anything happen purely by coincidence? Or do you believe that everything ...' he took his hand from the steering wheel and gestured expansively, 'everything unfolds according to a great master plan?'

'Definitely the latter,' she said, and then she laughed. 'Don't give me that disapproving look.'

'I'm not.'

'Oh, yes you are.' She mimicked his stern expression, and this made him laugh too. 'But of course I believe in random chance,' she said. 'So many things take place over the course of history, there are bound to be coincidences happening all the time.'

'I'm glad to hear it.'

'But are you giving me a dichotomy? Do I have to choose between random coincidence and ... I don't know ...' she was hunting for a word, 'destiny?' She screwed up her face. It didn't feel like the right word.

He nodded at that. 'How about *providence*?' he suggested.

'Providence?'

'Yes. *Pro-videre*. An incident that was foreseen. That was provided for.'

'Something that was supposed to happen?'

'If you like.' He offered a weak smile. 'If I toss a coin five times and every time it comes up heads – is that a coincidence?'

Azalea considered this carefully. 'If my maths is correct,' she said, 'then the chances of four coin tosses all being the same as the first coin are … one in sixteen. So yes, it's a coincidence, but not an amazing one.'

Thomas looked over from the driving seat. 'Interesting,' he said. 'So if I threw fifty heads in a row – what then?'

She smiled. 'Then I would say the coin was fixed.'

'So at some point you would cease to believe in coincidence and start to believe in some kind of intelligent intervention?'

She nodded cautiously, unsure where this was leading. 'I guess so.'

'Fifty heads means someone is messing with the coin?'

'Probably.'

They drove for a while. The gear changes were becoming so second nature now that Thomas didn't even have to say 'gear'. He would drop the clutch and Azalea would slip the gears and it didn't interrupt the rhythm of the conversation. They drove through Crediton and picked up the road to Stockleigh Pomeroy. The light was starting to fade.

'We never had much twilight in Africa,' said Azalea. 'One moment it was daylight, and the next – pfft – it was dark.'

'Just like that?' said Thomas. 'Pfft?'

'Pfft,' said Azalea.

'In 1912 a lady called Violet Jessop survived the sinking of the *Titanic*,' Thomas said, picking up the earlier conversation. 'And then, four years later, she survived the sinking of the *Titanic*'s sister ship, the *Britannic*. Was that a coincidence?'

'It was certainly unlucky,' Azalea said.

'Was it a coincidence, then?'

'If I had to choose … I'd say she must have had a helping hand.'

'At the time a lot of people claimed that Violet Jessop's survival was more than a simple coincidence. Some said it was proof of divine intervention.'

'Perhaps it was. Maybe she wasn't meant to die at sea.'

'Or maybe it was just chance. When we come to look at it, we find that Violet Jessop wasn't actually a *passenger* on the *Titanic*. She was a stewardess, employed by White Star Lines. A lot of liners used to sink in those days, so a stewardess like Violet might reasonably expect someday to experience a sinking. Then after the first disaster she retrained as a nurse, and she went to serve in the Great War. The *Britannic* had been commandeered as a hospital ship. It was because of her experience of ocean liners that she secured the job – so no great coincidence there. The ship hit a mine. No great coincidence there, either. The mines had been placed with the intention of sinking ships, after all.'

'So it wasn't a coincidence?'

'Oh yes. It *was* a coincidence. But more along the lines of tossing five consecutive heads than tossing fifty. It was an *acceptable* coincidence.'

'So what,' Azalea asked, 'does all this have to do with my coincidences?'

Thomas narrowed his eyes. 'Here's another one,' he said, ignoring her question. 'Shakespeare and Cervantes – the greatest writers in the English and Spanish languages – respectively both died on the same date – 23 April 1616. Was that a coincidence?'

She mused. 'I would say it's a pretty borderline one; say, twenty-five heads.'

'Divine intervention or no divine intervention?'

She shrugged. 'Why would it matter to God if they died on the same day?'

'And in fact they didn't,' said Thomas, 'because Spain and England operated different calendars in 1616. The Gregorian calendar in Spain was ten days ahead of the Julian calendar in England. So it looks like a big fat coincidence, but it's more of a coincidence based on wonky calendars than any kind of cosmic synchronicity.'

'Cosmic synchronicity? Is that the official term?'

'Maybe not, but it's quite a useful expression, don't you think? Coincidence relies on some synchronicity. Look at John Adams and Thomas Jefferson, the second and third presidents of the USA. Guess what? They both died on the same day, and that day was 4 July 1826, which was exactly fifty years to the day since the

Declaration of Independence – to which they were both signatories. John Quincy Adams was president when they died. He wrote in his journal that it could *not* have been a coincidence – it had to have been a manifestation of divine favour. A lot of people shared his view at the time.'

'Well, maybe it was. Divine favour.'

'Do you really think so?'

'I don't know what to think,' Azalea replied. 'That's why I came to see you.'

'And I'm not proving particularly helpful, am I?'

She didn't reply to this.

'Shall we stop for something to eat in Tiverton?'

They parked in the town and found a pub close to the canal. The menu was not especially enticing, but through the window they could see the welcoming glow of an open fire. It was enough. They bought beers from the bar and settled opposite each other at a small table, their knees almost touching.

'Looks like fish and chips for me,' Thomas said.

'That'll be two then,' she said.

'You can't beat a traditional English pub, can you?'

Azalea nodded in agreement. 'No TV,' she said, 'no jukebox.'

'No fruit machine, no pool table.'

A waitress came to take their order. Afterwards they sat and sipped at their drinks.

'Are you familiar with the concept of determinism?' Thomas asked.

Azalea raised an eyebrow. 'I've heard of it. Why?'

'Because determinism is what I study. That's my true field, not coincidences. My work is really about trying to look experimentally at a very deep conundrum in philosophy. There is a theory of the universe that is sometimes called the "billiard ball" theory. Do you know it?'

Azalea said she didn't.

'It's a bit of a depressing theory, really. What it suggests is that from the moment the universe came into being, you know, a zillionth of a second after the Big Bang – well, everything that

152

happened from that moment onwards was essentially predictable, like the movement of balls on a snooker table. When you take a shot in snooker, if you could know exactly the position of every ball and the mass and the speed and direction of the cue ball, and the air pressure and all the other things that might affect the impact, well then, you could predict exactly how the balls would cascade and bounce around the table. The balls don't have free will. They all follow the basic rules of physics – and so does every particle in the universe, including every atom in your body and every atom in your brain. So the billiard-ball theory suggests that every particle in the universe has simply been obeying a basic set of rules since the beginning of time. And the key thing is this: everything was effectively preordained right from the very first instant. So if you could have known the precise location and velocity and relevant property of every particle in that Big Bang, you could ultimately have predicted that you and I would be sitting here at this table and having this conversation, because all we are is clusters of fundamental particles and none of us has the power to alter the laws of science.'

'I think I need another drink already,' Azalea said.

'I told you it was a depressing theory.'

'And that's the theory of determinism?'

'Actually it's the theory of *pre*determinism, if we want to be picky. But everyone confuses the two, so we needn't worry too much. In any case, it's an idea that's been around for a long time. Democritus and Leucippus put forward the idea around four hundred years before Christ. Laplace thought up the billiard-ball idea in 1814. We call it "Laplace's Demon" in his honour. Hobbes, Leibniz, Hume – they all bought into it.'

'So free will is just an illusion?'

'Or a delusion,' said Thomas.

'So even though I feel perfectly free to chuck this beer over you and kick the table, you would say that I don't have that freedom at all, that I'm just responding to the colliding atoms in my brain?'

'I'm just explaining that this is one way of understanding the universe. Look at it another way: if we accept that you really do have the freedom to choose your own actions, then every time you exercise that freedom you must be breaking the laws of physics at some subatomic level.' Thomas took a long draught of beer.

'Hasn't quantum mechanics swept this theory away?' Azalea asked. 'You know, the Uncertainty Principle, Schrödinger's cat and all that?'

Thomas inhaled slowly. 'That misunderstands what quantum physics really tells us. What Schrödinger and Heisenberg showed was that we can never know the position of an elementary particle like an electron because the very act of observing it changes it. Their propositions don't really alter the arguments of determinism. After all, just because we can't know the position of an electron doesn't mean that it doesn't have one.'

'This is very deep stuff.'

'And even if we choose to interpret the science as telling us that nothing is really knowable, and that random events really can happen at the quantum level, we still don't have any mechanism that might describe how a bowl of chemicals – which is essentially all our brains are – can select or modify the way that matter will behave.' Thomas looked at her with the air of a man who had presented these arguments many times before. 'So imagine you wanted to prove the existence of free will in the universe. How would you do that?'

'I have no idea,' Azalea said. 'But I have a feeling you're about to tell me.'

'Well, it isn't easy. If we're thinking about whether the universe is predetermined or subject to free will, then I prefer to ask myself whether we can find out, empirically, if the universe is random or non-random.'

'Was it created, or did it just emerge from a big bang?'

'No. We *know* that it emerged from a big bang. That isn't at issue. What is at issue is whether the universe *behaves* in a way that might suggest some controlling mechanism.'

'I didn't know we'd be going back as far as the Big Bang.'

'That's where everything starts. So let's try a thought experiment.

154

Imagine there are two universes. We're allowed to explore both. We are told that in one universe free will exists. In the other, everything obeys Laplace's Demon and we're all just billiard balls bouncing around according to the laws of motion. Can we distinguish which of the two universes is which? What will *differ* between these two universes?'

Azalea shook her head. 'You tell me.'

'OK. So you'd expect that the intervention of an intelligence capable of interfering with the way that everything unravels would leave one universe measurably different to the other.'

'But we only have one universe,' Azalea pointed out.

'Exactly,' Thomas thumped the table. 'So let's extend our thought experiment to just one universe. What would be the characteristics of a universe determined by free will?'

'I don't know.'

Thomas grinned. 'Non-randomness,' he said, and he laughed at Azalea's perplexed expression. 'We need to look for things in the universe that ought to be random, but aren't.'

'What – like the distribution of stars, or something?'

He shook his head. 'No. We need to look at the areas where we might *expect* free will to make a difference. And there is only one area where we can realistically look for that – and that has to be in *human events*.'

Azalea took a swig of her beer. 'So we're looking for … what … miracles?'

'Miracles, well yes, perhaps … but I don't really like the idea of miracles; coincidences, on the other hand, yes.' Thomas spread out his hands as if coincidences might just fall into them from above. 'Look at it this way. Do you have a cleaner?'

'What – like a vacuum cleaner?'

'Like a person who comes into your flat and cleans?'

'You clearly haven't seen my flat.'

'OK, so you don't have a cleaner. But imagine if you did. Now imagine if you were to come back from work one day and look around your flat and you were to ask yourself, "Has my cleaner been here today or not?" How would you know? Easy.

You'd look to see if the place was any tidier than when you left it. Let's say, for example, that when you left this morning your books were randomly distributed over the carpet in your living room.'

'That's a fairly accurate description of my living room,' Azalea agreed.

'Now when you get home you find your books are no longer in a random sprawl. Instead they are in a neat pile. Maybe they're now arranged on your shelves in alphabetical order by author. Ergo, you can conclude that a supreme cleaning being has visited and cleaned up your room.'

'So,' she suggested, 'you are looking for non-randomness in a random world?'

'And they call that phenomenon "coincidence",' said Thomas, 'or sometimes "serendipity". Or sometimes they simply call it luck.'

'I see.' Azalea fell silent. The waitress arrived with two plates of fish and chips, and the subject fell off the radar for a while as they set about tackling the food.

'So maybe my coincidences prove that the universe really is non-random,' Azalea said when they were able to pick up the conversation again.

'Well, they're interesting,' Thomas agreed. 'But coincidences always are.'

'But you don't think they're significant enough to prove anything?'

'Well, it certainly helps if you can demonstrate how unlikely a coincidence is. But remember the case of Violet Jessop. It isn't always easy to measure.'

'I can imagine.'

'Sometimes we can pick a coincidence and assign a fairly accurate probability value to it. Take the case of Richard Parker, for example.'

'Richard Parker? Wasn't that the name of the tiger in …'

'*The Life of Pi*?' Thomas finished the sentence for her. 'Great novel. Yes it was. Yann Martel chose the name because of its association with a famous coincidence. It started with a novel by Edgar Allan Poe called *The Narrative of Arthur Gordon Pym of Nantucket*.'

'Catchy title.'

'It's the story of a whaling ship that sinks. All the survivors are adrift in a lifeboat and they draw lots to decide which one of them should be eaten. The unfortunate sailor who gets to be dish of the day is a cabin boy called Richard Parker. Then, forty years later, a real whaling boat called the *Mignonette* sank. And guess what?'

'They ate a real cabin boy?'

'Exactly. And his name was …'

'Richard Parker?'

'Spot on.' Thomas grinned.

'Quite a coincidence.'

'Yes.' He leaned back slowly, swinging his arms. 'The interesting thing is that we can calculate just how much of a coincidence it was. We can look up actuarial tables from nineteenth-century America to find out how likely it would be that the real cabin boy on the *Mignonette* would also be called Richard Parker. And it turns out that Richard was a fairly popular name. Around seventeen boys in a thousand were Richards. And Parker was a common enough name, too. So if we do the maths, we find out that about twenty-five men in a million were Richard Parkers. There's your probability.'

She mused on this. 'It's still a pretty startling coincidence.'

'Of course. But you can't always work things out like that. Human events are tough to unpick. I meet a lot of people who come to me with extraordinary stories. And the thing they want to know is nearly always the same – is this just a remarkable co-incidence, or is there something else at work here?'

'And the answer is?'

'… Very hard to supply.'

'Did you ever hear the story,' Azalea asked him, 'about the man who walks past a telephone box?'

Thomas laughed. 'And the phone is ringing …'

'You know the story then?'

'And when he answers the phone,' said Thomas, 'it's his secretary. She wanted to call him but she made a mistake and she didn't dial his phone number, she called his social security number because that was written on his Rolodex card ...'

'And it just happened to be the telephone number of the very phone box he was walking past!'

'Good story, isn't it?' Thomas said.

'It is,' Azalea agreed. 'Only when I heard it, it wasn't his social security number, it was his credit-card number.'

'It often is,' said Thomas.

'Often?'

'There are dozens of versions.' He laughed again, his goofy, deep laugh. 'I've found the story in about six different countries. Often the man has a name, but he's surprisingly difficult to track down.'

'So it's an urban myth?'

He nodded. 'Almost certainly.'

'What about Kennedy and Lincoln? I remember reading a whole set of coincidences that linked the way they were assassinated. Like Kennedy was shot from a warehouse and the guy ran to a theatre, while Lincoln was shot in a theatre but his killer ran to a warehouse. That sort of thing.'

Thomas bobbed his head. 'It's a famous set of coincidences – you're right.'

'And is there anything in them?'

'Well, according to the story Lincoln had a secretary called Kennedy and Kennedy had a secretary called Lincoln.' Thomas grinned. 'It's nonsense, of course. Lincoln had two secretaries – one was called John Nicolay and the other was John Hay. Kennedy and Lincoln were born a hundred years apart. Big deal. How is that a coincidence? Both were shot by Southerners. Except that John Wilkes Booth was born in Maryland, which is not very *Southern*, really.'

She laughed along with him. 'I always thought it was a strange coincidence,' she said, 'that two of the great civilisations of the

158

Mediterranean – Minoan Crete and Ancient Rome – turn out to be anagrams of each other.'

'Only in English,' Thomas said.

'Still, it's useful for the people who set crosswords.'

'The problem is, you can't run any statistics on one unexpected event. And you especially can't do real statistics on an event that has been selected *after* the event, because all it means is that you're selectively excluding a whole set of events that don't coincide. So we can say what a coincidence that Minoan Crete is an anagram of Ancient Rome, but we conveniently ignore the Ancient Greeks, or the Egyptians, or the Mesopotamians or Sumerians. We can marvel at the coincidence of Richard Parker's story, but ignore the fact that Poe's captain was called Barnard while the real captain of the *Mignonette* was called Dudley. Or we can say that Lincoln and Kennedy each have seven letters in their surname, but quietly overlook the less convenient fact that Abraham has seven letters while John has only four. It's like spraying a barn door with a burst of machine-gun fire and then finding the tightest cluster of bullet holes, drawing a circle around them and saying, "There's our target – look how many random bullets hit the bullseye!" And even if you *could* calculate the chances of an unusual event happening, well, it doesn't really help. We are all the product of a whole host of staggeringly unlikely events.'

She raised her eyebrows. 'We are?'

'Oh yes,' Thomas said. 'We are all fabulously luckier, and more unlikely, than any lottery-winner in history. Just consider that an average man can produce around one hundred million sperm a day – that would be about two thousand billion sperm in a lifetime, more sperm than there have ever been human beings on Planet Earth. Forget the one-in-fourteen-million chance of winning the English lottery – you had a one-in-a-thousand-billion chance of being born. So you, Azalea, are an amazing fluke of nature. And yet, here you are, sitting in a pub in Tiverton with another person who is also a one-in-a-thousand-billion lottery-winner. What are the chances of that?'

Azalea furrowed her forehead. 'I see,' she said. 'So what does this prove?'

'It proves that you can't calculate chance retrospectively,' said Thomas, tapping the table for emphasis. 'So when anybody comes to me and says, "Something astonishing has happened", or, "What are the chances of this big coincidence that happened to me?" Well, I can always answer these questions. If you tell me that you bumped into your old childhood sweetheart in a souk in Cairo, and you ask me what are the chances of that happening, the answer is one hundred per cent. It is one hundred per cent certain to have happened, because it *did* happen.'

'So you can't measure coincidence, then?'

'I didn't say that,' said Thomas. 'I said you can't measure co-incidence *retrospectively*. But we can if we measure it proactively. So if you already met your long-lost childhood sweetheart in a Cairo souk, then the chances of that happening are one hundred per cent. But if you were to tell me that you're going to Cairo next week, and you want to know the odds that you *will* meet your lost sweetheart – well now, that's a different matter.'

They left the pub and took a stroll into the town. A thin wind blew down Angel Hill. Thomas tucked his broken arm into his coat and thrust his good hand deep into a pocket. Azalea hugged her coat around her.

'Are we ready for the road?' Thomas asked when they had walked around the block and the pub came back into view.

They drove out of town with ease and were back on the motorway in less than ten minutes.

'I've enjoyed the day,' Thomas said.

'We've still got two hundred miles to go,' she reminded him.

'I know. All the same …'

'I've enjoyed it too.' She leaned across and placed a kiss upon his cheek. 'Thank you for taking me.'

'It has been a pleasure,' he said, and it was true at that moment, with the soft imprint of her kiss still on his face and the hint of her perfume in his nostrils.

'Do you know what you should do?' she said.

'What should I do?'

'You should set up a website.' She sank into her seat and lifted her feet up onto the dashboard. 'Somewhere where people can go and forecast a coincidence. People like me.'

'You mean, there are others like you?' He meant this in jest.

'There may be,' she said. 'Who knows?'

'And in what way, exactly, might they be like you?'

'They'll be people who've been afflicted by coincidences, just like me. They'll know in their bones that it isn't just … random, or chance. Something, or someone, is messing with their lives. That's the kind of people they'll be.'

'I see.'

She seemed taken by the idea now. 'What you have to do is to give people the opportunity to predict a coincidence … or something really unlikely that they think is going to happen to them. This is for people who've already noticed a pattern developing in their lives. This way you'll be able to measure the coincidence, and it won't be retrospective.'

Thomas nodded slowly. 'It's an interesting idea.'

'It's more than an interesting idea, it's a brilliant one.'

'If you say so.'

'I do.' Azalea fell silent, pondering. 'Then … what I shall need to do,' she said, 'if I want to convince you that my coincidences are more than just unfortunate throws of the dice, is to go onto your site and forecast something that might happen to me at some time in the future.'

'OK.'

'And if I do that, and if the prediction comes true, then will you believe that something strange is happening?'

Thomas wasn't taking this seriously enough. He gave one of his gentle laughs.

'So what if I predict that I'll have a chance encounter with a third man who claims to be my father?' Azalea pulled up a leg and began to unstrap her shoe.

'You could do that,' said Thomas, 'although it wouldn't constitute proof that the encounter – if it happened – was part of any predetermined destiny. It would still be anecdotal. It would be persuasive, I admit, but not necessarily compelling. Just because someone predicts that they'll win the lottery doesn't necessarily make it a miracle when they do.'

'No, but if they predict that they'll win the lottery on the first Saturday of October with the numbers five, seventeen and forty-two, *that* would be a miracle,' said Azalea.

'Perhaps.'

'So, what if I predict that he'll also be blind?' said Azalea. She pulled off one shoe and started on the other. 'John Hall and Peter Loak were both blind when I met them.'

'Well,' said Thomas, trying to be encouraging, 'details like that would certainly help.'

'So the more predictions I make that come true, then the more likely it'll be that …' she tailed off.

'That what?' Thomas asked her. She was placing her bare feet back on the dashboard.

'That someone – or something – is fucking with my life,' said Azalea.

'I'm glad,' said Thomas, 'that you're using the technical term.'

'Let's make it more interesting.' Azalea turned to look at him with a defiant expression. 'You set up the website, and I'll post my predictions. And I'll add one more.'

'And what will that be?'

'That on 21 June 2012,' Azalea said, 'Midsummer's Day, thirty years to the day after the death of Marion and twenty years after the deaths of Rebecca and Luke – I will die.'

18

June 1992

John Gropius Hall was fifty-one years old. He stood six feet one and a half inches tall in his heavy military boots, and he weighed sixteen stones. Most of that weight was muscle. He worked out. He had lost whatever hair he once had. In a lounge suit and tie you could have taken him for a nightclub bouncer. But he didn't dress like that. He wore loose camouflage trousers and a khaki t-shirt that struggled to accommodate his torso but allowed him to exhibit his muscles and his tattoos. John Hall was not the kind of man you would want to pick a fight with. You would avoid him if you saw him in a bar. He was a man who had flirted briefly with civilian life, but who now knew keenly where his skills lay. He was not made to stand behind a bar and splash gin into glasses; he wasn't born to wash out ashtrays or make polite conversation with drunken tourists. He was a fighting man, a soldier, a man born to bring about order through force. He was also a disturbed man, a morose man. He didn't smile a great deal.

John Hall was the man that Luke Folley met in the garden of the Acholi Inn on 21 June 1992. We, of course, have already met him. We know that he was one of the near godfathers of Azaliah Yves; one of the *candidate* fathers. We don't know why he left the Bell Inn at Port St Menfre on the Isle of Man. Nor do we know what became of the forgiving wife. Perhaps she was less forgiving than first appearances suggested. Maybe Marion Yves was only one in a succession of barmaids to be pressed up in the cellar against boxes of cider, while the unhappy wife pulled pints in the bar above. Perhaps Mrs John Hall lost patience with her faithless husband. We don't know, but it doesn't really matter. We can construct any number of stories to account for John Hall's translocation from the comfort of a Manx village to a mercenary army unit in Uganda. It matters only that it happened.

The mercenaries travelled by night. The unit numbered six men, no more. They drove in convoy in two nondescript lorries of the type that belched black smoke all the way across Africa; they travelled three to a vehicle, and they crossed the Nile River on the ancient Laropi ferry on the last crossing of the day and made the border post into Sudan sometime after midnight, leaving the border guards rather wealthier than they had been before.

There were two South Africans, a Belgian, two former Ugandan army officers and a Manxman. The Manxman was John Hall. They carried enough ordnance to equip a platoon.

They did it for the money. In the safety deposit box of John Hall's hotel were the envelopes that Luke Folley had passed to him. Inside one was a string-bound package of two thousand American dollars; inside the other was a document duly signed and witnessed that would transfer to John Hall the deeds of ownership to the Folley house in St Piran.

John Hall had told Luke that speed was essential. 'We need to do it,' he said, 'while we can still smell them.'

'How will you find them?' Luke had asked.

John Hall was checking the signatures on the deed that would make him the owner of an English Edwardian seaside home. Satisfied, he folded the pages and slid them into a long pocket in his trousers. 'We already know where they are,' he told Luke. 'Everyone knows where the bastards hide out.'

'I see,' said Luke. 'So why doesn't the Ugandan army just take them out?'

The mercenary feigned a look of indifference. The look said, 'This is Africa – why do you need to ask?' But then he said, 'There's a whole bunch of reasons why Museveni and his men might be perfectly happy to keep Kony alive. Kony's a madman. He captures kids, for Christ's sake. And the people up here think he's some kind of wizard. They're scared of him. They think he can do magic.' Hall spat carelessly on the ground. 'But one thing

Kony doesn't do is present any real Acholi opposition to the government in Kampala that the people here can identify with. Now *that* would worry Museveni and his thugs. All Kony has is a gang of trigger-happy kids and a load of home-made guns, so the Acholi are even more scared of Kony than they are of Museveni. That's a good position for the President. He likes that.'

Luke nodded. 'So where are they hiding?'

Hall laughed. 'Not in Uganda,' he said. 'Kony rounds up kids from villages in Acholiland and takes them across into Sudan. President Bashir lets the Ugandan army chase Kony across the border, but only as far as a line that runs across the country about a hundred miles north of the border. So Kony has his camps just the other side of the line.'

'Is that where they'll have taken Azalea?' Luke asked.

Hall looked off into the middle distance. 'I knew a kid called Azaliah once,' he said. He let the thought float. 'Is she your daughter?'

Luke hesitated. 'Adopted,' he said.

Hall nodded slowly.

'You won't put her at any risk?' Luke said. 'Tell me you won't go in there with all guns blazing?'

The big Manxman surveyed Luke through narrowed eyes. 'Everyone thinks our job is about going in and shooting people.' He paused. 'Fact is, we hardly ever do that. If we did, we wouldn't live very long.'

'So how do you intend to get her out?'

'Well, we have three options. Option One, we start a big firefight. Lots of people get killed. Some of our guys get killed. Maybe even your … Azaliah … gets killed.' He was lost again in a reverie. 'Mind you,' he said, 'it would be bloody revenge, if that's what you want. If we go for Option One, it only works if we kill every man jack of them. It could come to it.'

Luke waited.

'Option Two,' Hall said, 'we try to break in under cover of darkness and steal the kids out. It could work, but it's bloody dangerous. Those child soldiers have no idea when to shoot and when to wait – they just shoot. That's what Kony wants them to do.'

'And Option Three?' asked Luke.

'Ahh,' said the soldier, 'Option Three. We trade.'

'You trade?'

'Sure thing. We get there and we open up a dialogue.'

Luke nodded. He liked Option Three. 'What do you use to trade with?' he asked.

'Money,' said Hall, 'guns. Ammo.'

Luke winced. The peacenik was never far away. 'It would be good,' he said, 'if we could avoid giving them more guns.'

Hall grinned. 'Hell, if we give them money they're only going to spend it on guns. Why not make it easy for us both?' He laughed – a faintly cruel laugh. 'Anyone who thinks we can take the guns out of Africa never sat on my side of the table.' He rose from his chair. 'Are we done? Only we should get started.'

'Yes,' said Luke weakly.

'Final thing,' said Hall. 'No one gets to know about our arrangement. No one.'

'That's fine,' said Luke, 'I understand.'

'Good. Don't send anyone to look for us.' He lifted his eyebrows. 'If we never come back then the whole thing's a bust. You get to keep your pretty house, but you'll be damn sure that I'm dead, my boys are dead and all your kids are dead too.'

'I get it,' Luke said slowly.

'We only get one go at this. If we screw up the first time, there won't be a second time. Kony is the most merciless motherfucker on either side of the equator. If we screw up, we're dog meat – all of us.'

When the nondescript lorry crept up the approach road to the LRA camp, it would have been breakfast time back in Langadi. In the LRA camps there was no breakfast time.

There were just two men in the lorry, John Hall and one of the Ugandans. They let the vehicle crawl up to the first barricade. The gaggle of guards looked terrified. Guns were waving. The

Ugandan mercenary slowly wound down his window. 'Tell your boss,' he said, talking in Acholi, 'that we're here to trade with him.'

Guards began to gather round the truck. Most were teenagers. All were thin. Some wore flip-flops, but most had no shoes. All carried guns.

One man, who may have been the most senior, approached the lorry with hesitation. He stood a few feet away as if the whole vehicle might be a booby trap.

'What are you wanting to trade?' he shouted.

The Ugandan mercenary looked supremely relaxed. 'Two anti-tank guns and a box of grenades,' he said.

The LRA man looked doubtful.

'And one hundred American dollars,' said Hall, in English. The Ugandan translated.

The guards conferred loudly. Their spokesman needed to look important. 'Show me these weapons,' he demanded.

The Ugandan shook his head. 'We don't have them here,' he said. He made eye contact with the LRA man. 'But we have one gift for you. Just to prove our good intentions.' He nodded his head towards the rear of the lorry. One of the boys made as if to investigate but the lead guard yelled at him. He suspected a trap.

'It is OK,' said the Ugandan mercenary. 'He can get it.'

The LRA man was weighing up his options. Finally he yelled something to one of the boys, who disappeared into the back of the lorry. There was a moment of danger. Then the boy re-appeared with a whoop of excitement. He jumped down from the tailboard carrying an American-made Barrett M82A2 anti-tank rifle. At thirty or so pounds, it was almost too heavy for the frail boy to handle. He swung it around at knee height with feigned menace.

'Take it to your commander,' said Hall, while the Ugandan translated. 'Tell him this is a token of our good faith. We have ammunition and one more of these. And other weapons.'

The LRA man still looked hesitant. 'And what do you want in return?'

'Smart boy,' said the mercenary. 'You have some guests staying with you. Some guests visiting from a mission school in Moyo District.' He stared directly at the guard. 'We want to take them ... for a safari.'

For a few moments there was an impasse. The two men looked at each other. The boys around the lorry pressed in closer to share the excitement.

'Go and discuss this with your commanding officer,' said the Ugandan. He leaned back in his seat and pulled his beret down over his eyes as if now was a good time to sleep. 'We are patient men,' he said, 'we can wait.'

They waited as the day grew hotter. They had brought water and food. The cluster of LRA boys thinned a little, and after a while some of the boys grew bored and sat down to watch for further developments.

Then a Toyota truck came heading towards them from the camp. An LRA commander in full military uniform climbed out of the truck. He was carrying the Barrett M82A2. He swaggered over to the lorry, aware of his audience. 'Is this your gun?' he demanded.

The driver's window slid down. 'No, sir,' said the Ugandan soldier. 'This is your gun. It is a gift.'

The LRA man strutted round to the back of the lorry and tossed the anti-tank gun inside with a gesture of contempt. 'You can keep your gun,' he said, and he offered a toothless grin. 'We have no guests here to trade with you.'

The two mercenaries exchanged glances. Hall said something in English and the Ugandan soldier nodded grimly. 'In that case,' he said to the LRA man, 'we thank you for your time.' He ground the lorry into gear and started up the engine. The vehicle began to reverse awkwardly up the dusty track.

'Wait!' The customs and tradition of negotiation are the same worldwide, and the LRA man fell into line. He approached the lorry.

The mercenaries didn't kill the engine.

'We have just one guest,' said the LRA man. 'We will give you this one guest for four of these guns.' He walked around the lorry and retrieved the Barrett. 'And ammunition,' he said.

Hall shook his head. He held up two fingers. 'We have two guns,' he said in English, 'and twelve grenades. But we want all the guests.' He watched the LRA man's reaction as this was relayed to him. 'We have to hurry,' he added, 'before the army gets here.'

The LRA man laughed. 'The army are not coming here,' he said.

Hall looked impassive. 'Oh yes they are. The British are very angry. Very *very* angry. Museveni will do what they ask.' He let this sink in. 'They are one hour away, so why not let us take the guests to meet them?'

The lorry engine ticked over.

'Just the muna muna, then,' said the LRA man. 'But we need to see the guns first.'

Hall bobbed his head rhythmically. 'All of the guests,' he said, 'including the Acholi children. But we will add one hundred American dollars and …' he acted as if this concession was a struggle, 'one rocket launcher.'

This was translated. The LRA man's eyes were widening. 'How many rockets?' he asked.

'Six.'

'Eight. We have eight guests.'

John Hall raised his eyebrows very slightly. Luke Folley had only mentioned six abductees. 'We only have six rockets. I'm sorry.'

The man considered this. The crowd of boys was silent.

'Ten thousand dollars then,' the man demanded, switching to English.

'All of the guests,' repeated Hall very slowly and illustrating with his hands. 'All eight. For two tank guns and ammunition, one launcher and six rockets, twelve grenades and two hundred dollars.'

The two men held each other's eyes.

'Ten thousand dollars!'

'I only have two hundred,' said Hall, managing to look sorrowful.

There was a moment of consideration. 'What else do you have?' asked the LRA man.

Hall shrugged, 'Nothing else.'

'You have this lorry.'

'We need this lorry to take the guests for their safari.'

The commander gave a loud laugh. He had him now. 'You must have another lorry,' he said. 'Or where are your guns? Where are your rockets?'

Hall shook his head. 'We cannot give you the lorry.' He pulled a walkie-talkie from his pocket. 'We can give you walkie-talkies.'

The commander looked at this.

'Where is the other one?'

'In our other lorry.' Hall smiled. He pressed the call button. 'Just checking in,' he said into the device.

'Roger.'

The commander looked at this with relish.

'A range of ten miles,' said Hall, holding up ten fingers.

The LRA man reflected. Then he spat on his hand and held it out. 'Fetch me the guns,' he said.

Hall spat on his own hand. They shook hands through the cab window and the Ugandan mercenary did the same.

'You send one gun,' said the man, 'and we send one guest.'

Hall agreed. He spoke into his walkie-talkie. The LRA man shouted some instructions and boys ran towards the camp.

This was going to take all day.

A long time passed. Then a man came hurrying up the track. He was leading Tebere.

Hall spoke into the radio. A few minutes later, the second mercenary lorry approached slowly from the main road. The other Ugandan mercenary climbed out. He was carrying a box of ammunition. The exchange took place. The lorry, now with Tebere as passenger, reversed back up the track and a second hostage was sent for. Kila was exchanged for more ammunition. James was swapped for three rockets and Lubangakene for three more.

The Lord's Resistance Army were holding the English captives until last. But the mercenaries were holding back the guns, so honour was even. Anyeko came next. She earned the LRA a box of grenades.

This was taking too long. Hall began tapping his fingers against the side of the lorry. He was impatient to see Azalea; impatient to see this adopted girl with the name of a child he once knew. He could feel the impatience gnawing at his bones.

There was a long wait. A man came up the track with a white woman. Hall looked at her with interest. She was too tall, surely, to be Azalea. His Azalea, he thought, and then he checked himself for daring to entertain the idea. It was Lauren. She looked terrified. 'It's OK,' Hall told her. 'I'm not sure who you are, but it's good to have you with us.' He pointed towards the second lorry. She was exchanged for a Barrett anti-tank gun.

A tall, athletic-looking white boy – Ritchie – was swapped for another Barrett. Now the LRA had three.

'One more guest,' said Hall.

The LRA commander seemed to sense the mercenary's anxiety. 'Give me the money now,' he said.

Hall pulled two hundred dollars from his pocket. The money was counted once, twice, three times.

'More,' demanded the commander.

Hall puckered his lips and shook his head. 'No more,' he said. 'One more guest, and you get the rocket launcher.'

Did the LRA man want to keep the lengthy exchanges going? Was he loath to see an end to this day-long charade?

'What is the rocket launcher?' the man said, suddenly. 'What make is it?'

Hall contrived to look bored. 'It's an Israeli weapon,' he intoned, 'the B-300. It's a shoulder-launched assault weapon. Do you want it?'

The man held his stare, then broke away. The command was given and a boy was sent to fetch the final hostage.

It was growing dark as two men swaggered up the track with Azalea. In the low evening light John Hall could make out only the lissom, nondescript figure of a girl – just the *shape* of a girl in the gloom. The men held her at a safe distance while they waited for the lorry bearing the final trade. The equatorial sunset was nearly over. By the time the second mercenary lorry ground up the track towards the negotiation point, they were in a darkness relieved only by the flicker of a heavily shaded moon.

But now, as the whole operation was almost done, the LRA man seemed to be growing cautious. 'Show me the gun first,' he said.

John Hall considered this. He shouted to the second lorry and the Ugandan mercenary who had made all the weapons exchanges stepped out holding the launcher.

'Show me,' demanded the LRA man. 'Show me how to work it.'

John Hall climbed down from the lorry. He looked over towards Azalea, still only a shadow in the darkness. His heart was beating fast. He moved into the pool of light cast by the lorry's headlamps and gave the LRA man a cursory description of the B-300.

'Show me how to load it,' said the man.

'First give me the girl.'

The LRA man nodded agreement. Azalea walked forward alone towards the second lorry. In just the briefest flicker of moonlight Hall saw a stick-like girl wearing a long nightdress, with a shock of red hair – thick, curly red hair – the ghost, if ever there could be one, of Marion Yves. His heart skipped.

The moon vanished and Azalea was in darkness. John Hall reached out an arm as if to call her back and then checked himself. Another momentary flicker of moonlight, and in that fragment of time John Hall saw her face. He saw the face of a girl he hadn't seen since she was three years old. His hand flew to his mouth.

But something wasn't right. The LRA man was sliding a solid rocket with a high explosive tank round into the launcher. 'Like this?' he was asking.

'Azalea, run! RUN!' John Hall shouted. He leaped onto the

running plate of the first lorry. 'Go go GO!' He smacked his palm onto the windscreen. The Ugandan mercenary at the wheel hit reverse and the lorry shot backwards. Hall looked around to see what had happened to Azalea. She was visible now in the headlights of the second lorry – running towards it, her red hair flying out behind her.

'Run RUN RUN!'

The moon reappeared. In the cold light Hall could see figures in pursuit. Azalea jumped onto the footplate of the second lorry and now both vehicles were barrelling backwards. Somewhere in the light John Hall could see the LRA man raising the launcher to his shoulder.

'Spin the lorry,' he shouted to the Ugandan at the wheel. 'SPIN IT!'

The mercenary hauled down on the steering wheel and the lorry slid sideways in a hurricane of sand and dust. It came to a halt at a right angle across the track.

'Now get the fuck out!'

John Hall leaped from the running plate. The Ugandan in the cab wasn't quick enough. There was a whoosh and a flash of flame and an eighty-two-millimetre missile smashed into the side of the lorry. The force of the explosion picked Hall up off his feet and threw him backwards in a slew of flame and debris. Everything was very dark. He blinked.

Invisible hands grabbed at him. An Englishman's voice was barely audible over the ringing in his ears. 'Are you OK?'

It was too bloody dark. 'I can't see you.'

'Can you run?'

Hall struggled to his feet. 'I think so.' He reached out and caught the Englishman's arm. His eyes were stinging badly. His face was wet with blood. 'Lead me,' he said.

'Let's go.' The Englishman took his hand and they fled like lovers up the track, feet kicking up the sand. The Englishman helped the big Manxman into the back of the lorry, and with a roar of the engine the vehicle tore back towards the main road.

'What about Rico?' shouted Hall. His ears were humming.

'Was he the other man with you?' said the English voice.

'Yes.'

'I'm afraid we lost him.'

'Shit,' said John Hall, and he slumped down uncomfortably in a corner of the truck. 'Shit, shit, *shit*.' He put his hands to his face. His eyes felt as if someone had gouged them out with rusty nails. 'I need a doctor,' he said.

'I'm a doctor,' said the voice, and then it added, 'almost.'

The pick-up point was about three miles away – a roundhouse well off the main road. No wonder it had taken so long to choreograph every switch. The two South African mercenaries were guarding the place. All the other hostages and the Belgian mercenary were inside.

Hands lifted John Hall out of the lorry and carried him into the hut. There was no light – not that Hall would have noticed. They laid him down on a rug of goatskins. The vehicle was then driven away, to be hidden out of sight.

'What were you doing in the damn truck?' John Hall asked Ritchie.

'I went along for the ride,' Ritchie said. 'Just in case they needed a doctor.'

He tried to examine John Hall in the faint gleam of a cigarette lighter. The Manxman's face had been slashed by shards of glass from the exploding truck. This was not the kind of case Ritchie had ever seen at medical school. 'You're pretty fucked up,' Ritchie told him.

'Great bedside manner,' said Hall.

'I don't have any painkillers, any sutures, any antibiotics, anything to clean you up with,' said Ritchie. 'Actually,' he said, 'I don't have anything. We need to get you to a hospital.'

'Boy, am I glad you came along,' said Hall. 'Do you have any idea where we are? We're in the fucking desert. We're in the middle of a civil war zone.'

Outside, one of the South Africans called, 'Down!' There was silence in the hut. Careering down the main road came a truck. It shot past. On the back there were kids with guns.

'They're trying to follow us back into Uganda,' said Azalea.

No one wanted to respond to this rather frightening proposition.

'Down!' came a second command. More headlights, and now a convoy of trucks. One, two, three, four … and trailing them a Land Rover with armoured windows. The excited voices of the boy soldiers drifted across the void as the vehicles swept past.

'We can't stay here,' said John Hall.

'What do you suggest?' asked Ritchie.

'If we head east on the road to Kapoeta, we can cross the border into Kenya.' Hall forced himself to sit up. 'Let's all make our way to the truck. Keep low. If anything comes past, just lie down. We'll give them an hour and then we head east.'

They linked arms and filed out of the hut. A few hundred yards off the road they came to the lorry and climbed aboard. All of the children were silent. They waited in the perfect darkness with barely a whisper. After an age, John Hall tapped on the back of the cab and the engine started; they rolled slowly over the desert and back onto the potholed road to Kenya.

19

June 1992

In the bright light of an African morning, it didn't need a doctor for John Hall to realise that his face had been shredded by glass in an ugly, bloody stripe that had taken out both his eyes. Lauren knelt over him picking tiny fragments of glass from his face.

'Am I going to see again?' Hall asked her.

Lauren shook her head slowly. 'I'm not an eye surgeon,' she said. 'Can you sense light and dark?' She moved her hands in front of his eyes and then pulled them away.

'I think so,' he said.

'In that case, maybe your retina hasn't been too badly damaged. You might get some sight back with a good surgeon, but I really don't know. We do need to get you to a hospital, though. You need stitches. And there's a risk of infection.' Lauren tore a cotton fabric belt from her frock and tied it around Hall's face like a bandage.

They were parked about a mile from Kapoeta. The difficulty was a roadblock that guarded the entrance to the town. It may have been a Sudanese government barricade – or it might have been SPLA. The information had come from a driver they had met at Logirim, where the road starts to coil up towards the mountains. The mercenaries had stopped well short of the blockade so that one of their number could approach on foot and make an assessment of the risk it might present.

They breakfasted on flatbreads and pawpaws bought in Logirim. The mood of the six children had lightened now that the trauma of the previous day had passed. They all sat up in the back of the truck and everyone chatted at once, and it was like the noise in a playground.

This was a hostile landscape. Not quite desert, not quite mountains; great rocky hills burst free of the sand and occasional tenacious shrubs clung onto life. There was little tree cover. It was hot in the back of the truck. John Hall lifted himself up, feeling his age.

'Is Azaliah here?' he asked.

'I'm here,' said Azalea. She had been sitting alongside the big man, trying not to look too hard at the bleeding mess that was his face.

Hall held out his hand. 'Can you walk me out into the desert?' he asked. 'I need to move about a bit.'

'I'll help you,' volunteered Ritchie.

'Thanks all the same,' said Hall. 'But I'd like to speak to Azaliah.'

She took his hand and led him through the rocks onto the sand. She didn't question why he had asked for her. Maybe, she thought, he had a message for her from Luke.

They sat in the shade of a cliff. Azalea was still wearing the dirty nightdress she had worn for breakfast at the mission; her feet were still bare.

John Hall was shaking. His temperature was raised. In a few hours, he knew, this would become a fever. He had to talk to her now.

'What did you want to say to me?' Azalea asked.

Hall reached into a pocket and drew out a slim leather wallet. Slowly he pulled a photograph from the wallet and passed it to Azalea. 'I don't suppose,' he said, 'that I will ever see that picture again. Not in this life. Not with these eyes.'

The photograph showed a very young girl in a swimsuit on a beach. The girl had a shock of maple-red hair.

'Who is that?' John Hall asked.

Azalea looked at the picture for a very long time.

'Is it me?' she asked at last.

John Hall nodded. 'I think so.'

'I think so too,' she said. The child in the picture seemed a long way from the girl standing by a dry desert road in Sudan. The light in the picture was cool and grey and the soft, inviting sea swelled a deep blue. The hills that rose up to one side were so pure and so green and so unspoilt that they told of a land of an infinite, almost heartbreaking peace.

'This was before I was ... before I was adopted?'

'It would be. Yes.'

'So you knew me then?'

John Hall was quiet for a moment. He started to shake again. The fever was beginning. 'Do you have a scar?' he asked. 'On your face? Just here?' He ran his finger over his own bloody face – a face that, if it survived, would be a map of scars.

Azalea's hand went up to her scar and she ran the warm tip of a finger along its familiar valley. She looked at the face of the bleeding man, unafraid now to contemplate his wounds. 'Yes I do,' she said softly. 'I do have a scar.' She took his heavy hand and let him trace the line on her face.

'Then I did know you,' whispered John Hall.

He was breathing heavily, and she had to lean towards him to hear his voice clearly.

'How much do you know about your life before ... before you were adopted?'

Azalea looked away. The landscape here was harsher than Langadi, where everything was so lush and green. Here the rich and fertile soils of Uganda had given way to the arid sands and rocks of the Sudan. And yet, she thought, there was a beauty to this landscape, too. She tried to think back to that day at the fairground in Totnes. She had no memory of it. Could she, perhaps, have any recollection of a time before? Had she closed the door on a life before the Folleys and St Piran, and before Langadi? Had there truly been a time when she had stood barefoot on a beach in a blue and white swimsuit, and this big tattooed man had photographed her with the swell of the sea to one side and the utter tranquillity of the hills to the other? She closed her eyes for a moment. Were there shapes there? Shapes of a young,

young girl and the memory of the cool sea spray and the call of unfamiliar seabirds?

She opened her eyes again. 'Nothing,' she said. 'I don't … really remember anything.'

John Hall said, 'Do you recognise this tune?' He started softly to sing – it was a lilting tune, gentle, a rocking tune, but the words were very strange. 'V'ad oie ayns y Ghlion dy Ballacomish,' he sang. His voice was as rough and broken as his face, but his heart knew the melody and his lips knew the words. 'Jannoo yn lhondoo aynshen e hedd. Chaddil oo lhiannoo, hig sheeaghyn troailtagh orrin!'

'Bee dty host nish,' the words came out of Azalea's mouth. 'Ta mee geamagh er'n ushag.' She gave a little gasp and sprang to her feet. 'How do I know that?' she said, alarmed by the mining of this memory from her brain.

'It's OK,' said John Hall. He reached out for Azalea's hand. 'It's a lullaby … from the Isle of Man. Your mother used to sing it to you. She would sing you to sleep with it. Later you would sing it together.'

'I didn't,' she exclaimed, and she shook away his hand. 'I didn't. I never did.' But I did, she thought. I did. I knew those words, that tune. She blinked her eyes away from the fierce sunlight and looked away from the bleeding man.

He hummed the tune again, a gasping hum from a damaged throat.

'Bee dty host nish, ta mee geamagh er'n ushag,' Azalea whispered, '… geamagh er'n ushag.' She turned back to look at John Hall. He was leaning heavily on the rock as if the lullaby had worked its magic. 'What does it mean?'

'It means go to sleep, baby, the fairies are coming.'

She was disturbed by this memory. 'I've never been to the Isle of Man,' she said.

'You've never been to the Isle of Man and you never knew the words of that song,' said John Hall. 'And yet … and yet you have. And yet you did. You were born there.'

'I wasn't.'

'You were born on 8 August 1978, in a village called Port St Menfre. Your mother was a barmaid called Marion Yves. Your real name is Azaliah Yves.' He spelled out her name for her.

She echoed the words back. 'Port St Menfre. Marion Yves. Azaliah Yves.'

'All the boys loved Marion Yves,' he said. 'That was her problem. When you were christened you had three godfathers. There was a barman called Peter and a fisherman called Gideon Robertson, and then ... well, then there was me. The vicar dropped you into the font. That's how you got that scar.'

Azalea's hand went to her face. She touched the scar again, touched this physical memory of a time beyond memory. 'Marion,' she echoed quietly again. 'Marion Yves.' There was a dark familiarity to the words. 'Why did I have three godfathers?'

'Because any one of us ... might have been ... your dad,' said Hall.

Azalea looked at him, open-jawed. 'You?' she said. 'You might have been my dad? My real dad?'

'I *am* your real dad,' said Hall. He held out his hand. After a moment, Azalea took it. They were just a father and a daughter resting by a roadside; just an ordinary parent and child. There was no LRA and no roadblock. There were no guns. There was a sandy beach and the swell of a blue sea and a green, green hill and the haunting echoes of a lullaby.

'In the spring of 1982,' said John Hall, 'Marion Yves moved out of Port St Menfre and she took you with her. She never came back.'

Azalea thought about this. 'Where did she go?' she asked.

'I have no idea. She left the island, that's all I know. No one saw her again.'

A handful of sand swirled up in the wind and flicked its fingers at them. Azalea blinked the grains from her eyes. She thought back to what she had been told of that time. 'In June 1982,' she said, 'I was left at a fairground in Devon. No one could find my mother. That's how I ended up with the Folleys.'

Hall nodded. 'I guess that explains it,' he said. 'I guess she left you there for someone to find you.'

Azalea tried to remember the fairground but no pictures would form. 'Does that sound like Marion? Is that something she would do?'

Hall seemed to reflect on this. 'No,' he said after a while, and he said it with some finality.

Azalea noticed that Hall was sweating badly even though the sun was not fully upon them. She felt devoid of any energy or emotion, as if the desert heat had bleached all feeling from her soul, as if a plug had been pulled and her very humanity had drained away into the dust. The story was true, she knew that. The lullaby was true. The scar was true. The photograph was true and Marion Yves was true, and all of this meant that there really was a past in her life sometime before the world she now knew. But all the same, it didn't *feel* real. Not here, not sitting on this rock with this bleeding man with his damaged face and the blood-soaked bandage around his eyes. The fear she had felt in the LRA camp still lingered in the marrow of her bones; the terror as she ran towards the truck while the big soldier, who now said he was her father, yelled at her to RUN, the shock from that moment when the fireball swallowed up the truck. And Rebecca Folley, her heart yelled, was her true mother, her soul mother, and now she, Rebecca, would be crying out for her, would be desperate in her fear and her loss, because at that moment another mother seemed like a dreadful betrayal. And now the guilt of that betrayal and the unbearable weariness from these past two days and the aching from a hard, uncomfortable night in the back of the truck seemed to well up in the throat of the thirteen-year-old. But somehow her tears refused to run.

The man beside her spluttered and spat blood from his mouth.

'What should I call you?' Azalea asked the man who said he was her father. 'I can't call you Dad.'

'Just call me John.'

'Do you have a picture of my mother? Of Marion?'

Hall turned his bandaged eyes towards her. 'No,' he said. 'I never had a photograph of Marion.'

Slowly they walked back to the lorry. Hall was stumbling badly. Ritchie helped him on board and they waited. Water bottles were passed around. The mood that had been so good at dawn now grew tense. Some of the children were sleeping. John Hall also fell asleep in one corner and snored like an ox.

The mercenary who had been sent to investigate the road-block returned. They drove forward a couple of miles and then soldiers from the Sudanese army swarmed aboard. They poked at the children with bayonets fastened onto ancient Winchester .303 rifles. They flipped John Hall over to check that he wasn't concealing contraband. They were looking for money. Hall barely stirred from his sleep. The soldiers started to demand documents; but there were no documents. They were threatening to search the lorry; this wasn't a welcome development. They would find an arsenal underneath the planking. Something creative was required to prevent the situation from turning bad. In the end, it was Ritchie who provided it.

'I tell you what, chaps,' he said to the men of the Sudanese army in the voice of someone who had once captained the first eleven at cricket. 'We need to get this chap to a hospital. What we need is a military escort.'

Azalea, weary, with her head deep in her hands, translated for him.

'What we need,' said Ritchie, raising himself up to his full six-foot-two height and sweeping back his blond fringe, 'what we need … is one army vehicle ahead and one behind to take us all the way to the Kenyan border. That way, we can avoid bandits or SPLA. We need this,' said Ritchie, 'to prevent a diplomatic incident.' He surveyed their bewildered expressions. 'OK chaps,' he said, clapping his hands. 'Let's do it, shall we? Chop, chop.'

With this piece of colonial posturing behind them, and the military escort alongside them, the rest of the journey went as smoothly as the corrugated roads and potholes would allow. At the Kenyan border post there was consternation because not one passenger was carrying a passport. But the Sudanese army captain who had led the convoy pulled rank and waved them brusquely through. It was still light when they spotted the 'Welcome to Kenya' sign.

In the first town there was a rudimentary pharmacy. 'Do we have any money at all?' Ritchie asked the mercenaries. There were two hundred dollars in a plastic bag in the diesel tank. 'It's to buy fuel,' one of the South Africans explained. The men had some loose change, but all in Ugandan shillings. Lauren disappeared into the store and emerged with aspirins and alcohol wipes. She gave four tablets to John Hall and he swallowed them with some difficulty. 'They say there's a mission hospital in Kakuma,' she said. 'Sixty miles.'

The driver started up the wagon and they pulled back out onto the road.

In the back of the truck, Azalea slept. She was holding John Hall by the hand. Ritchie Lewis and Lauren Marks slept with their arms around each other. The mercenaries sat at the back, awake, smoking, with their feet hanging over the tailgate.

They made slow progress along the bad road. The sixty miles took three hours. When they got to Kakuma it was dark, and John Hall had sunk into a very deep slumber. They carried him into the mission hospital. His breathing was shallow.

There was no doctor present, only a girl in a dirty white frock who told them that she was the duty nurse. The doctor, she told them, would be there on a Monday. No one seemed quite sure which day it was, but it wasn't Monday.

'I guess,' said Ritchie to Lauren, 'that makes us responsible.'

They operated by the light of a single bulb, stitching every wound they could, cleaning away foreign matter and damaged tissue. They re-bandaged John Hall's eyes with clean white bandages.

The mission gave them space to bed down in the hall. It almost felt like being back at Langadi. There were straw mattresses, wool blankets, chicken-feather pillows. There was blissful darkness and the calling of crickets. In the morning a bell summoned them to breakfast, and they joined a happy throng of children and fed on boiled vegetables and millet meal and sweet milky tea.

Later in the morning the mission chaplain came to see them. 'Are you in charge of the orphanage here?' Ritchie asked him.

The chaplain nodded with a hint of reluctance. He knew what was coming.

'We need to leave the Acholi children here,' said Ritchie.

'They belong in Uganda,' said the chaplain.

Ritchie drew closer. 'Listen,' he said, 'these children were kidnapped by Joseph Kony. LRA. Do you know them?'

The chaplain nodded.

'Then you know they can't go back,' said Ritchie. 'It will never be safe for them.'

The chaplain seemed to consider this. 'Five Acholi children,' he said at last.

'Four,' said Lauren Marks, holding up four fingers. She shot a glance at Ritchie. 'Anyeko comes with us.'

Ritchie looked at her. 'Five children,' he said, sadly. He turned back to the chaplain. 'Anyeko will be safer here.' He put out his hand to touch Lauren on the arm. 'We can't keep her.'

Lauren looked away.

'Five children,' said Ritchie again to the chaplain.

Later that afternoon, the two young doctors sat outside in the garden of the mission under the shadow of a thorn tree drinking Fanta Orange through straws. One of the South Africans came and pulled up a chair. 'We're leaving you guys here,' he said.

Ritchie nodded.

'We need to get back to Gulu,' the mercenary said.

'I understand,' said Ritchie. 'What about Azalea? What about us?'

'We leave you here,' said the soldier. 'It won't be safe back in Langadi. Those LRA guys will go back to look for you.' He gave Ritchie and Lauren an apologetic smile. 'You're safer here.'

'And what about John Hall?'

'He comes with us.'

'He needs medical care,' Lauren said. 'Urgently. Or he'll die.

He needs antibiotics, blood. We haven't been able to do much for him.'

'We'll take him to the hospital in Gulu.'

'He won't be much use to you as a blind guy.'

'Oh, I don't know,' the South African said. 'We'll find something for him. We stick together. That's what we do.'

'I bet you do.' Ritchie offered his hand. 'Thanks.'

'Don't mention it.' They shook hands.

'Will you stick around here?' the South African asked.

Ritchie shrugged. 'I guess we'll stay here until Luke and Rebecca come for Azalea,' he said. 'We might be able to help in the hospital. And then we'll see if we can get a bus to Nairobi. Or we'll hitch a ride. We'll go the embassy – see if we can get a flight home.' There was nothing else to say. But there was. 'Can you lend us fifty dollars?'

The South African laughed. 'Twenty-five,' he said. He peeled off some notes and pushed them into Ritchie's hand.

'Thanks again.'

The mission nurse was hovering. 'Dr Lewis,' she said, 'Please, Dr Lewis.'

'I'm not a qualified doctor yet, Nurse Matu.'

'I know that, Dr Lewis. We have a woman who needs to see you. It is very urgent.'

'Well, if I can help ...'

'You can help,' said Nurse Matu, leading him away. 'And there is a man with a very bad fever.' She held Ritchie by the elbow and steered him towards the clinic.

John Hall was still asleep when his comrades-in-arms lifted him back into the truck. He was still snoring like an Ankole ox.

Azalea watched him being carried away. The man who was – who *said* he was – her father; the man who had lifted a camera and photographed her on a beach in a different lifetime. His face was barely visible now, wound with bandages. He wasn't a man any more. He was a thing, a sack being loaded onto a wagon. Nothing felt real. Still there were no tears.

Lauren came over and took her hand.

'I should go back with them,' Azalea told Lauren, although she made no move to go. 'My dad will need me.' She meant Luke. 'My dad,' she said again, 'my proper dad.'

The tears were close now.

Lauren squeezed her hand. 'Your dad wouldn't want us to send you back,' she said. 'Not yet. You saw the trucks. They were going back to Uganda. It wouldn't be safe.'

'But my mum ...'

Lauren looked down. The news of Rebecca's shooting had not reached them, but all the same she spoke with a deep disquiet. 'Your mum will be happier if you stay here. She needs to know you're safe'. She put an arm around the teenager. 'Come with me into town. I want to buy you some clothes.'

They took five dollars from Ritchie and walked out of the mission gate. A man sitting cross-legged beneath a tree, with a hand-cranked Singer sewing machine on a low wooden table, took about twenty minutes to stitch together a pale blue dress with a white cotton collar. It cost them three of their dollars. They bought pink flip-flops with flower-patterned straps from a woman who sold shoes alongside cactus pears and pieces of sugar cane. Another dollar. A real shop sold Coca-Cola from a fridge. They shared a bottle, and with some of the change Lauren picked up a newspaper, the Nairobi *Daily Nation*. She carried the paper back to the mission before spreading it out on the table under the thorn tree. 'Let's see,' she said, 'if any of this made the papers.'

The photograph on the front page was the one that the Olsen Press Agency reporter had lifted from the desk in Luke Folley's office. 'Mission Family Murdered' was the headline. Rebecca and Luke were dead, read the story, and it told of a hail of gunfire. Azalea was also reported to be dead, and five children, according to the *Daily Nation*, were missing.

That was when the tears began.

There is a postscript to this story. The mercenaries' lorry broke down on the long road back towards Uganda. They simply ran out of diesel. Their glorious anonymity as just another dirty truck on a dusty African road failed to protect them from what happened next. By unhappy chance, as Thomas might have explained it, the first vehicle that stopped to offer help turned out to be a detachment of the Kenyan army. There was no Ritchie present to pull colonial rank. Instead there were two hated Afrikaners, a bemused Ugandan, a belligerent Belgian and a comatose Manxman. This time the lorry was searched. The five were arrested for being in the country illegally and for carrying illegal weapons. They were handcuffed and driven for twenty hours to Nairobi. John Hall did not survive the journey. The Ugandan mercenary served five years in a prison near Kisumu. The Belgian and the two South Africans were deported. Before he boarded the plane, Pieter Van de Merwe, one of the South Africans, wrote a note and passed it to the Kenyan police official responsible for overseeing the deportation. 'Please,' he said, 'make sure this message gets delivered.' The note was addressed to Luke Folley. In the note Van de Merwe told Luke that the mission had been a success. Azalea and the rest of the hostages were alive. He would find them all in Kakuma.

'One of my men will deliver it personally,' said the policeman. 'Thank you.'

Van de Merwe kicked the dust of East Africa from his boots and never returned. But the policeman was not true to his word. No message made it to Langadi.

In Kakuma, Ritchie and Lauren did a bit of doctoring and they took care of Azalea. They telephoned home from the post office in Kakuma, and a few days later Ritchie's father showed up at the mission in a British Embassy Range Rover. He was a man with the same tall bearing and slow smile and the same flop of blond hair as Ritchie. There were hugs and there were tears, and the elder Dr Lewis became aware that his mission to rescue his son had become a mission to rescue a family.

They stayed for two more weeks. The man from the British Embassy was most obliging. If Azalea returned to England, he told them, she would go into council care, unless a family member could be found to look after her. It was easier to organise things from the Kenya end, he told them. He would make the arrangements.

Ritchie and Lauren married in the outdoor chapel of the mission at Kakuma, and the children of the school formed the choir; and with the ink still wet on the marriage papers, Azalea Folley became their adopted daughter. The embassy man witnessed the signing of the forms. 'There are some benefits,' he told them, 'to a career with the Foreign and Commonwealth Office. It opens a lot of doors.' From an envelope he produced three red passports. 'To replace the ones you lost,' he said. 'One for Mr Richard Lewis,' he slid it across to Ritchie. 'One for Mrs Lauren Lewis.' And then he smiled. 'This one,' he said, 'was the difficult one.' He flipped open the third passport. 'One for Miss Azalea Lewis. Now, shall we fly you home?'

PART THREE

The Coincidence Authority

You have brains in your head.
You have feet in your shoes.
You can steer yourself any direction you choose.

Dr Seuss, *Oh! The Places You'll Go*

20

May 2011

It takes around six weeks for a broken arm to heal. It took more than eight weeks for Thomas Post to defeat his gloomy reservations and to build up the courage to phone Azalea Lewis.

'Hello, stranger,' was how she responded to his call.

They met for lunch in the same cramped Bloomsbury café where they had once sat and nursed their broken bones; they found themselves on the same two stools at the same narrow table.

'Coincidence?' remarked Azalea.

'Far from it,' said Thomas. 'I told the maître d' to reserve our favourite table.'

She laughed, and he remembered, then, how musical the world could be when Azalea laughed.

'How's the rib?' he asked.

'Mended,' she said. 'And you?'

He held up his hand. 'My gear-knob hand,' he said.

'Gear!' she called.

He crunched an imaginary gear, and they both laughed.

'I enjoyed that day,' she told him.

'Me too.' Thomas thought back to the trip to Devon. They had bickered like an old married couple; they had suffered from their respective aches and pains; they had driven for long stretches in silence, had spent ten hours of the day on the road and just minutes at the cliff face; and once there, Azalea had railed angrily against the world. Had he really enjoyed that day? And yet he had felt uncommonly relaxed in her company. Even squabbling had been easy. Even silence. He had relished the time they spent over lunch and again over dinner – lingering over their conversations, catching her gaze and holding it in his own. He had shared, with this woman, stories about his life that would normally have remained locked away – and she had done the same with him. They had a connection. That was beyond doubt.

They ordered savoury pastries and muffins.

'I have two things to tell you,' said Thomas, when the small talk had petered out.

'Oh good,' Azalea said. 'I love to be told things.'

'Number one, we're going with your idea.'

She raised her eyebrows. 'I had an idea?'

'You did.' He grinned at her. 'Do you remember? Anyway, I thought about it.'

She dropped her head to one side. 'And what did you conclude … after all this thinking?'

He leaned towards her and draped his forearms over the narrow table. 'I did what you suggested,' he said. 'I've set up a new experiment. It's called *The Coincidence Authority*.'

'Good name.'

'Thecoincidenceauthority,' said Thomas Post, 'dot com.'

'It's a website?'

'It was your idea, remember? It isn't quite live yet. We're going to go global with this. We hope to recruit thousands of subjects.'

Azalea nodded approvingly, and this was an encouragement to Thomas.

'It's exactly as you imagined it. If anyone has the sensation that they're being afflicted by coincidence, they can go onto the site and make a prediction. A woman came to see me last week. She has two grandchildren, and both were born on her birthday. She's convinced that it must be more than just chance. So all she has to do is go online and forecast the exact date her next grandchild will be born. It's foolproof.'

'So all you have to do is write down your prediction …?'

'Exactly. In two hundred words or less.'

'Two hundred words or *fewer*,' said Azalea. 'Sorry.' She waved an apologetic hand. 'Force of habit.'

'Two hundred words,' said Thomas with emphasis, 'or fewer. Then you identify this as a serious prediction. And finally you agree to reply to an email questionnaire every month that simply asks whether or not your prediction has come true.' He took a healthy bite of his pastry.

'And afterwards you work out how many people's predictions have come true – and how many didn't?'

'Exactly,' said Thomas. 'And we can look for any that seem to be out of the ordinary.'

'And what will it prove?'

'Well.' Thomas wiped crumbs from his mouth. 'I expect the results to show that the world is a random and unpredictable place. I expect them to show that no one can exert any remote influence on events. I expect to show that no one is in control of our lives – except perhaps for ourselves.'

Azalea nodded her understanding. 'So no coincidences?'

'Oh yes. There will be coincidences. But only at the level that you'd expect them.'

'And what if you don't find that the world is random and un-predictable? What if predictions do come true?'

'They won't.' Thomas gave her a defiant look.

'What about wishes or dreams? Do they never come true?'

'Statistically, not more frequently than they would if the wish had never been made.'

Azalea gave a look of mock disappointment. 'Dreams never come true,' she echoed, '*statistically*. There speaks Mr Romantic.'

'I'm sorry.' Thomas Post almost mumbled this apology. 'But it isn't about romance. No one is messing with our lives. No one is making predictions come true. There are three fundamental theories of existence. The first is that everything is controlled by an all-knowing creator. This creator can tinker with the laws of physics and bend the future in any way that he – or she – wishes. The second theory is that everything is predetermined from the instant of the Big Bang, and no one can change the way that the universe will unravel – not even a supreme being. And the third theory is that everything happens more or less randomly and that we human beings have tapped into a clever mechanism that allows us to introduce free will into the equation. What we could do is eliminate theory number one.'

Azalea allowed her jaw to drop. 'You think your website can disprove the existence of God?'

This wasn't going well. Thomas retreated. 'No, no,' he said, 'not exactly.' He offered a smile to help recover the situation, and gave one of his anthropoid shrugs. 'But it might help show that coincidences – when they happen, like your coincidences – aren't the responsibility of any malign force – or even benign force. They're just things that happen from time to time. That's all.'

'I see.' Azalea looked reflective. 'What about me, then?'

'What about you?'

'Do you think this will help ensure that I don't die on Midsummer's Day next year?'

'This isn't about your prediction,' Thomas said quietly.

'No? So you don't want me to use the site?'

He leaned back and took another bite of his pastry. 'Of course you can use it. I can't stop you, anyway.'

'But …?'

'I thought we could use it to do an early test. Do you remember telling me that you expected to meet a third man who says he's your father? And you expect him to be blind? We could try that.'

'What about my midsummer coincidence?'

He dropped his face, breaking her stare. 'I think,' he said, 'that you're assigning too much significance to Midsummer's Day.'

'Too much significance?'

'It's only a number on a calendar.'

'It's the *same* number on the calendar,' said Azalea.

'Yes, but there's nothing magical about calendar dates,' said Thomas. This was an argument he had pressed before, on different occasions with different people, always confronting the same look of disbelief as he tried to explain the simple mathematics of synchronicity, but never before had it felt so personal. Never before had he cared about the outcome.

'Take an obvious objection,' he said. 'Our leap-year date is wholly arbitrary. We pop it at the end of February but we could equally have put it in, say, July. If that was the case, then Luke and Rebecca would have died on 22 June because they died in a leap year.'

Azalea gave him a look. 'But we don't have our extra day in July,' she said as if she was explaining this to a nine-year-old. 'We have it in February. So Marion died on 21 June, and Luke and Rebecca died on 21 June exactly ten years later.'

'But ten years is an arbitrary measure too,' protested Thomas. 'What if it was eight years? Or twelve? Would that be just as big a coincidence? We only think decades are special because we happen to have ten fingers, and so we count in tens. But there is nothing intrinsically distinctive about the number ten.'

'But the fact remains,' said Azalea, 'that we *do* count in tens and we *do* use a calendar that makes those two days significant.'

'OK,' said Thomas. 'So let's assume, just for a moment, that you're right. What about 21 June 2002? Why didn't anything happen on that date? By your logic *you* should have died *then* – ten years after Luke and Rebecca. That would have been quite an interesting coincidence. But you didn't. You're still very much here. So all 21 June 2012 will be is a twenty-year anniversary. What's so special about that?'

The exchange seemed to have exhausted Thomas. He half lifted himself from the uncomfortable stool and as he did so, his face passed uncommonly close to Azalea's and he caught a rush of her soft perfume; in one blink he could have touched her face and kissed her. 'I'll just go and pay,' he said.

'Do you want to know what I think?' she said.

'Of course,' he said, sinking back onto the stool.

'You won't like it.'

Thomas raised his eyebrows. 'Is it that bad?'

'What I think,' said Azalea, 'is that everything that happens, happens for a reason.'

'Everything that happens …' echoed Thomas.

'… Happens for a reason.' Azalea held out two open hands. 'That's it. That's what I think.'

'It isn't a particularly easy hypothesis to test,' Thomas said, making every effort to sound positive. But he felt disappointed by Azalea's observation. It was a familiar enough world view, and he had heard it expressed countless times. It was hitsuzen writ large. Deo volente.

'I was right, wasn't I? You don't like it.'

'Oh, I wouldn't say that.'

'Oh, I would.' Azalea neutralised his disappointment with a fetching smile. 'Thomas the Philosopher doesn't like New Age poppycock.'

'I didn't call it New Age poppycock.'

'But that's what you think. If everything happens for a reason, then there must be a planner. That's what you're thinking.'

Thomas nodded slowly. 'Maybe.'

Azalea laughed. 'You remind me of my father,' she said. 'You remind me of Luke.'

'I just prefer to believe that nothing is preordained.'

She moved close to him and touched him affectionately on the nose. 'I've put this out of joint,' she said.

Her proximity had brought back the faint aroma of her perfume, and the touch of her fingertip on his face felt like the breaching of a boundary. He reached up and took hold of her hand, and she didn't pull away.

'And what was the other thing?' she asked.

'The other thing?'

'You were going to tell me two things.'

'Ah.' He looked down, unsure, releasing his hold on her hand.

'What have you done?'

'I've bought some tickets,' he said. Something a little like fear was stalking his arteries.

'Theatre?' she asked. 'The ballet?'

'Do I look like the sort of person,' asked Thomas, 'who would enjoy the ballet?'

Azalea bit her lip, trying to look remorseful. 'Cinema?' she asked him. 'A Royal Garden Party?'

Thomas Post shook his head, enjoying the guessing game but nervous about the way it might conclude.

'What are you doing this weekend?'

21

May 2011

They took an early flight from London City Airport that brought them into Ronaldsway. The landing strip starts just a few dozen yards from the top of the cliffs, so the view from Azalea's window appeared to promise a bellyflop into the Irish Sea until suddenly the island was beneath them, and then they were on the ground.

'I've never been to the Isle of Man before,' said Thomas.

'I was born here,' Azalea murmured. What did she expect? She had glimpsed green fields and roads and rooftops. It could have been Somerset or Devon.

They hired a small car and set off towards the Parish of Castletown and Peel. The sun was shining. Azalea felt a numbing sense of anticipation, or was it dread?

'Do you recognise anything?' asked Thomas. She shook her head. How could she recognise this place – this island from her infanthood?

The roadway wound gently through this hamlet and that one, and then the sea was ahead of them and the lane descended past rows of white cottages to a harbour decked with pleasure boats and fishing smacks. There was a big square inn beside which they parked the car.

'Ice cream?' invited Thomas.

They walked up to the village shop and bought two vanilla cones, and then, like a pair of tourists, they strolled along the quay observing the boats and watching fishermen roll out nylon nets. They settled on a bench, and a kind blaze of May sunshine served to relax them. The tranquillity of the place after the bustle of London was almost unreal.

'I could live here,' announced Azalea.

'You once did,' Thomas reminded her.

She looked over towards the harbour, and the bobbing of the boats seemed to match a gentle rocking in her spirit, and a clean gust of sea air filled her lungs. Above her the herring gulls perched on a high wall waiting for scraps. Nothing about this place seemed familiar; but everything was familiar. She tried to remember the way she had felt at Peter Loak's house in Lakeland. There, she had sensed an echo from her distant past; she had seen in a forgotten corner of her memory the track that led over the stile and down the daffodil path to the beck; she had remembered – or half remembered – the old house and its big empty rooms. And in the background, at Buttermere, there had been a figure; the ever-present shadow of a person who could only have been Marion Yves, her mother. But the shadow of Marion wasn't here. Not here in Port St Menfre. Not yet. But the way the boats rose and fell, and the way the water lapped at the hulls, and the way the breeze came in from the harbour – all of these things, if not familiar, seemed at least to be truthful. They seemed real. And the scent of lobster pots and landed fish; and the hawking of the gulls. These were real too.

On a fishing boat way out in the bay a tall, gaunt fisherman wearing faded waders slopped water from a bucket along his decks. Azalea nudged Thomas. 'Look at him,' she said, conspiratorially. 'Do you think that's him?'

'Too young,' said Thomas. 'He would be in his sixties by now.'

'We should have brought binoculars,' she said.

They sat and enjoyed the moment.

'It feels wrong somehow,' Azalea said. 'Tracking him down like this.' She watched the gaunt fisherman as he stacked plastic crates on his deck. Did she have a father who worked on a boat like this one, in this little harbour, out in that blue bay? 'I always thought that I would just encounter him somewhere; somewhere at random – like I did with John Hall and Peter Loak.'

'Sometimes,' said Thomas, 'encounters need a nudge to make them happen.'

'Maybe we shouldn't look too hard for him,' said Azalea. 'Maybe we should just sit here and wait, and see if he comes to us.' The sunlight flickered on the waves like a soft strobe or an old film.

'He might be out at sea,' said Thomas. 'In fact, he probably is.'

'Do they fish on a Saturday?' Azalea asked, feeling immediately foolish. Of course they would fish on a Saturday. There were no weekends at sea.

They finished the ice creams and found themselves slightly at a loss for what to do next. There was no plan. Thomas had simply said, 'I've bought two tickets to the Isle of Man. I thought we could go and find Gideon Robertson.' And she had agreed. And here they were. But what should they do now?

They walked back up the quayside to the town. A little shop sold postcards and souvenirs: pottery emblazoned with the three legs of Man, Manx cats in many guises, ashtrays shaped like the Laxey Wheel, model motorcycles, tea towels embroidered with Celtic runes, seashells and nautical paraphernalia. Thomas bought Azalea a badge embossed with the Isle of Man motif, and Azalea pinned it to her lapel.

Back outside they made their way up the cliff path. Without knowing where they were, they walked right past 4 Briny Hill Walk where Marion Yves had lived and where Gideon Robertson had been her lodger, or something more. They came upon the Parish Church of St Menfre and rested on the bench, overlooking the rooftops and the bay, where once Marion Yves had sat and thrown bread to the seagulls.

'What do we do now?' Azalea asked.

'I suppose,' said Thomas, 'we ought to ask someone.'

But instead they sat and savoured the good things that the day had to offer as the sunshine stroked their faces.

An old man with a head of feather-white hair emerged from the churchyard; a very old man. He walked with two sticks. He appeared to be making for the bench, so Thomas stood to let him sit. The old man lowered himself down next to Azalea, who started to stand up, but he beckoned her to stay. 'Please don't leave on my account,' he said in a voice that was half whisper, half wheeze.

Azalea lowered herself back down. 'This is such a lovely spot,' she said.

The old man didn't answer. But he did turn his head to look at Azalea through watery eyes. And then he turned back to gaze out over the bay. 'I mistook you for your mother,' he said after a moment. 'You do look very much like her.'

Azalea felt a wobble in her world.

'Is she still with us?' asked the old man. 'Is Marion still alive?'

Azalea shook her head.

'Alas, my dear. I'm so sorry.'

How strange it seemed to meet someone who was sorry about Marion. 'You knew her?' Azalea asked.

Again the old man sat silent, but he nodded in response to her question. A warm sea breeze heavy with the smell of landed fish wafted up the hillside. 'I hope,' wheezed the old man after a while, 'that you have forgiven me for the scar.'

Her fingers fluttered over the familiar line.

'You were wearing a very glossy christening gown. You just slipped through my arms.'

'You're the priest?' Azalea said.

'Yes, my dear,' said the Reverend Doctor Jeremiah Lender, 'I am the priest.'

Out in the harbour, the fishing boat with the gaunt fisherman was making its way between the harbour walls, out into the Irish Sea. Azalea was struck by the timelessness of the place. Even the pleasure boats and souvenir shops and cafés couldn't conceal the thread of continuity and tradition that clung to this village. That fisherman would be the son of a fisherman, and he the son of another, and so it would go back into the past and perhaps into the future as if the pages of the book had already been written. And was she, Azalea, the daughter of just such a fisherman? She was certainly the granddaughter of a man who had sailed out every day between those same harbour walls, and the great-grand-daughter of another. Did the sudden comfort she felt about this place hearken back to a calling deep within her genes, the same calling that had summoned the first of her kin to this bay, to these waters?

'What was she like – my mother?' she asked the priest.

'Oh, my dear,' said the reverend, 'has she been lost to us for some time?'

'For twenty-nine years,' Azalea said.

The Reverend Lender leaned forward upon his sticks and contemplated the view. 'The last time I saw your mother must have been around then,' he said at last. 'She looked a lot like you do now. She was an outspoken young woman, but she had a good heart. A very good heart.'

Azalea told him Marion's story. She told him about HMS *Sheffield* and Peter Loak. She told him about the fairground in Totnes and about Carl Morse and the cliffs at Millook.

After this, they sat for a while in silence. Then Lender told Azalea more about Marion. He told her the story of the dropped baby at the font and asked again for her forgiveness.

'Of course I forgive you,' Azalea told him. She took his hand. His skin felt like paper.

'She came to me,' Lender said, 'when she was first expecting you. She wanted to ask God for guidance. I'm afraid I wasn't much help.'

'What guidance did she need?'

'Oh …' Lender hesitated. 'This and that.'

'Was it to do with my father? Was it because she wanted to know who my father was?'

The old priest nodded slowly. 'Did she ever tell you the story of the seagulls?'

Azalea shook her head. 'I barely remember her,' she said. 'But I have heard the story. I heard it from Peter Loak.'

'I was angry with her.' His voice dropped, and it seemed as if the breeze would whip his words out across the bay.

Azalea found herself leaning closer to hear him.

'I shouldn't have been angry, but I was. I told her this was no way to put your problems to God. But Marion didn't see things the same way I did. In her view, everything happens for a reason. That's why it made sense to her to make a serious decision about her life based upon nothing better than a seagull and a piece of bread.'

This made Azalea smile. 'I can understand that. I think perhaps it's something I might have done.'

'We were sitting on this bench,' the priest told her.

She tried to imagine it. She had, in a sense, been there, unborn, just a bundle of cells in a womb. On the rooftops today the gulls were perched, scanning the ocean. Perhaps these birds were descendants of the gull that saved her life. She smiled at the thought.

'So is Peter Loak your father then?' asked Lender. 'Your real father? Just as Marion believed God had told her?'

Azalea shook her head. 'My real father was a man called Luke Folley.' And she felt a tear appear unbidden in her eye. She blinked it quickly away. 'He was my real father because he loved me and he raised me; and in the end, he gave his life for me.'

'Then he truly was your father,' said the priest.

'But as for the man who lent me just one cell from his body, I don't know who that man was. When I was a child I met John Hall. Do you remember him?'

The old man nodded.

'He believed he was my father, and I believed him too. Then seventeen years passed and I met Peter. He also believed himself to be my father, so what could I say? Maybe he was. Maybe the seagull told the truth.'

'And what of Gideon Robertson? Are you here to find him?'

Azalea nodded, and as she did the tear reappeared in her eye.

'Are you all right?' asked Thomas, who had been listening to the conversation.

The old man gave him a gentle but reproving look. 'There are times,' he said, 'when it is prudent not to ask.' Slowly he raised himself up on his sticks. 'You had better come with me,' he said.

They followed him at his hobbling pace back through the gate of the churchyard.

'Are you still the vicar here?' asked Thomas.

'Oh no,' the wheeze was almost a laugh. 'No, indeed. I've been retired for many, many years.'

Azalea was holding Lender by the arm as they toiled up the three or four shallow steps to the great oak door of the church.

'They built this church,' said Lender, 'in 1425.' He stood, perhaps to admire the building, perhaps to recover his breath from the steps. 'The island had just been transferred from the rule of Scotland to the rule of England. Then in 1405 King Henry IV gave the island to his friend, Sir John Stanley. It was a very amiable arrangement. All Stanley had to do was provide a gift of two falcons to every new king of England on his coronation. Of course, Stanley hardly bothered to visit the island; but he did give the Church a very free rein, and hence,' Lender waved a stick up towards the church, 'we have magnificent places such as this.'

They stepped out of the spring sunshine into the cool shade of the church porch. Slowly they followed the Reverend Lender, down past the font where Azalea had slid from the preacher's arms and earned the scar that would line her face for life; up the aisle and through the nave where once Marion had bowed her head and prayed to God for direction; and through the chancel past the choir stalls. Azalea wondered for one moment if the Reverend Lender was about to ask them to kneel and pray. Instead he led them to one side and into a transept chapel behind the organ.

They stood in the transept, which was lit by a stained-glass window depicting the gospel fishermen, each with a halo, pulling in a net from a small boat. The Reverend Lender sank into one of the pews. Azalea helped him down. 'Why have you brought us here?' she asked.

The old man nodded very slowly. Then he raised one stick and pointed to a brass plaque beneath the window. 'We put this here because of the window. It seemed the right place.'

The engraving on the plaque also bore the image of a fisherman with his net; and the words below read, 'In Loving Memory of the Men of Port St Menfre who Gave their Lives to the Sea'.

Beneath this was a text that read, 'For thou hadst cast me into the deep, in the midst of the seas; and the floods compassed me about: all thy billows and thy waves passed over me'.

And now the tears were in Azalea's eyes again and she could read no further. She let go her grasp on the arm of the Reverend Doctor, and instead she found a hand reaching for Thomas. She slid her hand within his.

Beneath the Bible text came a list of names and dates.

'Read them to me,' she said to Thomas in a whisper.

'All of them?'

'Yes. All of them.'

'Fintan Kissack,' read Thomas, 'aged 43. Lost at sea December 12th 1841. Joshua Kissack, aged 21. Lost at sea December 12th 1841.'

'They must have been brothers,' said Azalea very softly.

'They were father and son,' said the Reverend Lender.

'Abraham Clague, aged 61. Lost at sea March 1st 1876; Christian Costain, 42, November 12th 1901; Peter Kissack, 27, December 24th 1936.'

'Christmas Eve,' whispered Azalea. The transept seemed to swallow up her words.

'John Joughin, 40, March 6th 1949; David Joughin, 44, March 6th 1949; Samuel Yves, 38, March 6th 1949.'

'He was your great-grandfather,' said Lender.

'Abraham Yves,' read Thomas, 'aged 33. Lost at sea June 21st 1962.'

'June 21st!' Azalea sat upright. 'Midsummer's Day?'

'He was Marion's father,' the priest explained.

Azalea started to rise from the pew. 'I think we should go now,' she said. Her heart was beating too fast for this place. It was too silent. There were too many ghosts.

Thomas squeezed her hand. 'Wait,' he said. 'Just one more.' He paused for a second and then he read, 'Gideon Robertson, aged 54. Lost at sea. 2002.'

'What was the date?' asked Azalea.

Thomas hesitated.

'It was a June day,' said Jeremiah Lender. 'It dawned very bright and clear. Sometimes the men on the small boats go out for two tides when the day is so long. There were three men on the boat, Gideon Robertson and two brothers – the Clagues – Adam and Tom. Around early afternoon a dreadful squall came over the sea. They had a good catch, and all three men were on deck tying everything down before the wind grew too high. Gideon must have seen these conditions a thousand times. While the Clagues were aft, Gideon was at the bow and a high wave broke above him just as the boat fell to the side. No one saw it happen, but it must have been that wave that took him. When Adam and Tom discovered he was missing, they turned and searched the sea. Air-sea rescue came out, and a helicopter from Anglesey. They searched until dark and were back at first light. The Clagues were out all night. But alas, he was never found.'

The silence of the transept consumed them. Then Azalea asked again, 'What was the date? What was the date in June?'

'It was June 21st,' said Thomas, and he felt Azalea release his hand as he spoke. 'It was Midsummer's Day.'

22

June 2012

'So what are the chances,' Clementine asks Thomas, 'of all those dates coinciding?'

It is a summer evening in Clementine Bielszowska's ground-floor office at the university. It is the Monday following her Friday visit to him in his little room on the fifth floor when he told her the story of Azalea. Clearly it has been on her mind over the weekend, as this time she has summoned him. He sits like a disobedient student, his big hands trapped between his knees. He looks sullen.

'And don't tell me that the chances are one hundred per cent,' she adds. 'I *know* your answer to this question. History happened, and we all live extremely unlikely lives. I don't want to hear that. I just want to know the particular probability in this case. Wind back to 1962. Now tell me the chances of every significant date in the life of Azalea Lewis crashing into Midsummer's Day.' She is hunched up in a deep leather armchair, watching him like a patient predator.

'In most of Europe,' Thomas says miserably, 'people don't even celebrate midsummer on 21 June. They celebrate it on 24 June.'

'Well that,' Clementine says, 'is plain stupid. But it doesn't answer my question.'

Thomas rises from his seat. There is a flipchart propped up against the wall. He writes 'Midsummer' in faint red marker pen at the top.

'Midsummer's Day 1962,' he says, 'Abraham Yves is lost at sea.'

He writes this down.

'Midsummer's Day 1982, Marion Yves is murdered at a fairground.'

'Twenty years later,' Clementine says.

'Yes.'

'So what happened on Midsummer's Day *1972*?'

'Nothing. So far as I know.'

'Good.' She taps her walking stick on the floor. 'Next.'

'1992. June 21st. Luke and Rebecca Folley are gunned down at the Langadi Mission in Uganda.'

'Are you sure?'

'Am I sure of what?'

'Are you sure they were gunned down? How do you know?'

Thomas thought about this. 'Because it said so in the newspaper.'

'Which paper?'

'The Nairobi *Daily Nation*,' Thomas says, but his expression is troubled.

'You've seen the article?'

'Yes. I've been researching Azalea's coincidences. I found a library copy.'

'Do you believe everything you read in the papers?'

'Not always, but this was a pretty authoritative article. It had a photograph ...'

'A photograph of the bodies?'

He stalls a little. 'No,' he says. 'A photograph of Luke and Rebecca and Azalea standing outside a building.'

'All alive?'

'Well. Of course.'

'And this photograph proves what, exactly?'

He looks uneasy. 'I guess it proves that the journalist who wrote the article must at least have visited the mission. Someone must have given him the photograph.'

'You've just assumed,' the elderly psychoanalyst says, 'that John Hall and a group of mercenary soldiers simply took off after Azalea and risked their lives to save her. Why? Why would they do that?'

'I don't know. I've never really thought about it.'

'Someone must have paid them. Isn't that what mercenary soldiers are – paid muscle?'

'I guess …'

'So who paid them?' She fixes him with a glare. 'Less than twelve hours after the abduction, someone is paying mercenaries to rescue Azalea. Who would do that?'

Thomas gulps slightly. Clementine's forensic intelligence makes him nervous. 'Someone else from the mission?' he suggests. 'And we aren't sure it was just Azalea they were after.'

Clementine leans forward and slides open a narrow drawer. She pulls out a sheet of paper. 'Do you remember the report you saw in the Kenyan paper about the mercenaries being deported?' she asks.

He nods.

'Did you make a note of their names?'

Thomas looks surprised at the question.

'One name is notably absent,' she says. 'John Hall. It seems that he died before they could deport him. But the other names were given, and I tracked one of them down.' She gives him a satisfied grin.

He looks at her in disbelief. 'You tracked … How did you do that?'

'Google. A lot of international phone calls, a friend in Johannesburg and some serendipity.' She waves the printed page at him.

'What's that?'

'It's an email from our friend,' she says. She pulls on her spectacles. 'Pieter van der Merwe.'

'*The* Pieter van der Merwe?'

'The same,' she says. 'Pieter van der Merwe, mercenary and rather unpleasant alumnus of the Johannesburg police.' She tosses the page across the room and Thomas snatches it up.

'Have you spoken to him?' he asks with urgency in his voice.

'I have.'

'And what did he say?'

She grins. She is enjoying this. 'He told me that a man came to a hotel in Gulu to meet with John Hall. An Englishman. No one else met this man. It's a long time ago and his memory is shaky, but Pieter is reasonably sure it was Luke.'

'It might not have been.' Thomas's hands are shaking.

'Whoever it was paid for the transaction with the deeds of a house in Cornwall,' she says. 'Those deeds are probably still in a safe somewhere in Uganda. The boys never did anything about it.'

'Oh my God.' Thomas straightens up. 'Luke had a house in Cornwall.'

'He did.'

'So Luke is still alive?'

'We don't know that. But we do know that he *was* still alive on the afternoon of 21 June 1992,' Clementine says. 'Several hours after Azalea was abducted.'

'Shit.' Thomas begins to pace up and down the room. 'Shit, shit, shit.'

She permits him this rush of expletives.

'So if Luke survived the shooting in Langadi ...' Thomas tails off again, struck by too many new thoughts to process them all. 'Why didn't he go looking for Azalea? I mean, after the mercenary thing went belly-up? Why didn't he try to track her down?'

'How do we know he didn't?' Clementine removes her spectacles. 'Just think about it. The trail must have been cold. According to Van der Merwe, John Hall told Luke *not* to come after them. He made that very clear. If no one made it back from the LRA camp with Azalea or any of the hostages, then they *all* had to be dead. So just imagine you're Luke Folley. What do you do? You wait around for a few days, desperately waiting for news. It never comes. Eventually, what? What do young men do in such circumstances?' She taps her stick as if it is helping her to think. 'I would expect him to head north into Sudan looking for the LRA camp himself. But how would he find it? The mercenaries knew where it was – Luke probably didn't. And the chances are that after their encounter with our dogs of war, the LRA would have moved the evidence anyway. But even if they hadn't, what would Luke find? A bombed-out truck? A dead driver?'

This is sinking in. 'But what about Ritchie and Lauren?'

'What about them?'

'Luke could have tracked them down. He must have had ways of contacting them.'

'Why would he think to do that? So far as Luke knew, Ritchie and Lauren had fled the mission compound. He told them to go. He probably saw them go. He'd have expected them to be on the first bus back to Kampala and then the first plane back to London. He didn't know they'd been abducted too.'

Thomas remains silent, absorbing this.

'And even if it did cross his mind to contact them, he could never have imagined that they would have known anything about Azalea – or where she was, because if they did know, they would surely have tried to contact *him*.'

'One phone call,' Thomas says, emphasising this by stabbing the air with a long finger. 'One cheap, lousy phone call to Ritchie Lewis and he could have been back in touch with his daughter.'

Clementine nods. 'Luke couldn't track down Azalea because he didn't even know if she was alive. He would calculate that if even one mercenary had survived – just *one* – they'd have come back to him with news. He probably checked all the reports from Sudan and Uganda to see if there was any news of them. He'd probably never dreamed they'd fled to Kenya. Or that Ritchie and Lauren were with them. Or that the mercenaries would all end up dead, imprisoned or deported. Or that Van der Merwe's message would be lost. Or that Azalea would have changed her name. Even a very sharp detective would run aground on all of that.'

'Not if the detective were as sharp as you,' Thomas says.

Clementine ignores this. 'And then, Luke would also have assumed that if Azalea *was* alive, and if she had made it out of the clutches of the LRA, then *she* would be in touch. She was thirteen – quite old enough to find her way back to Langadi – or at least to tell someone to get a message to her parents. She was a resourceful teenager, by your account. Luke knew that. But he would never have known that a newspaper in Kenya had told Azalea that he and Rebecca were dead. He would never have known that she'd mourned them both for twenty years.'

'Clementine, you're a wonder. Why didn't I come to you before now?'

She nods, enjoying this appreciation. 'Why indeed?'

'What an extraordinary set of circumstances.'

'Would you call it chance?' she asks, 'or providence?'

'Guzen or hitsuzen?' he echoes. 'Either way, it was one almighty helping of crumby bad luck.' He whistles slowly through his teeth and flexes his long arms. 'You might even call it coincidence,' he says.

She grunts agreement. 'You may pour me a glass of red wine,' she says.

'It would be a pleasure.' He crosses her office to a set of bookshelves. He has done this before. There are volumes here by Freud and Jung, by Reich, Lacan and Schimek. He runs his finger down a row of spines.

'Try the Pleasure Principle,' she says. '*Jenseits des Lustprinzips.* Freud.'

He locates the volume and slides it forward. The book is a fake. Behind the false spine stands a bottle.

'Chateau Talbot,' she says. 'Named after a Shropshire earl who died in the Battle of Castillon.'

He retrieves the bottle, and a corkscrew. 'Is it a claret?' he asks.

'My dear boy. Have you ever known me to drink anything else?'

He pulls the cork and pours two generous glasses.

Clementine savours the wine slowly, swirling it round the glass and inhaling the bouquet. 'So Azalea went off to England with the Lewises,' she says, 'thinking that Rebecca and Luke were dead. But Luke – at least – was alive.'

'And Rebecca?'

'Who knows? It seems possible that she really was killed. But who knows?'

Thomas releases a long whistle of a sigh. He swings his arms around behind his head.

'Now,' Clementine says, 'can we get back to the maths?'

'I need to get in touch with Luke Folley,' Thomas says. 'If he's still alive, and if he's still in Langadi, then Azalea would have seen him ...'

'When would she have seen him?' Clementine asks. 'What do you mean?'

'Well, that's where she went when she left in February. Back to Langadi. Oh my God!' He claps his hands to his face.

'I see. Always assuming he survived this long.'

'It was twenty years ago.'

'How old was Luke when ...?'

'He would have been forty-something. Forty-three. Or forty-four.'

'Not so old, then.'

'No.'

They look at each other.

'He probably wouldn't still be in Langadi though,' Thomas says.

'Why not?'

'Because the mission doesn't exist any more.'

'Are you sure of that?'

'One hundred per cent. I've googled every possible combination of "Langadi" and "Mission", and there's no listing. I even had a letter from the Church Missionary Society. They say the St Paul Mission was closed down in 1992. They don't have any record of any new mission in its place.'

Clementine fixes him with a stare. 'All the same,' she says, 'I would expect Luke still to be living in Langadi. He has to stay there. He has no choice.'

'Why?' Thomas looks puzzled.

'Why do you think? In case Azalea ever comes home.'

This is almost too much for Thomas. He covers his face with his hands.

'Can we get back to my list?'

'OK.'

He lifts himself up and goes to the chart.

'Two thousand and two?' she prompts him.

'Midsummer's Day 2002, Gideon Robertson is lost at sea,' Thomas says. He writes this down.

'And finally?'

He pauses, and breathes in slowly. 'Two thousand and twelve. Midsummer's Day ...'

There is a long silence. 'You know the rest.'

'I want to hear it from you.'

'Azalea Lewis dies,' he says. There is another long pause. 'Or else she doesn't.'

'And what do you think will happen?'

'I don't know.' He feels a pressure on his chest. He screws up his eyes. 'I don't know. I don't know. I don't know.'

'Perhaps it would help if we were to finish the calculation,' she says.

'OK.' He drags his attention back to the scrawled list of names and dates.

'Each of the events involves a death,' Clementine says. 'Every death is brutal and unexpected. No one dies in comfortable old age in the saga of Azalea Lewis.'

She raises an eyebrow as if anticipating a challenge from Thomas on this point, but he shrugs agreement.

'All the deaths happen on the same day of the year, at the same point in a decade.'

Thomas nods.

'Do me some sums,' she tells him.

'OK.' He is at least on familiar ground here. 'We should assume that the first death – the death of Abraham Yves – was a random day of the year. So we don't need to calculate the odds for him.'

'Very well. And for the record, we should note that Samuel Yves died on an altogether different date.'

'March 6th 1949,' Thomas says.

'Exactly. So we start with Marion. What are the chances that she would die on exactly the same day of the decade as her father?'

'Say there are three thousand six hundred and fifty days in a decade,' says Thomas, 'plus a couple of leap years – then those are the odds. One in three thousand six hundred and fifty-two.'

'Excellent. Long odds, but not astronomical. Like having the winning ticket in the village raffle. So now we add Rebecca.'

'Multiply three and a half thousand by three and a half thousand.'

'Which makes ...' Clementine rummages on her desk and finds a calculator.

Thomas punches in the numbers. 'Thirteen point three million.'

'About the same odds as winning the lottery. Now what if we add Gideon Robertson?'

'Forty-eight billion.'

'And now ...' she pauses to catch his eye, '... we add Azalea.'

Thomas exhales deeply. 'So the chances of that are ... one in one hundred and seventy trillion. Give or take.' He drops the calculator back on the desk.

'And you're still worried about this?'

'Well it doesn't look very random, does it? If you throw five heads, it's chance. If you throw fifty, then someone is messing with the coin.'

'Maybe, Dr Post, you just proved the existence of God.'

Thomas grimaces. 'But what kind of God? One who kills people off at regular intervals just to taunt us?'

'What if there's another explanation?'

It's getting late. They walk out of the university and stroll up towards Euston Road.

'Do you take the tube?' Thomas asks.

'My dear boy.' She gives him an indulgent look. 'With this leg?'

'We could share a taxi.'

'I thought you lived in Hackney.'

'I do. But I'm not in a hurry. Let me travel with you.'

They climb into the back of the cab. 'Primrose Hill,' Thomas tells the driver. 'Elsworthy Road.'

The taxi pulls off into the evening traffic.

'What you said,' Thomas says, 'reminded me of something.' He reaches into his bag for a newspaper. 'Look. It's the *Telegraph*. I try to do it every day,' he says. He turns the paper over for Clementine to see.

'The crossword?'

'I'm a cruciverbalist.' He smiles. 'Do you know the famous coincidence associated with the *Daily Telegraph* crossword?'

'I'm not sure.'

'There was once a crossword compiler for the *Telegraph* called Leonard Dawe,' he says.

'When was this?'

'During the Second World War.'

'Ah,' she says. 'Then I think perhaps I do know the story. Didn't he spook MI5 by putting all the code-words for the D-Day landings in a crossword?'

'Almost. In the crossword on 16 August 1942, Dawe included the clue "French Port", six letters. Innocuous enough, you might think. Then the next day the paper published the solution.'

'Which was?'

'Dieppe.'

'And the relevance was?'

'The very next day, the Allies mounted a raid on Dieppe. It was a disaster. Three and a half thousand men were killed or captured. They lost over a hundred planes.'

She is tapping her walking stick again. 'And they thought the crossword may have been responsible for giving away the location of the raid?'

'Not right away. The War Office did notice the coincidence. They looked into it, and decided it was just a fluke. But then two years later, more unlikely words started to appear. First Juno, then Gold, then Sword.'

She nods in recognition. 'Code names for the D-day beaches.'

'Exactly. Then came Utah, and then, on 22 May the clue was "Indian on the Missouri", and the solution was …'

'Omaha?'

Thomas grins. 'Five days later one of the answers was

"Overlord", which was the code name for the whole operation. Then three more days and there was a clue which was "The bush in the centre of nursery revolutions". Eight letters.'

'English is not my first language, dear boy,' she rebukes him.

'Of course. Well the answer was "Mulberry", as in, "Here we go round the mulberry bush". Nursery revolutions, you see. Anyway, Mulberry was the code name given to the floating harbours they used on the landings.'

'I see.'

'And finally, on 30 May, the crossword included the answer "Neptune", which was the code-word for the whole naval assault.'

'Quite a set of coincidences,' she observes. 'And did the authorities look into it?'

'Oh yes. And they concluded it was just a huge coincidence. They questioned Leonard Dawe and he seemed convincing. "Why shouldn't I use these words?" he said.'

'I see.'

'What would you have made of it?'

She shrugs. 'I don't know. I'm not the coincidentologist.'

Thomas laughs. The taxi turns into Regent's Park Road, and he leans towards her. 'The War Office believed Dawe when he told them it was all an embarrassing coincidence.' His eyes are twinkling.

'But you don't?'

'If I had been around at the time, and if they'd sought my advice ...' he pauses for dramatic effect, '... I'd have hanged him.'

'Good gracious! So it wasn't a coincidence at all?'

'Consider the likelihood of the eight most significant code names all turning up within six months of each other,' he says. 'Each crossword had thirty to forty answers, so we're looking at around four thousand words. What are the chances that all five Normandy beaches would appear in those four thousand clues?'

She shakes her head again. 'I'm guessing you've already done the maths.'

'I have,' he says. 'The sums aren't easy. We need to go back through thousands of crosswords to see, for example, how often the word "Juno" naturally crops up, or how often "Gold" appears. But let's make some generous assumptions; let's say the chance of "Juno" appearing in those four thousand clues is about one in twenty.'

'OK.'

'So the chances of both Juno and Gold appearing is about one in four hundred.'

'If you say so.'

'And the chances of all five beaches is around one in three million.'

'Still,' she says, 'would you hang a man on those statistics?'

'Maybe not. But let's add Overlord, Mulberry and Neptune,' Thomas says. 'The chances of all eight words randomly showing up in the months before the invasion would be less than one in twenty-five thousand million. Or, to put it another way, if they'd been publishing the *Telegraph* crossword every weekday since the earth was first formed, it would probably never have happened. But it did happen. And it happened in the months before D-Day.'

She narrows her eyes at him. 'Are you telling me the man *was* a spy?'

'Some coincidences are so outrageously unlikely that there *has* to be another explanation,' Thomas says.

'So you would have hanged him?'

Thomas mimes the tightening of a noose around his neck, and laughs. 'I would,' he says. 'I would have hanged him. So it's just as well they didn't consult me, because I would have been wrong.'

'Wrong? Are you saying it *was* a coincidence then?'

'No. But there *was* another explanation, although it didn't come out until quite a few years after the war had ended. Leonard Dawe wasn't just a crossword compiler; he was also the headmaster of a school in south London. He sometimes let the boys fill in some of the crossword grids for him, while he composed the clues. And it just happened that some of the boys had overheard the code-words from American soldiers billeted at the school. So they sneaked the words into the crosswords as a prank.'

'Some prank!'

'Indeed.' Thomas looks pleased with Clementine's reaction. 'I often tell this story to students who come to me with coincidences that are astronomically unlikely,' he says. 'And I tell them to look for another explanation. There's always another explanation.'

The taxi pulls up outside a large Georgian building. Clementine is reaching for her purse.

'Let me pay for this,' Thomas says.

'My dear boy, I wouldn't hear of it.' Dr Bielszowska thrusts some coins into his hand. 'Are you aware what date it is?'

'What *date* it is?'

'It is the eighteenth of June. You have three days to work this out.'

Thomas looks gloomy once more. 'I know.'

'I want you to come and see me tomorrow,' she says. 'Come here to my house. Five o'clock. I will make you tea.'

'Thank you,' he says.

'We will sort this out,' she says, and she clambers awkwardly from the taxi. 'Hackney,' she tells the driver. She swings the door shut.

23

June 2011–February 2012

Azalea Lewis and Thomas Post started dating in June 2011, a month after the Isle of Man trip. Thomas appeared unannounced at the office in Birkbeck College that Azalea shared with a colleague. The colleague, a moon-faced woman with dreadlocked hair, sat respectfully at her desk and tried not to giggle when Thomas produced flowers from a carrier bag. The stems had been damaged somewhat, and so had several of the flowers themselves. 'I'm sorry,' Thomas said. 'I didn't want to carry them too openly.'

'You were *embarrassed* to carry them too openly,' Azalea said accusingly while her colleague pretended to look out of the window. 'I don't have a vase,' she said.

The colleague slid a jug along her desk, still feigning unawareness of the conversation. Azalea swept it up, thrust the flowers inside and put the whole arrangement on her desk. 'There.' She gave a wide grin. 'Lovely.'

They went to see *Hamlet* at a West End theatre, and later they went to a French restaurant in Soho where they discussed the play. Thomas talked about predetermination. '*Hamlet* explores free will,' he said, while struggling with a Coquilles Saint Jacques. 'But his destiny defies him. He wants to commit suicide but he can't. He wants to kill his uncle but he can't. He has to play out his father's instructions, but he can't seem to do it.'

'But that isn't free will,' said Azalea. 'That's dithering. That's prevarication. Hamlet can't do the deeds because he's weak.'

'So the moral is …?'

'The burden of Hamlet's responsibility becomes the reason

for his inaction. You have to act in order to be. Don't you think that's what the play is telling us? We may not be born free, but what we do defines us.'

But Thomas Post was made of weaker stuff even than Hamlet. He didn't consummate a relationship with Azalea that night, nor did he after sitting through one of her evening lectures on Futurism in Poetry; afterwards, they ate a simple pizza on Tottenham Court Road and walked together all the way to Marble Arch. They didn't go home together after an afternoon at a Thames regatta, where Thomas wore a borrowed blazer with arms too short and a boater that perched on the top of his head. In the end, Azalea offered to cook a meal at home. Thomas came to her flat near Highgate with another bouquet; this time the flowers were unbroken. She made an African stew and he told her that he loved it. In truth, he loved her. In truth he wanted her so badly that his body no longer knew how to behave. He had become drunk on thoughts of Azalea. He sat and watched her through sheepish eyes.

She served up a trifle from Marks and Spencer's. 'I don't have much time to cook,' she explained.

It was the finest trifle ever.

'Shall we watch a DVD?' she asked him.

He nodded, wholly mute.

They squeezed together onto her small settee and tried to watch *Winter's Bone*, but he couldn't concentrate on the film. He let his arm creep around her like a teenager, and she snuggled her head into his shoulder. And finally, after hours in each other's company, five months after they had sat together in much the same configuration on the floor of a tube station, finally their human reserve ran out and human nature flooded in to replace it.

'Can I ask you something?' Thomas said, as they lay in bed in the early hours of a London morning listening to traffic noises through her open window.

'Ask away.'

'Why don't you do relationships?'

221

She lay silent for a long time. Far too long. 'I don't know.' It was a whisper.

'Is *this* a relationship?'

'I don't know.'

'Would you like it to be?'

You could measure time in heartbeats, Thomas thought. Some heartbeats came and went so fast, while others could last a lifetime. Once, for each of us, there must have been a first heartbeat, a quickening in the womb, a tiny electrical spark and a twitch of muscle and the engine has started that must now flex and pump without rest like the click of a metronome, one beat, two beats, a million beats, a billion beats, until one day the spark never comes and the muscle discovers that it was nothing but frail meat all along.

'I don't know,' whispered Azalea. And then, a thousand heartbeats later, 'Perhaps.'

The sun that rose over Highgate was a different sun to the one that rose every day over Thomas Post's apartment in Hackney. It was a bigger sun, a yellower sun. The sky was bluer, the clouds were lighter, the air was a different mixture of elements, the wind blew with a different purpose. The world even smelt different. It smelt new. It smelt of lilac and lime and toast and honey. Thomas made breakfast and carried it through to the bedroom and he kissed Azalea all the way up from her navel, and when he reached her mouth she was waiting.

They fitted as a couple. Azalea could rest her head on Thomas's broad shoulder. They could walk hand in hand down Regent Street, window-shopping for things that they could never afford. They could sit together in little coffee shops so that Azalea could breathe in the rich aroma of roasting beans. They could lie close together on Azalea's little sofa and tackle the cryptic crossword in the *Telegraph*. 'Five across,' she might chant, 'company in police before Conservative leader is taken in by directions, is synchronicity. Eleven letters.' And Thomas could look over her shoulder and say, 'coincidence', and then laugh and ruffle her hair. 'Synchronicity is coincidence. "Co" is company, "in CID" is "in police", and Conservative leader is C buried in east-north-east.'

It seemed not to matter that Azalea read poetry while Thomas read crime. Or that Thomas listened to indie rock while Azalea liked folk. Or that he rose early while she rose late. Or that he liked to stretch out with a beer and watch the test match on TV while she, well ... didn't. They were, in a sense, two solitary people who had become used to their own company, relaxed in their own company, but who longed nonetheless for another heart to beat alongside their own.

'Do you do relationships yet?' Thomas would ask.

'I don't know,' she would whisper. But she would wind her arm around his waist and whisper the words into his ear so that he could feel her breath.

So why did Azalea leave?

They gave it their best shot. One weekend they flew to Glasgow and they took a bus from the airport down the Clyde to a little town called Gourock, and they caught a ferry from Gourock to Dunoon, and there they met with two doctors who ran a general practice in a village north of Ballochyle, and the doctors were Ritchie and Lauren Lewis. Azalea called them 'Ritchie' and 'Lauren'; they were not her mum and dad. They were more like her elder siblings, eminently sensible, delightfully settled, with two teenage sons of their own.

'How long have you been here?' Thomas asked them.

'Just two years,' they said. But they loved it.

Would they ever go back to Africa?

Ritchie shook his head, and he glanced across at Lauren. 'Azalea told you about Africa, then?' he said. He still had his quiff of blond hair and his raffish manner. 'We shall never go back.' The month they had spent in East Africa had provided enough fireside stories for a lifetime, and the three weeks they had practised medicine as if they had been qualified doctors at the mission in Kakuma had given them a confidence and a grounding they could hardly have earned elsewhere.

When they stayed with Ritchie and Lauren, Azalea and Thomas slept together on a horsehair mattress in a spare bedroom looking out over Loch Eck. And in the morning they walked out like a family with the old family dog, taking the forest tracks up the hillside until high above the loch they could marvel at the views. And they sat together like a family in the snug bar of the village pub, while Ritchie showed off his knowledge of single malt whiskies and Lauren and Azalea shared a hundred stories. And they strolled back along the seafront at Dunoon watching the ferries haul out across the sound.

'It's a little like West Nile,' Azalea told Thomas, and he raised his eyebrows in surprise. 'No, you're right,' she said, 'it's nothing like West Nile. Except that it's a part of the mainland, but you need the ferry to get here. Once, in Langadi, when the Laropi ferry broke down for a month the only way to Gulu without crossing a border was a two-hundred-mile detour via the only bridge at Pakwach. And the roads were terrible. If there had been heavy rain, you wouldn't even think about trying to drive it. Here when the ferries stop running at night, the only way to Gourock just across the bay is the long drive up through Argyll Forest Park and all the way down the coast to Helensburgh and back over the Clyde at Erskine, and that's around ninety miles, just to cross a two-mile strait.'

They spent a day in Edinburgh, climbing up to see the castle, strolling like an old married couple down Princes Street. Alongside the Scott Monument Thomas balanced on a low canvas stool while an artist sketched his likeness in charcoal. Azalea, Ritchie and Lauren stood and watched the drawing take shape, laughing at the licence shown by the artist. In the evening, Ritchie and Lauren drove them out from Dunoon to a ceilidh where all three Lewises knew all the steps, and Thomas lurched in his uncoordinated way unable to remember a move from one round to the next. And at night they lay on the horsehair bed with the view out over Loch Eck, and Azalea flung open the windows as she always did and they listened to the tangible silence of the glen.

How good might it have been if every day was like that?

Azalea in her cotton frock and sandals, her skin glowing from the summer sunshine; no deadlines, no alarm clocks, no emails, no phone calls.

Yet how like Hamlet was Thomas Post? He procrastinated. He should have acted, should have leaped in like Laertes, but something deep within his psyche forbade him; or maybe he was just a fool. Back in London, the mismatch of their working hours was winning its battle with their regime. Azalea would work evenings and take the tube back home to Highgate. Thomas would work days and then kick around the evenings in his lonely flat in Hackney, occasionally venturing out to take on the squash ladder, or drinking late in the Hawley Arms. Azalea would often work at weekends, and Thomas would be left to watch sport on the television, catching up with his ironing and his laundry in front of the Grand Prix or the golf.

Oh Thomas, Thomas. He would sit at his desk for hours running statistics on the trends from *The Coincidence Authority* website. He would plot his projections and his forecasts on graphs, and then he would collapse them, for they were not ready; not yet.

Some nights Thomas would spend at Azalea's flat in Highgate, squeezed up against her in her three-quarter bed with his long legs reaching out over the end. Once she made the journey out to Hackney and climbed the four flights of stairs to his flat, but she was uncomfortable in his unfamiliar bedroom without her wardrobe of clothes and her armoury of cosmetics close to hand. It should have been easy and casual, but somehow the arrangements were awkward and faltering. His day finished so much earlier than her day – should he travel alone up to Highgate and sit for hours in her feminine flat, waiting for her to arrive home? He did this sometimes, but it made him uneasy, tiptoeing up her stairway, sitting alone on her sofa. So how should it work? Should she move in with him? Or should he move in with her? Or should they find a new flat together? And if they did, then what would this say about the permanence of their relationship, and were they ready for this yet? Hackney and Highgate. So close in the alphabet, so near on the page, yet the gulf between these two

London boroughs was threatening to tear them apart. Thomas owned a car, but he kept it parked in a lock-up in Clapton. So he could as an option walk to the lock-up, drive for half an hour, find somewhere to park in Highgate and all should be well; and this he did too, on occasion, trying to time his arrival at Azalea's apartment just as she would emerge from Highgate tube. But it seemed a very deliberate and mechanical set of arrangements. And then it gave him a problem for the morning after, because parking in central London was too expensive to contemplate, so he would have to drive back to the lock-up, walk to his flat, climb the four flights, change and then set off on the bus journey into Bloomsbury arriving into work after two hours of travel. The wonderful benefits of London living, the multifarious travel options of Underground, Overground, bus, cycle, car and taxi all transformed into burdens when faced with the reality of disparate work shifts and six miles of separation.

And then there was another thing. This thing was a mystery to them both. This thing belonged more in Clementine Bielszowska's domain – the domain of human psychology – than in the curious philosophy of Thomas or the cryptic poetry of Azalea. This thing was a barrier that was growing between them based not on their natural human chemistry, or even upon their obvious desire one for another. There may not be a lexicon to explain this drifting apart of Thomas and Azalea – two individuals who seemed in so many respects to have been divinely created for each other – but there was an inevitability about it. Perhaps, Thomas might have concluded, the luckless collisions of Laplace's Demon were to blame. Maybe free will was not enough to defeat a providence that was destined to separate them. They were two travellers, each on a different trajectory. Like satellites in different orbits, they had come together almost miraculously, but now their revolutions were drawing them apart. Partly it was temperament. 'Everything that happens,' Azalea would say, 'happens for a reason.' Thomas, with his outsized feet rooted in unwavering rationalism would gently mock this world view, and when the subject came up – as so often it did – they would end up with a glass pane of silence between them.

'You're too arrogant,' Azalea would accuse him. 'You can't simply dismiss my views just because they make no sense to you.'

And he *was* arrogant. Of course he was arrogant. But even when he tried to conceal his arrogance with counterfeit understanding, she would see through the gambit and this would upset her even more. 'I don't need you to pretend,' she would say.

'Then what do you need?'

What indeed?

She had sought him out to explain her coincidences, but she couldn't accept his explanation.

'Everything happens for a reason.'

'Then why,' he would ask, 'do bad things happen? Why do people die young? Why did Marion die? Why did Luke and Rebecca die? Why did my mother die?'

'I never said ... that the reason was a *good* reason.'

'So some things happen for an evil reason?'

And she would look at him with sorrow in her large eyes. 'Sometimes. Yes.'

Then this would awaken the arrogance. 'Post hoc ergo propter hoc,' he quoted to her. 'Are you familiar with this aphorism? It means "After this – therefore because of this". It's an expression we use to describe lazy logic. Because A happened *before* B, therefore A *caused* B. Because I stepped on the lines between the kerbstones, that's why I failed my maths test. Because the rooster crows, that's why the sun rises. It's faulty reasoning. You see something happen, and then later something else happens, and you conclude that the second event was the *reason* for the first event.'

'So you think I'm stupid?' Azalea would say.

But Thomas had yet to learn that questions beginning with 'so' were a trap.

And if all of this was one explanation for the orbital drift between the lovers, there was another reason; far more prosaic, but even harder, somehow, for Thomas to accept.

She would never admit to it. Not aloud. Not in an intimate

moment. When Thomas would whisper, 'Why don't you do relationships, Miss Lewis?' she would murmur, 'I don't know. Why don't you do poetry?' Only in open conversation could she try to hide the truth. Only when she knew that Thomas wasn't really, truly listening could she conceal her reasons in plain sight. One evening they snatched a drink in a pub on the Tottenham Court Road, when she had just a few short minutes before a lecture and his day was all but over. They stood in a corner with a glass each, and the noise of a jukebox made conversation difficult.

'You do understand why I can't do relationships, don't you, Thomas?' Azalea said, and she said it with such a smile of affection that he could only return it.

'Explain it to me.'

'I'm not really a Lewis. I'm a Folley.'

'Should I call you Miss Folley?'

'If you like. But I'm not speaking legally. I'm speaking metaphorically.'

'So Folley is a metaphor, then?'

'No, not really.' Her smile turned a little more sorrowful and Thomas pulled her close and kissed her.

'You do understand, don't you, Thomas? You understand the burden? The Folley burden?'

Thomas probably didn't, but of course he nodded. She wanted him to understand.

'Good. Because a time will come when I have to go. It will come soon.'

He looked at his watch. 'You have at least five minutes.'

She kissed him on his nose. 'Bless you,' she said. 'I knew you'd understand.' But she knew he didn't.

Another time, they were in her flat in Highgate. She was marking a pile of essays. Thomas was idly watching football on TV. They were batting comments back and forth across her living room.

'Where would you go,' she asked him, 'if you could go anywhere?'

'Florida,' he said too quickly.

'Why?'

'I don't know, really. Lots to do. Beaches. Things like that. Or Hawaii, perhaps. Great for a holiday.'

Azalea was silent for a while. 'What if you had to *live* somewhere else? Where would you go?'

'Oh, I don't know. Italy probably. Tuscany is lovely. Or maybe up by Lake Garda. There's a restaurant on the harbour front at Malcesine with a view over the lake to Limone. We could eat there every night.'

Another long silence. On the TV someone missed a goal.

'Maybe we could,' she said.

'And what about you?'

'What about me?'

'Where would you live?'

'You know where I'd live.'

'No I don't.'

He turned away from the TV screen to look at her, and again she disarmed him with a smile.

'I'd live in Uganda. West Nile.'

'But you've already lived there. Bad things happened to you there.'

'I know.' Azalea shrugged. 'But I'm a Folley, remember?'

'You're a Lewis now.'

'My passport says I'm a Lewis.' But her heart, she might have added, still called her a Folley. And the calling had to come to the Folley young. Sooner or later, it would come.

But that was in the early autumn, and there were still long evenings to enjoy; still weekends. They took the train to Paris, booked into a poky hotel alongside the Gare du Nord and tried to find their way on foot to Notre Dame. They ended up footsore and cold in a café near Bastille. Azalea told him she wanted to go home.

'I'll get a taxi,' he said.

'No … not home to the hotel,' she said. 'Home. I want to go home.'

But where was home for Azalea Lewis? Not a poky hotel by

the Gare du Nord, certainly – but was it a first-floor apartment in Highgate, or was it a bedroom with a horsehair mattress and views out over Loch Eck? Or was it, perhaps, a mission house high in the hills of a distant country, a country of heat and dust and conflict?

In February, she told him, at last, that she was returning to Langadi. It was an atrocious day. They'd planned to walk along the South Bank, to buy some second-hand books and visit a gallery. In the end they shivered in the window of a soulless coffee shop in a concrete block of a building and watched the sheets of rain wash up along the pavements. Thomas was preoccupied. His programmer and research assistant on *The Coincidence Authority* had gone home to India, and now there was no one who could so readily handle the maintenance of the website. He poured out his worries to Azalea, who sat avoiding his eyes. And then she said in a quiet voice, 'I'm going back to Langadi.'

He blinked. Had he even heard her? 'That's nice,' he said.

'In twenty years I haven't spoken or written to anyone from the mission,' she said. 'I don't even know if the mission still exists. I expect it closed down when Luke and Rebecca were killed, but I don't know for sure. I'm thirty-three years old. I've been running away from the place since I was thirteen. It's time I went back.'

Thomas still didn't get it. Not really. He simply bobbed his head. 'Jolly good idea,' he said. 'Put a few demons to bed.'

Oh Thomas, Thomas. Why didn't you say you would go with her? To hell with your stupid experiment. To hell with determination and free will. Why didn't you sweep her up and march together to the travel agent and purchase two tickets? Why didn't you buy some flattering shorts and a khaki safari shirt and some expedition sandals and a commodious rucksack and board that plane alongside her?

We can ask these questions of Thomas, but the truth remains: he sat in that coffee shop just a little bewildered and he prevaricated.

'I wonder,' said Azalea, 'if they all think I'm dead. I do wonder that sometimes. John Hall could have tracked us down. He knew we were at Kakuma, and the people at Kakuma knew how to contact Ritchie. But he never did. I wonder, sometimes, if John Hall ever made it back to Gulu. And even if he did, who would he have told? Luke and Rebecca were dead. He would have to have told Pastor David. I should have written to Pastor David, don't you think? Don't you think so, Thomas? I should have written to Pastor David.'

'You could write to him now,' said Thomas.

'He was sixty-something years old when I left,' Azalea said. 'He would be in his eighties now. I doubt if he's still alive.'

'So write to someone else,' Thomas suggested.

'I've googled the mission,' she said, 'but it doesn't seem to exist.'

'Well then,' Thomas said; and he may have imagined that the crisis was over.

'But that doesn't mean anything, does it? It's just a little farmstead on the Sudanese border. Why would they have a computer, let alone a website? The country's had twenty years of civil unrest; they've had a God-almighty war to the north; they've had Joseph Kony stealing their kids and weaving his magic spells; they've had AIDS and TB and malaria and malnutrition. Why build a fancy website?'

'They probably wouldn't,' agreed Thomas. 'Or maybe the mission simply isn't there any more.' Maybe, he thought, when Luke and Rebecca died, everyone else gave up and the place was turned back into little parcels of farmland the way it had once been before progress and the white man ever found his way up the West Nile to Moyo District. 'So who will you write to?' Thomas asked.

'I won't,' Azalea said. 'I'll fly into Entebbe and take a bus to Gulu, and then another bus to Moyo, and then I'll get a bicycle taxi to take me ten miles to Langadi and then I shall walk up the main driveway and if no one is there, then I'll knock on the door. Someone must be living in the mission house. It is too nice a place to be empty.'

'And what about Kony and his people?'

'From what I've read,' said Azalea, 'they're still around, but not so active in Acholiland. Things are more peaceful now. Uganda had elections in March. Museveni is still in power, of course, but presidents in Africa don't get thrown out by elections. Not often. The country has a fairly free press. Some vocal opposition. The place is getting back on its feet. And now the war in Sudan is over, well, anything is possible.'

'Well,' Thomas said, 'I think it will be good for you. How long will you go for? A week? Two?'

Azalea looked out of the window at the grey curtain of rain and she thought of the red dust of Africa and the yellow sun and the dark green fields and the olive hills. She thought of the children in their blue uniforms and the women in the queue for water and Odokonyero and his cassava porridge. She thought of Anyeko and the goats, and the farm boys and Matron Maria. She thought of the bright fruit in the trees, and the scarlet flash of the gonolek bird, and the ding ding ding of the mission bell and the smell of fresh roasted coffee. She thought of the bed-time stories that Rebecca would read, and the songs that Luke would sing, and the sermons that Pastor David would recite and the hymns the congregation would chant. She thought of the multitude of voices, and the brightly coloured garments, and the billboards for Omo and Fanta, and the noise, and the smell of the two-stroke scooters. She thought of the lizards that would flicker up the walls, and the precious comfort of a mosquito net over the bed and the smell of pyrethrum spray at bedtime. And the images that had haunted her dreams for so long, for so very long, seemed on that grey morning in that grey concrete café to dissolve in the rain. The memory of the guns and the thumb ties and the cold, impassive faces of the boy soldiers. Those images had gone. The memories of the missile smashing into the truck, of John Hall shouting, 'Run run RUN', of the wall of flame and the deafening sound and the smell of burning; she could compartmentalise these memories now. Maybe this was the first time. Maybe she had been running all these years: running from Joseph Kony, running from the picture in her mind of

Rebecca and Luke lying dead in the red dust of the mission yard.

Thomas was nodding his foolish approval, but he was a long way away. She knew now that he would never understand. He would never see what she could see, never hear the call that she could hear. He was stuck here in a city that was as cold and as wet and as unfriendly as a gravestone. He had once been engaged to be married, she recalled. But he had chosen this city. He chose to stay here. He was an anchor here, in this city of colourless rain, chained to the buildings, and his routine, and his work. He was an anchor she could never hope to reel in. It would be unkind to take him away from all of this. This was where he belonged, with his books and his numbers. She hadn't seen it clearly until now. He was a tree stump in her path. Without knowing, she had always known. There was only one thing she could do, and she had to do it. Azalea scooped up her phone from the coffee-shop table and pulled her coat tight around her. 'I'm sorry, Thomas,' she said, 'but I have to go.'

He was suddenly alarmed. 'You have to go where?' he said. He was reaching for his coat.

'No, no, no.' She reached out a hand to stop him. 'I have to go,' she said again.

He was confused now. 'Wait. I'll come. Where are you going?'

'Please stay here. Please stay. Drink your tea.' She planted the briefest of kisses on his forehead. 'I love you, Thomas,' she whispered, and she held his head for a moment in her hands and took a long last look at his goofy face and his confused grin. 'I love you. But I have to go. There will never be another time.' She gave him a longer kiss, and then she pulled back. This was the Acholi way. This was the way that Luke had walked away from his brief rebellion in a street in Ladbroke Grove. Like the hyena she had been defeated by two roads, and her life had become one long equivocation. The time had come to choose a path and continue on running. She had run into a tree stump, but the stump hadn't killed her. It had been one hell of a tree stump. It had been a stump of brutal abduction and violent liberation. It had been a long search for three fathers. But in the end, none had been her father. John Hall had rolled out of her life in the back of a truck. Peter Loak was trapped in his Lakeland cottage scribbling out his simple rhymes. And Gideon Robertson had embraced his destiny in the cold, unforgiving waters of the Irish Sea. Ritchie and Lauren were well on their way to happy-ever-after. And Thomas … Well, Thomas would always be Thomas, with his unfathomable research projects and his tables of statistics, with his laundry and his ironing and his afternoons of televised sport.

It was raining hard as she walked out of the coffee shop. On the Hungerford Bridge she drew her phone from the pocket of her coat and she cast it over the rail. Above the grey waters of the Thames a rainbow had formed. She looked at it with satisfaction. The hyena was on its way.

24

February 2012–June 2012

In the weeks that followed that rainy February day when Azalea Lewis had walked out of the riverside café, Thomas Post was forced to come to terms with the vacancy in his life that Azalea had created. Clementine Bielszowska might have recognised the symptoms, might have been able to offer a diagnosis of Thomas's condition during those weeks. She might have referenced a familiar psychological pathway, the Elisabeth Kübler-Ross grief cycle. The five stages – denial, anger, bargaining, depression and, finally, acceptance – are not unique to bereavement; they can equally apply to personal life changes. In the case of Thomas Post, they could tender to the break-up of a relationship.

Denial, the first stage, infected Thomas even as he sat in the dismal coffee shop, even as Azalea's final words to him echoed in his ears. He took his time, waited for the rain to abate and then he strolled east along the Thames pathway and across the river on the Millennium footbridge. Denial defined Thomas Post at this moment. He would give Azalea an hour or so to work out whatever it was that was bothering her, then he would telephone. Perhaps later they could meet up in Highgate. Maybe they might go to see a film. He walked the three and a half miles back to his flat, up past Shoreditch, cutting through the park to London Fields. In the park he tried to call her. Her number was unobtainable. Perhaps, he told himself, she was on the Underground somewhere. He didn't leave a message.

He didn't visit her flat that night. Nor the next. But something was up. Her phone, he decided, must be out of order. At lunchtime on the Monday he popped his head around the door of the little office at Birkbeck College. 'Do you know where Azalea is?' he asked of the round-faced, dreadlocked woman who had once slid a vase across a desk to accommodate his damaged flowers.

'Apparently,' said the woman, 'she has resigned.'

'Resigned? What do you mean ... resigned?' Denial.

'I thought you might know about it.' It was almost an accusation.

There was a removal van parked outside Azalea's apartment building in Highgate that evening. Two men were heaving the last of a pile of boxes into the back. Thomas ignored the van – barely noticed it – as he pushed past to the front door and scaled the steps to Azalea's flat. His key still worked, but the flat was bare.

Even denial on the scale of Thomas's must admit some evidence to the contrary. He descended the steps two at a time. The removal van was pulling away from the kerb.

'Wait!' Thomas found himself knocking desperately on the window of the cab. 'Where are you taking this stuff?'

One of the removal men slowly wound down his window. 'Is it yours?' he asked.

'No,' said Thomas. 'Yes ... No ... I mean, I know the woman who lived here.'

The removal man proffered a meaningful smile. 'It sounds to me, mate, as if she doesn't want you to know.' The window slid back up.

Denial.

Trudging back to Highgate tube, Thomas tried to remember their closing conversation. What had Azalea said? Two weeks in Africa, wasn't that it? Hadn't she said she would be gone for two weeks? He could wait for two weeks. Two weeks would be nothing. Maybe, when she got back, she would move in with him. Maybe they would find a flat together.

But something was gnawing away at him. He was at that stage in the cycle when denial passes the baton onto anger.

The letter arrived at his house a week later, and was pushed underneath his front door by a neighbour. It seemed hastily written, in fading biro, on the notepaper of a Kampala hotel. *Dear Thomas*, it read.

And he flung it down without reading further. In his mind he was already composing a reply. Hurt and angry, his letter would demand some answers. 'Why didn't you tell me?' he would write. 'Why couldn't you let me know you were moving out, or where you were going? I thought we had something. I thought we *meant* something to each other. Clearly I was wrong.' He left Azalea's letter unread on his welcome mat as he stormed down four flights of stairs and set off for work. Halfway to the bus stop he relented. He turned back and climbed the steps to his flat. There, he sat on the floor of his living room and read the letter.

Dear Thomas,

First, you must know that I love you. If this letter brings you hurt and pain, know, my love, that it wounds me too.

You, my dearest Thomas, were ever the rational one. I would not change that in you. You understand the clockwork cogwheels of our lives, the tick and the tock of the universe; you can fit together the pieces and count the clicks. You know how the numbers stack up and how the dice will fall, and when I hear you say it I know you speak the truth, and there is nowhere I would rather be in my deepest despair than in your arms, listening to your voice, feeling the beat of your heart.

But there is, I fear, another truth, and this is one that I can know, and you with your calculations never can. I know, in a way that you do not, that my life has a beginning and a middle and an end. And I know that my destiny does not obey your rules and your logic. I was born because the universe decreed that it should be so. I lost my mother when I was three because the universe decreed this too. I know this to be true. I don't know, my love, if this was the work of God, or the Devil, or a force that we have never chosen to name. I only know that the pages of the book were written before I was even born. By chance, or by design, I met two men who claimed to be my father; one in a wet and windswept valley, and one in a violent battle in the deserts of Sudan. My grandfather died on a midsummer day in the third year of a decade. My real mother died on a midsummer day in the third year of a decade. The man who must have been my father died at sea on a midsummer day, in the third year of a decade. And the parents who adopted me died nine years and eight months ago, and they died on a midsummer day, and that midsummer day was a perfect day, a Langadi day with a clear blue sky, and the year was 1992, the third year of the decade. And not a day goes by, my love, when I do not rise and think of that day, and think of another day just four months away when the pieces of the clockwork will come together again, and then there will be only one person left to die. And that person will be me.

When I talk of this, my love, you dismiss this, as, of course, you must.

But I cannot run away.

Maybe you are right. Maybe this is all a random mess. But every day I count down the days.

I failed in one prediction. This might give us hope. I failed when I said that I would meet another man who called himself my father, and I failed when I said that this man would be blind. Gideon Robertson is at peace beneath the grey waves. I never met him, and he never lost his sight. This gives me comfort, because this is your voice, Thomas, the voice of reason, the voice that says that I have been seduced by a cruel concatenation of events that has no meaning.

Yet every day the sun must rise. And every day I will count the days. And every day brings me closer.

I have to go back, Thomas. This is no place for you. I don't know if the mission at Langadi is still there, but there are hundreds of missions in Uganda. One of them is calling me. I will find it.

It is not cruelty that makes me leave you, Thomas. It is the call of something greater than us both. It is not cruelty.

It is love.

My wish is for us to be together. But the universe does not always grant our wishes, does it? And dreams, as you would say, don't necessarily come true.

So take good care, my love. This letter is my goodbye. Hold me in your heart, and I will hold you in mine. But do not look for me over your shoulder. I will not write again. If we meet again, whichever way the universe decrees it, it will be in a better place.

Azalea

In the Elisabeth Kübler-Ross grief cycle, anger will morph into a state of mind that Kübler-Ross calls 'bargaining'. Thomas Post, after all, was not by nature a man given to anger. He was an easy-going man, a conciliatory individual, someone for whom bitterness and self-pity would sit uncomfortably upon his large shoulders. Bargaining is a feature of the grief cycle that should have applied more easily to Thomas than anger. But how do you bargain with an absent lover? And how, more appositely, do you bargain with the universe?

Thomas's bargain with the universe was his website. He set to it with a new sense of vigour. The experiment, so the bargain went, would prove to humanity that only chance and purpose govern the unfolding of our lives. No supernatural being or fantastic illusion can spell out our destiny for us; can say, 'On this day you will meet your long-lost father', or 'On this day you will surely die'. If this was a bargain, then it would seem to break all of the natural rules of contract; but Elisabeth Kübler-Ross might have recognised it all the same. Thomas's covenant with the cosmos was fuelled by defiance. 'I will prove you wrong,' Thomas seemed to be crying. 'I will prove you wrong, and Azalea will live.' At another time, in another set of circumstances, Thomas might have seen the folly of his enterprise. But this wasn't, at its heart, an attempt to challenge the cherished beliefs of religionists or New Age thinkers; it was, for Thomas, more of a mathematical challenge, an empirical snub of the nose towards the universe itself. Effect will follow cause, reasoned the philosopher. The hand will pull the tiller and the boat will turn. But there is no invisible hand. There can be no invisible effect.

For if there was, then Azalea might be right.

And if Azalea was right, then the calendar would spin on its evil wheel.

And on Midsummer's Day, Azalea would die.

Depression will follow bargaining. It is a part of the cycle. Thomas spent Easter at an aunt's home in Belfast. She was his mother's only sister. They sat down, just the two of them, to a roast dinner as sleet lashed the windows of the little council house.

'What became of that girlfriend of yours?' asked his aunt.

'We're not together any more,' said Thomas. It was the first time he had used these words. It almost shocked him to be saying them. It surprised him, too, how true the statement felt.

'I'm sorry,' said his aunt.

'Don't be,' said Thomas reflexively. 'We weren't right for one another.' And that, of course, felt like a lie.

He was going to phone Ritchie and Lauren. He was going to ask them about Azalea. He would ask where she was. Had she found a mission? Had she found somewhere to live? Was she in touch? Did they have a telephone number? An address?

But depression prevented that call. Depression inhibited his fingers from dialling their number. Depression is the enemy of action.

He walked into Belfast on a day when the clouds seemed heavy with rain, past the Harland and Wolff shipyards on Queen's Island, with their gigantic steel gantries and their sense of desolation. This is where they built the *Titanic*, he thought. And he thought about Violet Jessop, who had boarded the *Titanic* as a stewardess, here in Belfast docks. He walked across the Queen Elizabeth Bridge and into the city. He knew these streets from his childhood, but how they had changed. The roadblocks and checkpoints were gone. There were new buildings of steel and glass. There were billboards, and cheerful lights, and crowds hunting for bargains in the sales.

The shoppers should have lightened his mood, but they served instead to magnify his loneliness. He wasn't a Belfast boy any more. His accent was more Bloomsbury than Sandy Row. 'Where do any of us belong?' he wondered. Azalea was a Manx girl who could only feel at home in the heat and dust of West Nile. Where was home for Thomas Post?

Still, just as anger was never a defining trait for Thomas, neither, thankfully, was depression. Back in London, as April spent out its days, as routine and habit asserted their hold, so the darkest days of Thomas's winter began to lift. Depression was giving way to acceptance. The numbers were starting to clock up for his experiment as early users began to register outcomes. It was far too early, of course, for any real conclusions, but Thomas built his spreadsheets and constructed his graphs in preparation. Yet there was also a sense of hopelessness about the enterprise. He was struck by the triviality of the incidents he was trying to compute. Here was a woman who lost a book on a train, and found another book, of the same title, abandoned in a hotel room. Then she lost the second book. She registered onto *The Coincidence Authority* website and forecast that she would find a third copy of the book. Then she wrote again with an outcome. She had discovered a volume by the same author on her sister's bookshelves. Only the title was different. Thomas hunched over his computer and hazarded some mathematics. What were the chances, he thought, that sisters might share an interest in the same author? High. And his interest would wane. He would score down the outcome and turn to another. A woman had visited two psychics and both had predicted that she would come into a fortune. She'd been onto Thomas's website to forecast that a third psychic would make the same prediction. Now, two weeks later, lo and behold, the impossible had happened. A Gypsy fortune teller had painted the same rosy picture. Thomas sighed. What odds would you offer on a psychic *not* predicting a fortune? He punched his keyboard. Trivial, he thought. Trivial, trivial, trivial.

He would stare for long minutes from his attic window, would throw breadcrumbs to visiting pigeons, would make endless cups of weak tea, would sit at his desk with his head buried in his hands. He would deliver his lectures, conduct his tutorials, mark student papers. But all the magic, the sense of discovery, the drive to experiment seemed to have deserted him. Only one coincidence now mattered. Sometimes he could imagine the universe turning, like great brass cogwheels in a cosmic clock, and a pendulum swinging among the galaxies, and giant hands sweeping across all of creation, and all of this to deliver one bitter judgement every ten years to the bloodline of Azalea Lewis.

No. No.

He would pound his desk with a fist.

No.

The universe didn't work like that. There was no hitsuzen. Only guzen. No stars directing our fate. No evil watchmaker. No magic.

But still his eyes would flash to the calendar, to a single date. The twenty-first of June. He never needed to count the days. He had started the countdown in his head almost from the day that Azalea had left. Now he knew. He always knew. 'Twenty-seven days,' he would whisper. 'Nineteen days.'

'Eleven days.'

He would stalk morosely down the corridors of the university, would sit alone in the cafeteria with his crossword and his desolate thoughts. Thomas Post, the Coincidence Man, was withdrawing into a shadow, a pensive, waiting presence. And every tick of every clock was part of the great machinery of providence, the inexorable, inevitable collisions of atoms, of billiard balls and human beings, thrown off course by the impact, but only into new trajectories – ones that had been preordained by science and mathematics and eternal logarithms, tick tock, tick tock.

Eight days.

Seven days.

Six days.

25

June 2012

Thomas walks from his office to Primrose Hill. It is a beautiful afternoon. He takes the footpath through Regent's Park, up through St Mark's Square under the canopy of trees. There are tourists picnicking on the lawns and couples enjoying the sun. He has plenty of time. He sits for a while on a bench, watching a squirrel inspect a waste bin. Four months have passed since Azalea walked out of his life. He feels a longing for her now, an aching to see her face, to touch her hair, to breathe her soft scent. If he closes his eyes he can see her. There are little crease-lines round her eyes; a tilting asymmetry to her smile. There's a frown she makes when he catches her deep in thought. He can hear her soft laughter.

There are few places quite as solitary as a park bench when thoughts like this invade. Thomas feels the depression of Azalea's loss returning and he stands up with resolve.

The pathway takes him up past the zoo and down along the canal towpath. He can see the swaying necks of the giraffes.

Clementine is at her front door even as he rings the bell. 'Come in, dear boy, come in.' She bustles him down the hallway and into her library. 'Take a seat.'

He's in a book-lined room. There is heavy oak furniture, and an upright piano bearing upon it the marble bust of a bearded man. He lowers himself tentatively onto the edge of a chaise longue.

'I promised you tea,' Clementine says. 'So tea you shall have.'

'Really, you don't need ...' he protests.

But she waves him down. 'Wait there.'

She bustles out of the room, walking, he notices, without her stick. He considers following. Perhaps he should offer to help. But her instructions were clear. He must wait. He casts his eyes about the room. He has been here before, but only once. Clementine is his mentor, assigned on the day he joined the university. He met her here and they talked into the night, drank a great deal of claret, shared a good many secrets. Since then she has become less of a mentor and more a friend.

She re-emerges with a tea tray. He is relieved to find that her definition of making him tea does not extend to a meal. She has brewed tea in a pot, and provided a plate of Polish placek and petits fours.

'Clementine, you are a wonder,' he says.

She pours the tea, and as Thomas helps himself to a cake, she settles into an armchair. 'Are you familiar with Dr Freud's concept of fixation?'

He shakes his head. 'Should I be?'

'Not necessarily.' She waves a dismissive hand. 'You know what I think of Herr Freud. Anyhow. Freud saw it as a psychosexual neurosis. I'm far less sure.'

'Clementine, what are we talking about, exactly?'

'Ah.' She gives him a smile. 'I think perhaps all these coincidences surrounding Azalea, I think perhaps it gives you a fixation. Would you agree?'

'I might,' he says, 'if I knew what you were talking about.'

'Number one,' she raises a slim finger, 'you have a fixation on this girl. You think about her all the time. Am I right?'

He shakes his head. 'Clementine, you promised not to psychoanalyse me.'

'This isn't psychoanalysis,' she protests, 'this is helping a friend.'

'But you're talking about Freud.'

'Then let us forget him. Let's talk about you.'

He sighs, giving in to the inevitable.

'Number two. You have a fixation on this date. Midsummer's Day.' She arches her eyebrows. 'Am I right?'

He finds himself nodding.

'If anyone else were to come to you, anyone in the world, with a trillion-to-one prediction, would you give it serious consideration?' She cocks her head gently.

'Perhaps not.'

'Most certainly not.' She claps her hands. 'But this is Azalea, and she is the one person – the *only* person – who could convince the Coincidence Man to believe in the unbelievable.'

Thomas shrugs his shoulders. It is never easy to disagree with Clementine Bielszowska.

'So how do we cure a fixation?'

'Does it matter?' he replies. 'In two days it'll be midsummer. After that it won't matter what I believe.'

'Maybe so. Maybe so.' She raises her teacup. 'But maybe we can break the fixation before then.'

He is uncomfortable. He shifts on the chaise longue.

'Do you think she will kill herself?'

The question surprises him. 'Azalea?'

'Of course Azalea.'

'Why would I think that?'

'Because she is convinced that the day after tomorrow should be the day of her death? Because she has persuaded herself?'

Thomas shakes his head. 'No. She wouldn't do that.'

'Good.' Clementine seems happy with this answer. 'Then let us consider your fixation. It is consuming you from within. And how shall we address this? Hm?'

'I don't know.'

'We must demolish the logic. We have to unpick this set of coincidences. Would you agree?'

He feels a sense of reluctance. Does he really want to explore this again? 'I don't know,' he protests. 'I have been over it a hundred times.'

'I'm sure you have.' She puts down her tea. 'First,' she says, 'shall we demolish this one hundred and seventy trillion figure? Now I'm not the expert, but it seems to me that your sums don't work.'

'Why not?'

'Because first, all of the deaths up to and including Rebecca Folley's death had already happened when Azalea made her prediction. So the chances of them happening were …?'

'One,' Thomas says.

'Good. So Azalea's prediction – if it is worth anything – should be based on the actuarial tables of her life. What are the chances of a healthy thirty-three-year-old accurately predicting the day of her death?'

'I don't know.'

'Indulge me. Do some sums.'

'Well I don't have the tables, but let's say she might reasonably have expected to live for fifty more years. Fifty multiplied by three-six-five is … I don't know, but it isn't anywhere near the trillions.'

'No,' Clementine agrees. 'It isn't. So here's another thing.' She turns some papers over on her tea table. 'This was hard to find.' She hands a page to him.

'What is it?'

'Weather records. For the Irish Sea, in 2002.'

He looks at them, uncomprehending.

'So when was the squall?'

'Which squall?'

'Thomas,' she says kindly, 'do you have to be so slow?'

'I'm sorry.' He sits upright. 'The squall that killed Gideon?'

'Yes,' she says. 'When was it?'

He looks at the page.

'About midday,' she tells him. 'Midday on the twentieth of June. The boys stayed out all night looking for him. They radioed the coastguard and they searched all that night and again at first light the next day. He was officially listed as dead when the Clagues moored up without him. That was on the morning of the twenty-first. But do you think he was swimming around in the Irish Sea in a gale for twelve hours?'

Thomas is shaking his head slowly in disbelief.

'Neither do I.'

'Which means,' Thomas says, inhaling audibly, 'that he probably died on the twentieth.'

'Now we're getting somewhere.' Clementine finds another set of papers. 'Thank heavens for the internet,' she says. 'How would we manage without it?'

She passes him a document stapled at the corner. 'I have friends in the police force,' she says with a smile. 'I used to do some work for them.'

He is looking at the document in disbelief. 'The police report on Carl Morse?' he says.

'In which Morse says that the woman he abducted from the fair at Totnes came of her own free will. But we have our doubts about free will, don't we? Anyhow, he claims to have taken her from the fairground at around nine o'clock. Now he didn't know the date because he made this confession some years later – but we *do* know the date. We know that he abducted Marion on 21 June 1982. In his confession Morse says that he drove her to a lock-up garage in Launceston – where, he says, he entertained her. Then eventually, according to his statement, he left in the early hours of the morning and drove her to the cliffs at Millook. There they argued, and she inconveniently leaped over the edge. What is the key point there, dear boy?'

Thomas is leafing through the report. 'So she probably died ...'

'On the twenty-second of June. Is it all looking quite so coincidental now?'

Some colour seems to have returned to Thomas's face. 'Is there any more of that cake?'

She passes him the plate and he helps himself.

'Have we addressed the fixation?' she says, smiling.

'I'm not sure.'

'Well then. There is one more thing. Something I need from you.'

'Anything.' He feels as if a weight is slowly lifting from his shoulders.

'Five hundred and sixty-two pounds and forty-eight pence,' she says.

He experiences a moment of dissonance. 'Five hundred and sixty-two pounds?'

'And forty-eight pence.'

'I … I … don't have it.'

'My dear boy, I don't expect it now. You may pay me when you get back.'

He looks befuddled. 'Back? Back from where?'

'You need to be at Heathrow tomorrow morning at six thirty,' she says. She hands him a final set of papers. 'You might want to go home and get some sleep.'

'Where are we going?'

'Thomas,' she says, 'you are a wonderful friend and a very fine human being; one of the best I have known. But sometimes you're incredibly slow. *We* aren't going anywhere. You are.'

He is looking at the printout. 'Uganda?'

'Treat it as part of your research. Go and see if Luke Folley is still alive. Go and find Azalea. Make sure she is well. You have two days.'

He looks doubtful. She waves him away. 'Now get yourself out of my house. You need to book a taxi for three forty-five.'

26

June 2012

Uganda takes Thomas by surprise. It is a whole lot brighter than he'd expected. Greener. More lush and more fertile. It is noisier, dirtier. It is busier. He is startled by the intensity of the place. The bustle of traffic on the road into Kampala; the swarming, weaving throngs of motor scooters with their blaring hooters, the flocks of matatu minibuses packed tight with commuters on their way home, the grinding gears and dust of ancient lorries piled unfeasibly high with produce, the shoals of bicycles flooding into every empty space. He is taken by the shiny, round faces; the beaming smiles of schoolgirls in pristine uniforms and Victorian bonnets and bright, glass earrings; the warm and open faces of the walkers – those thousands who, perhaps, can afford neither a bicycle nor matatu to get home from work; the relaxed and easy faces of the roadside traders sitting alongside giant heaps of shoes or boxes of unidentifiable vegetables, negotiating with raised voices and waving hands. He is struck by the businessmen walking the dusty roadsides in starched and ironed shirts, by the women in their colourful cotton frocks, by the policeman at the junction blowing his whistle and waving his arms, to little avail.

Thomas sits in the back of his taxi, the tourist who should have taken a front seat, gazing through the soiled window and perspiring into his polo shirt. He has nothing but a vague plan. It has all been too quick. It is almost evening. He will make for a hotel in the capital, stay the night, freshen up and find a way to travel north to Langadi. Tomorrow will be Midsummer's Day.

The taxi swings into the leafy courtyard of a reassuringly modern hotel.

The next morning, with clear instructions from the hotel receptionist, he sets off for the Old Kampala Bus Park. It isn't even seven o'clock, but this part of town is already filled with a density of crowds that Thomas has only ever seen outside a football stadium. The taxi picks its way through the press of people and drops him, apparently at random, when the crowd becomes too dense to navigate.

'Tell this man where you're going,' the taxi driver says as Thomas counts out the unfamiliar bills for his fare.

'This man' is a youth who has swung open the car door and has helped himself to Thomas's duffel bag.

'Er ... Gulu,' says Thomas, as the youth sets off purposefully with the bag. Thomas, uncertain what to do, gives chase.

He ends up, reunited with his luggage, on a huge yellow bus already heavy with passengers. His duffel bag is squeezed into an impossible space on the luggage rack. The youth pulls him towards a middle seat in a row of four hard seats, and he squeezes improbably between a thin man wearing a white lace hat and a large woman in her Sunday best. By now he is ridiculously hot, sweating into the armpits of a second polo shirt, and asking himself what in heaven he is doing in this far-flung corner of the Commonwealth. Yet it's an adventure. He is no more crushed here than he might have been on a Northern Line tube train to Charing Cross.

It is an hour before the bus pulls away, with accompanying cheers from the passengers, and it feels like another hour before they break free of the Kampala traffic.

'How long is this trip?' Thomas asks the man in the white lace hat. He points to his watch.

'To Gulu?' the man asks.

'Yes. To Gulu.'

'It is very short,' the man reassures him. 'Very short.'

Thomas feels himself relaxing. It is Midsummer's Day. He feels an urge to find Azalea before nightfall.

'Six hours,' the man says, helpfully. 'No more than seven hours. No more than seven.'

'I think it will be eight hours,' says the woman in her Sunday best.

'Eight hours?' Thomas groans.

'No more than eight hours,' says the man in the hat. 'No more than eight.'

'Thank you,' says Thomas. He wants to stop the conversation before the journey gets even longer. How far is it, he wonders, from Gulu to Langadi? He is worried now. What if he should arrive too late? What if Azalea's prediction were to come true?

But of course he mustn't think like this. He checks himself. It is a simple fixation, he tells himself. A psychosexual neurosis.

'We will be there by six o'clock,' the man in the hat confirms confidently.

Thomas looks at his watch. It is almost nine in the morning.

'Unless,' the woman adds, 'we have a breakdown.'

The roadway is tarmac all the way to Gulu. Thomas stares through the window on the long, straight stretches as the farms and fields of Africa roll past. He feels like a child now, struck with an innocent awe by the ancient scenery, by people whose way of life barely seems to have changed for centuries. 'What are those?' he wants to ask, spying the tall sacks of charcoal for sale along the route. 'And what is that?' as an Ankole cow with unfeasibly long horns crosses the road in front of them. Every village seems to be baking bricks. Children line the roadsides selling fruits. Every now and then they pass through a township and passengers disembark. And every town has half a dozen shop-fronts advertising mobile-phone networks; and every town, large or small, displays a forest of painted signs announcing schools, missions, hospitals, churches or NGOs. Thomas feels encouraged by these. There seem to be countless missions on the road from Kampala to Gulu. Perhaps, he imagines, the Holy Tabernacle Mission of St Paul to the Needy of West Nile might still be there. Perhaps he will find it intact. Perhaps Azalea will still be alive. Perhaps she might come out to greet him.

It is almost dusk when they reach Gulu. 'How do I get to Langadi?' he asks the bus driver.

'Langadi?'

'Near Moyo.'

'Ah. Moyo. You need a matatu,' the driver says. 'A taxi.' He points to the minibuses all around the bus station. 'Tomorrow,' he says.

'No,' Thomas is anxious now. 'Not tomorrow. I need to be there today.'

The bus driver places a hand on his shoulder. 'Not today,' he says. He wags a long finger. 'Tomorrow.' He catches Thomas's crestfallen expression. 'Look,' he takes hold of Thomas's wrist and points to his watch. 'No ferry,' he says, and he shakes his head in sorrow.

'No ferry?'

The driver lets go of his arm. 'No ferry,' he confirms. 'The last one is at six.'

Thomas finds a room at the Acholi Inn. It is a little oasis of calm in a dusty township that has been within a war zone for almost three decades. It is the same place where Luke Folley passed his envelope to John Hall.

Twenty years have passed since that day.

Thomas Post sits outside in the pool garden in the cool of the evening and listens to the cicadas and the grumble of city traffic. He looks at the faces of the hotel guests sitting at tables around the bar, drinking African beers, putting the continent to rights in alcohol-fuelled conversations. Despite everything, he feels peculiarly at home here. He imagines Azalea visiting this garden as a girl – swimming in the pool, eating sliced pineapples in the shade of the jacaranda trees.

It is the day after midsummer. The sun still rises. His heart still beats. He takes a matatu minibus to Moyo, squeezed up by a window. The tarmac is no more. The matatu leaves the road for detours through every village, and sometimes on the whim of a single passenger it barrels off to destinations miles from the main route. But by now Thomas is more relaxed. Infected by the amiable and easy-going ways of the people, he leans back in his seat and watches Africa bounce past.

They rest in a town called Adjumani, and Thomas sits at a roadside bar and drinks three bottles of water. The landscape is changing. The hard red dust of Africa is giving way to the softer, whiter soil of the desert.

Another hour in the minibus, and they are at the Nile River. The ancient ferry breathing dense, black fumes clanks its way across the water towards them. This must be the Laropi ferry, Thomas thinks, remembering all that Azalea told him about this fragile lifeline to the people of West Nile Province. There is a wait of almost an hour, but Thomas relishes the opportunity to stretch his long legs and watch the slow, heavy waters of the Nile slide past on their way to the deserts of Sudan and Egypt.

After Laropi the road climbs dangerously into the mountains. Thomas should really have brought a camera. He tries to photograph one of the villages with his mobile phone but it comes out as little more than a blur on the tiny screen.

And then, at last, they are in Moyo. The matatu empties of people, and Thomas finds himself standing, slightly dazed, in a busy town square. He feels unsure quite what to do. He is aware now, as never before, of just how remote this place is. Never in his life has he travelled so far, or for so long – and his destination, now that he is here, seems disappointingly anticlimactic.

He slings his duffel bag over a shoulder and ambles into the town. No one seems to notice him. The presence of a tall, angular Englishman is clearly unremarkable even in this far-flung outpost of the old empire.

'Excuse me?' he catches the eye of a young man strolling in his direction. 'Do you know the St Paul Mission?'

The young man seems eager to help. 'The St Paul Mission?' he says, nodding his head emphatically. 'The St Paul Mission?'

'Yes,' Thomas says. 'It's in Langadi.'

'You want the hospital?' says the young man, helpfully. 'I shall show you the hospital.'

'No, no. I want the mission in Langadi. The St Paul Mission.

To the Needy. Here.' Thomas pulls from a pocket a card on which he has written the name of the mission. He hands it to the young man who surveys it gravely.

People are arriving from all directions to help.

'I can take you to the hospital,' says one man. 'Come. Come with me.'

'No, no. Thank you all the same. I don't want the hospital.'

'We have a very good hospital here in Moyo.'

'I'm sure you do.' Thomas is feeling flustered. 'But I don't need the hospital. Here.' He points to the card. 'I want this place. This mission. In Langadi.'

The card is passed around among the growing cluster of helpful bystanders.

'You want Langadi?' one man says.

'Yes,' Thomas nods. 'Langadi.'

'This is not Langadi. This is Moyo.'

'I know,' says Thomas. It is midday and uncomfortably hot now. He really should have brought a hat. Or held this conversation somewhere in the shade.

The bystanders are conferring loudly, and Thomas feels strangely removed from the hubbub. He reaches out and retrieves the card.

'There is no mission in Langadi,' a woman says firmly.

'Was there ever a mission?' Thomas looks around at the young faces. No one would remember a mission that might have closed two decades before.

'No.' The crowd seems to agree on this.

'There is a mission here in Moyo,' offers the first man. 'I shall take you there.'

'No, but thank you all the same,' Thomas says. 'I want to go to Langadi.'

A young man approaches on a bicycle.

'You want this man,' one of the locals tells him. 'You need to take this bicycle.'

But it isn't easy for Thomas with his dangling limbs and his heavy bag and his awkward sense of balance. He perches uncomfortably on the luggage rack and they wobble away from the crowd.

'How far is it to Langadi?'

'Ten miles.'

Can he endure this discomfort and this dreadful heat for ten long miles? The bicycle hits a pothole and Thomas feels as if his abdomen has been thrust up into his ribcage. His foot hits a lump in the road, the duffel bag swings heavily against his side and then he is falling – Thomas Post, and the young cyclist, and the bicycle – into the dust of the road to a chorus of amusement from the crowd.

He dusts himself off and pays the boy. 'I'll walk,' he says. He buys a bottle of water, almost aware as he does that it will be insufficient for a ten-mile walk in this heat. But now he is feeling reckless. Some of the bystanders offer to show him the way, and some walk with him for a while, but a hundred yards or so from the town he has shaken them all off and is on his own.

He sits beneath the shade of a mango tree and does some calculations. How long will this take him? Two hours, perhaps, at a jog. But never in this heat. Three hours, then. He checks his watch. It is nearly three o'clock. He reproaches himself for having abandoned the bicycle taxi quite so easily. Perhaps, he thinks, if another bicycle comes past, he could flag it down and make another attempt. But the few that do come by have passengers already. They glide effortlessly past with the feet of their customers soaring above the dust of the road.

He sets off again at a brisk pace, but the heat is gruelling and the shade intermittent. Half an hour into the walk and his water bottle is empty. Damn. He curses himself for being so impetuous.

There is a large tree ahead. Perhaps he should wait there and cool down. Maybe he will pass someone selling water.

And so it is, for an hour, and then for two. He buys a pair of mangoes from a barefoot boy and devours them like apples. Five o'clock. Surely, Thomas thinks, the sun will start to set. All along the road are the little farmsteads of the Acholi; round huts of baked brick topped with cool black thatch. It isn't correct to think that the Acholi live in mud huts, Thomas realises. This is a European perspective. The Acholi people, he sees, live outside. They simply *sleep* in their huts. These are their *bedrooms*. An Acholi man, Thomas sees, has a bigger house than any Englishman because his house is the great wide panorama of the West Nile, his roof is the blue sky of Africa, his lighting comes from the sun and the moon and the Milky Way. An Acholi man can rest in the gentle shade of his own mango tree and feast off the fruit, and then he can retire to the dark comfort of his roundhouse and let the soft smoke of his charcoal keep away the insects. Is this really so bad?

But then, of course, the Acholi have to labour. They have to rise early and tend to their animals, and they have to bend at the waist and work their fields, and they have to carry water and firewood and bundles of produce; and here there are no weekends or bank holidays, no coffee shops or supermarkets, or escalators or tube trains. They have to work, these people of Africa, Thomas thinks. Or else …

Or else what?

Or else, perhaps, they die.

He sits down to rest again. A great weariness after three days of travelling is starting to descend. He isn't used to this intolerable heat. The weight of his bag is making his shoulders ache. His feet hurt. He is painfully thirsty. What is he doing here? He is a pale, urbane philosopher used to little more than the corridors of Bloomsbury and the commuter routes of London. His natural habitat is a seminar room overlooking Gower Street, or a squash court in Camden, or a coffee house in Soho, or the dusty back room of a bookshop on Tottenham Court Road.

Perhaps – just perhaps – it is getting cooler. He throws the bag across his shoulder and sets off again. A trudge this time. A slow, methodical plod. One foot in front of the other, then another, that's a yard. Then again, that's two yards. Counting the paces, watching his shadow.

Some way ahead of him on the same side of the road a woman sits on a stool in front of her hut, selling something. Whatever it is, he shall buy it. Unless it's charcoal, of course. But if it's water, or mango, or prickly pear, hang the cost, he will buy it. One foot in front of the other; then another. How faint he suddenly feels. His head is beginning to spin. Heatstroke, he thinks. I really should have brought a hat.

One hundred yards to go. The Acholi woman is motionless on her stool. Her face is turned away.

Fifty yards and he can see. She is selling beans of some sort. Pulses. He feels a crushing disappointment. Then she turns her face towards him and for a moment his heart stops. She has no lips.

He closes the distance between them and makes himself look at the gums and teeth that define her face. On impulse he scoops up a handful of beans. 'How much?' He pulls a banknote from his wallet, an indefinable sum of money, and thrusts it into her hand. She must be a survivor of Joseph Kony, he thinks.

'Do you have any water?' he asks. He mimes the request for her. 'Water?'

The woman rises and disappears behind the roundhouse. She returns with water in a tin mug. Thomas drinks it all. He thinks about all the infections that he might catch. Amoebic dysentery, perhaps. He doesn't care. He passes back the mug.

'How far is it to Langadi?' he asks, not sure if the woman will understand; or if she will even be able to reply.

But the lipless woman holds up her bony fingers. 'Langadi,' she says, 'three.'

'Three what? Three miles?'

The woman nods mutely.

'Is there a mission in Langadi?' Thomas asks.

She gives him a piercing gaze as if computing the question.

'A mission?' he asks again. 'St Paul Mission?'

Very slowly she shakes her head. 'No.'

'No mission? Are you sure?'

She looks as if the question has alarmed her. 'No,' she says again.

Thomas releases a long and heavy breath. What stupid, futile thing has he done? He is a day late, anyway. Azalea will be dead. Or she will be alive. Like Schrödinger's cat, she is maybe dead and alive at the same time. Maybe she will be alive until he finds her. Maybe he will never find her. There are countless villages in this part of West Nile. He can't search every one.

The heat is making his head swim. He looks up and down the long dirt road, but even now, turning back seems less attractive than going on. He slips the handful of beans into a pocket and hefts the bag back onto a sore shoulder. One more foot in front of another.

And then the ring of a bell. A bicycle bell. Coasting down the gentle slope behind him comes the bicycle boy from Moyo with a wide grin across his face. 'Boda boda?' he calls to Thomas, knowing well what the answer will be.

This time as they wobble off, Thomas keeps his long legs out of the way. I'm such a fool, he thinks. This is what I should have done all the way from Moyo. Ahead of them is a little township.

'Is this Langadi?'

'Yes.'

'And is there a mission here?'

The boy shrugs and shakes his head. Thomas pays him and feels a new wave of energy. A cluster of low buildings with shops and workshops are strung out along the road. No mobile-phone stores here, Thomas notes. West Nile seems still to be holding out against the encroaching technology. He lost the signal on his own phone sometime after Laropi.

There is only one direction to go, and that is onwards. He walks the length of the town and the buildings begin to peter out. But somewhere, he thinks, the old mission must still be standing. He should at least try to find them. Someone would have seen Azalea when she came here in February. Someone, surely, would know what had become of her.

A young man is walking towards him. There is something un-gainly about his gait. As he draws closer, Thomas can see that he has no arms.

'Good day to you, sir,' he says in clear English.

'Good day to you,' Thomas replies.

'Can I help you, sir? Are you looking for something?'

'I don't know,' Thomas says. 'I was looking for a mission. But it seems that there is no mission in Langadi any more.'

'No, sir. There is no mission in Langadi.'

'Then I think perhaps I've had a wasted journey.'

The young man shakes his head sympathetically.

'Do you know how I might find someone to take me back to Moyo? A taxi perhaps?'

The young man smiles. 'There is an Englishman at the Centre,' he says. 'He has a car and a driver. I'm sure his driver can take you.'

Thomas feels the first stirrings of relief. 'Thank you,' he says. 'Can you show me where I might find this man?'

'Of course. Just follow me.' The man with no arms turns around and starts down the road in the direction that Thomas had been heading.

'You speak excellent English,' Thomas tells him.

'Thank you. I had a very good teacher.'

'Where did you go to school?'

'Here in Langadi,' the man says. 'At the Centre.'

A bright red bird flies across their path and for a moment Thomas's attention is diverted. Thomas looks at the man. 'How did you lose your arms?'

'They were cut off, sir. When I was just a boy.'

'Cut off?' It seems almost too appalling to say. 'By Joseph Kony?'

'You know of Joseph Kony then?' the man says.

Thomas nods.

'It was his men. His men did it.'

Something is surfacing in Thomas's mind. 'What is this Centre you mentioned?'

'It's here, sir.' They have rounded a corner and there in front of them is a signboard, one of the thousands of signboards that decorate the roadways of Uganda. This one reads, 'The Rebecca Folley Centre for the Children of Conflict'.

Thomas's heart begins to race. 'This is it!' he cries. 'This is the mission!'

'No, sir. This is a rescue centre.'

'A rescue centre?'

'Yes, sir.'

'A rescue centre for children who were abducted by the LRA?'

'Yes, sir.'

A dirt driveway leads from the road to a cluster of buildings almost hidden among trees. Around the compound is a high wooden fence, and topping the fence, a coil of barbed wire.

'It looks like a prison,' Thomas says.

'No, sir, it isn't a prison,' says the man with no arms. 'The wire is to keep the LRA men out.'

The driveway is protected by a high wire gate. A tall man, wearing fragments of a uniform, lets them through. They walk up the murrum drive. A cluster of children gather to watch them. Most of the children, Thomas is relieved to see, are undamaged.

As for the 'rescue centre', it isn't quite how Thomas has pictured it. It is shabbier, somehow, than the mission in his imagination. The buildings are dusty and rather unkempt; the once whitewashed walls are stained the colour of overripe bananas. The vegetation grows wild and the grass is sparse. But ahead is an inviting, open-sided building that can only be the mess hall. This would be the place where Kony and his men first confronted the Folleys. There are tables and benches and a kitchen space where a large, greying Acholi man is stirring a huge stewpot over a charcoal stove. He is barking commands to a clutch of teenage assistants, and one is setting out forks and knives on tables in preparation for dinner.

In a winged wicker armchair, looking out over the compound, sits a European man; his mirrored sunglasses, weathered face and long grey hair lend him the look of an ageing rock star.

The man with no arms addresses him. 'Mr Boss,' he says, 'I have a visitor here to see you.'

The grey-haired man turns in his chair to face them. 'You'll forgive me if I don't get up,' he says.

Thomas holds out his hand but the man appears to ignore it.

'I don't get many visitors,' he says. 'Do I know you?'

'No, sir. My name is Thomas Post,' says Thomas.

'Ah,' says the man. 'Then I do know who you are.'

'You do?'

'Of course I do. Can I offer you a drink? You must have travelled a long way.'

Thomas feels the weariness flood over him again. He sinks down onto a stool. 'Yes please. I should love something to drink.'

'I'll get one of the boys to fetch it,' says the man with no arms. 'Tea, coffee, or something stronger?'

'Tea,' says Thomas. 'Tea, please. Not too strong. And water, if you have some.'

'Of course.'

'Azalea told me you're a tea drinker,' the grey-haired man says.

Thomas feels his head spinning. 'Azalea told you?'

'Indeed. She tells me everything.'

Tells me. The glorious present tense. Thomas finds himself choking on his words. 'Azalea ... so she ... she's ... still alive?'

The man looks puzzled by this remark. 'Of course. Why shouldn't she be?'

Thomas shakes his head. His eyes have filled with tears and he turns his face away, not wanting to be seen. He feels a sob emerging like a deep eruption within his chest and he fights to keep it from bursting to the surface. Instead he manages just a whisper. 'Azalea is alive. She's alive.'

'My dear young man, what were you imagining?'

'I don't know. I'm not sure. I ...' Thomas can't turn to face the man in the wicker chair, not yet; not with his eyes brimming so. Instead, he looks out over the compound, over a raggle-taggle of buildings and trees. That low building there must be the old mission house. And that long rectangular structure – the school, perhaps? Or maybe the hospital? A man is washing a minibus with water from a bucket. A group of children are tethering some cattle to a tree. Somewhere he can hear voices singing. Children's voices.

'You must be Luke Folley,' he says.

'I am.'

'Azalea thought you were dead.'

'I know.' The man who is Luke Folley nods slowly. 'She thought I was dead, and I thought she was dead. And so we wasted twenty years.'

The voices of children are coming closer. Thomas feels a sudden sense of urgency to understand everything; to know everything. 'Why didn't you track her down?' he asks, aware as he speaks that his voice is cracking, but aware too that it doesn't matter any more. Nothing seems to matter any more. Azalea is alive. The thirty years since Marion's death are like the lost pages of a manuscript telling an ancient story that no longer has any relevance.

But Luke answers all the same. 'No one called Folley ever left Uganda, or Kenya, or Congo, or Sudan.' Luke says. 'Not one soldier of fortune ever returned to Uganda. I tracked down Kony's men and they told me that all the children had been blown up on the truck. They showed me the burned-out lorry. What was I to think?'

'I'm sorry,' Thomas says; and he truly is.

'Worst of all,' says Luke, 'Azalea never came home.'

Thomas nods.

'This place was a war zone for twenty years. We had LRA and SPLA and Uganda government forces all at each other's throats. You couldn't move in or out for a long time. The roads were blocked; the airfields were closed.'

'I see.'

'I was abducted myself by the LRA.'

'You were?' Thomas is surprised. 'I never knew that.'

'Why should you? Until four months ago Azalea didn't even know I was still alive.'

'How long did they hold you?'

'Two months. I drove up into Sudan to find them, and when I found them they were afraid I might tell the authorities where they were. So they held me captive.'

'Did they ...'

'Did they what?'

'Did they ... mistreat you?'

Luke gives a snort and his shoulders shake in a silent laugh. 'Oh yes,' he says. 'Oh God, yes. They mistreated me.'

'What did they do?'

'You don't want to know.'

There is an awkward silence. And then a group of children come around the corner of the big rectangular building that might have been the schoolhouse. They sing and call to one another gaily as they start to file into the mess hall.

'You will join us for dinner?' Luke asks. The discomfort of their last exchange has passed.

'I should love to.'

The shadows are growing longer.

'Is Azalea here?'

'No,' Luke says, and then he smiles. 'But she will be.'

'When?'

'Soon.'

The mess hall is noisy with voices now, and alive with movement. Someone rings a bell, a slow, persuasive, ding, ding, ding. Thomas finds that his face has drawn itself into a wide smile.

'The mission bell,' he whispers.

'Not any more,' says Luke. 'This isn't a mission any more.'

A girl arrives with tea in a teapot, milk, sugar, a china cup and a bottle of water. Thomas thanks her, and pours himself a cup. 'Do you want some?' he asks Luke.

'No thanks. I'm a coffee drinker.'

'Of course.' Thomas grins even wider. 'Azalea told me you liked your coffee.'

'Did she now?' This seems to please Luke.

'When did you say she'd be here?'

'Soon,' Luke says.

'Did Azalea ever tell you ... about her prediction?' Thomas asks.

'What prediction?'

'It was a … a … thing that we did on the internet.'

'Ahh yes.' Luke is contemplating this. 'I have heard of the internet,' he says. 'Never used it, of course.'

'No.'

'Nothing like that in Langadi.'

'No. I just wondered, you know, if Azalea ever mentioned …'

'Mentioned what?' says Luke. He is looking somewhere off into the distance, somewhere where the deep green hills roll away into the valley of the Nile.

'I thought that Azalea might be dead.' How foolish this sounds. How petulant the logic that might lead to such a thought. Yet saying the words wounds him still.

Luke turns his face from the vista of the mountains and the valley. 'You did?' he says, with a measure of surprise. 'Now why ever would you think that?'

Why indeed? Thomas tries to picture the great clockwork universe, the brass cogwheels, the cosmic pendulum. But no image coalesces in his mind. The elegant model that seemed so easy to visualise in the cool comfort of a London office has evaporated here at the equator. 'She predicted it.' It seems a weak response.

Luke turns away again. The red of the sunset is reflected in his glasses. 'I'm not sure why she would do that,' he says, softly. 'But I think you'll find it had something to do with you.'

'Something to do with me?'

'I think so.' Luke shrugs. 'Does it matter?'

Thomas casts his eyes around. There are thirty or forty children in the mess hall now. Some have injuries like the ones he has seen on the roadway – like the woman who sold him beans. One or two walk with crutches. One is in a wheelchair. All are crowding around the tables, ready to eat. A little yellow bird no larger than a sparrow is hopping between the tables, experienced in the search for crumbs.

'I don't know,' Thomas says, and as he says it he knows what the answer ought to be. 'No,' he corrects himself, and he contemplates this dawning truth. 'No. It doesn't matter. It doesn't matter at all.' His experiment, he realises at that moment, will be inconclusive. That is the honest outcome. There is no God. Or maybe there is. No one is messing with our lives. No one is pulling the strings. Or maybe they are. Coincidences happen. Wishes come true. Or maybe they don't. He would prove nothing. But, he realises for the first time, maybe that is the right result. The truthful result.

'I think,' Thomas says, and his grin is beginning to fade, 'that I may have been a bit of an ass.'

'Occupational hazard of the English male,' says Luke.

'Not on this scale.' He stirs sugar into his tea and tries a sip. 'Azalea predicted that she would die. Yesterday.'

Luke looks surprised. 'And you believed it?'

'I don't know. I don't know what I believed. I think she just wanted to survive Midsummer's Day.'

'I see.' Luke nods. 'Twenty years after Rebecca died?'

'Twenty years after Rebecca. Thirty years after Marion. Ten years after Gideon.'

Luke rocks slowly in the big wicker chair, and for a moment Thomas wonders if, perhaps, he has said too much.

'She told me about Marion,' Luke says, after a moment. 'And Gideon.' He turns his face away so that Thomas cannot see his expression. 'And about Peter Loak, and John Hall.'

'Azalea told me she feared that she would die on the same day as Rebecca and Marion and Gideon.'

'She told you that?'

'Yes.'

'I see. It sounds like something Azalea might say. Azalea would say that everything that happens, happens for a reason.'

'I know. She used to say that to me too.'

'And you don't believe that?'

'Do you?'

Luke takes some time to answer. 'Once I believed it,' he says softly, 'then I stopped believing it; and now I'm not sure what to believe.' Once, he might have said, a very long time ago, when I played my guitar for money and wore flowers in my hair and read the writings of Trotsky and Marx; then I might have believed it.

But a time came when I lost every fragment of belief that I ever held. And now?

'If everything happens for a reason then someone must be in control,' Thomas says.

'That's the bit,' says Luke, 'that I find hard to believe.'

The two men sit motionless for a time. It is growing cooler. Thomas pours himself a long glass of water and drinks it in a single draught.

'I expect you might be ready for a beer,' says Luke, and he gives a slow smile. 'A cold beer?'

'I'd love one.'

Luke calls out a name and one of the older children comes running up. 'Lakwo – could you bring a cold beer for this man – and one for me too?'

'Of course, Mr Luke.'

'They seem very fond of you,' Thomas says. 'The children, I mean.'

'Are they? I'm not sure. They've all had a terrible time.'

'Why did you change the place from a mission to a rescue centre?'

'It seemed like an important thing to do,' Luke says. He leans back in the chair. 'Some of the kids coming down from Sudan were Muslims. Some had no religion. It occurred to me one day that we were part of the problem. We were making this into a religious conflict simply by helping to sustain the ridiculous social convention that every child is born with a set of beliefs and that every child has to stay loyal to those beliefs until the day they die. All the missions in Africa – they all share part of the blame.'

'And was it ... a religious conflict?' Thomas asks.

'In part. One man with a set of mumbo-jumbo beliefs decided that God had spoken to him, so anyone who disagreed could be shot, or have bits of their body hacked off.'

'I see.'

A boy comes to the table with two bottles of cold beer. He has wide eyes and a beaming smile.

'Thank you.' Thomas takes a long draught. A year of anxiety

is starting to dissolve. He feels relaxed sitting here, with this man he feels that he knows.

'Would it be all right if I stayed here a night ... or two?' he asks.

'Of course,' Luke says.

Thomas has not planned much beyond this moment. 'What time will Azalea be here?'

'Soon enough. She's been to Arua. Reuniting a child with her mother.'

'Ahh.' The enormity of this responsibility fills Thomas with a sudden feeling of tenderness. Azalea is reuniting a child with her mother. A child who, presumably, has been separated from her family by war and by terror is being delivered back into the arms of her family. By Azalea. He takes another mouthful of beer.

'So what do you believe, Thomas?' Luke asks. 'Azalea thinks that everything happens for a reason. What do you think?'

'I think,' Thomas says, 'that this is what came between us. Between Azalea and me. We were compatible in so many ways, but never, somehow, in this.' He thinks about it. 'I believe that the world is a random place. If I see a rock falling down a hill, I don't imagine that anyone is controlling the way it bounces, sending it this way or that. If there were a child at the foot of the hill, then I wouldn't think that the fate of that child would be in the hands of anything except for the laws of gravity and physics.'

'So no overseeing angel? No great plan?'

Thomas shakes his head. 'If there were, then I find it hard to imagine how it would work.'

'So who *is* in control of our lives? Who manages our destiny?'

'No one.'

Luke clicks his tongue. 'Maybe Azalea couldn't live with such a nihilistic idea.'

'Maybe not.'

'The Acholi have a saying: "Each rat has its own whiskers".'

'Which means?'

'It means we are all responsible for our own problems.'

'I see.' Thomas reflects. 'I think I've been responsible for a few problems of my own.'

'I daresay we all have.'

'I convinced myself that Azalea's prediction would come true. I just assumed ...' Thomas lets the thought hang in the air.

'Do you love Azalea?' Luke asks.

'Yes, sir. I do.'

'Perhaps not enough, though? If you really love her, then why weren't you here for her yesterday?'

'I should have been.' Thomas looks sorrowfully into his beer. The scale of his stupidity is looming into focus. 'Is that what she wanted? Is that why she did this? Did she want me to be here?'

'I don't know. You shall have to ask her.'

'I wish she was here.'

'She will be. Soon.'

How fast the sunsets are here, Thomas thinks. Azalea told him this. 'Pfft,' she had said. Pfft, and it would be dark. Soon, he knew, the great blanket of African darkness would settle over the landscape, and all the way down the valley barely a flame would flicker in the void. And a great sweep of stars would litter the sky.

'In my job,' Thomas tells Luke, 'people often come to me with a story about a coincidence; something that happened to them. That's my field, you see. I'm an authority on coincidences. So someone will knock on my door, and the next thing I know they'll be telling me about the man they met on holiday who turned out to have been at the same school as their neighbour. Or else they went to buy a car, and the person selling it just happened to share the same name as them. I've heard so many of these stories. People will catch me at a dinner party, or even in the street, and they'll expect me to explain. Two sisters both married a man named Ron, and both sisters called their dogs Poppy, and both Rons have the same birthday. I'm supposed to be amazed by these stories. But I never am. I always explain that this is the way a random universe works. Sometimes when you throw two dice, you'll throw two sixes. It isn't a coincidence. It's just mathematics. And that's what I always thought. Until one day the person who came and knocked on my door was Azalea.'

'I see.'

'Azalea's coincidences seemed to be off the scale. They seemed to define her life. No wonder Azalea thinks that everything happens for a reason. In her universe, that is how it looks.'

'I suppose it does.'

'But I think I can get her to see that it isn't like that. She *did* survive midsummer 2012. There's a big question mark over some of the other dates, anyway. No one is pulling her strings.'

Luke is rocking gently in his chair. The hubbub of voices in the mess hall is making it difficult to hear the conversation. 'Maybe,' he says, so softly that Thomas has to lean forward to catch his words, 'she wants to believe it?' He makes this into a question. 'And if so, maybe you need to be comfortable with that?'

Thomas looks at him.

'If it came between you last time, why let it come between you again?' Luke says. 'Maybe there's another way. Did you ever consider that?'

'I'm not sure I quite understand ...'

'Azalea's life is a mess of contradictions and coincidences and peculiarities; things that shouldn't have happened but did; things that couldn't possibly have happened, but did. You're the expert, Mr Thomas Post. Stop trying to explain it. Start trying to embrace it. Don't poke around looking for evidence of a conspiracy. But don't try to dismiss it all, either. Enjoy it. Relish it. Look forward to the next big shock. Because there will be one. If Azalea's life teaches us anything, it at least teaches us that we need to be prepared – because anything can happen, and it probably will. Azalea came to you looking for an explanation, and you've been busy trying to provide her with one. But perhaps you don't understand what is really going on, Mr Post. Perhaps you don't really understand Azalea. What if Azalea doesn't want an explanation at all? What then? What if the thing that Azalea really wants is support? Or understanding? Did you ever consider that? What if all Azalea wants is someone to face life's surprises with her?'

It is a long speech, and it seems to have tired Luke out.

An ancient-looking man with a white beard stands up at the far end of the mess hall and taps loudly on the table.

'Time for grace,' Luke whispers. 'A bit of a hangover from the days when this was still a mission.'

The voices of the children subside and everyone stands politely.

'For those of us who believe in God, let us thank Him for this meal,' the old man intones in heavily accented English. 'And for those who do not believe, let us thank the farmers who grew the food, the donors who paid for it, the kitchen staff who cooked it and the friends who brought it to our table. Amen.'

'Amen,' chant fifty voices.

'I've never heard a grace like that,' Thomas tells Luke.

'It is our compromise,' Luke says. 'Will you help me to the table?'

'Why yes,' says Thomas, surprised. He lifts himself clumsily off his stool and holds out a hand. 'Are you in some difficulty?' he asks, painfully conscious of the tactlessness of the question.

But Luke rises effortlessly from the wicker chair with a chuckle. 'It's these sunglasses,' he declares. 'They fool a lot of people.' He holds out an arm. 'It helps if you take hold of my shoulder.'

Thomas grasps Luke's upper arm.

'Now,' Luke says, 'we have a democratic seating arrangement here, apart from me.' He swings his free arm to point in the direction of one of the tables. 'There should be a couple of spare seats at the head of that table.'

Thomas leads Luke to his seat. 'When did you ... lose your sight?'

'Oh, you know. A long time ago. Long enough to be fairly used to it, anyway.' Luke lowers himself carefully into his seat. 'Have you thought about how long you're going to stay?'

Thomas looks around. The children seem to span an age range from possibly nine or ten through to late teens. All wear simple blue uniforms and plastic sandals, and Thomas notes that there is a crest badge in white embroidered cotton on every breast pocket. The badge reads, 'The Rebecca Folley Centre for the Children of Conflict'. There are a dozen adults too, one wearing the uniform of a nurse, one in a business suit with a starched shirt, several dressed like the security man at the gate. They all have cheerful faces, the stoic yet jovial expressions of men and women who follow a calling. The big cook is ladling stew onto tin plates, a younger cook in a tall chef's hat is straining potatoes, two of the older girls are delivering jugs of water to the tables. It is a scene of practised routine, of comfortable, homely domesticity. But in the eyes of the children, Thomas fancies, just for the brief flicker of a moment, he can see something else. Something burns in those eyes, in those nervous, fleeting expressions that tell of a different, darker narrative. Every child in this hall has their own story, Thomas thinks. And every story is one of violence and unhappiness, of pain and loss.

Luke is facing him, waiting for an answer to his question.

Outside the mess hall the sky is the colour of bougainvillea.

'Have you given it any thought?' Luke asks.

And truly Thomas hasn't. 'It depends,' he finds himself saying.

'Upon what?'

And to this question Thomas Post possesses no answer. Outside, and up the driveway, a rusty old car is approaching the gate, and even now the gate is being swung open to let it pass. Along the drive it rattles with its slipstream of dust.

27

November 2012

far far out on ocean's swell
and all is well
all is well

the clapping of the klaxon bell
and all is well
all is well

the crack of boots on iron deck
a silent twisting of the neck
the echo of a distant yell
and all is well
all is well

the slamming of a steel hatch
the sliding of a heavy latch
a crashing hammer blow from hell
and naught is well
naught is well

and thirty years of darkness pass
black paint upon my looking glass
and time placates that lethal shell
all will be well
all will be well

a visitor from long times past
unlashed me from the mizzen mast
she led me from the deathly knell
to where a young man never fell
to where the memories dispel
and all is well
   all is well

so let cruel providence compel
the exodus of personnel
and when the mysteries foretell
the coming of the sentinel
then send for me
and I will tell
that all is well
all is well

p. j. loak

Explaining Azalea

This story is a work of the imagination. All the characters in this book are fictional, and none is based on any person, living or dead. Except:

(1) Joseph Kony is a real person. While none of the incidents in this book happened as depicted, Joseph Kony and his cult-like Lord's Resistance Army (LRA) have nonetheless been operating in Uganda, Sudan and the Congo for over twenty years. The BBC reports that tens of thousands have been killed by the LRA and one and a half million people have been displaced. Thousands of children have been abducted. No one knows how many have been mutilated. As far as we know, Joseph Kony still lives and still evades capture.

(2) The abduction of children from the Sacred Heart Secondary Boarding School for Girls and the St Mary's Girls School were real events. In March 1989, the LRA raided St Mary's Girls School and abducted ten schoolgirls and thirty-three seminarians and villagers. Nine of the ten girls eventually escaped. The tenth was killed some years later.

(3) For a very readable account which touches on the LRA and the Gulu abductions, I recommend Jane Bussmann's *The Worst Date Ever – Or How it Took a Comedy Writer to Expose Africa's Secret War*, a book which pulls very few punches when it comes to exposing the murky presence of the LRA in Uganda. *The Wizard of the Nile: The Hunt for Africa's Most Wanted* by Matthew Green also provides a harrowing personal view of the search for Kony.

(4) As recently as Christmas Eve 2008, according to the United Nations peacekeeping force, the Lord's Resistance Army massacred 189 people and abducted twenty children during a celebration sponsored by the Catholic Church in Faradje, Democratic Republic of Congo.

(5) Joseph Kony is ranked as the seventh most-wanted criminal in the world. Like me, you may be left wondering who the other six are, and how their crimes could possibly exceed those of Kony.

(6) The BBC reports that Kony has created an aura of fear and mysticism around himself. His rebels follow strict rules and rituals. They are commanded always to make the sign of the cross before fighting. They are also instructed to take oil and draw a cross on their chest, forehead and shoulder, and to make a cross in oil on their guns. They believe that the oil is the power of the Holy Spirit.

(7) In 2003, Uganda's parliamentary defence committee proposed hiring South African mercenaries to 'eliminate' LRA rebels. Uganda's president squashed the idea, saying that the suggestion to hire mercenaries showed a lack of confidence in Uganda's army.

(8) The missions depicted in Langadi and Kakuma were invented for the purposes of the story, and are not intended to resemble any missions present or past.

(9) No one can tell you for certain if we have free will or we don't. Neuroscientists have developed ways of measuring brain activity that seem to suggest that the unconscious part of the brain is active in making a decision around half a second before the conscious brain, and some have theorised that this is proof of determinism. Not every neuroscientist accepts these conclusions, and you may prefer to go along with Søren Kierkegaard, who argued that God would hardly have wasted his time creating us if all we were going to do was to follow a predetermined path. Whatever you choose to believe, you will probably want to agree with the philosopher John Locke, who argued that the whole debate is largely irrelevant.

If it feels to us like free will, then let's treat it as free will and get on with our lives. A lesson that Thomas Post, eventually, may have grasped.

... there's a special providence in the fall of a sparrow.
If it be now, 'tis not to come;
if it be not to come, it will be now;
if it be not now, yet it will come:
the readiness is all:

William Shakespeare, *Hamlet*

READING GROUP NOTES

FOR DISCUSSION

- *'Everything that happens . . . happens for a reason'*
  How far can Azalea and Thomas control their destinies? Do you think Thomas's attitude to fate changes during the novel?

- Although they are 'strangers in a city of strangers' when they first meet on the escalator, Thomas feels a certain 'familiarity' towards Azalea. Can you explain this?

- *'There were altogether too many choices for Marion to make a decision herself'*
  Do you judge Marion for letting God decide the fate of her unborn child?

- Have you ever struggled to make a difficult decision? Did you ask someone for help?

- Does Azalea really owe her life to a seagull?

- How much did you know about Joseph Kony and the LRA before reading *The Coincidence Authority*? Do you find the acts of violence and abductions more upsetting because they are based on real events in Uganda?

- What's the strangest coincidence in the novel?

- Marion wanted to call her daughter 'Hazel' but the vicar chose 'Azaliah' which then became 'Azalea'. She is also known as

'Girl A' at the beginning of the novel. What impact does a name have on identity? Do you imagine your life would have been different with a different name?

- How is religion presented throughout the novel? Do you find anything surprising in the author's portrait of the Reverend Jeremiah Lender?

- Thomas tells his story to his friend and colleague, Clementine Bielszowska. Does the narrative framework affect the way you see Azalea? What is Clementine's role in the novel?

- Are we free to make our own choices or is there a higher power directing our actions? Does it matter?

- Why do bad things happen?

- *'The stump of a tree can fell a running man'*
  What does this mean?

- There are lots of sayings, ancient proverbs and pieces of wisdom within the book. Do you have a favourite?

- Thomas Post is a rationalist and a mathematician; Azalea teaches literature and believes everything happens for a reason. Do you think they are compatible as a couple? What do you imagine the future holds for them?

- When Azalea goes to see Thomas, she is looking for an explanation for the coincidences in her life. Does she find one? Do you discover who Azalea's real father is? How important are answers, explanations and solutions in *The Coincidence Authority*?

FURTHER READING ON FATE AND COINCIDENCES

Classics

Hamlet by William Shakespeare

Endgame by Samuel Beckett

Moby Dick by Herman Melville

Tess of the d'Urbervilles by Thomas Hardy

Of Mice and Men by John Steinbeck

Beyond Good and Evil by Friedrich Nietzsche

Kierkegaard: A Very Short Introduction by Patrick Gardiner

The poetry of p. j. loak

Modern novels

The Humans by Matt Haig

Salmon Fishing in the Yemen by Paul Torday

Eleven by Mark Watson

The Unlikely Pilgrimage of Harold Fry by Rachel Joyce

Enduring Love by Ian McEwan

The Universe Versus Alex Woods by Gavin Extence

AN UNLIKELY ENCOUNTER:
JOHN IRONMONGER SHARES HIS STORY

My editor at W&N called me while she was reading the manuscript for my second novel, *The Coincidence Authority*.

'We're thinking of compiling a list of interesting coincidences,' she told me, 'to help promote the novel. Do you have any big coincidences that have happened to you?'

And do you know, I couldn't think of one.

I was busy at that time doing some research for my third novel. I don't want to give too much away here, but I had this idea in my mind of a young futurologist who becomes persuaded, by his own computer forecasts, that the whole world is about to collapse. He flees from the city to a remote village where he convinces the villagers to shut themselves away from the outside world to weather the economic storm. Trust me on this. It will work. Now the thing is, I needed to research my idea if I wanted to make it convincing, and so I went onto Amazon and bought a book called *Collapse* by the Pulitzer Prize-winning writer Jared Diamond (subtitle: *How Societies Choose to Fail or Succeed*). It's advertised as a No. 1 International Bestseller, and Jared Diamond himself is the undisputed world authority on these things.

Well it's a heavy book, almost six hundred dense pages, but I worked my way through it. At the end I wanted to ask Professor Diamond a question. I wanted to describe the conceit in *Not Forgetting the Whale* (that's the title of novel three) and ask him if he thought my scenario was possible. I toyed with sending him an email. But he's a professor at UCLA! Why would he take the time to read my fanciful musings?

So instead I went off on holiday with my lovely wife Sue. We spent three nights in a remote forest lodge close to Way Kambas National Park in Sumatra. It isn't a typical tourist destination (this isn't really a tourist park), and in fact we were almost the only people there. But not quite. There were two serious birdwatchers also staying, and so we shared a table at dinner. One was an Australian, and the other an American. And the American . . . (you may have guessed this already . . .) was Jared Diamond.

And while this doesn't exactly compound the coincidence, the day we met was his seventy-fifth birthday.

So there it is. I did have a coincidence to report to my editor. And of course I did bend the good professor's ear about my story, and he nodded very sagely. 'Absolutely,' he told me. 'That's a very legitimate scenario.'

But the story isn't quite over. When I told my editor my coincidence, she had one more twist to add. 'I used to be Jared Diamond's publicist,' she told me. 'I once took him to Cambridge.'

So how about that?

LOVED *THE COINCIDENCE AUTHORITY?*

Turn over to enjoy the first chapter of John's new book.

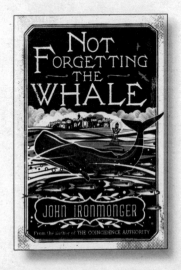

When a young man washes up, naked, on the sands of St Piran in Cornwall, he is quickly rescued by the villagers. From the retired village doctor and the schoolteacher to the beachcomber and the owner of the local bar, the priest's wife and the romantic novelist, they take this lost soul into their midst. But what the villagers don't know is that Joe Haak worked as an analyst and has fled the City amid fears of a worldwide banking collapse caused by a computer program he invented. But is the end of the world really nigh? And what of the whale that lurks in the bay?

Intimate, funny and deeply moving, *Not Forgetting the Whale* is the story of a man on a journey to find a place he can call home.

Hardback and eBook available from
Weidenfeld & Nicolson in February 2015

PART ONE

*Can You Catch Leviathan
with a Hook?*

PROLOGUE

In the village of St Piran they still speak of the day when the naked man washed up on Piran Sands. It was the same day Kenny Kennet saw the whale. Some say it was a Wednesday. Others seem sure it was Thursday. It was early October. Unless it was late September. But almost half a century has passed since the events of that day, and the turmoil of the days and weeks that followed, and no one, at that time or since, thought to write it all down. So memory is all we have, fragile though this may be. There are some in the village who claim to recollect every detail, as if perhaps it happened last week. They would have been young when these things happened, and their stories are part of a web of tales that echo of the old days, and the world as it was, and they all tell of the naked man, and they all tell of the whale.

Many who shared in these events are no longer with us. Old Man Garrow is long since dead. So too is Dr Mallory Books, and Martha Fishburne, and the Reverend Alvin Hocking, and Jeremy Melon, and many of those who helped to rescue the whale. But their stories survive and are told by the children and the grand-children of the villagers, by neighbours, and by friends. They are told too at the Festival of the Whale held in the old Norman church every Christmas Day. So if you should ever find your way to St Piran (which might be hard to do), you will hear the story in the streets and in the bars; and if you should stop a villager or two and ask, they might sit you down upon a bench with a view out over the swell of the ocean, and there they might recount the tale, about the beach, and about the whale, and about the naked man. They might, perhaps, walk you down along the ancient harbour wall and the rocky path around the headland to where the shingle and the sands begin, and there they might show you the rock where Kenny Kennet stood when he saw the whale; and just a clamber away they will point out the stretch of sand where the man named Joe was found. They might look out to sea, to the uninviting rocks that garland the beach like a giant's necklace. 'How,' they might ask you, 'could any man float among all those and not be cut to shreds?'

'It was an unconventional entrance.' That's what Jeremy Melon, the naturalist, would say of Joe Haak's arrival in St Piran when he gave the annual address at the Festival of the Whale. 'Trust Joe to get carried naked onto the beach by a whale! Other people ask for directions and drive politely onto the quay in daylight. But not Joe. Oh no. Joe wants to make a dramatic entrance. So he sneaks into town in the middle of the night, swims all the way out to sea and rides back in on a bloomin' great whale.' And every time Jeremy Melon told this tale he would bow his legs wide like a cowboy straddling an enormous horse, and he would swing one arm as if holding a lasso. You could picture Joe, mounted on the great beast, steering it through the rocks and up onto the sands. Jeremy would know, as well as anyone, that very little of that story was true; but there were tiny fragments of truth in there somewhere, and fragments of truth are often all we need to help us understand reality. Jeremy's story would make people laugh – even those who had known Joe Haak. And that, in the end, was what mattered. 'Sometimes exaggeration can be closer to the truth,' Demelza Trevarrick the novelist would say. And it seemed to Jeremy Melon that this was the way St Piran preferred to remember Joe Haak. They didn't want the serious Joe, the geek who had spent his life bent over his computers, working out the mathematics of Armageddon. They didn't want the slick, spoilt city boy who wore silk ties and drove fast cars and earned more in a month than they could earn in a year. They didn't want the Joe that none of them had known – the insecure, troubled Joe, the Joe beset by demons, the solitary Joe that lurked in the darkness fighting his private fears. None of these is the man they remember at the Festival of the Whale. The man they celebrate was a *hero*. He was a prophet. He was the man who saved the world. And if you live in the village of St Piran, then St Piran *is* the world – for you at least. And so, as the years have passed, the real memories of the man called Joe have become confused with the stories. There would be children at the Festival of the Whale, listening to Jeremy Melon speak, who would now always picture the young Joe Haak, naked, astride a whale, and perhaps, when all who knew him have died, this will be the image that remains.

1

The Day Kenny Kennet Saw the Whale

It was Charity Cloke who saw him first. Just seventeen she was then, so fresh of complexion that her cheeks shone like clover honey. They would say in St Piran that she was 'late to blossom', but a summer of soft Cornish sunshine and warm Atlantic winds had swept away any lingering trace of adolescent spots, and scowls, and rolls of baby flesh, and the girl who took to the beach with her dog on that October morning (or was it perhaps September?) was truly a girl no longer. 'Trees that are late to blossom,' Martha Fishburne would say, 'often blossom best.' And Martha was a teacher, so she would know.

Charity Cloke was walking her dog along the strip of dry shingle that ran between the beach and the cliffs, just above the litter of seaweed discarded by the tide. The few autumn holiday-makers who might, on a warmer day, have ventured onto the sands were muffled up, walking the clifftops instead. The beach was all but deserted. To hear the stories now, you might believe that half the village was there, for many claim to have seen the man, or to have helped him away from the sea, but when you sort through the accounts, and when you listen carefully to who saw what, only five people, including Charity Cloke, can be said, beyond doubt, to have been there that day; six, if you include the naked man himself.

There was Kenny Kennet, the beachcomber. He was prowling the shingle at the east bay looking for mussels, and crabs, and flotsam, and driftwood. He would, if the finds were good, turn the driftwood into works of art he could sell to next summer's tourists. The mussels and the crabs he would cook up and eat.

And the flotsam – well – that would depend upon whatever he found.

Old Man Garrow the fisherman was there, but, as villagers would say, Old Man Garrow was *always* there. He would sit on a bench for much of the day when the weather was fine and the winds were low, his knitted hat pulled over his ears, and here he would smoke his pipe and gaze out across the waves, drawn by the swell of the waters and the slap of the salt spray and the call of the herring gulls; and here, perhaps, he would dream of the years when the ocean was his home.

Aminata Chikelu, the young nurse, was there. She worked the night shift at the cottage hospital in Treadangel, so the morning on Piran Sands was, in a sense, the *evening* of her day. Aminata would unwind, when the morning was fair, with a walk along the narrow path that hugged the coast. Here she could let the stresses of the night shift evaporate away. 'What do you *do* in the hospital at night?' people might ask. 'I watch sick people sleeping,' she would say. And so she did, out on her rounds with her dim torch and shoes that didn't squeak, checking the drips, and the drugs, and the pulses of her long-stay, elderly and (often) dying patients. Few of us live quite as intimately with death as nurses do; and the Cornish coast, Aminata would tell you, was one of the places where people *came* to die. There are worse places to live out your twilight years. But would you imagine, if you swapped your city home for a cheap retirement cottage by the sea, that one night you might exhale your final breath within the antiseptic confines of an overheated hospital ward, with no one to hold your hand or watch your parting but a willowy nurse from Senegal? And even for those possessed of sufficient imagination, it might be hard to picture a fairer face, or a softer voice, or warmer hands to ease their passing than those of Aminata Chikelu. She was blessed with the coffee-and-cream complexion that spoke of a cocktail of genes within her ancestry, a little bit of Africa, and a little bit of Europe, and a little bit of who-knows-where. A hybrid confection that had favoured her with the perfect combination of features – dark sub-Saharan eyes, thick hair that she wore beribboned in braids, a slight Celtic nose and a beguiling gypsy smile.

Last of all on the sands that day was Jeremy Melon, the naturalist and writer. A lean and singular figure, Jeremy came to the cove, or so he would tell you, for *inspiration*. Sometimes he would set up an easel and daub at a canvas with watercolours, but this was never especially his thing. Words were his thing. Stories were his thing. More often, he would pick his way across the bay at low tide, contemplating the creatures in the rock pools, imagining the stories of their lives. How curious it must be, he would think, to be a worm, or a fish, or a seashell, in a pool. At high-tide your life would become a part of the great ocean that girdles the planet. You could come and go as you choose. You could sail out on a wave and float or swim to the beach at Port Nevis, or over the seas to Tahiti. Then the very next moment, the tide has abandoned you, the sea withdrawn; and now you occupy a fragile kettle of water with no refuge from the desiccating powers of the sun, or even from beachcombers such as Kenny Kennet, who might scoop you into a bucket and fry you. One day, Jeremy Melon would think, he could write a story about this.

Six people then, and one dog; and one of the six was lying naked, face-up and looked to be drowned.

People would ask of Charity Cloke, 'Was he as beautiful . . . you know . . . *down there*?' and they would flick their eyes suggestively downwards. What they meant, of course, was, 'Was he as beautiful below the waist as he undoubtedly was above it?' And Charity Cloke would respond with a coy smile, and her honey cheeks would blush. 'I'm not telling,' she would say, and she would lift her eyebrows just so – happy to be possessor of such intimate information, but never inclined to share it.

Above the waist, the man on the sand would be said, by many, to be beautiful. Cold from the sea, his flesh seemed translucent, his blue veins like a secret map beneath the pale paper of his skin, his hair strewn across his face like wet wheat after a storm. But what the villagers who mooted the subject with Charity Cloke already knew (because the rumours had clearly told them) was that the naked man had exhibited, on that day, a physiological phenomenon quite unusual for any man drawn from cold water. Dr Mallory Books would use the proper medical term when explaining this to Charity. The man from the sea, he would say, was 'priapic'. Very cold water, he told the young woman, can, in some circumstances, cause vasodilation. And vasodilation can result in the reaction that Charity Cloke observed. Don't worry, Dr Books told her, the tumescence was involuntary. 'These things don't last long,' he said. And sure enough, within minutes of his arrival at Dr Books's little surgery in Fish Street, the effect had receded, the man's erection subsided and Miss Cloke's further blushes were spared.

You could, if you were a visitor to St Piran, piece together the sequence of events on Piran Sands and the village of St Piran that autumn day by overlaying the stories told by Charity Cloke and Kenny Kennet the beachcomber, and Casey Limber the net maker. You could add to these the reported accounts of Jeremy Melon, and Dr Books, and Old Man Garrow. If you were to do this, you might, with some confidence, be able to unravel the true course of events on the day when everything started.

You could begin with Kenny Kennet, the beachcomber, picking among the rocks at the east end of the bay with his plastic sacks, his pond nets, his oddments of equipment. These were rocks he knew well. He had been scouring this cove, and a dozen others around the coast, for ten or fifteen years now; since leaving school, if his account is to be believed. His hair, rarely cut, was dreadlocked, coiled and stiff, like strands of rope bleached by the salt and the wind; now that the days were growing cooler he held the unruly locks in place beneath a linen gendarme cap. He wore jeans from Oxfam rolled up to the knee, and a Guinness T-shirt, and a pointless cotton scarf. He was bent, prying mussels from a rock with a flat-bladed knife, when, on an impulse, he straightened up, scrambled a dozen feet or so up the headland and, from this commanding position, gazed out towards the sea.

What was he looking for? 'Nothing in particular,' he would say. This was simply something he did. He was hoping for drifting debris perhaps, for floats he might sell back to the lobstermen for the price of a glass of beer, or for scraps of net for Casey Limber.

What he saw, however, was the whale.

At first it might have been a dolphin. Or even a harbour seal. It slipped into view like a shadow beneath the waves, like the grey-green hulk of an ancient wreck, rolling slightly, sucking the sunlight from the water. It seemed to Kenny as if a hand had waved in front of the sun, sending a slice of darkness scudding along the deep. And then with barely a ripple, the leviathan sank, and was gone.

The water was dark and deep at the headland. Kenny Kennet knew that, but he'd never seen a dolphin quite this close to shore. He stared at the empty stretch of sea, reflecting on what he had, or hadn't, seen. It must have been a dolphin, he thought. Unless . . . unless perhaps it was a whale? There was a sheen now to the water where the giant shape had been, as if a thin film of glass had been left upon the sea. The beachcomber turned his face away to see if anyone else was there who might confirm his sighting. And there, just a hundred yards or so away, was Charity and her poodle.

'Hey!' Kenny waved both arms. 'Hey!'

His cries caught the attention of Charity Cloke, and also of Aminata Chikelu, who was further up the shore, and of Jeremy Melon too, who was still exploring rock pools.

'Hey!' Kenny called again. 'I think I saw a whale!'

'A what?' shouted Charity. Jeremy and Aminata were too distant to join in the exchange.

'A whale.' Kenny made a beckoning gesture.

Charity Cloke broke into a run across the sand towards the headland. There were several spits of rock to negotiate.

'Quick!' Kenny could see the shape again, emerging slowly from the depths.

'I'm coming.' Charity used her hands to steady herself around a spear of barnacle-encrusted rock.

'Quick.'

In the ocean the leviathan was surfacing. The tide appeared

to be rising with the beast, a waterfall of spume and foam flooding from its flanks. Now it was a discernible shape, a striated barrage balloon flexing and rippling. Could it be a submarine? The thought struck Kenny, but in an instant the suggestion was dispelled as the great, grey back of the cetacean surged above the surface, and with a monstrous snort, a plume of water flew from its blowholes.

'Oh my God!'

A few yards from the shore Charity Cloke was screaming.

'It's all right,' called the beachcomber, his eyes transfixed by the whale. 'He isn't going to hurt you.'

But Charity wasn't screaming at the whale.

Later, Charity would say that it wasn't the man's nakedness that caused her to scream. Nor was it his prominent erection; his 'priapic state', as Dr Books had called it. 'It was just a shock,' she would say. 'I came around the rock, and there he was – lying there. I thought he was dead.'

The man on the beach may not have been dead, but he was certainly cold, and very still. Jeremy Melon was the second to arrive on the scene. If anything, Jeremy seemed even more shocked by the man's appearance than Charity had been. Then Kenny came down from his rock still flushed from his encounter with the whale.

'What the . . . ?'

'I think he's dead,' said Charity.

Three people now stood looking at the body on the sand, and not one dared touch him. It was the terrible inertia of crisis that held them back. The immobility of indecision. It was a man . . . of course – his terrible tumescence was proof of that – but his skin was so white and so bruised with sand that at first Charity had thought he may have been a porpoise. Or a seal. Or a dead thing dredged up from the depths and deposited like debris on the beach.

'Who is he?' Kenny asked, as if knowing this might help.

'I've never seen him before,' said Charity.

Jeremy shook his head slowly. 'Me neither.'

'Should we . . .' Charity started.

'Do what?'

'Give him the . . . kiss of life?'

The pause was awkward. Neither of the two men seemed anxious to administer such a therapy.

'I'll do it,' said Jeremy after a moment. He was sinking to his knees.

'No. I'll do it,' called a voice from behind. Aminata the nurse, glowing from her run across the beach, had arrived. She pushed between them and dropped to the sand. 'Hold his arms for me.'

They did as they were told. The castaway was cold and soaking wet; he hadn't been out of the water for long. Perhaps the surge wave from the whale had driven him ashore.

'Get him onto his front. We have to empty his lungs.'

This was a team activity now. They flipped the body over, ignoring the impact this would have on his erection. Aminata thrust her palms down hard on his back. Water spluttered from his mouth. She pressed again. He seemed to choke.

'I think he's alive,' Aminata said. 'He didn't have much water in his lungs. Flip him back.'

Clumsily they turned him over.

'I think he's breathing,' Kenny said.

'Let's make sure.' The nurse squeezed shut the man's nostrils and closed her lips around his mouth, exhaling into his lungs. His chest rose, and then, as she released her hold, his chest fell. She blew again.

'He's definitely breathing,' Jeremy said.

'One more time.' Another lungful of warm Senegalese air expelled into the cold alveoli of the man who wasn't dead. And this time, as Aminata released Joe and his body fell slowly away, their lips seemed to separate reluctantly, like the desperate mouths of parting lovers.

'He's freezing,' said Charity.

'It's the cold that's kept him alive.' Aminata was peeling off her coat. 'But all the same, we have to warm him up. Let's put this on him.'

'Where did he come from?' Kenny asked.

'Does it matter? Here. Give me a hand.'

'He needs some . . . trousers,' said Charity. It was as close as she would get to referencing the man's condition.

'He's not having mine,' said Kenny.

'He can have mine.' Jeremy pulled his belt loose. 'Don't worry. I'm decent.'

'More decent than he is,' said Aminata.

They pulled Jeremy's trousers over the castaway's wet legs. Jeremy, in his wind jacket and boxer shorts, surveyed their handiwork. 'Now,' he said, 'we'd better get him to Dr Books.'

Old Man Garrow, sitting on his rock, tapping down the tobacco in his pipe, watched the foursome struggle to lift the man. At first each rescuer took a limb, dangling the stranger sack-like between them, but this proved cumbersome. They stopped and made a basket of their arms and slung the man between them. It wasn't elegant, but it was easier.

Garrow tapped his pipe on the rock. 'Did ee zee yon whale?' he asked, as they made ponderous progress up the sands.

'I saw him,' said Kenny. 'He was as close to me as you are now.'

'Ee's bad news,' said Garrow rising heavily to his feet. He gave a deep and throaty cough. 'Ee shawn't be this close.'

'No,' said Kenny. 'Mr Garrow, we have to take this man to Dr Books.'

'A whale in the cove, ee's bad.'

'Yes,' said Kenny. 'We have to go.'

'Fishermen in't goin' to like it.'

'I don't suppose they will.'

'It wasn't a fish-eating whale, Mr Garrow,' said Jeremy. 'From what I could see, it was a fin whale.'

'A fin whale is it?'

'They don't eat fish. It's a type of baleen whale.'

Aminata broke in. 'Mr Melon, much as we'd all like to stand around and discuss the biology of whales, I really think we need to get this man to the doctor.'

'Of course. Of course.'

The path along the beach at Piran Sands leads around the rocky headland then turns immediately inland onto the great granite stones of St Piran village harbour. Here a pair of sea walls reach out like protective arms, holding away the ocean from the unimposing strip of low whitewashed buildings that line the quay. It was around this headland that the rescue party stumbled with the body of the stranger suspended awkwardly between them. On the dockside they drew the attention of every villager with a view of the harbour. Casey Limber, the net maker, was the first to spot them. He had been walking along the harbour wall in the direction of the beach when he came upon them. They were soon joined by Jessie Higgs the shopkeeper, and the fishermen Daniel and Samuel Robins, and the landlord of the Petrel Inn, Jacob Anderssen, and two of the girls who packed fish, and Captain O'Shea the harbourmaster, and Polly Hocking the vicar's wife, and Martha Fishburne the teacher, and a dozen more if we are to believe the stories.

'Who is he?' was the cry from many, anxious that the body from the sea might be a lover, or a brother, or a cousin, or a son.

'We don't know,' Jeremy told them.

'A stranger, then?'

'Indeed.'

Behind the stretcher party came Old Man Garrow, waving his walking stick in one hand, his pipe in the other. 'Ee's an omen, I'm tellin' ee. Ee's a bad sign.'

Eager for more information, the villagers settled upon Garrow. ''Twas a whale,' he told them, waving with great exaggeration. 'Ee came from the waters like a devil from the deep. Bigger'n a house ee was. Bigger'n a row of houses.'

This report was confusing. 'What are you talkin' about, Old Man Garrow?' someone said. 'That in't a whale. That's a man.'

'An 'ansum one,' said someone else. This may have been Polly Hocking, the vicar's wife.

''Twere a WHALE, I tell ee,' cried the old fisherman. 'I saw 'im. Ee come out the sea, and ee looked at me with 'is eye.'

This revelation was considered with suspicion by the crowd on the quay.

'You were nowhere near the whale,' offered Kenney Kennet, keen, now that the conversation had turned to the whale, to ensure that his own part in the events was not overlooked. 'I was right next to him.'

'I saw ee as close as I see you,' said Garrow.

'Can we please get this man to the doctor?' said Aminata.

'Here, let me help.' This was young Casey Limber. He stepped in to relieve Charity of her share of the burden, but so strong were his arms that he lifted the unconscious man clear and carried him alone.

And so the crowd swept along the harbour keep, past the fishermen's houses that fronted the quay, into the narrow square and up along a narrow cobbled street to the door of a terraced cottage. Many of the people who had joined the original four on the dockside attempted to follow them indoors. 'Are you ill?' demanded Jeremy of Mrs Penroth, the lobsterman's wife. 'No? Then please stay outside.'

The door of the house in Fish Street closed behind them and the interested bystanders were left in the road with their theories.

Visit thecoincidenceauthority.com

Watch John talking about how
The Coincidence Authority came about

Find out more about Thomas and Azalea and
the fact behind their fictional story

Read other people's stories of unexplained
coincidences and tell us yours

Win a proof copy of John's new book
Not Forgetting the Whale

You can also tweet @wnbooks and @jwironmonger

blog and newsletter

For literary discussion, author insight,
book news, exclusive content,
recipes and giveaways, visit the
Weidenfeld & Nicolson blog and
sign up for the newsletter at:

www.wnblog.co.uk

For breaking news, reviews and exclusive competitions
Follow us 🐦 @wnbooks
Find us 📘 facebook.com/WNfiction